NEW YORK, MY VILLAGE

ALSO BY UWEM AKPAN

Say You're One of Them

NEW YORK, MY VILLAGE

A Novel

Uwem Akpan

W. W. NORTON & COMPANY

Independent Publishers Since 1923

Copyright © 2022 by Uwem Akpan

Printed in the United States of America
First Edition

For information about permission to reproduce selections from this book, write to Permissions, W. W. Norton & Company, Inc., 500 Fifth Avenue, New York, NY 10110

For information about special discounts for bulk purchases, please contact W. W. Norton Special Sales at specialsales@wwnorton.com or 800-233-4830

Manufacturing by Lakeside Book Company
Book design by Lovedog Studio
Maps by David Lindroth
Production manager: Devon Zahn

Library of Congress Cataloging-in-Publication Data

Names: Akpan, Uwem, author.
Title: New York, my village : a novel / Uwem Akpan.
Description: First edition. | New York : W. W. Norton & Company, [2022]
Identifiers: LCCN 2021022378 | ISBN 9780393881424 (hardcover) |
   ISBN 9780393881431 (epub)
Subjects: LCSH: Nigerians—New York (State)—New York—Fiction. | Publishers
   and publishing—Fiction. | Africans—United States—Fiction. | African
   diaspora—Fiction. | GSAFD: Satire. | LCGFT: Satirical literature.
Classification: LCC PR9387.9.A3935 N49 2022 | DDC 823/.92—dc23
LC record available at https://lccn.loc.gov/2021022378

W. W. Norton & Company, Inc., 500 Fifth Avenue, New York, N.Y. 10110
www.wwnorton.com

W. W. Norton & Company Ltd., 15 Carlisle Street, London W1D 3BS

1 2 3 4 5 6 7 8 9 0

[A writer] should always try for something that has never been done or that others have tried and failed. Then sometimes, with great luck, he will succeed.

—ERNEST HEMINGWAY

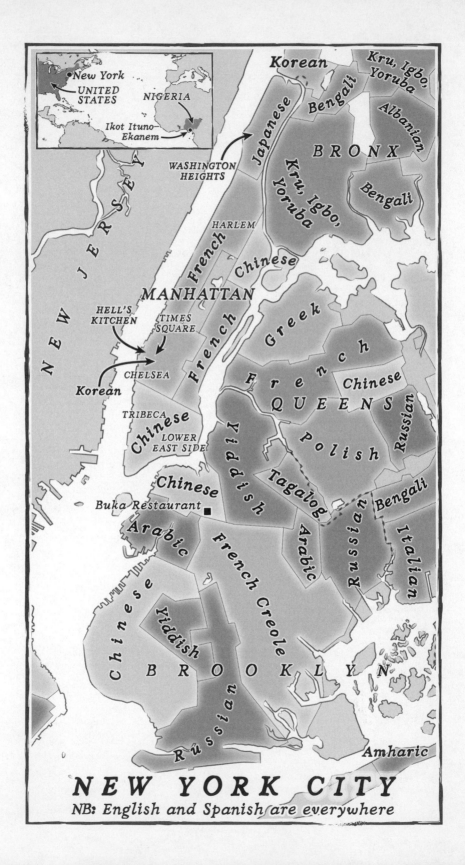

NEW YORK CITY

NB: English and Spanish are everywhere

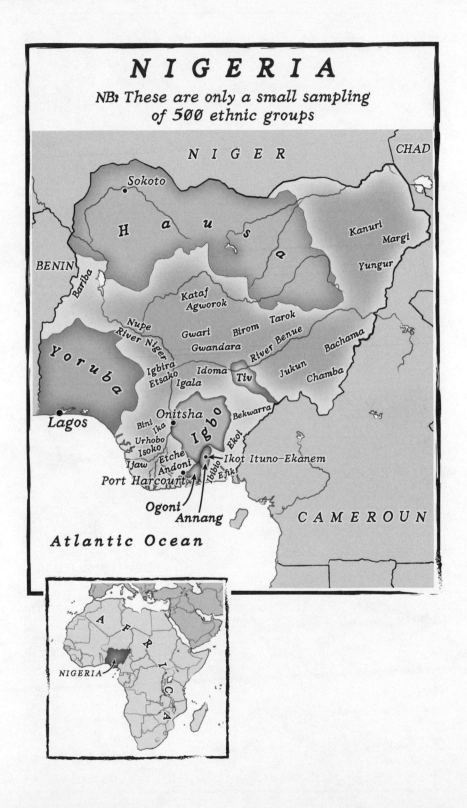

NEW YORK, MY VILLAGE

Santa Judessas vs Lagoon Drinkers, huh?

NOTHING WAS GOING TO STOP ME FROM ENJOYING NEW York to the marrow, as we say back home in Ikot Ituno-Ekanem in the Niger Delta of Nigeria. I was the managing editor of Mkpouto Books in Uyo, after I left my job as a literature lecturer at Ikot Osurua Polytechnic. With a Toni Morrison Fellowship for Black Editors I was on my way to Andrew & Thompson, a publishing house, to understudy their operations for four months. I would also use that time to edit an anthology of stories by minority writers on the Biafran War, the fiftieth anniversary of which was going to be the following year. This ethnic war rang deep in my soul: I was born a year into it, 1968, hence my mother naming me Ekong, which means "War."

It was to be my first time in America. I had seen a lot of America on TV and spoke American English, so it was not going to be that complicated. Better still, we had dozens of Americans, Europeans, Asians, and Latinos in our local church, Our Lady of Guadalupe; they worked in the oil fields of the Niger Delta. Though they lived in walled fortresses, the church was our meeting point, where our children and theirs attended the same First Holy Communion classes and were featured in nativity and passion plays.

I had wanted to travel with my wife, Caro, but her bank job got in the way. So our consolation was that I would be back for Christmas.

As the visa interview at the American Embassy in Lagos approached, I had already sorted out my accommodation in New York. Usen Umoh, a childhood friend, who was a super in the Bronx, had warned me that looking for housing in NYC was a mess and invited me to stay with him. But after learning he lived with his wife and two kids in a one-bedroom apartment, I was not keen. Worse still, Molly Simmons, who would be my supervisor in America, hinted that the Bronx was also a little dangerous and suggested I "live near *things*, so you could really enjoy your short stay." I made the mistake of relating this to Usen. Offended, he complained to the entire Ikot Ituno-Ekanem village that I was looking down on him.

Tuesday Ita, an older "brother," who lived in New Jersey, would have allowed me his spare room, as he had done for many of our villagers, but Molly made New Jersey sound like some distant violent Third World city. I had never met Tuesday, though we all loved him for paying the tuition for a host of orphans and digging wells for clean water in the eight surrounding villages. I was only seven years old when his late uncle who worked with American Red Cross/ Catholic Charities brought him to America in 1975, five years after our civil war. But it was Tuesday, an anesthesiologist, who settled the quarrel between Usen's extended family and mine in the village over my "rejection" of Usen. He accomplished this by leaking the news of Usen's secret party plans to welcome me to NYC during Thanksgiving.

I felt more than honored, and was relieved that village relations were restored.

On the phone, Molly, who was the publisher and editor-in-chief, had the sweetest and most reassuring voice I had ever heard, though Caro did not like her one bit and insisted I put the phone on speaker as we enthused about the pleasures of putting a book together and discussed the overlap between my job at our Mkpouto Books and her role at her publishing house. Anyway, we were relieved Molly knew someone who knew an old gentleman, Greg Lucci, who was ready to sublet a furnished one-bedroom apartment in Hell's Kitchen, three blocks from Times Square. The white lady, who had seen the place, said it was romantic because the bath was in the kitchen, like in the old movies. She said the rent was also great, half the market price.

✕

IN EARLY APRIL, a day before my visa interview, I flew out of Akwa Ibom International across southern Nigeria to Lagos. That evening, in my pretty Yaba hotel, after a quiet meal of *atama* and *garri*, I unzipped my sky-blue waterproof folder to ensure I had *everything* for the interview. Though the embassy website asked for only my passport, the invitation letter, and proofs of accommodation and financial resources, conventional wisdom said you could be asked any question by the consular officer. So I also had the originals of my birth certificate, baptismal card, certificate of origin, driver's license, letters from the university, the National War Museum, and the Federal Ministry of Information and Culture vouching for the importance of my work in memory preservation, my expired marriage certificate, divorce certificate plus two police reports attesting I had been a victim of domestic violence, a clearance letter from the National Drug Law Enforcement Agency, a certificate of ownership of our new home in Ikot Ituno-Ekanem plus its architectural design, a Certificate of Minor Chieftaincy Title from Afe Annang, transcripts from secondary school through my master's program, three years' worth of tax documents, membership cards of professional associations, etc.

Next, I stood up and walked around the room, rehearsing my answer to the most important question everyone said the consular officer would ask: What proof could I offer that I would return to Nigeria after my fellowship? Usen, whose wife, Ofonime, flunked four interviews before she could join him in the Bronx, had helped me build my answer around my coveted position at Mkpouto Books, my excitement over grooming local writers, the books I had published so far, and my ongoing war research by way of recording oral interviews of our Annang war victims, which had to be done in Annangland, not America. Molly also said I should add that her company was thinking of establishing a professional relationship with Mkpouto.

By the time I finally slept that night, my mind was already in New York. I scrambled up many times before the hotel service woke me at five a.m. I had no appetite, though they were already serving their complimentary breakfast at that hour.

Thirty minutes later, I was dutifully seated in a Benz Uber, eager to beat Lagos traffic for my eight a.m. appointment on Victoria Island. My folder lay beside me as I responded to all the text messages from Nigeria and abroad wishing me good luck as if I were going to court or taking a bar exam. I restricted myself to answering only texts from Caro, Molly, Usen, and Father Kiobel Baribor—our beloved parish priest and friend—because I was beginning to be restless; though my driver had said the traffic would be okay, it was dangerously building up. I called Caro to say how tense I was. She said it was unbearable for her. After she sobbed and said three Hail Marys slowly into the phone, which brought tears to my eyes, Usen sought to distract me by asking for pictures of "the poor man's skyscrapers of Victoria Island"; I snapped and sent them to him. He asked to see how I was dressed; I took a selfie of my charcoal-colored *senator* outfit and black shoes for him and Caro. He grumbled that I looked too glum; I said I was saving my smile for the embassy.

I GOT OUT NEAR Walter Carrington Crescent, near the lagoon, which emptied a few streets away into the Atlantic Ocean. The heat of the dry season had woken up, too. It was going to be a hot, dusty day. The taxi berth was already like a mobile open market, as if nobody had slept the night before. There were all kinds of businesses: folks hawking stationery, groups running locker depots to house your phones and bags because you could not enter the embassy with them, photographers taking last-minute passport photos, restaurateurs serving assorted Nigerian breakfast dishes as though it were a mini–food carnival. The police here were more energetic than those at any country's independence day celebrations. And there were too many folks in this neighborhood walking their huge muzzled dogs, as though to advertise a new fad, because I could not believe there were no smaller dogs in Victoria Island.

But, as I deposited my phone, what intrigued me the most was the number of touts trying to sell me colorful pamphlets on how to nail American visa interviews. I wore down the crowd haggling for my attention to two ladies who trailed me through the half-mile-high security no-vehicular zone leading to the embassy.

"Uncle, do everyting to get the Latina visa interviewer!" counseled a lady in bright red culottes, carrying a huge bag of pamphlets on her head. "She *dey* merciful. We *dey* call *am* Santa Judessa. She *dey* wear blue-rimmed glasses. She be our personal person for de embassy."

"Okay," I said.

"Avoid de white man, Lagoon Drinker," her partner in an immaculate white dress said. "Dat one just *dey* drink water nonstop as if liquid no *dey* America. He *dey* bully our people too much, especially if you want visit New York, his village."

"*Mbok*, I'm headed to New York!" I said.

"Please, just say you *dey* go New Jersey or Connecticut," the other said.

"Thanks, ladies, I love your humor," I said, chuckling confidently. "Let's see: Santa Judessas vs Lagoon Drinkers, huh? Sounds like an exciting soccer match!"

"Uncle, dis Yankee embassy no get funny bone inside *o*," the former warned me, sweeping her braids off her face. "Soon you go see how inside embassy be . . . *meanwilee*, make you give us tip *na*."

"Tip?" I said.

"You look like first-timer," she said.

"Yes, I am," I said.

"Then give us small change, little appreciation for decoding de color game for you!" the other one said impatiently. "*Abi*, we done give you valuable info to get visa to go make dollar *nyafu nyafu* for America!"

"I didn't ask you for anything, did I?" I said.

"Good, just buy our pamphlets, then," the culottes lady said. "Uncle, we no be beggars. We no be touts. Just serious External Visa Processors, EVPs!"

I impatiently pushed past them, pointing to my folder to signal I had everything I needed. They apologized and went to find someone else.

By the time I arrived at the embassy, the angry sleepless gritty dust that filled the air had settled on me. And then I began to sweat. By ten a.m., after more than an hour at the processing line, I received my number and was among the first batch to enter the large interview hall. I took my seat and put my folder on my knees as the embassy apologized via a public-address system that due to "technical difficulties the interview lines are going to be a bit slower than usual." I clenched my jaw and went through all the documents again.

My neighbor, a beautiful and tastefully dressed woman in her thirties, shuddered. She brought out her *tesbih*, Muslim prayer beads, closed her eyes, and started to rub them between her fingers. She was naturally fair-skinned, and her hands were covered with delicate black hennas designed like gloves. The other neighbor, an old man with a gold tooth, would not even answer my greeting, as though I were a bad omen. Yet he smiled often. He was in a black-and-white-striped cotton dashiki and matching cap. People were already lining up to use the restrooms, others to drink from the water fountain. And there were those who were too cold because of the powerful air-conditioning. When the old man complained, the guards said if he could not stand this little breeze, he should tell his interviewer he would not survive the American winter.

You did not push your luck with these folks, these our compatriots in sharp uniforms and boots. These guards moved about the packed hall like they ran America.

BEHIND THE GLASS WALL, I could see six interview booths. In front of them were thirty or so seats reserved for the next batch to be interviewed. These were as solemn as jury chairs. But, as soon as only two interviewers arrived and took their places in the booths, I knew we were in for a long day. Someone complained that in London and Beijing, America always filled the booths. Another said they had enough interviewers, too, in Sydney and Riyadh, and were nicer. Another said we should thank our stars things had really improved these days, unlike ten years ago when our people used to literally sleep outside the embassy because the consular officers did everything to delay the lines. When security moved toward our murmuring section, we all hushed and avoided their eyes.

Though I could tell one interviewer was a white American, I could not ascertain whether he was the dreaded Lagoon Drinker. I was also too far away to figure out the rim color of the glasses of his lady counterpart, to determine if she was Santa Judessa, *the* Latina. It took a long time for security to move a group forward and even longer for the interviews to begin. And when they did, I studied the patterns of rows being relocated by security to the pre-interview zone, without understanding what was going on. Sometimes it was this row, and then that row.

It was pure voodoo.

What I could see very well, though, were anxious people approaching the booths like their knees were popping with fear. You could tell who was triumphant by their smiles and thumbs-ups. Some got their visas within a minute and waved the pink slips with details on when to pick up their passports. Some succeeded after a tug-of-war between them and the interviewers. Others failed. There were shrugs; there were tears. Two families who broke out in total confrontation with the interviewers were escorted out by security, the children wailing like their parents had died. As more folks from the lady's booth were celebrating, I suspected she was Santa Judessa.

The only problem was you did not choose your interviewer. You said your prayers.

By two p.m., my nose was running because of the cold and hunger. The old man went to the restroom, returned almost immediately, and tried to negotiate a seat exchange with me. Since he spoke no English and I neither understood a word of his native tongue nor knew what language it was, someone behind us volunteered to interpret. The old man wanted to be interviewed by Santa Judessa, too, not the white man. I said no and explained it was too early to tell who would interview whom, since we were still very far from the booths. He said his dead grandmother had assured him in the restroom he would get the lady if I relinquished my seat. He said his doctor had told him he needed a serious checkup in the U.S., so he could not afford to fail the interview. He opened his file to show me batches upon batches of frayed receipts for medications he had been taking since 1980 and a health insurance card listing him as a dependent of a son in Jamaica, New York.

I was about to oblige when security arrived, a man and a woman. They said we could not change seats, even if I agreed. "You eider obey ASAP because America *na* country of laws," the lady warned, "or we go bundle you out!" The interpreter translated the message; my neighbor sat down immediately, with hands in between his legs. I was helping him rearrange his receipts when the security man asked whether he would promise not to cause any more trouble. He nodded and looked up smiling, tears coming down his cheeks.

FINALLY, AT 3:07 P.M., they invited my row to move into the pre-interview section, skipping five rows. And they pulled ours out from the direction I did not expect, so that the old man was ahead of me and the Muslim lady behind. I did not mind the disorientation, so long as we were moving.

At the booths, the white man wore a blue suit. I knew he was Lagoon Drinker because three bottles of water stood in front of him.

The lady's blue-rimmed glasses assured me that she was our beloved Latina. She wore a white dress and her brown hair was pulled back in a ponytail. She had a calm friendly demeanor, something not even the officiousness of diplomacy could distort. In the short twenty minutes since we took our new seats, she had enhanced her image further by giving four visas out of six while Lagoon Drinker gave none. As I scudded forward from seat to empty seat, I could hear snatches of the interviews. However, the thing I heard the most clearly was when the interviewer said, "Next!" and in the same twenty minutes, I had looked over my documents seven times and changed the order of them four times. The Muslim woman beside me was exhaling and groaning each time we moved forward.

When we got to the front of the line, the security guard asked the old man to wait, as the official interpreter had gone to the restroom. So I was beckoned forward, and I stood up and confidently walked up to Santa Judessa.

"Good afternoon, madam," I said, bowing and placing my folder on the ledge of the counter with my two hands over it.

"Good morning . . . Mr. Ekong Otis Udousoro?" she asked with a smile.

"Yes, madam."

"Please, what tribe are you?"

"Oh, I'm Annang."

"Annang?"

"Yes, Annang."

"Does that mean you're not Hausa-Fulani or Yoruba or Igbo?"

"That's what it means, madam."

When she smiled and nodded and jotted something down, I thought my stock had appreciated and shifted my weight from one leg to the other. I was secretly celebrating the fact that I was not a member of these behemoth ethnic groups of thirty million each, these big bullies who had plunged our dear country into the Biafran War—the Biafrans, mainly Igbos, squaring off against the other two, the Yorubas and Hausa-Fulanis. We the minorities had been crushed in Nigeria for far too long even though most of the oil, Nigeria's main resource, was in our territories. But now, I thought, for once being a minority or minority of minorities had got me out of jail.

In the next booth, Lagoon Drinker screamed that his interviewee did not have sufficient documentation. She pleaded that she had given him everything the embassy website demanded. The man *nexted* her and sipped his water. As she asked what else she needed to bring, he stormed out of the booth.

Santa Judessa looked up and said to me: "Sir, it means then that, unlike your compatriots, you're not going to America to fill up the prisons, are you?"

"I'm going to understudy a publishing house, not the prisons," I said.

"Well, just to confirm what you said in your application, you're not going with the intention of committing any crime, right?"

"Absolutely not!"

"Excellent. You're not going there to scam anybody?"

"No, madam, I'm not a criminal."

She was staring at me, nodding slowly. I maintained eye contact and nodded, too.

"Please, madam, would you like to see my invitation letter?" I said.

"Not yet," she said.

"I mean, I'm not saying we are better than other ethnicities or anything like that."

She took off her glasses. "I understand there are two hundred and fifty tribes. But in what part of the country is this tribe of yours located?"

"The Niger Delta."

"Excellent." She bent down and wrote furiously and said without looking up: "But can you prove there's such a tribe?"

"What tribe?" I said.

"*Your* tribe . . . could you convince me there's such a people, Mr. Udousoro?"

I folded my arms and searched the ceiling. *But can you prove there's such a tribe?* No one had ever asked me such a ridiculous question before. *Your tribe . . . could you convince me there's such a people, Mr. Udousoro?* Which one is better: to be known as a *criminal* or not to exist at all? Who invents a new ethnic group for the purposes of getting an American visa? I thought this Latina woman was insulting all the Annangs in the world. And she was someone whose people had themselves migrated to the United States! She even asked the foolish question twice!

I was about to suggest that she google *Annang* for herself when she said, "Sir, may I have your passport, please?" I put the passport in the tray, but she did not pick it up. "Your application says you're going to New York to edit a six-hundred-page anthology of stories about the Biafran War. I want to know what side of the war your tribe was on."

"Well, unfortunately, we were forced into and trapped in Biafra," I said.

Lagoon Drinker returned and called the old man and his translator forward.

"And, Mr. Udousoro, when was this tribal war again and why?" Santa Judessa asked.

"From 1967 to 1970," I said. "The Biafrans claimed they went to war for self-determination."

"Excellent, excellent. So, next year is the fiftieth anniversary of the start of the war, yes?"

"Correct. They said they wanted their own country because Nigeria had killed thirty-five thousand of them in genocide. But we, the minorities, knew they just wanted our oil and our lands. This war affected us a lot . . ."

"Please, just one moment."

She started typing into her computer. This bought me time to prepare to tell her how Biafra, this Igbo-thing, had dragged more than thirty minority tribes into war, how Chief Okon Essien, our village head, was buried alive for saying no, how General Odumegwu Ojukwu, the Biafran leader, subjected our minorities to a brutal regime of divide-and-rule, how Father Gary Walsh, the old rugged son of Dublin, fought to protect us, how the Nigerian army who claimed to have come to liberate us—as opposed to fighting for oil—had raped Eka Utitofon, our neighbor's pregnant mother, how the Nigerian government then deported Father Walsh for mentioning it to the international press. I thought I would do better to offer these few poignant details than to venture into the tragic story of how my father was disappeared, or to rehash the coups and genocide before the war.

But before I could say anything, Santa Judessa grabbed my passport, opened it, and pinned it to the desk. "Mr. Udousoro," she said, and cleared her throat, "I'm sorry to say we cannot, at this time, process your visa to the United States, because you've completely failed to prove you'd return to Nigeria."

"No, I swear by the Blessed Sacrament I shall return!" I said.

The stamp of denial on my passport sounded like a gavel.

"Mr. Udousoro, you may reapply anytime . . . Next!"

I looked up and down, confused. I tried to see her face, but she was writing away with the intensity of a street artist trying to draw me. I looked behind me. The other applicants hid their faces. I looked at the next booth. The interviewer was drinking noisily as the translator helped the old man search for a document, because his hands were shaking like tailor ants. As I turned toward Santa Judessa again, the next interviewee, the Muslim lady, gently touched my shoulder. "Dear, don't worry," she said, holding my hand and pointing me toward the exit. "You'll get it next time. Just reapply tonight. Be strong." Her kind words helped me to recover, collect my passport and yellow denial slip, and move away before security reacted. The whole thing had lasted four minutes.

OUTSIDE, I WAS DIZZY. I quickly bought Maltina and *moi moi* from some hawkers and snacked, leaning on an electric pole. I avoided looking at my folder, which felt like a bag of shame.

"Uncle, no vex," the pamphlet ladies consoled me. "Dese Yankees can destroy even God's dream o."

"Thanks," I said.

"Be strong, if not, dese professional sadists go push you enter early grave o."

"I know."

They said their different pamphlets could help get me the visa next time—so that I did not have to keep paying the exorbitant application fees. "Lagoon Drinker just *dey* make money for America!" they complained. They wanted to know what questions I was asked, whether I greeted my interviewer, whether I made eye contact. They wanted to know, if I was Christian, whether I had prayed that morning and if I had fasted and gone to confession and paid my tithe regularly; or, if I was a traditional shrine worshipper, whether I had gone for the shrine cleanup before the interview, or shared the sacrificial food with the poor; or, if I was Muslim, whether I did *zakat* for the needy. "Dese pre-interview divine tips *dey* our pamphlets," they said. I did not respond, for it felt like another interview. I handed them some money to get them off my back.

And after retrieving my phone, I sat down on a bench to a meal of "assorted" peppersoup and *ekpang nkukwo* with smoked Norwegian mackerel while watching the boats in the lagoon. One belonged to the police guarding all the Western embassies on the island. The officers looked very efficient. Some on the deck had binoculars and were monitoring everywhere. I had never seen our police so consumed in their work.

Then another group of External Visa Processors arrived, to drive away the two ladies who were still waiting for me. These new ones were more organized and in blue uniforms.

"Sir, don't mind our police," they said, pointing to their boat. "They only know how to protect white folks and their embassies. These embassies bribe them . . . but, hey, pamphlets alone won't get you the visa! You need an advanced visa course!"

"A course?" I said, finishing up my meal.

"Of course. Look, if you'd contacted us before this interview, we would've suggested General White Visa 101."

I suppressed a laugh. "Okay."

"We hope, though, you were interviewed by that New Yorker prig, because our data show our clients have had more luck over-turning his denials."

When I said it was Santa Judessa, they said my situation was less hopeful, that their data also showed they rarely overturned her deci-sions, for she was kind. "We like to be honest, but no problem," they assured me. "We've got the expertise to fix it. We highly recommend Aggressive American Visa 605. You need to raise your game."

They put down six complimentary cards on the bench, spreading them out in a fan as in a game. I did not touch them. Two of the touts sat down with me, one on each side. I moved my wallet from my back pocket to my breast pocket. "Sir, relax, we're all univer-sity graduates, not pickpockets!" they said, and explained that the Visa 605 package came with an esteemed pastor, imam, or juju man who would personally fast for me for a week. I told them to leave me alone, because I had never liked this new spirituality of renting prayer-warriors for visas.

"Well, seeing your trauma, we can give you what's called the Depression Discount," they bargained.

"I am not depressed!" I shot back.

"Visa rejection usually comes with instant depression."

"Go away!"

They ignored my outburst and said I could pay for the course in installments. They even produced a little point-of-sale machine and said I could swipe my credit or debit card in case I was short of cash. To get rid of them, I lied that I was not reapplying for a visa.

Then I saw the old man being held up by relatives, some of whom were buying different pamphlets. One relative was echoing what the old man was saying in English for the benefit of other relatives who could not understand his native language. He had failed his interview because he could not explain to Lagoon Drinker why his American son had bought him an expensive gold tooth while people were starving in his village. He said he had tried to change his seat to meet the Latina instead of Lagoon Drinker but could not. His family was already calling his son in Jamaica, New York, to send money so that he could have the tooth removed before he reapplied for the visa. They blamed the New York son for giving his father the tooth five years before when he had last visited America.

One of the visa touts said the old man was Bekwarra, another minority group in defunct Biafra. My heart jumped because, though I had heard of them, especially their war stories, I had never met any of them before. We had grown up hearing of how their Ogoja group, the Ogonis, and other minority associations had fought forever for autonomy from the Igbos even before Nigeria's independence in 1960.

WHEN THE OLD MAN began to weep, I broke through the scrum of touts and stepped forward to sympathize and to say Santa Judessa also did me in. I introduced myself as a fellow minority in defunct Biafra, which made his family warm up to me. But no sooner had he recognized me than he accused me of stealing his interview spot. The family apologized and told me their patriarch was senile. In a bid to be inclusive and transparent, they translated some of his rant and begged me to play along.

But when he called me *Biafran*, all the relatives quickly berated him into silence. They explained that each time the man had a little misfortune it just had to be the fault of Biafra. His Igbo in-laws had learned to live with this. In the end, the whole family shook hands with me, and after reminiscing about important minority soccer players, past and current, we exchanged email addresses and strategized about reapplying for our visas that very night.

"CALL YOUR FRIEND Molly Simmons immediately!" Caro advised me on the phone as my Uber drove off. "From the way you talk on the phone and exchange emails, I think she'll push your case. I don't think she's the kind of white person who would mock our African *savagery*." Caro added that if she were in my position, she would tell Molly a bit about my family tragedy, so she could see how personal this fellowship was to me.

Since it was already too late to call New York, when I got back to my hotel I emailed Molly about my embassy experience, expecting a reply in the morning. But since Usen was my friend, I phoned him to simply say I had failed to prove to America that we, the Annangs, existed. "Oh no, I don't think it's personal," he explained. "You know, out here, the few Americans who know about Nigeria only know of the Igbos, Yorubas, and Hausa-Fulanis. If you say you're something else, you may confuse them." He said Tuesday Ita had strongly suggested I ask Molly to send the embassy an attestation from competent American ethnographers and anthropologists that we existed. But then suddenly anger entered Usen's voice: "No, Ekong, wait . . . if we can't even prove that we exist, fuck, how can we say anybody hurt us in any war?" He called the embassy all kinds of unprintable names. Usen's feelings over the war were rawer than mine. As a kid, he had stabbed a Biafran classmate because he learned their soldiers had forced his grandpa to eat shit for not thanking them for commandeering his Raleigh bicycle.

After reapplying for the visa that night, I went out to stroll around the vicinity of Yaba Market, texting a customized "Bad news" to all my friends. Though the main market was locked up for the night, the streets were crowded with shoppers and lined with tables full of groceries and lit kerosene lanterns, in case the electricity went out. I was watching moviegoers coming in and out of a theater and bubbling crowds feasting away in boutique restaurants when Molly called. Of course, she was furious with her embassy. She assured me that

Andrew & Thompson would fax the embassy directly. "Ekong, this is bullshit tribal profiling, pure and simple!" she fumed. "But we've rebranded and exported it to you guys. The courts have knocked down racial profiling in America."

By the time I flew home the next day, Caro had brought Father Kiobel into the picture. He was our friend and we told him everything. We were also comfortable because he did not believe in using these *Visa Condolence Visits* to cast out embassy demons or extort money.

He was our huge handsome avuncular pastor at the Church of Our Lady of Guadalupe. He had a round babyish face, made even more so because he always shaved his head. He was a minority from a different tribe—the Ogonis, one of the minority groups which had been fighting for autonomy from the Igbos long before the war. His people and ours shared borders. He smiled often and had won everyone's admiration by speaking our Annang language and dialects and visiting homes, even those of juju worshippers. He loved the beautiful four-bedroom home that Caro and I shared. Unlike other priests, he did not scold us for not wanting to have children. He also ensured that the expat oil workers were an integral part of the church community. While we were Liverpool fans, he was a die-hard Manchester United fan. These things were important in our villages, but he knew how to handle the rivalries.

The only thing we did not like about Father Kiobel was his rabid obsession with new clothes. He was always in the most expensive liturgical vestments, made of silk or damask and richly embroidered with floral designs. His cook told us most of these were given to him by the Italian oil workers in our parish. It was also an open secret that Father Kiobel was always buying clothes from the Shoprite Mall in Umuahia. But, as I have said, we loved the unity he had brought to the parish and surrounding villages. He was also a great homilist and storyteller, though he never told war stories.

Nobody knew what he thought of the war or our hopeless Nigerian politics. He never talked about his childhood or parents even when the rumor surfaced that he himself had been a ruthless Biafran child soldier. In fact, the previous month, when our minority youths started planning for a fiftieth anniversary commemoration of the beginning of the war and made me a keynote speaker, he quietly vetoed it. Next, he used his influence to get the village chiefs, the Awire Womenfolk, and the police to discourage the clamor in the larger community. The leader of the youths, Gabriel, aka Two-Scabbard, and I were quite angry with this and I told the priest so. When he met my protest with his customary silence about everything relating to the war, what could I do? I disliked this part of him—and wished he had even an iota of interest in my anthology.

But his attitude sat better with my wife: because Caro did not like talking about the war with me or with anybody, for that matter. My wife hated the war because her grandfather, who voluntarily joined the Biafran army, was publicly executed with nails hammered into his head when Nigeria finally overran Biafra. In fact, sometimes she was more anxious than me about the war anthology, but for another reason entirely: nobody had submitted any stories that explored her trauma—the endless village taunts and barbs that her entire extended family had a traitor's blood coursing through them. It was a form of internal banishment.

The priest was the only person she felt understood the pain of her family's memories of her grandpa's murder. Caro and I had a fiery jealous love that had burned down village objections to unite us in a secret sacristy wedding in Lagos. That love was still strong, though folks still taunted me that I had allowed her sheer beauty and gray eyes and "long buttocks" to confuse me. But discussing my father's or her grandpa's fates was still awkward. It was a part of our lives we did not talk about.

Anyway, that night, to avoid the priest's and Caro's awkward silences, I did not mention anything about the old Bekwarra man and the war. We enjoyed Father's loud, crazy laugh while we played Ludo and ate *mmansang ikpok* and drank Coke. Dinner was chicken peppersoup and *mmun-mboro* with smoked shark, *ata anyim ewa*.

CHAPTER 2

Both God and *utere*, the vulture, can never abandon the corpse

IT HAD BEEN RAINING ALL WEEK AND THE MOST RECENT national power cut and internet dysfunction were three days old when I hit Lagos for my repeat interview. I was as prepared as I could be. Andrew & Thompson had written in. Molly said they had attestations by experts from Yale and Columbia Universities that the Annangs existed. I did not mind this humiliation as long as I got the visa.

When I arrived at the embassy that drizzly windy July morning, I took off my shoes and socks and rolled up my trousers to my calves, for the street was flooded. Others had done the same. I put up my umbrella. I held my footwear and my folder almost above my head and stepped out into the rain. Despite the weather the "market" near Carrington Crescent was booming. Even the street photographers had set up huge lit transparent balloons on podiums above the floods to do business. They looked quite upbeat, as though they had figured out how to generate electricity directly from the deluge.

I was glad the embassy let us into the first part of the building. I found space to put back on my socks and shoes. Though some warmth had returned to my feet, the place smelled of wet shoes and clothes and damp perfumes. Mercifully, someone had turned down the air conditioner.

In this packed space, I recognized a few people from last time, but the most striking was the old Bekwarra man. His neck revealed he had layered on two sweaters to beat the cold, but it was still easy to see he had lost weight. Sniffling and sneezing, and without his gold tooth, he looked quite different. His smile was gone, too. Now, when he was not running his tongue over his new tooth, he was touching his mouth gingerly in a way that suggested he was still recovering from the dentist's visit. When he coughed, it sounded like a truck's busted exhaust pipe, causing everybody around him to grumble and jostle. As soon as he saw me, he instinctively moved away.

It did not take long before the loudspeakers informed us again of the "technical difficulties" and how they were doing everything to fix them. Luckily, when I got to my seat, I was with neighbors who wanted to chat. So we warmed our mouths talking about Nigeria, how wonderful it was to be African soccer champions again in 2013, how the Buhari government was backing Fulani killer herdsmen Janjaweed-style, how the Calabar Carnival and Ake Book Festival were spotlighting the country.

WHEN THE INTERVIEWERS ARRIVED, they were a Black man and Lagoon Drinker. As the security started ordering rows forward, in their random pattern, to the pre-interview enclosure, the buzz around the hall was that the Black man was more difficult than Lagoon Drinker. Those who were hearing of this for the first time, like me, were angry with the Black man, because we expected him to be the most lenient.

When someone exploded in a dry slow sneeze, I knew immediately it was the old man. I discovered him at the end of my row. Those around him murmured and asked for relocation while an old woman lent him a blazer to keep warm. The noise died as security moved in. The kind unflappable intelligent Muslim woman who had helped me manage my visa denial was in the row before mine. She was in a lace blouse and single-layer *wrappa* and headtie and wristwatch and bangles—all lime-green. I longed to go thank her for her compassion. But she was studiously comparing notes from six differ-ent pamphlets.

At 1:37 p.m., as the rain pounded the roof, my batch was sum-moned to the pre-interview space. I could see the Muslim woman ahead of me, her beads out and the pamphlets gone. She was the most sober interviewee in this enclosure.

As I hopped from seat to seat, my heart began to pound due to the rate people were being denied visas. I was a sweaty mess. I pulled out my handkerchief and mopped my face and neck. Even my palms were sweating, and they had never sweated before. I quickly wiped them on my trousers, like one trying to warm his hands. I looked at my neighbors; they avoided my eyes. I looked behind me; they also looked away—except a six-year-old boy in the company of his young mother. Tired of changing seats, he wanted just to remain standing. His lips were trembling, his eyes beclouded by tears as his mother, avoiding his face, scolded him in sharp whispers to treat this like a version of his beloved musical chairs. When he said he was hungry, I dodged his eyes, too, for I did not know what to say. Such was the tension, like we were approaching a battlefront. Then I felt some moist heat on the soles of my feet, which convinced me I was sweat-ing down there, too. It was like my toes were going numb or the cold rain had finally entered my shoes. This was not the space to remove your shoes because the security was watching every gesture and you had to keep moving.

This time I had no prayers for which interviewer to meet: white American, Black American, what did it matter? My mind looped back to the first interview. Was there anything I could have said differently? Had I angered Santa Judessa by offering to show her my paperwork? Was my eye contact too aggressive, betraying overconfidence?

My vision steadied when the Muslim woman put away her beads and stood up and *catwalked* up to the booth. I could see now she also had on lime-green heels. She was in front of the Black man, a guy in a black blazer, white shirt, and brown tie, with a shaven head and everlasting scowl. She put her file on the counter. He asked for something; she produced a letter from the file. It was clear to everyone the interview was not going well. Now she was trembling so much I exchanged glances with my neighbors. You could see sweat coming down the back of her neck. She was gesticulating with her hands, and the consular officer was pushing back, as if they were two people haggling over Cameroon pepper in the market.

Feeling the heat, the Muslim lady choked and coughed and signaled to excuse herself. Her interviewer obliged. She climbed down from her heels and bent down to push them aside. With her feet on solid ground, she rolled her shoulders and lifted onto her toes, a wrestler about to spring on the opponent. The soles sported laces of solid henna that went as far as the calves where the *wrappa* stopped. The security officer laughed and beckoned to another to come catch the fun.

The interviewer asked for her passport, which she put in the tray. He ignored it and bent down to write. Her body started to tremble again. She shifted her weight from leg to leg. Then she shuddered uncontrollably—till her beautiful lace *wrappa* weakened and unraveled and fell slowly to the floor, revealing a ropy gold G-string juggling large wonderful balls of buttocks that glistened with sweat and vibrated like the rest of her body. The henna climbed above her knees, thigh-high gladiator sandals. Now you saw her little triangular thigh gap, now you did not.

The whole embassy gasped and held its breath. The young mother stood up to gawk. But the old man pulled her back down. Lagoon Drinker glared at them over the shoulder of his interviewee.

WE ALL STARTED TO MURMUR, because the half-dressed lady had two amulet belts around her little waist, like the bells of a native wrestler. Something that looked like a dried-out vulture head hung from one of them, its beak right on the crack of her butt. The beak had a bright red ring. However, when it became clear that she was oblivious to her state of undress—or had sacrificed everything to win an eye-contact contest with her interviewer—a security man stepped up. But the fear of the juju did keep him from steaming in as usual. Instead, he signaled to the Black interviewer from a safe distance, who in turn asked her to pick up her clothing. Suddenly conscious of her situation, she panicked and splayed and swooped on the *wrappa* like a hawk.

Some in the hall complained of indecency; others said they had not seen enough. What pained me most was Lagoon Drinker's ringing laugh even as he hid his face.

To tie the *wrappa* back, the lady stood with legs apart. This was how women did it to create room for their legs, but as she threw the cloth back over her body, some sighs of disappointment went up, as though a beautiful movie scene had been cut too soon. When she finished, she was more nervous than before; she was full of exaggerated bows and loud apologies to the interviewer. He did not even appear to have noticed he had run this gentle soul ragged or naked.

WHEN HE RETURNED HER DOCUMENTS and *nexted* her, she shook her head slowly. She refused to leave.

The embassy went berserk.

Some were rooting for her, others against her. As she hung in to beg, a loud debate swept the place. Some said she must be given the visa because she had been harassed to nakedness. Others said she should be thrown into the rain and banned from future interviews for trying to juju-rig the process. The Muslims said that at the very least all the Christian women should be forced to undress to prove that they were not beyond belts-*ibok*, otherwise the headlines would demonize Muslims alone. The Christians said the Muslims were accusing them without evidence. The juju worshippers said both Muslims and Christians were spoiling their reputation by day but patronizing them by night, like this lady. The two foreign religions turned on them.

When security managed to calm things by menacingly fanning out into the hall, some people in an unpoliced corner called the interviewee a prostitute for donning "Lucifer panties." And they were quite loud about this. But others said they loved this kind of evil on themselves or on their ladies and warned them to stop policing how women dressed. The other group retorted that it was un-Nigerian to even talk about lingerie; others reminded them the embassy premises were America, not Nigeria. The debates spread like an *ekarika* fire till the loudspeakers boomed, telling everyone to hush, otherwise they could cancel our interviews for "breaking diplomatic/embassy protocol."

Total silence.

But because of the woman's juju sacramentals, neither the next applicant nor security went near the booth. Even Lagoon Drinker did not get anybody, because the person would have had to stand close to the juju woman. He sat there sipping his water and calling, "Next!"

"Hey, juju woman, stop terrorizing de embassy!" a security woman growled as more security arrived. "Leave dere, ASAP!"

The Muslim turned to her and shouted: "But the officer is insinuating I'm traveling for prostitution. Same thing they said last time. What's their proof? I'm not a prostitute!"

"Look, even fellow Nigerians *dey* accuse you, too," they said.

"You want make we bring out de security dogs?"

"You no see on TV how American cops *dey* shoot Black folks . . . ?"

This seemed to bring the Muslim back to her senses, for she picked up her documents, then her shoes. She did not put them back on but carried them on her head, turned around, and sobbed through the hall. There was another wave of commotion as people scampered away from her juju.

The embassy warned everyone again.

I GOT LAGOON DRINKER. He was in a red tie and white shirt. His large eyes were almost malaria-sick green, and there were two bottles of water in front of him.

"Okay, Mr. Udousoro, do I understand that you're reapplying?" he said after I greeted him.

"Yes, sir," I said.

I put my passport in the tray.

"Why were you denied a visa?" he asked, paging through the passport.

"I was not told," I said.

"You were not told?"

"Yes."

"Yes, what?"

"Yes, I was not told."

He shook his head and then drank some water.

"No, you were told," he said. "Your record says my colleague dutifully informed you, you wouldn't return from America. Do you remember anything like this?"

"Ah . . . ah . . . sir, yes, sir."

"She also noted you were talking to the ceiling when she asked you about your tribe. No eye contact whatsoever. Correct?"

"No, sir. I wasn't talking to the ceiling."

"Which definitely meant you have something to hide or are crazy. Do you have any documentation verifying your mental health status?"

"No, sir. It wasn't mentioned in the requirements."

"Well, let's just say you could've invented your tribe . . . just too many tribes in this beautiful country."

"Please, sir, I wish to put it on record that, one, I'm not the founder of the Annangs. Two, I have nothing to hide. And, three, I'm not crazy."

"Come on, this tribe stuff is just a fake question. If it weren't, it would be on the application form, okay? It's just how you handled it. And there's no need for Andrew & Thompson to insult our intelligence by sending copious documentation from Ivy League universities on your precious Annang people! You don't expect us to know everything about your hundreds of tribes, do you?"

"Sir, you're right."

"You're an editor traveling to edit an anthology of war stories and to learn publishing in America. But it's not clear how you will use this knowledge back in Nigeria. Anyway, do you have a table of contents for the book?"

"Yes. 'Biafran Warship on the Hudson,' 'Ojukwu's Divide and Rule'—"

"Wait, wait. *Hudson* like in the Hudson River in our U.S. of A.? Are you kidding me?"

"Please, sir, don't be offended. I believe the author wants to show the international dimensions of our war and the effects on our diaspora. There's another story, 'Biafra in Rome,' that shows the same thing about Europe."

"Well, I can assure you the world out there is tired of reading about all these senseless wars. We can never understand why you guys can't stop killing each other—so much violence! Even your soccer team, once the pride of Africa, is going down, crippled by tribalism. Don't get me wrong: I love to eat *suya* and Agege bread, because I've always loved brioche. I just think the only things lacking in your country, if you ask me, are order and constant electricity like in this embassy. See how happy you are in this serene and clean space?"

I swallowed his wicked irony like a stubborn wad of phlegm.

"I am a happy, peaceful, and clean person, sir," I said.

"But, Mr. Udousoro, did you not buy those pamphlets out there warning applicants not to fold your arms so you don't appear defensive, or how to avoid Lagoon Drinker, the demon? I mean, how many years is it going to take you guys to learn that Americans appreciate eye contact while your cultures think humility and honesty is staring at your feet when you speak to authority? And didn't they tell you I deny visas to folks visiting New York, my village?"

"I heard something like that outside. Sir, the only reason I want to go to New York—"

"Naah, not when you *lied* about the previous interview."

I said I meant to say I was not told why she thought I would not return. He said those were two different things and accused me of dishonesty. He wrote something down on a piece of paper and seemed to underline or cancel it a hundred times. Then he abruptly stood up, excused himself, and left the booth with my passport.

The Black interviewer was quizzing a young man heading to college in Montana on a scholarship. The boy said the school had offered to pay his flight ticket. He wore white flip-flops and red socks and a pink *asine-ata-ukang* and yellow shorts. He was color-blocking, for no Nigerian ethnic group dressed like that. But what stood out for me was the way he had bleached his skin. Whatever creams he was using had lightened it almost to the color of his nails, except around his knuckles and elbows and knees and lips. They stood out like black islands on a sea of whitening skin and intensified the color scheme of his total appearance.

The interviewer asked him what he knew of Montana. Without blinking, he replied the place was more tropical than Lagos, never snowed, and belonged to the grandfather of Joe Montana, the American footballer. When the man nodded and smiled and approved the visa, it was further confirmation the whole process was pure bullshit.

The successful applicant gathered his things and thanked his interviewer profusely. Then the boy turned and bowed to the applicants behind us. They responded with smiles and thumbs-ups. Sashaying into the main hall, he lost it altogether and started to sing, holding up the slip like a winning lottery ticket. Then he stopped and put everything down on the floor and started dancing to Alanta moves, then Azonto, then Ndombolo, and then back to Alanta. His footwork was impossibly intricate and caught security completely by surprise. But the hall was cheering, urging him to register for *America's Got Talent*.

Even the Black consular officer abandoned his current interview of the young mother and her son, loosened his tie, pointed at the dancer, and broke into a crazy laugh. When the hall caught on to the diplomat's blatant "breach of diplomatic/embassy protocol," applause rang out, loud and sustained and solemn. Some stood up. It was like church. However, this really got security mad. They tackled the dancer and bundled him out into the rain.

The little boy peed on himself; the mother wept and searched for the restroom with her eyes. Their interviewer stopped laughing and left the booth. When the urine spread toward the mother's shoes, the boy squatted and pushed her away and covered his face with both hands. Before I could react, security and cleaners arrived and screened them off in a yellow contraption that smelled of chlorine, then dragged the whole thing to the restroom. As the PA brought us back to the embassy we knew, cleaners mopped and air-freshened the spot in the most efficient of operations.

"OKAY, MR. UDOUSORO, when you filled out the United States of America visa form, you promised under penalty of perjury to tell the whole truth," Lagoon Drinker said when he returned, opening my passport. "Look, you even wrote down in your second online application that my colleague didn't believe you'd return. So I don't understand why you'd just so blatantly sabotage yourself and lie to me this afternoon that she didn't tell you why you flunked your interview. Sometimes the stupidity, the craziness of Nigerians still baffles me!"

"Again, sir, I wish to humbly and categorically state that I did not lie. If I wrote it down on my application and could not initially understand your question today, could you not see this as an honest mistake? I can also get psychological certification that I'm not crazy."

"I regret to deny you the visa to the United States of America the second time." This time the rejection stamp sounded like a muffled gunshot. "It's my considered opinion that if we processed your visa you will lie your way to remaining in America . . ."

I snatched up my passport from the tray and walked out on him.

The security stepped forward to drag me back to swallow every last word of my humiliation. But Lagoon Drinker stopped them.

OUTSIDE, THE RAIN HAD NOT MELLOWED, and the skies were darkening. The flood smelled of the sea, as though the Atlantic had overrun its beaches.

When I had gathered myself, I put up my umbrella and started wading toward the taxi berth. I was too sad to remove my shoes or roll up my trousers. I did not know whether I was crying or not because the wind drove and battled the rain so hard I was completely wet. I was startled when the pamphlet ladies ducked under my umbrella, clad in raincoats and rain boots.

They said they had heard about the dancer who made the consular officers laugh. They asked whether I thought the student got the visa because of his bleached *onyibo* skin, whether they should recommend bleaching in their updated pamphlets. I said it had nothing to do with his color change. They assured me they had advised him to do everything to avoid using O'Hare International Airport, Chicago, as port of entry because the internet chat rooms had listed it as the most notorious for turning back Nigerians.

"Uncle, as courtesy for helping you debrief, could you share *your* interview details?" they said.

"No!" I said.

"We're sorry. But if de sadists no want you for deir country, don't be mad. Look at us. We *sef* shall never even see de inside of dis beautiful embassy whose visas we *dey* help process daily."

"Go away."

"*Chai*, you selfish man o . . . it's like embassy soccer match: Santa Judessas/Lagoon Drinkers ten-uncle-zero!"

Before I could kick them out from under my umbrella, they put a pamphlet in my hand, pushed my fingers to clasp it, and fled. I slogged away, embarrassed and angry.

A broom of lightning swept the skies, applauded by a procession of thunder. When a wedge of wind snapped the umbrella, I tossed it in a trash can and held on to my waterproof folder and pamphlet. Now the damn pamphlet was getting soaked. I was not going to open my folder to stick it in. I stormed back to the trash can and smashed the pamphlet inside. But the wind deflected and landed it in the flood. In frustration, I pursued it down the road. An embassy car splashed water on me and created waves that drove the pamphlet farther away.

"Stupid pamphlet, you're not also allowed to mock me!" I said, pointing, chasing. "As our people say, both God and *utere*, the vulture, can never abandon the corpse. Two interviews, and I couldn't even get to present my documents . . . excellent!"

I waved at the old man's relatives, who were huddled under big umbrellas. They did not wave back but looked at me like I was a madman. I walked toward them. They moved away toward a trio of cops. Hearing folks laughing behind me, I turned sharply to see the Depression Discount assholes tracking me under two big green tarpaulins. They said God had punished me for lying to them that I was not reapplying. They said if not for the police they would have tossed me and the juju woman into the lagoon, like the Yorubas did to the Igbos during the genocide and war. When I groped the flood for stones to haul at them, they scattered.

CHAPTER 3

Daddy, when is Thanksgiving?

THE FOLLOWING WEEK, MOLLY TOLD ME HER CONGRESSMAN had put in a call to the State Department, which had asked the embassy "to review" my visa application. And when the embassy emailed me an invite to a third interview, everyone insisted it would not hurt to try again, especially since I did not have to fill out another form or pay a new fee. They told me to remember the endless interviews of Usen's wife, before she was allowed to join her husband.

This third interview turned out to be a mere formality, though I had gone with a letter from a psychologist to prove that I was sane. My regret was that the pamphlet ladies did not show up that day. Though the new visa was scented like a newly minted dollar bill on my passport, I had suffered so much already I could no longer feel the joy of coming to America. This accentuated the emotional farewell between Caro and me before the flight to Lagos, from which I would get on a New York flight. The old Bekwarra man did not crack his second interview. His son told me this in an email, in which he expressed shock that I had gotten my visa and apologized for "not responding to your greetings after the second interview on that rainy day." He said his father's health was deteriorating. This weighed on my mind until the stern JFK immigration folks took me in and asked their thousand foolish questions, as the embassy touts had predicted. They said they were calling to verify my proof of accommodation with my landlord. They said they were calling Molly to verify whether she was my supervisor and whether I was truly editing a war anthology. When they got angry that they could not reach her with the office number, which was what I had put down on my visa application, I panicked and offered her cell phone number. They called her in New Haven, Connecticut, where she was visiting her retired Yale professor parents for the weekend.

That Saturday afternoon, August 27, 2016, in my navy-blue Nigerian *senator* wear, I did not feel any relief even when they finally said, "Welcome to America!" and stamped my passport. I did not stop trembling till I cleared customs—after more questions and a search of my belongings—and finally arrived at my address in Hell's Kitchen in a taxi.

Stacking a huge bag, a boom box and a carry-on on my head and strapping a blue-red bulky computer bag behind me, I hiked and panted up the tight stairwell to my floor, the steepest steps I had ever climbed, since each flight went straight to the next floor. It was worse than climbing a steep *mbod irim*, and I had to shorten my strides to avoid ripping my trousers. My door was one of the three forming a semicircle around this stairwell of rusty twisted vertical bars with sharp edges. The ceiling was a low sky, its leak stains ominous clouds, the round light fixture half filled with dirt, a dying moon. A hallway linked up with this open area, like the tail of a noose.

My apartment was unlocked and painted a light blue, the blinds off-white. It was much smaller than I had thought. When I gave Caro a video tour on WhatsApp, she did not think much of the kitchen because it was much smaller than ours. But she appreciated the fact that Lucci had left bread, eggs, peanut butter, Coke, and Budweiser in the pink orchid Whirlpool fridge to welcome me, and, on the lovely little dining table, instructions about the local shops. He weighed the note with three keys, with further instructions to always use all of them. This table was surrounded by three old beat-up chairs. In the living room, there was a bookshelf, a chandelier, a green recliner, and a Sony TV. Atop the shelf, there was a black-and-white portrait of a smiling old man with large friendly eyes, dried lips, and a black earring and thick silver hair. The windows opened onto the street, where a twenty-four-hour parking sign twinkled nonstop. All the windows had gaps, hence the few mosquitoes buzzing in the apartment. Caro and I had not worried about mosquitoes but about the coming winter when we had discussed New York. Besides, we had been told since primary school that American mosquitoes did not give malaria.

Apart from the whole place having, in my opinion, too many wiring pipes running along the dusty walls, there were also too many taped wires and electrical sockets, as if it were some improvised recording studio. The tapes came in many bright colors, like the plumage of *nsasak*, the sun bird. My bedroom looked like a little storage area between the living room and the kitchen, exactly the length of the full bed and a footpath; it had one of those beds you fold into a cabinet fixed to the wall. I liked the small bed and its navy-blue sheets and multicolored bedcover. I put most of my clothes in the ample cabinet shelves above it, while my sweaters and suit were in the big closet in the living room. I left the boom box I had brought by the bed, which was how I loved to listen to my audiobooks. The wooden floor was old and scraggy, and glued together with a dirty yellowish filler in places. This was not exactly the glistening floor of the New York apartments we saw on TV or in magazines, but I was not going to allow this little inconvenience to spoil the excitement of living by Times Square. "Ekong Baby, the most important thing in a bedroom is the bed," Caro consoled me.

I was elated when Usen rang to welcome me and to say he would bring his family to visit me the next day. He could not come to the airport because of a crucial meeting with his landlord.

Molly herself called to say she could not wait to see me at work on Monday. And I could have hugged her when she added, "I really gave the JFK immigration a-holes a piece of my mind when they phoned to say they'd detained you and asked me all these stupid questions about the usefulness of your fellowship! And why is it their business whether your relatives were personally hurt in the war? They made it sound as though Andrew & Thompson were helping you apply for asylum. Even I felt humiliated listening to them. God knows what shit questions they asked you." She said they only let me go when she lost her cool while rehashing my torrid visa interviews for them.

But now, because she was still fuming, I could not say how angry the officers themselves were with me after that call. I could tell right away she was quite an expressive and passionate lady who called things as she saw them.

Next, Molly said to call Gregory Lucci in Purchase, New York, to arrange to pay rent. However, when I did, he was still seething from his own run-in with the same immigration authorities. "These thugs interrogated me for thirty long minutes as if I'd stolen my apartment or something," the old man said in a trembling voice like he wanted to cry. "Buddy, I'm so relieved you called, because now I know you're safe. They were so rude they threatened to send you home or stick you in quarantine if I didn't cooperate. And can you believe they tried to trip me up by asking me to corroborate some of what Molly had told them? Claiming she was too upset for them to understand her?"

When I responded that he was a very understanding man, it seemed to console him. Then he eagerly confided in me he had rented my apartment for thirty years, and how much he loved it, though the landlord, Tony Canepa, was refusing to renovate it just to provoke him to leave. He said something about "rent stabilization" but I did not understand. He asked about my family and age and was happy to hear I was married. He promptly said the married usually treated his space better. He was shocked when I said we did not want children. But, giggling with embarrassment, he scolded himself for nursing this stereotype that Africans could never decide not to have children. Then he added that I could remove his crucifix above the door and his photo and hide them somewhere. When I said it was fine because I was also Catholic and liked the photo anyway, he was pleased. He spent a bit of time trying to pronounce Ikot Ituno-Ekanem, my village.

I wanted to know whether there was paperwork on the subletting to be filled out or signed, but he said no. "You mean I don't have to sign anything with you or the landlord or the city?" I pushed for clarity. He assured me that, according to the law, he had informed the landlord, which he did in writing as soon as Molly had contacted him. He praised me for being a stickler for laws, just the kind of subletee he and the landlord preferred. We agreed on when and how to get his rent to him, the first installment being the rent for both August and December.

Finally, he was really moved that I had come all the way from Africa to understudy publishing. It meant so much to him that I was a Morrison Fellow; he told me when he first read *The Bluest Eye* in 1970 it felt as though he were being thrown into a distant country and culture. "Buddy, I've been meaning to say you must be a really special person!" he said, laughing. "I'm an avid reader myself. I'm so honored to host you in my humble abode. I apologize on behalf of our crazy immigration officers."

But what stayed with me was his weak, wavering voice. I could tell he was a kind old man. His voice seemed weaker the harder he laughed, yet it was a comforting, trusted grandfatherly presence in a strange land. I texted Molly to say how pleasant he was. She replied with a thumbs-up emoji.

I ATE BREAD AND COKE and napped till the sun came down. When I stepped out with Lucci's cart to shop at the Food Emporium in Times Square, I ran into my two nearest neighbors chatting by the stairwell, one Asian, one white. I stopped to greet them, but they ignored me. The Asian was a tall sinewy man with a flat shaven head and a goatee whose strands you could count. His teeth had a double gap. He was wearing black jeans and a white long-sleeved T-shirt under a red short-sleeved shirt. Though both men shared the same height, the white guy was broad-shouldered, with thick heavy lips and thick glasses in brown round frames. He had a yellow long-sleeved T-shirt over tight white trousers that revealed his calves were bigger than his thighs.

I went nearer and said another hello. But it did not earn me even a glance. I was ashamed and lost. The place suddenly seemed too small for me and them. So I backed off slowly and lugged my cart down the stairwell, glancing over my shoulder to the mailboxes. However, the voices of the two men actually seemed to be getting louder, their laughter chasing me from the building—or maybe it was in my head. I was sweating and my back ached as I rolled into the streets.

But seeing the majestic skyline, "the rich man's skyscrapers," to use Usen's description, up close set my heart pounding. I was always crazy about Times Square. After Caro and I attended the long midnight Mass that ushered in the New Year in Nigeria, we would not go to bed until six a.m. Nigerian time, when we had witnessed the New Year ball hit Times Square on CNN. It was like experiencing New Year's twice. It was always a special private thing between us; now I missed her so much the pull of the square felt raw, as though she would suddenly show up if I hurried and burst into it. But I was impeded by cars and tourists clogging the streets, the restaurants overflowing onto the curbs. New Yorkers and their tourists came in all manner of colors and races and sizes and clothing and languages. It was intense. The air around Hell's Kitchen was full of the assorted beautiful scents of ethnic food. Though I could not place the cilantro smells, those of curry reminded me of the Indian restaurants of Abuja, and those of baked overripe plantain fleetingly of my village.

Yet entering the square was more surreal than anything TV could conjure. The atmosphere sparkled with life and images and sound, whole sides of skyscrapers covered by screens. Sometimes these screens were interactive as the same advertisement exploded and splashed from screen to random skyscraper screen, like the ball in ping-pong doubles. The square was the glare of a lacerating kaleidoscope.

The sheer energy alone from the diversity of people pouring in from all over the world could have lit up the place. It felt so global, so democratic, as though all these lights had already boiled and refined every soul down to essential humanity. From the glow on the faces, the excitement from even the American accents around me, I could see that even Americans found this as fascinating as the foreigners. And the cops were everywhere, armed like soldiers. I was shocked to see all these beautiful ladies in cowboy boots and colorful bikinis shaking their boobs like bells. But when I got near enough to realize their breasts were merely painted like they were in bras, I knew the square was even wilder than I had thought.

The only thing that remotely reminded me of home was the statue of Father Francis Duffy behind the cross in Father Duffy Square. The face of this fine Irish American soldier, who had meritoriously served as chaplain in the Spanish-American War and First World War, had the same sharp features and seriousness of the Irish priests and nuns who sacrificed everything to plant the Christian faith, Western education, and hospitals in southern Nigeria. His eyes and lips really resembled those of Father Gary Walsh, who defended the people of Ikot Ituno-Ekanem during the Biafran War. I would not have wanted to remember the war here, but the atmosphere was like an anesthesia and this seeming familiarity was like a precious opening, a doorway into the unbridled effervescence that was Time Square.

I BOUGHT TWO BASEBALL CAPS from Forever 21 and a set of long satin pajamas from Victoria's Secret for Caro. Of course, she was excited; we texted back and forth. Then I parked my cart and joined others in climbing to the top of the red and silver bleachers of Father Duffy Square, where a camera projected my face on a thirty-foot screen. It was all so sudden, like my head was sucked out of all proportion by a magnifying mirror. I recoiled from the horror in my eyes, but before I could smile like others were doing, the camera had cut to something else. I was still feeling my face when a big cheer washed over me. Without knowing what was going on, I scrambled down and grabbed the cart to join the jokers in front of the Marriot Marquis Hotel. They sounded like fun.

There was a giant screen atop the latter that showed miniatures of everyone standing there. A titan of a girl was superimposed on the screen and she would pick up these miniature images from the screen as if to bite them, like King Kong, but then she would just kiss the image and put it back down. I wanted to be picked up. But I was not lucky. When staying in one place for a long time did not favor me, I moved about and waved to the girl. As our people say, you cannot stand in one place to watch the masqueraders. Nothing. When she picked one baby whose family was eating hamburgers on one of the little red dining sets outside a McDonald's, the mother held her precious baby closer. As I watched folks eating, I had no guts to ask the family whose images got picked up what it felt like, because if my neighbors could not answer my greetings, why should these random folks?

When a cop politely tapped my shoulder to move my cart for it was inconveniencing others, I apologized, got ahold of myself, and disappeared into the Food Emporium. I packed up as many groceries as possible, because hauling stuff to my apartment was not something I wanted to do often. But what I remembered most was buying yams, a common food in Nigeria. While the name rang with nostalgia, these yam tubers were nothing like what I knew. Our Nigerian yam could be as big as a human thigh, whereas these ones were a little bigger than potatoes.

YET A HEAVINESS, a discomfort, a homelessness descended on my heart as I pushed my purchases home. It was the fear of my two neighbors.

It worsened the farther I got from the conviviality of the square. I texted Caro about it, who said the best thing was to ignore them. But I kept thinking about whether I had greeted them the right way, whether I had moved too close to them during the second hello. Were all my neighbors like this? Though I decided to be checking my peep-hole before leaving home, how would I avoid them going up to the apartment? Should I ask Lucci for advice?

When I got to my building, I breathed in, steeled myself, opened the front door, and entered. I stood quietly by the mailboxes, listening and scanning the stairwell. In my village you greeted your neighbor, unless something was wrong. How do you live close to people who do not want to greet you?

An African American man walked in behind me. Though he was struggling with eight different breeds of dogs, all on leashes, he nodded and smiled and greeted me warmly and introduced himself as Keith Jim-Stehr. We connected right away. He was a slim friendly guy with a neat fade haircut. He was wearing green cargo shorts and a blue sleeveless top. He told me his great-grandparents were from Alabama. The dogs were excited, some licking my hands, others jumping about. Though I did not like dogs, today I appreciated their welcome.

"Hey, Ekong, I got to know you were here when I overheard your neighbors—I'm sure you've met Jeff, the Asian, and Brad, the white guy, and Alejandra Ledesma, his girlfriend. . . ?"

"Not the girl . . . yes, yes, any problem?"

"Well, I heard them talking about *the African* carrying his luggage on his head. I thought they were going to call the cops on you. Last year, someone on the second floor called the cops for a Black guy who came to visit his Latino friend."

"Really?"

I was noncommittal, for even in my village it was unwise to jump into neighborhood gossip. I changed the topic and told him how much I loved the city already. I eagerly accepted his firm handshake when he could finally move all the leashes into the other hand.

He was a middle school teacher and walked dogs on the side, an occupation I never knew existed. I was happy when he asked me to wait for him to take his dogs to his apartment so he could help carry my cart. He apologized that the dogs would be noisy some nights, especially since his apartment was directly under mine. I said it did not matter, for I was a deep sleeper. Be that as it may, I did not understand why someone would go to the trouble of having dogs and then pay another to walk or keep them.

"Ekong, where should I visit in Africa?" he said cheerily when he returned.

"Big question—fifty-four countries!" I said, as we began to trudge up with the cart.

"That trip has been on my bucket list for centuries, man. Tourists' reviews online all sound the same."

"It's confusing. Even I know so little of my continent."

"And I know so little about my roots in the South. Some would even say I look down on southerners. But it's a bit more complex, because I'm proud of my grandpa, who fought gallantly in the Second World War in spite of the bruising racism back in Alabama . . . well, I've never had the good fortune to be near *you* guys, bro."

"The feeling is mutual, bro. Let me think carefully where to visit."

When we reached his landing, the dogs growled and pounded his door. I smiled an empty smile to assure him it was nothing. "But, hey, Ekong, you know what, maybe I should start with your country. I read somewhere Nigeria is *the Giant of Africa*. Now, that's my kind of tourist spot!"

"Let's just say the so-called giant is a bad mess right now . . . I'll get back with you on where to go, okay?"

"No hurry."

When we gently put down the cart before my door, I thanked him for his hospitality. As soon as he was gone, I locked up with the three keys and bolts, as Lucci had instructed. I polished the peephole with my index finger and peered out through it. *They* were not there, but I had a clear view of things.

THE NEXT DAY, I woke up late and tired. After breakfast of eggs and bread, I set about dressing up in my native Annang attire for the midmorning Mass. I put on my male *wrappa*, *ofong-isin iden*, and *asine-ata-ukang*, traditional dress, and cap. The peephole assured me outside was okay. But then when I took the first few steps down the stairwell, I realized it was too steep for my own good. I was like a lady riding with her skirt up to her waist; I was in the wrong clothes for this sport.

When I persisted on continuing down, I slipped and grabbed the banisters. I gave up. Luckily nobody saw me. I scrambled back up to change into a pair of trousers and shirt and blazer. With a map app, I found my way through the square's madness to the famous spires of St. Patrick's Cathedral.

But, as I would tell Caro and Father Kiobel later, though the familiarity of the Mass brought nostalgia, this space was not for me. It was too beautiful, too hallowed, too imposing, and trafficked in too much history and tradition and tourists moping at the altar like a magic show gone bad. Folks just sauntered in like it was a Wendy's or a stadium—no genuflection, no pre-Mass rosary recitation, nothing. And no matter how much I begged God to save me from Brad and Jeff, I myself was distracted, goggling at this or that part of the picturesque architecture. Moreover, instead of listening to the homilist, my mind kept replaying the booming arresting voice and the unforgettably poetic imagery of the cathedral's late archbishop Fulton Sheen, whose homily tapes we had listened to in our youth, long after his death. Today, the preaching felt intolerably flat, the whole liturgy as hurried as bad fiction, like these diverse worshippers could not wait to eat Communion and jump back into the Big Apple. It reminded me of John Updike's "Packed Dirt, Churchgoing, a Dying Cat, a Traded Car," where he wrote, "In Manhattan, Christianity is so feeble, its future seems before it."

On my way back, a text from Molly asked how I was settling in, repeating how she and her colleagues looked forward to meeting me the following day. Of course, I talked about my fascination with the square. She politely said it was not her favorite part of town and pitied me, for I would endure this twice daily to and from work. "But it's still better than coming in from the Bronx daily!" she insisted. I changed the topic, because I loved *my* square and was actually already roaming it, angling to be picked up by the King Kong lady. But she avoided me, even when I cupped my hands around my mouth and shouted and jumped and waved in the brilliant afternoon sun. I only ran home when Usen texted they were already on our street.

We exchanged big hugs and were as loud and dramatic as only Nigerians can be, so much so that the street stopped and paid us attention. The Umohs were in matching red Nike sneakers, black jeans, and red Liverpool soccer club home jerseys. The wife, Ofonime, a graduate student at CUNY, even completed her outfit with a red headband. Being a Liverpool fan myself, I was so moved by their display I asked for a group selfie.

Though I had not seen Usen for decades, he was still the short lean fierce boy of my childhood with alert eyes and big nose. Now the only big difference in his physique was that he had grown a funny stomach, a kind of hard *garri* bag that slumped from the chest, like all the fat in his body had settled into a soccer ball therein. Ofonime shared the same height with him, though her complexion was as fair as some of white New Yorkers, or the embassy Muslim.

In my apartment, Igwat, their toddler son, refused to leave Usen's lap and kept pointing and screaming at the broken floor each time he set him down. He equally eyed me with suspicion, like I came out of the cracks. I was shocked at how Usen promptly dumped him on Ofonime and scudded closer to me to chat; I thought every man in America had learned to carry a child. However, their eight-year old daughter, Ujai, was the most excited to meet me and said her father had told her so much about our childhood. She was all over the place, like this was her second home. She was a tall inquisitive confident willowy girl, so different from her dad. In fact, if the parents did not stop her, she would have unplugged the yellow fillers or thrown something down the cracks, to satisfy her curiosity. She was as unyielding as Usen and I, when we were her age, when we were poking cricket holes with broomsticks under the full bold moons of Ikot Ituno-Ekanem of yore.

She immediately took to calling me Uncle Ekong, which surprised Ofonime, who said they could not get her to prefix *Uncle* to Tuesday. Each time I spoke, this American girl listened consumed like I had brought the undiluted truth from the mythic village of her parents', a place she had never visited before. She wanted to see photos of Ikot Ituno-Ekanem in my phone. I had none.

I was really glad, though, that they had brought me two portions of delicious *afang* soup and *poundo* flour, a frozen pack of shelled periwinkles, goat meat *mm'ikpa*, rings of dried smoked catfish, and ground crayfish and bottled palm wine, which Usen said he bought in Little Senegal. Though I was an alcoholic and had gone cold turkey for ten years, I wanted to open this wine immediately because I was quite curious about its taste. But Usen suggested I refrigerate it for the best outcome. Yet it was the palm oil, "with zero cholesterol," as Ofonime gloriously proclaimed, and the great spice we, the Annangs, call *ujajak* that filled my place with Ikot Ituno-Ekanem scents.

When Usen called up Tuesday Ita on speakerphone, he addressed him as "Hughes," his American name. Both Usen and Tuesday were unbelievably excited I was going to publish our war stories. And I thought Tuesday's ringing *nsasak* laugh was exactly as folks described it back home, though he had never visited since 1975. I could not help but gush about how his scholarships had made sure no child was left behind in Ikot Ituno-Ekanem, how his wells had given us clean water, or how his money had helped the widows of Awire Womenfolk to start up small businesses.

"Ekong, I have a very vivid image of your father!" Tuesday cut into my tales. "Before the war, he was one of our primary school teachers and a wonderful choirmaster at Our Lady of Guadalupe." Usen quickly explained that Tuesday was uncomfortable with being praised and moved the conversation to why I left my teaching job. I told them I had always wanted to be an editor, especially after noticing our schools did not have minority war literature in our syllabi. But when Tuesday volunteered to write the foreword to the anthology because of his experiences in the war as a ten-year-old, Usen and Ofonime exchanged glances and fell into silence. I simply thanked Tuesday, promising to discuss his offer when we eventually met.

After Tuesday praised Father Kiobel for running a wonderful parish, we reminisced about our seasonal festivals, and argued about who among Governors Godswill Akpabio, Babatunde Fashola, and Sam Mbakwe was better at fixing up roads and hospitals in their respective states. Ujai wanted to know who these folks were, and we took time to explain, not because we expected her to get the politics, but because the parents said she was really into anything African and had been asking to visit Ikot Ituno-Ekanem.

But Ofonime became very bitter about my embassy experience, especially about the health of the old Bekwarra man. It got worse when she heard how the embassy had accused the Muslim of prostitution. Ujai sat still for the first time and avoided my eyes.

Obviously, this was the same accusation that had made the embassy deny Ofonime a visa several times. She started detailing how the consular officer had asked how many divorces she had had "before faking this American marriage to Usen," whether she had ever known any pimps, how many prostitute friends she had. Ofonime sounded very much like the compassionate Muslim lady at the embassy. "I had four damn repeat interviews with this same crazy Asian American consular lady!" she sneered. "Each time, she said I was lying and stormed out and came back as though to wear me down. Are they going to hand me over to the Nigerian police for prostitution? Has someone stolen my identity? Are they going to examine my body? If not for Father Kiobel and sleeping pills, I would've lost my mind the days preceding the interviews. Each time she asked me the same questions about divorces and a prostitution past I never had—"

Ujai jumped up and whispered loudly in her ear: "Mommy, you're seriously embarrassing me with all this sex stuff!" The mother apologized and hugged her.

"Da Ekong, please, you shall be with our family for Thanksgiving, okay?" Usen invited me before they left. "In fact, it will be your official welcome to New York. Tuesday and our friends are invited. We shall serve both turkey and *ekpang-nkukwo*!"

"*Sosongo o*!" I thanked them. "I've been hearing of American Thanksgiving all my life."

"Daddy, when is Thanksgiving again?" Ujai asked.

"In just over three months," he said.

"Okay," she said, shaking her head.

"No, what's on your mind, my daughter?" the mother asked.

"Mommy, please, could Uncle Ekong visit us before Thanksgiving?" Ujai said, searching our faces.

The parents said I could visit anytime.

"Yes, my daughter, I will visit you guys soon," I promised.

WHEN I ESCORTED THEM downstairs that evening, Ujai skipped ahead of us, singing that Uncle Ekong's house was ancient and ugly and had no elevator, while theirs was modern and had two elevators. She waited for us on each landing. Keith Jim-Stehr exploded out of his apartment and took a position on the landing, recording us with his phone. He was in such a hurry he was barefoot and his shirt buttons were undone. I wanted to tell him to put away his stupid phone, but Ofonime pinched me. Then, twice, we heard Ujai greeting people on their way up the stairs. They did not respond. We and the silent people met on the landing like two opposing waves clapping into Ujai.

My two neighbors!

Jeff, the Asian American, had tears streaming down his face; he was in wine-red trousers and a black sweater. Brad, the white American, was in black corduroy shorts and a tight green long-sleeved T-shirt, which showed all his muscles. He said a belated hello to Ujai. It was tense. Keith cleared his throat, as though to warn them we had backup. We squirmed against the rails for them to pass, and Usen hugged his daughter with one hand and gagged her with the other. Ofonime whispered to me to hush, that this was not Ikot Ituno-Ekanem where everyone greeted everyone anyway. Jeff and Brad also squirmed to get past Keith, who had established himself like a colossus.

I felt like following my Annang folks back to the Bronx.

However, Keith gave Ujai a thumps-up and pocketed his phone and, buttoning his shirt, descended to join us. He apologized that he had to whip out his phone to record things because he had seen our neighbors from his window returning from the city very distraught. "I knew I had to be here in case shit happened," he said. "As I told you, Ekong, last year someone called the cops on a Black visitor . . . horrible, horrible situation. That's what actually put me in touch with Mr. Canepa, the landlord. We talk. He's a friend. I'm going to let him know what happened here, in case things escalate, okay?"

"Thanks, bro, you understand our situation," Usen said.

"So thoughtful of you to record," Ofonime said.

"Thank you, sir!" Ujai said.

"You're all welcome," Keith said.

When introductions were completed, Keith repeated his desire to visit Africa. Ujai blurted out he must go to Ikot Ituno-Ekanem. We all laughed while she went on to impress him with features of our two seasons and her favorite village flowers—the simplicity of ixora, the resilience of mother-in-law's tongue through our six-month dry season, the jasmine scent of the queen of the night—all rain forest facts they said she had been googling. She unlocked her phone and showed him pictures, like she lived there, of our beautiful Our Lady of Guadalupe Church and school, the lip of the valley, the palm trees.

Nostalgia came over me. It was not so much what the phone could show Keith, but what it could not capture. I thought about our Ikot Ituno-Ekanem valley, which was thick with cashew and guava and mango trees, and one of these was always heavy with fruit, their treetops buzzing with birds, bees, and gnats drunk on the sweet smell of fermented fruit. From the top of the valley, the practiced eye could pick out folks moving on the tracks underneath the canopied meadows, like ants burrowing their way through the green clayey ground, the dark blue river dyed olive-green by the sun in the rainy season and a yellow-green in the dry.

The picturesque river lay there at the bottom of the valley, gracious to both the native and stranger, guarded by its narrow white sandy beaches. Even when fog covered the entire valley and obliterated its beauty, it was still spectacular. It was as though it had been stuffed with light cotton to shield our ancestors as they bathed in its depths.

But, on a clear day, you could see beyond the valley to the open market, to the mission with the church marked by a white cross atop it and the cement-colored life-sized Stations of the Cross in its fields, to the bridge that now connected the two parts of the village. Behind the church were our Guadalupe primary and secondary schools, my alma maters, wartime barracks. If you looked sideways on our own side of the valley, you caught how far in both directions property development had eaten into the slope and, the further you went from the village, into the thick forests.

✖

Keith thanked Ujai for the photos and, winking at me, announced that someone had finally convinced him where to visit in Africa. We all laughed.

As he returned to his apartment, I was touched by how he had rushed out to protect us, how he had made my guests feel welcome. I felt lucky to have another Black person around. But, as Usen knelt to retie Ujai's shoelaces, I was getting increasingly angry with Brad and Jeff and hated the stairwell like a shithole. Twice now I had met them here, and twice their nastiness had taken me unawares. I made the decision to confront these amateur sadists.

These four months, no one was going to make me feel like I did in the American visa interviews or during the JFK detention. It was no fun to be squeezed by tribalism back home and then by racism out here. Being a minority wherever you went in the world was no joke. I could endure personal humiliation, but not an insult against my guests. A red line had been crossed.

Like she knew my thoughts, Ofonime said if I let trifles like this get to me, I would never enjoy this country. "*Iyo*, I'm not worried," I lied. "I shall take care of the situation." She pleaded I should ignore it.

"My dear childhood friend," Usen said, "you can't fight everything in America. What have you seen yet? I say: just concentrate on what brought you here: the fight to prove that we exist back home, so that the Yorubas, the Igbos, and the Hausa-Fulanis—the huge ethnic groups—can get off our backs. I say leave American racism to us. We're okay."

"Well, I was only worried about Ujai," I said.

"No, Uncle, I'm fine," she said, swallowing hard. "Just that I greeted them twice."

"I'm sorry," I said.

"Oh well, it's difficult to be a Black kid in America," she said.

Her last words silenced everyone; the parents avoided my face. They tried to look at each other but failed at that, too, as though they could not protect me from the shame of America. The girl herself clung to me till we got to the mailboxes.

Outside, Igwat finally relaxed, giggling and clapping and waving like he was celebrating an escape from some haunted house. And by the time we got to the subway on Fiftieth Street, his sister had recouped her spirits. We were as boisterous in our goodbyes as when they had arrived in my place, and as we hugged and took more selfies, Ujai said we should have taken a selfie with Keith. When she said she had a big secret for me, I thought she was going to ask me to bring Keith along when I visited the Bronx. But Ujai pulled me down and whispered she did not like the three mosquitoes she saw in my apartment.

I promised to kill them that night.

I HURRIED HOME to try the palm wine, in spite of all my guilt of drinking, in spite of knowing Caro would not have found it funny if she knew. I pounded the 110 steps upstairs, ready to mow down anybody bent on belittling me. I drank straight from the bottle. Well, it was nothing like the real thing, but, as our people say, in the absence of an alligator a lizard will do. It was not even that potent; it tasted diluted.

Soon the water for the *poundo* was boiling on the cooker and the *afang* soup hummed in the microwave, the whiffs of home spices and flavors finally ripening all over the apartment. By the time I finished making the *poundo* and stood it was like a small steamy jagged white mountain in a flat plate beside the soup bowl, memories of the stairwell bullshit were almost cleansed from my head. I washed my hands and cut and worked the *poundo* and soup with my fingers like I had not eaten for years. Though my taste buds immediately concluded this Annang food had been Americanized, I was continually licking my fingers. I could neither resist the spinach used in place of our tropical *mmung-mmung ikong* nor the bales of succulent *ati-napa* mushrooms nor the generous crumbs of deboned dried bonga fish nor the tenderly baked drumsticks.

It was only when I was almost done that I realized I was chowing down both portions instead of one, like hungry folks who suddenly remember to add salt to a meal at the end. Also discovering I was sweating, I paused to cool myself with more wine. But then one swallow continued to call on another insatiable swallow—till I tilted the soup bowl and cocked my index finger to scoop and lick everything. The bowl was as clean as though I had tongued it. I was very full, as though the balls of *poundo* had found their way to my toes. Sitting back, I sighed and consoled myself that Thanksgiving would be another chance to enjoy their outstanding cooking. I raised the wine bottle in a silent cheer to the immutable friendship between me and Usen, before shaking it to stir up the dregs and then, throwing back my head, poured everything down my gullet in one long gurgling swig. When the last drop hit my tongue, I smacked my lips, put down the bottle, and, out of habit, placed the empty bowl in the plate, our way of signaling that one was done.

When I washed my hands, I did not use soap. I wanted the heady smell of the fresh Cameroon pepper and palm wine to stay with me.

CHAPTER 4

I loved Starbucks

THAT FOGGY MONDAY MORNING IN LATE AUGUST, my first day of fellowship, I left early for breakfast at Starbucks. Jet lag had not allowed me to sleep a wink. I was in a brown Nigerian *senator* dress. After grabbing my laptop bag, I shone my eyes through the peephole and slipped out.

I was happiest away from my block.

I readily found a café on Forty-Seventh Street and Ninth Avenue. It was as enchanting as I always thought it would be from the ads I had seen on the internet, magazines, and global TV. Seeing its green mermaid logo and intense colors all over the shop reminded me of the powerfully energetic paintings of my namesake, Ekong Emmanuel Ekefrey, the Ibibio artist. I felt at home with the café's chirpy morning music, reminiscent of our 1970s Radio Calabar's Music While We Eat. I stood at a corner, carefully studying what others were getting before ordering a double-smoked bacon, cheddar, and egg sandwich and Salted Caramel Mocha Grande. And, hearing another customer tell the salesperson, "No whipped cream, no foam, please!" on his order, I repeated it. I just wanted to know what *salt* and *caramel* together tasted like; only children would combine both in Ikot Ituno-Ekanem.

I sat by one of the big rectangular windows facing the avenue and read home news from my laptop while I ate. I loved my mocha; the salt did not get in the way of the syrup. And this was the perfect calm perch from where to absorb the city, I thought, instead of being sucked into Times Square's whirlpool right away. I was disgusted by crazy NYC taxis hooting their horns so early like in Ikot Ekpene Motor Park. New York was already overwhelming; each minute, each experience, each location had the power to sink me deeper into the immensity of this city. I took refuge in watching Nigerian hip-hop on YouTube, entertained by all our dance moves.

I loved Starbucks.

I called Caro. She was still saying how jealous she was of my Star-bucks' ambience when I was startled by a gaggle of cartoon char-acters, Scooby-Doos and Mickey Mouses, on the street. They had zoomed against my window like I was sitting too close to a big TV screen. I fumbled my precious mocha, spilling some on my shirt. In another moment, they were gone. As I quickly dabbed the spill with napkins, the salesgirl came over to sympathize, wipe the table, and compliment my outfit.

I was not angry with the clowns. They brought me nostalgia, because as a child I had always loved them on NTA Channel 6 Aba and NTA Channel 10 Calabar in Usen's house on the other side of the valley, the only TV of our childhood. But too many of them in one place was a bad idea; they appeared to be competing among themselves for best character rendition—and too rowdily, like they had been woken too early to cheer up all these little groggy NYC kids being dragged to kindergarten by their parents.

When I saw the clowns' jaywalking had drawn angry hooting from taxis, quickly I excused myself from Caro, packed up my things, and, like folks trailing benevolent *ekpo* masqueraders, followed to see what morning show they had for the square. But the cartoon characters had not combusted into action like on TV but dawdled around, daily laborers waiting for an employer. Their attempt to be funny toward folks going to work looked like harassment, because this crowd was more serious than the weekend revelers. Everyone was in a hurry.

Not me. I looked up and around like one who had a whole open-air theater to himself, until I was bowled by the urchins in a *Newsies* commercial for Broadway. As they pirouetted, ghosted, and glided from building to building, I spun like a cone to follow the spectacle. Next, the rascals seemed to sprint at me from all directions as if they would fly off the screens. Then the screens momentarily darkened, burying them mid-flight. Immediately I knew I must visit Broadway soon. Then I went to wave at the King Kong lady. I expected to be picked up since I was, perhaps, the only attentive audience. But she ignored me again and picked up an empty MacDonald's chair. I sat on a nearby chair; she went for the table. I quickly pinned it down with my butt, yet, like a witch, she had already extracted the image. "Dude, it's too early for this stupid musical chairs!" growled a mother with a weeping child on a purple leash. "Go fucking get yourself a job or something, will you?" I was too disgusted with her and wanted to scream at her to carry her child instead. I had never seen a child on a leash before. But I shrugged and ignored the busybody.

AT VANDERBILT and Forty-Seventh Street, I rode an elevator to Andrew & Thompson, my heart swelling with joy. *I'm finally here!* I told myself several times to calm down. The place was even smaller than I had thought, one big square room partitioned into cubicles and fringed by a few offices and conference rooms. The walls were lined by shelves and art, and the floor had a blue-black carpet. It smelled of new books. Everyone was excited to see me. Molly was at a meeting in her office when I arrived, but the rest had risen to the occasion, like they had been waiting for me for years.

My new colleagues were all so nice and sweet. They were modest about their publishing house and, in self-deprecating humor, they merely pointed to the water fountain and the restroom in the hallway and the big printer in one of the conference rooms in the name of showing me around. Except for a few remarks about the uniqueness of my accent, I could not have found a warmer reception in my village.

Still, I was a bit more nervous than I needed to be on the first day of work, culture shock or not. Slowly it began to register that it was the first time in my life I had inhabited this kind of white space. While I could hope to avoid my two Hell's Kitchen neighbors, this feeling of being enclosed in a white bubble high up here in an NYC skyscraper was really out of this world, as it were. It was not the New York I had come to know in the past two days. When I looked out the window, my sight was beaten back by fog, and when I glanced at my body it was as though I myself had become darker.

Moreover, I did not like the fact that I was already blaming myself for my shock. When my eyes kept lashing the hallway where the nearest thing to diversity hung, Henri Matisse's *The Moroccans*, I knew I was allowing myself to be distracted by mere skin color, instead of appreciating the warmth of my new friends and environment.

So I exhaled and willed myself to calm down as they showed me my cubicle, which was in the nearest cluster of cubicles by Molly's office. On the desk was my schedule of rotations through the publishing house's various departments, starting with editorial.

We were all still gathered around my cubicle chatting about my first impressions of America, Nigerian hip-hop, and the Nollywood movie industry and the great strides of the American national women's soccer team when Molly emerged from her meeting and gave me a great hug and complimented me on my height. She was a petite white lady with a beautiful face, cropped blond hair, and freckled skin, and great perfume. She was as fiery in person as she was on the phone. I also liked her immediately because her heels rolled her little waist like a former girlfriend of mine's. And from the reaction of everyone, I knew straightaway she was a good boss.

"Hey, I want to add my voice to the enthusiastic welcome of everyone here!" Molly said before introducing me to those she was meeting with, Angela Stevens and Jack Cane, from the marketing and publicity departments, respectively. In a very short time, I already knew Angela was loquacious and gesticulated a lot when she talked, while Jack was quiet and introspective. Angela was taller than everyone except me. She was in her early sixties, with long brown hair. I also thought I got the measure of her expressive personality when a visitor from another publishing house stared at me like I was out of place; she quickly asked the guy to leave, that they were in the midst of a private reception for me. Jack, who was in his mid-thirties, nodded and gave her a thumbs-up. He had a beard that was redder than his hair. He liked to stroke the beard like it might catch fire, and his sense of humor came through the little he said.

THEN MOLLY LED ME into her office and closed the door. We sat down in a red velvet couch by the wall, while her hobo bag full of manuscripts and a handbag were on her desk. I thanked her again for all she had done to bring me here and mentioned how cool everyone was. Of course, when she asked how New York was treating me, I talked up Starbucks like I lived there. "Oh, New York is splendid, I must admit!" I concluded.

"Marvelous!" she said. "Are you hearing from your folks back home?"

"Yes, yes, even my Bronx folks visited yesterday. The *afang* soup really made me feel at home."

"Wow, how nice! By the way, could I offer you some water or something?"

"No, I'm fine. Thanks, though."

"Do you like your apartment's kitchen bath in reality as you did on the phone?"

"Even more, I'd say."

"Wonderful! Then you're really settling into the city."

"Even I surprise myself. Everything is so different here—big, intense!"

"Well, Andrew & Thompson is small, right?"

"And that suits me just fine."

"Oh, well, I've been there, done that at the big publishers, you know," she said, leaning back and pouring out a résumé that seemed to have taken her through all the powerful publishing houses already.

She said she had started off at Little, Brown and Company. Then she moved to Farrar, Straus and Giroux, or FSG, which she said was a branch of Macmillan, the popular one in Africa. She was enjoying her best stint there surrounded by a brilliant group of editors, but then Alfred Knopf tempted her away with higher pay. But she did not like her new bosses and ended up with Harper Wave, an imprint of HarperCollins, where she was fired within months. Next, Penguin hired her, but then it became Penguin Random House and someone who engineered her firing at Harper Wave became her boss and squeezed her ass till she lost her thrill for making books. She said then she became depressed because nobody would speak up for her, and when word got back to her nemesis that she was scouting for a new job, things only got worse. Then she got fired. "Oh well, there are worse tales out there," Molly said, shrugging and laughing.

She freelanced for six months before moving to Andrew & Thompson three years ago, where she said she was happy to have more editorial freedom, though they did not have the kind of money those other empires paid to their prized authors or put into publicizing their books. "So, yep, we'll get there someday," she concluded, giggling. "No stress, the most important thing is we're publishing really cool books and turning heads and winning prizes. Maybe financial rewards will follow, who knows?"

When she saw how surprised I was at her odyssey, she said American publishing was like that, cutthroat and insular, and that our Nigerian version would be this way once we had serious competition. "Everyone gets fired or poached, except the owners!" she joked. "Look, people move so much it's safe to say you have no permanent enemies. My only big regret was always leaving the authors I signed up. You work so hard to land the newest talent and establish a bond. And then, boom, you're gone. How do they know their next editor will share your enthusiasm? But I think it's worse when you're fired. You cry twice!"

"That's so sad," I said, squirming.

"Well, relationships are everything. The life of an editor is such that you'll have to run into everyone in the endless meet-and-greets, prize ceremonies, readings, festivals, end-of-year parties, and so on. If you don't recover quickly, or if you bitch too loudly, you're done." That infectious laugh I used to hear over the phone now filled the room. "By the way, you'll attend our editorial meetings, which are every two weeks. So, apart from editing your big anthology, you'll read some of our manuscripts for a second or third opinion."

"Oh, I really look forward to that! It will also give me a break from our crazy war stories and minority woes. You know, I must say I'm a bit nervous about the anthology."

"Who wouldn't be? But you'll be okay. I believe you have plenty of motivation to edit these stories. I like the table of contents you emailed to me. It's great.

"By the way, I forgot to tell you on Saturday where I got the war details to fight off the JFK folks and their stupid questions about your anthology . . . !" She brought out a copy of Chinua Achebe's recent Biafran War memoir *There Was a Country* and brandished it before me.

"Oh, you've read it?" I said, pulling up in surprise. "Some of the stories I'm editing are a direct reaction to the book!"

"This also helped me write your appeal letter to the congressman."

Molly said *There Was a Country* was one of the books the Columbia University professor who wrote one of the Annangs-exist attestation letters had recommended to her. She said it was an easy choice for her because ever since she read *Things Fall Apart* in high school, she had always loved Achebe's beautiful and spare style. I totally agreed with her, though I did not like how the weight of the war had already blighted our first meeting.

She praised the book for its capture of the trauma of the Achebes and their fellow Igbos from the 1966 genocide to the war to the evil postwar atmosphere of distrust. I said, yes, our murderous Nigerian government wanted to wipe out his family and had bombed his wartime publishing house, so he had to move his young family often to stay alive.

"Someday," Molly said, "you'll tell me whether you agree with how, as a Biafran War ambassador or propagandist, Achebe presented Biafra. It seems a different place altogether from the brutally divided Biafra of your project."

"You're totally right," I said. "But now I'm not in the mood to dig into Achebe's Biafra—this Igbo thing. They said it was about self-determination, independence, freedom of worship, freedom from genocide, all those noble things, but to us it seems just a grab for power and oil money. My country hasn't recovered from the war yet. Or my family! Don't ask me to talk about what happened to my father."

"Your father . . . ?"

"Yes."

"Oh, then your project is more personal than I'd imagined! I'm sorry to hear that."

"It is."

"But have you ever thought of writing a memoir?"

"I did not witness any events. I was a mere two-year-old when the war ended."

"Then a memoir of inherited trauma? There aren't many African autobiographies or memoirs out there, and I would be immensely interested. You know, I also edit memoirs. I can get you a really good agent!"

"Can't handle it!"

"Okay, well, you must write a foreword or introduction to your anthology. An autobiographical piece, something really personal? Maybe a poignant memory of how war stories shaped your childhood? I think it would be wonderful . . . we could help you place it with *Longreads* or *LitHub*. Maybe even *The New Yorker* or *Paris Review* would be interested!" I bit my lip, folding my arms, shaking my head. "Oh no, Ekong, I'm sorry, I didn't mean to push so hard. It can only work if you're comfortable. I got carried away."

"It's okay."

TO GET HER OUT of her guilt silence, I assured her it was okay to talk about these matters, as I was already confronting them in my editing. I told her today our ethnic relations were so bad our stupid government had proscribed the teaching of history in high school, to block serious conversation about the war. She said, well, her parents and grandparents remembered the war very well. She told me how they organized relief in their church for what the media reported as Biafran or Igbo genocide in real time. "So, naturally, they would be shocked to know they were minorities in Biafra, not to mention the abuse of these minorities!" she said.

Finally, she told me her door was always open and that she would show me a few not-to-be-missed sights of NYC, outside the insanity of Times Square, on Saturday. "We've got a great bunch of nice folks here," she said. "Ask them, too, for anything you need. The embassy mess has probably taught all of us more about international politics than any college course could." Molly added that we might be able to attend a few book events together, to give me a bigger picture of American publishing.

BUT BY THE TIME I arrived in my cubicle, I was already disappointed in myself for not sharing my family war tragedy with Molly. Shame and anger had blocked me.

I was still trying to arrange my desk when Jack, the publicity guy, stopped by and gave me a fist bump. He said he was really looking forward to reading my anthology. I said that meant a lot to me. We went on to make small talk about jet lag and my first impressions of America.

"You know, Ekong, the abuses in our embassy got us to research a few things about Nigeria," he said. "Really interesting history. I'd love to know more. Anyway, you should've seen the powerful protest letter Molly sent to the embassy, explaining at length how insulting it must be to Nigerians to turn to us, the same folks humiliating you at the embassy, for proof of their existence."

"Well, my country is quite a place, isn't it?" I said nervously.

"It's really rich in diversity."

"Complex."

My closest neighbor, Emily Noah, an editor, a big girl with short spiky hair of different colors, stood up to join the conversation. She looked tired, and given all the manuscripts piled up in her cubicle, I knew she was overworked. She was leaning on the partitioning of our cubicles, almost pressing against Jack. "Well, some internet sources say there are two hundred and fifty ethnic groups while others say three hundred seventy-one," she said, and revealed she was actually the one who contacted the anthropology departments at Yale and Columbia universities to get the Annang-existence letters. "Yes, we were all so terribly upset about those crazy visa interviews!" she continued. "Angela and Jack also added letters to the package. You can only imagine how upset we were when you were denied the second time!"

"We were all Nigerians that day!" Jack said.

"Jack is understating it," she said. "He wanted to lynch Lagoon Drinker, *the* New Yorker, ha!"

I thanked them, bowing and shaking her hand and then Jack's.

"Well, my friends, I've seen the three hundred seventy-one figure, too," I said. "I've even heard the figure five hundred. Mommy said she learned Nigeria had only a hundred and nine ethnic groups in school."

"What accounts for such large discrepancies, if I may ask?" Emily said.

"It's a mess, to be honest," I said, as two more people arrived. "Look, as it is in the eyes of the international community, once Nigeria finishes counting her three big ethnic groups, the rest can go to hell! Besides, nobody knows why we're a country beyond the fact that the Brits, our colonial masters, wanted it."

"It's really complex, then," Jack said ruefully, stroking his beard with the back of his fingers.

I nodded. I was comfortable with them, because when I had expected them to say, "Well, if you cannot count huge things like tribes, how could you count people or why should we believe in your two hundred million census claims," instead they wanted to know of our six distinct vegetation zones, from the Sahara in the north to the Atlantic in the south, where Annangland, my ancestral land, was located. Suppressing the urge to sing about the unique features of our terrain like Ujai singing about our flowers, I merely told them we were close to the ocean, roughly south of the Igbos, the owners of Biafra, and northeast of the Ogonis, Father Kiobel's people. Also, I could see my colleagues had carefully digested what they read about Nigeria, for when I feared they would bring up the country's gargantuan reputation for corruption, they talked about the endless diversity of food and clothing and music and festivals that two hundred and fifty or five hundred ethnicities and cultures must yield.

"You know, Jack and I would really love to try your food," Emily said when the others were gone. "We've just discovered online the battle royal between Nigerian jollof rice and Ghanaian jollof rice. It would be an unqualified honor to taste either of them." Excited, I assured her I had enough Nigerian groceries from the Food Emporium and Usen's gifts to make them a buffet.

By the time I stepped into the restroom, I knew they were genuinely interested in my background, co-fighters in the war to recognize our minority existence and dignity. In the mirror, my face looked happy and fresh and relaxed, the harvest of all the conviviality and nostalgia the conversations had brought me. I needed no one to tell me that Molly, Jack, and Emily were going to be my closest friends here. I felt so at home that, in my cubicle, I removed my shoes and my socks and put my feet on the blue-black carpet, symbolically grounding myself in my new world. I sent Molly a text to thank her again for everything, to which she responded instantly.

I exhaled and tried to focus right away on what brought me to New York.

I decided to begin with the novella "Biafran Warship on the Hudson," written by an Efik accountant in Sacramento, California. It was not my favorite, but one of its passages had the kind of precise historical information I could share with Molly, Emily, and Jack, to help them understand my background. It was a story that dealt with the pass-on trauma of the war on our diaspora children. It was narrated by someone Ujai's age. But, unlike her, the child characters never wanted to visit Africa again, afraid of war. Each time they saw a picture of a ship, even an ordinary boat on the Hudson, all they could think of was a Biafran warship.

While the terror of the war came through, my problem with it was the child narrator knew too much about the history of the war, complete with dates and figures, things beyond the scope of a child's mind.

In January 1966, Igbo military officers, graduates, were accused of leading a coup that assassinated democratically elected Hausa-Fulani and Yoruba and minority leaders—42 people—but spared their own. They claimed to fight universal corruption and tribalism, blaming the Hausa-Fulanis, the owners of the Sahel desert, for destroying military standards by insisting their high schoolers and illiterate herdsmen must join the officers corps.

This northern tribe, the Hausa-Fulanis, had married the most ruthless feudal system to a most horrible type of Islam, an amalgam that hates Western education and has finally resulted in Boko Haram. Their elite, whose children are educated in the best Western universities, have ensured that even today 20 million minors are systematically being taught to beg on the streets and sing Koranic verses. They use the kids in under-age

voting to rig elections and deploy the boys to burn churches,
while the girls are married off once they reach puberty.

General Ironsi, the Igboman who took over power after
the coup, worsened things by refusing to try the coupists but
detaining them in Igboland, where they didn't even lose their
military fatigues or pay! In There Was a Country, *Chinua*
Achebe defends Ironsi, his tribesman, arguing he couldn't try
the coupists because he was a "mild-mannered man." But, as
someone has pointed out, can you imagine the assassins of
JFK, Anwar Sadat, or Yitzhak Rabin not being tried because
of their "mild-mannered" successors?

Six months later, in a countercoup, northern Hausa-Fulanis
had sent their soldiers not only to kill Ironsi but to wipe out his
entire tribe, as though every Igbo child had planned the coup
and sheltered the coupists . . . the security forces and northern
herdsmen and masses didn't make a distinction between the
Igbos and our minorities. They claimed they mistakenly killed
us because they didn't know the difference.

More than 35,000 people lay dead.

After noting why the author must get rid of this history passage,
nonetheless I sent it to my three new friends, since they were already
invested in our nation's history. They acknowledged it helped them
see how tribalism led to our war. When Emily distracted me by
handing me two boxes of Andrew & Thompson books, all souve-
nirs from Molly, my heart swelled with gratitude. I had never had so
many new books at the same time. I admired the cover of each book
and inhaled their pleasant smell.

I STOOD UP and went to knock on Molly's door, to thank her for
the books. But Emily said she had left while I visited the restroom.
I emailed my edits to the author of the Hudson story. I skipped
lunch and apologized to Jack and Emily, who had invited me along.

When they pulled long faces, I promised to join them the following day. I needed to be in a group WhatsApp call to Caro and our new landscaper.

Jack, on his return, brought me a chicken burger and Coke. Then Emily forwarded me four novel manuscripts for my opinion. She told me my reports were due in two weeks, at my first editorial meeting. "Hey, we all read or moonlight this stuff at night or weekends!" Jack said, laughing at my alarm over the deadline. After Angela had stopped by to ask how my first day was going, I went back to tackling "Biafran Warship on the Hudson."

When I rode the elevator down at work's end, I thanked my ancestors for giving me a welcoming workplace and my new books. Once in the streets, though, my eyes struggled to readjust to diverse peoples again. When I turned and stared up at our beautiful building, it seemed to stare back at me, like a stranger smiling at me behind dark glasses.

I WAS SO HUNGRY I could not be distracted by the wonders of Times Square. I googled restaurant menus till I saw something familiar, *Baked ripe plantain* at Out Latin's. I hurriedly crossed the square to this Mexican storefront hole-in-the-wall in Hell's Kitchen. I ordered a to-go plate of roasted pork, white rice, and black beans and plantain. Then, fretting at the prospect of running into *those* neighbors, I whistled and strolled over to the Starbucks, where the salesgirl recognized me right away with a tired smile. In the absence of the morning rush, I relaxed to study the menu. I recognized and ordered Earl Grey tea.

I was jealous of the one or two people who looked like they had spent their whole day there, for I had seen them earlier. Already I felt emotional and worried these others could boot me out. This was *my* location, *my* Starbucks. I sat down where I sat before and ate this delicious Mexican thing.

I began to think of how to share the peculiar war story of our minorities with my colleagues, how we all escaped south across Rivers Niger and Benue back to our ancestral lands after the thirty-five thousand were killed, how we coped with this loss. But when I got to the attempted secession of Biafra from Nigeria and the maltreatment of minorities within Biafra itself, I lost interest and pushed my food aside.

What sort of country in the twenty-first century cannot even count its ethnic groups? How do you know who is who? Does the price for the lack of this basic knowledge have to be being *mistakenly* slaughtered along with others? How does one become a minority? How does one stop being a minority?

Feeling defeated, I left *my* Starbucks and returned to douse my despair in the bubbliness of Times Square. After buying three "Lucifer Panties" at Victoria Secret and a pair of earrings at Swarovski's for Caro, I roamed the neighborhood till I got to DeWitt Clinton Park, where seeing folks play pickup soccer lifted my mood. And when I finally arrived home, I balled my fingers and sprinted upstairs like someone going to war, each step or squeak reverberating through the stairwell, a warning to my enemies to steer clear. I did not mind if my trousers ripped or not.

CHAPTER 5

A Native American
cop peered into my food

MY EYES WERE BLOODSHOT WITH SLEEPLESSNESS WHEN I knocked on Molly's door first thing Tuesday morning. She greeted me enthusiastically from behind her desk.

"I'm so sorry, you must be suffering from terrible jet lag," she said. "Thanks again for the historical passage you sent."

"I've come to tell you about my father!" I said.

"Ekong, you know you don't have to do this."

"I know. But I'm actually intrigued, fired up by your suggestion that I do a full autobiography of my childhood. You also edit memoirs, so, who knows, you may be my editor someday. And you've promised to get me an agent. What I have to say would also give you an insight into why I'm not able to do the foreword . . . you already know so much about the war anyway, and nobody has contributed more to helping me get our story out."

When I closed the door and sat down on the couch where I was yesterday, she came to join me. As I gathered myself, twiddling my fingers, she said: "You know, Ekong, I was thinking someday we could go somewhere comfortable to talk . . . ?"

I shook my head and assured her I did not mind telling my story here. As our ancestors say, when a woman is overtaken by labor in the market, you cannot blame her for opening her legs. Besides,

I did not think my family shame was worth dragging around beautiful NYC.

"Molly, a year after the genocide and days after the Declaration of Biafra, our fortune in the new country was already grim!" I said. "Our folks fleeing home from the coastal Okrika had no words for what they were fleeing from, except to mumble about seeing local youths—who refused to join the Biafran army—being tossed down oil chutes to drown." I told her those who fled from Benin City, a part of Nigeria already invaded by Biafra, cried about public rapes when the women leaders roundly rejected Biafra's request for comfort women.* And rumors from our riverine towns like Ekoi, Essene, Oron, Onne, and Tungbo-Sagbama were all about *sabos* being dragged down forest trails and valleys, asked to dig their graves, and then lined up, shot, and buried during the day or stabbed and tossed in the unforgiving rivers at night.

Ikot Ituno-Ekanem woke up one morning and discovered that we had been overrun by tense and angry Biafran soldiers. Our folks started to fast and pray. Seeing Biafra turn a part of Our Lady of Guadalupe School into barracks meant our kids could not study in peace. When the soldiers raised the Biafran flag and started to teach the school their national anthem, many children wept. By the time they showed up in the valley and forced people to fetch water for the barracks, we became afraid to visit our beloved valley. Then there was pandemonium as they started killing people who did not obey them with military precision, burning down homes and conscripting young men. We did not know they had bought out some of our elders by promising them positions in the new country, until Caro's grandpa ratted on Tuesday Ita's two cousins who pulled down the Biafran flag at night and defecated on it. The "saboteurs" disappeared immediately.

Then the soldiers started calling everyone saboteur, or *sabo*.

* Orobator, S. E., "The Biafran Crisis and The Midwest," *African Affairs*, 1987.

Afraid of rape, Papa had hid Mama in the forests every morning—where, to forestall pregnancy nausea, she ate termite hills, wild fruits, and *mbiritem*—and sneaked her back at night. "Mama said I started kicking against Biafra in the womb, perhaps because of this Biafran diet!" I said.

The Biafrans imposed a curfew and sprayed even some sleeping dogs with bullets, for fear they would bark. Our people murmured that actually the dogs could have alerted the patrols of curfew breakers. But the Biafra army sent Caro's grandpa to explain that it was important for everything to be totally silent so that Biafran patrols could hear the stealth approach of the real enemy, the Nigerian army. The carcasses of these pets were left in the open in some places, to be buried by children, since adults, like Papa, were mobilized to plant bamboo stakes in school and church fields and village squares to keep away Nigerian army helicopters.

MOLLY GRIPPED THE COUCH when I told her how the patrols had raped Papa one night in our living room. I told her how he was unable to meet my brother's eyes as the boy kept asking why he was crying or why he was wrestling five soldiers. I told her how our pregnant mama stepped in to tell the boy they were military doctors giving him a painful type of multiple injections on his butt, which was why they had to hold him down each time.

When they were done, Mama got him off the floor. She pulled up his light blue trousers covered in blood and shame. Seeing they were bent on taking him away, all she could do was beg to give him a change of clothing. Mercifully, they obliged as she helped him into fresh black trousers before Biafra, this Igbo-thing, dragged him out of the house, down the street, down the trails of our thick forests, and herded him across our tribal borders.

"Molly, since you specifically suggested a foreword about how the war shaped my childhood," I said, "I can assure you my childhood was haunted from learning that Papa was among the accused *sabos* or saboteurs being frog-marched near Umuahia while Igbo crowds attacked them with sticks and crowbars for betraying Biafra, for not supporting their 'war of self-determination.' His crime? Mama said my querulous father was turned in by our Igbo neighbors for insisting that Igbo officers led the first coup, something the Igbos are still denying to this day."

I told Molly that for the longest time I could neither express any anger nor knew how to share this, because Mama herself had refused to judge my father's rapists. All she ever wanted to talk about was how much I kicked in her womb as they raped him. If you pushed her, she said many of these soldiers looked hungry and tattered from rushed military boot camp—and arrived in our Annang villages angry and afraid. If you pushed her more, she told you how many times, between Papa's capture and news of his death, she voluntarily cooked for the patrols, unlike other relatives of the disappeared. She had hoped they would in gratitude give her some hint of her husband's destiny. If you pushed her even further, she laughed a hopeless laugh and asked you to prove that the Nigeria that won the war has been fair to the oil minorities today, or that my anger or "minority war-stories activism," as she put it, would bring back my brother, who died of kwashiorkor in the last year of the war.

Papa's discarded bloodstained blue trousers had stood in for the corpse at the requiem Mass; it was a private arrangement in the sacristy of Our Lady of Guadalupe so our Igbo parishioners would not be offended. The night Mass was celebrated by our parish priest, Father Walsh, after he had gathered my extended family to say his fellow priests in Igboland reliably told him how Papa was executed.

Mama had taken time to perfume and iron these trousers and had folded them neatly in a little brown carton box and given them to the priest, like an offertory gift. And he, in turn, had placed it on the edge of the altar, by the crucifix. The cross was hastily written on the four sides with charcoal by the emotionally wrought Father Walsh, and the top was covered with a square white linen, the Corporal, the shawl for the remnants of the Blessed Sacrament. Over the years, I got to know that the priest had asked the sacristan, Usen's father, to leave because he was wailing for my father, his childhood friend. Caro's grandpa, an Annang who voluntarily became a Biafran soldier, had staunchly disobeyed the priest and stayed on to spy on who did or said what. The man was already hated for masterminding the disappearance of two of Tuesday's uncles, after he learned they had defecated on the Biafran flag.

There was no incense, no flowers, no songs for the soul of my father. Usen's mother said she heard from my father's cousin that Mama, after Communion, had burst into one of those powerful Annang Catholic dirges. Papa had once been a choirmaster. But, when she mentioned Biafra, our relatives had quickly gagged her until she choked and fainted. They begged Caro's grandpa never to report her to Biafra.

I told Molly even the holy water that was sprinkled on the box tasted fake, because it had no salt. Most of our salt had been diverted to make Biafran bombs. Yet, all the same, even if the corpse had been there, who could dare sing at the burial of a saboteur, or *sabo*? Who could ring the church bell after his summary execution?

This was only the beginning of the so-called war of self-determination. And Biafra had already changed the way we buried our dead . . .

I STUTTERED AND STOPPED, because Molly was sweating like I was torturing her. She stood up and hugged me and told me to be strong and praised my marriage to Caro for surviving such family enmity. I stayed with her in the office till she recovered and dried her eyes and reapplied her makeup. "Such stories really get to me," she apologized. "All this reminds me of the history of . . . Never mind." Whatever she wanted to say was making her too emotional, so it was my turn to say I would not press her.

Thus, I also held back telling her what I knew of the silent burial procession from the sacristy and interment by the *atama* plant beside our house: how Papa's trousers were hurriedly buried like some little treasure in a hole, or a yam head hastily planted in the first dusty drizzle of our long rainy season; how Mama could not attend because I was pounding her womb like the bombs falling in Aba, which was precisely when she made the decision, if we survived, to call me Ekong, war; how, after the burial, Father Walsh had diplomatically resorted to scolding the soldiers in private, because each time he broached Biafran brutality in his homily, some Biafrans, soldiers and civilians, had stormed out of Mass; how angry our people were to see their Igbo neighbors, the owners of Biafra, had better salt rations. I could not tell her Caro and I did not discuss Biafra because of her grandpa's surveillance of my dad's funeral. Though we loved each other, and she supported my work, it was prudent not to dwell on such things. We kept mute each time Biafran quarrels flared up in our extended family.

That day in New York, when I came back to my cubicle, I felt better, if totally exhausted. But the musky scent of Molly's perfume was so over me that Jack cocked his eyes and joked I smelled too much like her. I slouched on my desk, too sleepy to join those who laughed.

I WOKE TO THE BEEP of Molly's text. She suggested I go home to sleep properly and thanked me again for sharing. But I stayed on, for she had no idea how comfortable these offices were—as opposed to Hell's Kitchen, where I feared a confrontation.

I liked the Japanese buffet where Jack and Emily took me. Eating my smoked blue fish with a can of Crush, I shared a bit about my project; they asked some questions as they ate their grilled Spanish mackerel and Chinese *tong choy*. When they brought up the passage I sent them the previous day, nothing angered them more than the stupidity of the Hausa-Fulani elite's self-sabotaging refusal to educate their masses or decision to keep forcing ten-year-olds into being someone's third or fourth wives. Once Jack knew nothing had changed in the fifty intervening years since the war, he was very disappointed. "The shit reminds me of pre-1880 Delaware," he hissed, "when the age of consent was seven!" His anger was such that Emily moved the conversation to our village life. They both said they wished they could visit. "That would be really wonderful!" I said.

I told them about our complex multi-ethnic, multi-racial parish church, and they seemed fascinated by Father Kiobel's personality and ability to manage such a diverse congregation. But they were offended that he had no interest in my publishing project. They went on to tell me about their volunteer work in animal shelters and blood banks, through the local Humane Society where Angela was on the board. I was so impressed I promised I would join them for a day.

I said how much I wanted to hit Broadway for the spectacle of seeing if the *Newsies* urchins would live up to the Times Square mega-ads. They said they were interested, too, and would love to go with me.

I GOT HOME WITH too much energy for my own good.

I could not sit down to work. Not even listening to audiobooks or drinking Lucci's two Budweisers settled my spirit. To cope, I started cooking. I pulled out the Food Emporium yam tubers and started peeling, to make porridge, *mmun-edia*. Though they were different from our yams and even smelled different, I felt I could swing it, though I was not much of a cook.

Like I was practicing for the day I would cook for Emily and Jack, I improvised, chopping the tubers into big dices. A badly cooked *mmun-edia* was better than no *mmun-edia* at all, I encouraged myself. I made a stock from two dried smoked catfish, palm oil, onions, Maggi cubes, ground crayfish, and periwinkle—from my Sunday gifts from the Bronx. With a cleaver, I broke an *ujajak*, the spice, into three, to unleash its strong flavor, and tossed them in the pot. When the pot boiled and floated a froth of crayfish and the skin of the catfish softened and swelled and the *ujajak* scent bloomed, I knew the broth was ready. The only setback was, since I had no *real* pepper, I had used Lucci's black pepper: it skewed the taste.

Well, undaunted, I poured the diced yam into the stock and closed the pot for a short while. Certain that the spice had "entered" the food, as we say, I opened the pot to add dried *nton-aku* leaves, another spice, and chopped lettuce. But I intentionally overdid the spice, trying to cover the black pepper defect.

When I caught myself eating from the pot as I waited for the food to thicken, I burst into laughter. I was already drunk on the scent of the spices. I went over to the boom box to play Solototo and Timaya.

Of course, this American yam did not taste like our Nigerian yam at all. But I was bent on enjoying whatever I found in my sojourn. I had finished the first serving and was about to begin the second when Lucci called out of the blue to say he was just checking in on me. He started out by admiring my background music, and when he learned of what I had just cooked, he was so thrilled he sounded like he might crash my dinner. "Just great, how quickly you've made yourself comfortable around here!" he said.

He was happy I had thrown myself into my work and my colleagues liked me. And since he was sniffling, I asked whether he had seen the doctor, and that attention pleased him as well. When we discovered we both shared a love for soccer, I put my food aside. He was very tickled as I explained what world soccer and Roman Catholicism meant to our 1970s Nigerian childhood. I told him how we learned about the samba dance from watching Brazilian fans at World Cups, how we learned of the greatness of Italian footwear because we heard Gucci made the Pope's red shoes, how we learned of the enduring tensions of the Spanish Civil War from following Real Madrid–Barcelona rivalries. "Oh Lord, my friend the landlord and I are also soccer fanatics!" he said, his laugh as pleasing as his photo on the shelf. "Caught a few games together in the Red Bull Arena in New Jersey."

Lucci was proud of the U.S. women national team, praising them for winning the World Cup many times, these ladies whose profiles we knew so well in our villages. And he was not only calling up past legends like Mia Hamm, Michelle Akers, or Christine Lilly, but extolling the versatility of Megan Rapinoe and Hope Solo. I was equally touched when he took time to applaud goalie Briana Scurry's resilience as "the only minority on all those snow-white teams across so many World Cups and Olympics."

I loved his worldview.

I DUG INTO MY READING for the editorial meeting. *Trails of Tuskegee*, the title of one of the four manuscripts I was given, grabbed my attention. It was a black comedy fictionalizing the Tuskegee syphilis experiment on Black men by the U.S. government, something I had faintly heard about in college. The manuscript was sponsored by Emily.

Like some of the stories in my anthology, the book was full of biting humor, which I loved, especially whenever the charming boy narrator, who was two years older than Ujai, described the needles that were used to supposedly draw blood samples, or when he captured the victims' initial excitement as they thought their government had brought them free health care. I loved how he slowly made sense of the tragedy from eavesdropping into adult conversations. The cast of vibrant characters showed how this terror had trashed this community for forty long years and through seven American presidencies, progressively altering the bones of the narrator's father and grandfather's faces, as it boiled and ate away their genitals. The narrator's anger was tangible as he slowly discovered why the men of his community could no longer ride their bicycles or dance the Twist or cut their lawns. Yet, I was lifted by the author's vivid exploration of what hope the people of Tuskegee held on to even after discovering the war waged against them.

So, midway into *Trails of Tuskegee*, I resolved to support this book at the editorial meeting—if an outsider had a voice. Tuskegee took away a bit of my Biafran War victim's shame. I googled the

American presidents who were in power during this Tuskegee mess. When I counted the iconic Dwight Eisenhower and John F. Kennedy among them, it humanized America for me.

I wanted to send a text to Emily, to give her a heads-up. But since it was late, I began to take long notes on how to fix the novel's flaws. I got on the internet to learn more about syphilis and the subsequent public reaction to the experiment. I yearned to know about the "collateral damage" on, say, the women who got the disease from their men, or their congenitally deformed babies. I made suggestions on the possible evolution of the single white character. But the pain from the novel's final scenes, of the protagonist peeping through a keyhole to see his dickless uncle tearfully negotiating sex with the aunt, seeped into my bones and clogged my lungs.

I needed distraction. I needed fresh air.

It was past midnight when I stood up, scooped out, and microwaved my *mmun-edia*. I spooned it into a thermos, which I put in a plastic bag so I could go eat in the square, like I had seen some folks do. I knew the crowd's vivacity would revive my drooping spirits.

MY PEEPHOLE REVEALED Jeff and Brad chatting and yawning by the stairwell. I opened the door with so much force it shocked them. I jumped out, my face as blunt as a mallet, my mouth ready to scream the roof down at any sign of provocation or disrespect, my feet like unpinned grenades. This time I was ready. My sights set on them, I mightily slammed the door shut. This also jolted them, like giving someone two quick slaps.

They stood frozen as I slowly locked my door, one key after another. Alejandra, Brad's girlfriend, came out, smiling. She was in lacy white pajamas, and her hair looked like Santa Judessa's. She began to speak but the tension stopped her midsentence; she rushed back in and closed the door. I unlocked my door and locked up again. Then, whistling, I skipped downstairs, my heart warmer than the thermos.

In the square, no red table was free, so I walked around till I remembered to take photos of the beautiful war citation of uncommon service on Father Duffy's statue. It would help me invoke Father Walsh's dedication to our minorities during the Biafran War when I wrote the promo copy. It was great to be already thinking about publication, though the book was far from completion.

When I finally sat down to eat, I ignored all the stares—until a cop I thought was Latino peered into my thermos to ascertain that it was not a terrorist's last meal. Now I was ashamed, because the world began to gather like I was a spray-paint artist. Nonetheless, I smiled and asked the cop for a selfie. He readily agreed and pulled me into a pose. He asked where I came from and proudly told me he was Native American. He clowned and held up my fork and thermos, as though he enjoyed my *mmun-edia*, his mouth as if filled with food and laughter.

Suddenly there was a huge cheer, with folks pointing at the King Kong lady, who had extracted an image of the two of us, as if she were going to swallow us eating *mmun-edia*, or like she was going to smell it. Though I had longed to be picked up, it was so eerie. I wanted to join those screaming in excitement, but I got a lump in my throat: the display of my steaming food on that big screen, the fish and periwinkles tender and succulent. I could not breathe as the camera kept zooming into the food till it momentarily filled the screen. It was as if the Statue of Liberty lady had finally freed me after a long and arduous trial.

I flinched and staggered, trying to figure out where the camera was. The cop left, a bit embarrassed, as though he had overstepped his professionalism. My startled face on the screen covered the square in laughter. Before I remembered to photograph the screen, my image was gone.

SOME TOURIST, who had been recording the whole thing, asked what kind of seafood I was eating. "Seafood *mmun-edia*, or yam porridge seafood!" I announced. She said she thought as much; she said she was from Indonesia and a lover of anything seafood. She was more excited than me to see yam on the screen and went on and on about the many ways she cooked it. Her family gathered. I was grateful she promised to send me the recording. I was even happier she asked to taste the food. And she was already bending and complimenting the spices when her family said I had an African accent. She lost her composure and backed off. Then she threw my fork on the table, which rolled and fell to the ground. She disappeared.

On my way back, I ran into Keith and his dogs. I excitedly showed him the cop selfie with date, time, and place. But he pushed it away like another look might blind him, mumbling expletives about cops and African Americans. I disliked his reaction, especially since my food was involved.

Yet I held back as he went on to ask what time of the year was best to visit southern Nigeria and what prophylaxis he could use against malaria. Well, while talking about visas, we got into my embassy shit. Shocked, he said I must immediately sue the U.S. government for "tribal profiling." I said it would be useless. He insisted some sharp American lawyers could find a legal loophole, not just to sue on my behalf, but to bring the old Bekwarra man and the G-string-belt-*ibok* Muslim to America. He bit his lips as I explained that American immigration was not in a hurry to change its ways and cited Ofonime's torment a decade earlier.

"As an African American, I thought I understood everything about profiling!" he said. "Teach me, because I don't want to be totally lost when I visit *home*, Africa!"

"Immigration is protected even against the sick, like the old Bekwarra man. And, you know, as our ancestors said, even if you are homeless you cannot sue your neighbor for locking his doors!"

He laughed and repeated the proverb, like he was cramming for a test.

"Is that a real proverb?" he asked.

"Yes, but I made it up," I said.

"Then why attribute it to the ancestors?"

"Because ancestral attribution gives it power, like a biblical quote!"

By his apartment door, he stopped and took one long look at my empty thermos.

"What?" I said, bracing myself.

"Oh, nothing," he said, stepping back.

"No, hey, spit it out, bro."

"I like the scent from the thermos. You know, I've seen so many Nigerian dishes online. Please, is there any chance I could try your food . . . if you don't mind?"

"Absolutely!"

I relaxed, realizing he had only been disgusted with the selfie— not my food. I asked for time to plan a meal; I was excited by the prospect of having him, Jack, and Emily over.

Pulling him closer, I whispered that I had intimidated Brad and Jeff, so they were no longer a threat. He gave me a rigorous hand- shake with both hands. "Hey, you don't need to tell your friend the landlord about our Sunday stairwell shit!" I said. "I've taught them a few lessons." When he asked how I had accomplished that, I silently shook my head. He unleashed a huge laugh that echoed through the building. We did bro-fists and he quickly ducked into his place.

I called up Caro. Because she showed no interest in my *mmun- edia* tales, I knew I was in trouble. After saying she dreamed that I was overwhelmed by New York, she told me she had found a church in the square for me, in place of the cathedral. The Google link to the Actors' Chapel she sent showed diverse groups of worshippers, like in the cathedral, but in more informal gatherings. I was taken aback by the front, a nondescript thing you could not tell was a church from outside.

CHAPTER 6

Why really did the dogs die?

ONE WARM SATURDAY AFTERNOON, TWO WEEKS AFTER my arrival in New York, my back began to itch in the Hibernia Bar on West Fiftieth Street, an Irish sports place, where I was watching a Liverpool vs. Hull soccer match. I was in my red bell-bottom long-sleeved Senegalese caftan, which came down to my ankles.

The itch made me lose interest in my corned beef and cabbage sliders and Guinness Blonde. I had already been disappointed Molly could not show me around NYC two weekends in a row because, as publisher, she had to attend book events in Boston and Chicago. Usen was texting me nonstop to celebrate because Liverpool was leading by two goals. But I could not chat with him, as it became increasingly difficult to get to the little itch. I promised to call Usen later.

Just then the itch suddenly grew screaming wild, and I hurriedly pushed back my chair and shot up, but failed to reach the itch with my right hand. It was below my shoulder blades, almost at the midpoint of my back, stuck like unreachable trash in the gutter. I resorted to my left hand but could only hit the margins, which just worsened the itch. For a moment I wanted to pull off my red Senegalese caftan. But when I remembered I had just tight boxers underneath, I dashed to the door, leaned heavily against the frame, and rubbed at the itch like a stubborn goat.

The manager, a short man with sharp eyes, a stubble of a haircut, and an accent like the Irish priests of my childhood, looked at me in openmouthed shock. The other customers looked away. But before he could react, I was back at my table, ashamed. When he brought the bill, he was so tense his Irish accent almost mangled his words.

I apologized.

By the time I got home, all I could think of was the periodic fire near my backbone, not the match. When I called the Bronx, Usen and Ofonime eagerly put the phone on speaker and passed it to their daughter, like folks who were happy to get a break. She told me all about her school and church friends. She asked me about her parents' siblings back home and her cousins and the river and forests and Our Lady of Guadalupe Church. And then, unexpectedly, she asked me how I flew out of the country with the Biafra War still raging.

"Sweetheart, the war ended almost fifty years ago, after three years!" I said. "When Daddy and I were two."

"Then, Uncle, how come Daddy and Uncle Hughes talk about it nonstop like it's still going on?"

"Because people talk about wars forever."

"Mommy, though, never wants to hear about it. But these two are always drinking and saying dogs died in the war."

"Yes, many dogs."

"Did our relatives lose their dogs?"

"Some."

"Why really did the dogs die?"

"They made too much noise, I guess."

"How did they die?"

"I don't know."

"Who buried them?"

"I don't know."

"Uncle Ekong, hey, they said children buried them! Children like *me*. I caught them saying it, so they couldn't really change the story. Yep, my grandparents confirmed they were buried in our beautiful valley."

I told her we heard the same thing as kids and apologized for the mix-up. She wanted to know whether it was difficult to bury dogs. I responded I did not even want to bury lions. She said her parents said I was in NYC to edit war books and asked whether it was difficult. I said yes. In the background, her mother was laughing and saying Ujai finally had an uncle who would put up with her endless questioning, unlike Tuesday. The father was watching highlight clips of recent spectacular Liverpool performances and told me in English this was what he usually did whether we lost or won. And yet, in Annang, he warned me not to tell Ujai about other war atrocities, because she was prone to nightmares. When the daughter pressured me to interpret, I said something else in English. Then Ofonime said in Annang that Ujai hated being described as a minority in America.

"So don't tell her in Nigeria we're not even just minorities but minority of minorities," she said.

"*Mmekop*, I understand," I said.

"By the way, Ekong, work *abarie*?" Usen said, as I heard him switching off the TV.

"I love it," I said. "Great, man, great experience!"

"Many Black asses there?"

"None."

"Excuse me?"

"One. Me."

"Fuck, not in New York!"

"But if I'd had a bad experience, I would've said it!"

"So you don't know yet that being the only one is a bad experience?" He sounded like I was stupid. I heard him clear his throat, before turning the TV back on.

OFONIME SAID UJAI took great pride in the traditional saying about the Annangs being folks who hold eloquence and peace in one hand and machetes and stubbornness in the other. Usen had helped her find a parallel with the U.S. coat of arms' eagle, which clutches an olive branch in one set of talons and arrows in the other. "So hearing that Biafra even took away our machetes in some parts of Annangland would kill our daughter!" she warned. "I don't know how long we can protect her from these atrocities."

Usen said they would figure out a way in her teenage years to break Ujai into the conversation about being minorities in Nigeria. I returned to asking the impatient girl about her school and friends.

THAT SATURDAY EVENING, knowing my manuscript reports were due the following Tuesday, I began to read the second novel, *Sea Mistress*. But I could not get into this beautifully written historical novel, no matter how much I tried. It was a short novel set in the Aegean Sea, sponsored by Molly. I had never seen a defter portrayal of the sea or of the rugged lives of pirates. I could feel the fears and frustrations of the pirates, especially when their ship, *Sea Mistress*, broke down in the middle of nowhere. With flashbacks, this close third person narrator did a great job of showing the powerful sex lives of these hardened men coupled with their longing for the beautiful Greek islands.

But, as I have said, it was not my kind of book. I resisted sleep, made myself a cup of hot chocolate, and tied myself down to read. I googled some of the islands and marveled at how developed they had become over the centuries. Yet, beyond the obvious flaws in the book's characterization and pacing, everything still felt too distant. Perhaps, after reading *Trails of Tuskegee*, everything else was bound to sound distant and pointless.

I was halfway through when my back began to itch, and all sleep disappeared from my eyes. It was 9:23 p.m.

I got up slowly and tried to use the inside doorknobs to scratch the itch, but all were too smooth to be of any good. When I peeped out into the dimly lit stairwell a crazy idea crossed my mind. I opened the door slowly and thought of sneaking out to squat and grate my back against the sharp vertical bars of the stairwell handrail, ready to flee if a door opened. However, even the itch went away, embar-

rassed by such plans. I mean, I did not want to give my neighbors a
real chance to insult or hit back. As our people say, when the gods
want to kill you, you do not climb the palm tree with broken ropes.
Or, you do not challenge a lion and then refuse to lock your doors.
I believed these folks could make a viral video of me to shame Black
immigrants forever. I felt stupid for even standing there.

I locked the door.

But the maddening itching returned and was so bad that, to
remove every temptation, I used the two dead bolts. I convinced
myself the whole thing was the change of weather and environment.
I lay down and attempted to sleep, covering myself from the powerful air conditioner.

Still, late that night, like a ghost who could walk through walls,
I found myself tiptoeing around the stairwell. After ascertaining
everything was calm, I squatted with my back to the rail and went to
work. And, *iya-mmi*, were the feelings good!

Though I knew I had bruised myself, the itch was implacable. The
more I rubbed against the rails, the deeper its bite. Tears filled my
eyes, and seeing that an entrenched warfare had been declared on my
back, I pulled my pajamas, consisting of a long shirt, up to make a
direct contact with the metal. Then I sat on the floor, my legs pushed
out in a V to steady myself, my back flat against the rails. I tilted my
head forward so a bar could totally align with the gutter of my back,
a real whip against the itch. When the pain finally surpassed the itch,
I smelled blood and rust.

I stood up and went back inside and madly skimmed *Sea Mistress*
to its boring end. I decided not to endorse this novel.

THE ITCHING STOPPED ME from going to church that Sunday.
And I wrote Emily and Jack to say I could no longer join them at the
Brooklyn Book Festival, to which they had invited me.

By now I had some spots on my ankle, left forearm, and thigh.
And since I could see the affected areas, I studied them carefully.

There was not much to them, except that they rose in three unhappy welts, perhaps from my scratching. But they did not itch. Maybe they had nothing to do with the back itch. Maybe the crazy thing had afflicted me so much in my sleep that I scratched everywhere, and hence these three marks. Maybe, I had been bitten by the mosquitoes Ujai had complained of. Meanwhile, my back itch gave me a little kick, like it was listening to me, and sent a spasm through my body. And all day, periodically, it sparked into life. Yet it could not really match last night's unquenchable blaze.

When I looked at the three marks again that night, though they had not emitted any itches, they were looking angrier. I ignored them and put my energy into scratching my back. Then I picked up an old newspaper and started fanning everywhere to get the mosquitoes out of hiding, from the bath to the toilet to the kitchen to the bedroom to the living room, till I reached the door. Nothing. On my return journey, in the kitchen, I saw four mosquitoes and smashed them.

I was really relieved when the itching disappeared. In that bliss, I sat down and finished the edits for "Biafran Warship on the Hudson" and emailed them to the author.

After laying out my clothes for work the following day, I called Caro. It was two a.m., eight a.m. in Nigeria. Yet, she could tell all was not well in Hell's Kitchen, though I assured her I was okay.

"Or would you rather tell Molly!" she taunted.

"Caro, baby, I only *dey* meet *am* for office o."

"I know. I love all the sweet things you buy me from the square. Hey, I just *dey* jealous, okay? I miss you so much."

"I'm so sorry . . ."

"Please, don't tell me sorry. Tell me you miss me intensely!"

"You didn't allow me to finish. I miss you more."

"I've just been having bad dreams about you drinking with Molly Simmons. I can imagine you two talking Biafran War nonstop. You know how you get once you find someone who can listen to your war stories!"

"I wish you were here."

"Please, don't go drinking with her. Ekong Baby, you know, if you get drunk anything can happen?"

"You know I no longer drink, darling."

"*Nko asoho se* go to Actors' Chapel?"

"Yes, *mfon-mfon!*"

⚔

How I hated American mosquitoes when the itching continued Monday morning. I had never suffered like this from their malaria-bearing tropical relatives. I sent a text to Molly, Emily, and Jack saying I was staying home because of a stomach bug. The itching was not something I wanted to confide to anybody yet, until I knew better what was going on. They replied I should rest and take it easy though they would miss me.

By ten a.m., I was already too tired. I ate fried yam, *akamu mme* Nido, and scrambled eggs for breakfast. Of course, I could not attempt to use the rails to scratch my back in the daytime. But I worried what the welt on my back must be like, since I could not see it with the bathroom mirror. Whenever my affliction subsided, I tried to sleep. When I could no longer sleep, I attempted to read the two remaining manuscripts in time for the editorial meeting the following day.

I loved *Children of Elijah Moses*, another Black novel, because of its strong opening, memorable characters, and suburban setting. It was sponsored by Bob Hamm, a tall editor with frothy brown hair and large brown eyes. The race tensions among the Black and white and Asian and Latino workers in this huge bakery was palpable. The detailed descriptions of the smell of burnt cinnamon and of freshly baked giant chocolate chip cookies made me salivate. They were as evocative as the beauty of the sea captured in *Sea Mistress*. I liked the writer's usage of *nigger, chink, wetback,* etc., in the dialogue. I enjoyed the suspense that came from the fact that someone was stealing big quantities of bread without detection. But I thought the narration was rushed in places, like the author was afraid to escalate the race tensions and mutual suspicions. Because it was acutely disappointing, my imagination birthed a thousand ways to fix this major flaw. *I shall recommend this book!* I told myself.

Late that afternoon, as I was jotting down my thoughts, Jack and Emily sent me photos from the previous day's festival events. "Listen, if you need anything, let us know," Jack wrote.

Then Emily texted that she was looking forward to my reaction to *her* manuscript, *Trails of Tuskegee*, that she and Molly really loved it. When I wrote it was my favorite, she responded as though I were in their camp. She confided her roots were from a little town fifty miles from Tuskegee and that someday she would share with me the impact of the experiment on her extended family to this day. "This was part of why I was so touched when you shared at the Japanese buffet how the Biafran War continues to affect your family," she texted. I sat up, but before I could call to ask about the women and babies of Tuskegee, she fired another text, excusing herself. Her boyfriend needed her attention. I felt better when Molly checked in to suggest I get Imodium from the pharmacy, if I was still suffering.

I promptly visited Rite Aid on Fiftieth and Eighth. A salesman helped me find a tube of Cortizone-10. When I saw *The itch medicine doctors recommend* and *1% Hydrocortezone Anti-Itch* written on it, I nodded contentedly. He gave me another option, extra-strength first-aid anti-itch spray. I also bought two cans of insecticide and a little mirror.

Back home, I applied the Cortizone ointment generously on my whole body, especially the welts. Then I sprayed the anti-itch on my whole back. When the artificial cold of the analgesic got into that first back welt, I felt a sharp sting. That was how I knew that the stairwell bar had cut a real gash. A study of my back with the new little mirror against the wall mirror confirmed this. I applied more anti-itch on my back. One moment, I was in panic, and in another I was elated, surprised the pain felt so good. It frightened me that I wished it could even hurt more, to counter the itch.

I sprayed the apartment with the insecticide. I was surprised by the number of heavily-pregnant-with-my-blood mosquitoes peeling off from behind the pipes and colorful wires, flailing, bopping and tumbling in the fumes. I dutifully killed them, even pursuing one smart aleck till I had blasted it out of its frenzied flight. When its corpse hit the bed, it had long been dead. Still, I blasted it onto the floor so I could stomp it. But it disappeared into a crack. I returned to spraying, walking across the apartment twice—like the air hostesses who disinfected the flight cabin before we took off from Nigeria—till both cans were finished. Now I felt truly euphoric that I had finally "taken care of business." I resolved to kill all American mosquitoes, in life and dream, for these three days of menace had felt like three long years.

As a giant sneeze built in my chest and my eyes became watery because of the fumes, I locked up and went to bury my homesickness and nausea in Starbucks. Even the itches respected my right to be happy there. I bought an almond croissant and Very Berry Hibiscus Lemonade to celebrate my victory over my first American crisis. When Starbucks closed for the night, I relocated to the square with a cup of black tea, to stroll around like a man inspecting his vast estate.

When I got home, I read the fourth and last manuscript, *The Thunderous Sundays of Washtenaw County*. Like *Trails of Tuskegee*, it had a strong child narrator, but like "Biafran Warship on the Hudson," the voice was damaged by too many historical and esoteric facts, which a child would never know. I did not like this book.

For the first time since the Liverpool game, I slept deep and long. I knew because, as I came awake Tuesday morning, I was rattled hearing myself snore—something I had believed I never did.

CHAPTER 7

Trails of Tuskegee

THE EDITORIAL MEETING BEGAN AT TEN A.M. WE WERE nine people around a brown table. I felt really special in my gray minimalist batik attire, top-and-bottom, as though I were representing the entire Black race. I sat next to Emily, who was in a red dress and a black beret that hid her colorful hair. Jack was directly opposite her in a blue-striped sweater. I stayed farthest from Molly because of my addiction to her perfume. She wore a cyan-colored pantsuit and white blouse, while Angela was to her right in a rose print dress and a black blazer. Bob Hamm sat next to her; he was in a brown turtleneck and brown jacket.

Molly, the publisher/editor-in-chief, was moderating. She welcomed me again to Andrew & Thompson; I thanked them for their warm reception. When she introduced *Sea Mistress*, the pirate novel, everyone was up for it. They talked about how solid the plot and structure were, how it was a psychological thriller, how they enjoyed the brilliance of the character portrayals, the light touch on the themes. Then they spent quite a while juxtaposing *Mistress*'s tender description of the Aegean Sea with the brutal daily life of the pirates. They even read out some of the lines. They sounded so excited it seemed I had read a different thing entirely.

"In all my vast experience in publicity," Jack said, touching his beard, "I can tell you this book is going to fly off the shelves! I'm really, really excited about this one."

"So are we all. Except, perhaps, Ekong," Emily said, looking at my face.

"Yeah, Ekong, what's your take?" Bob Hamm said.

"Maybe it's because he's not been exposed to this kind of writing," Jack cut in, laughing. "I'm sorry, Ekong, I just wanted to chip that in before you speak!"

I shrugged and said, "Well, it's not exactly my thing. I'm not saying it's not good or anything like that . . . but there are so many flaws."

"And, yes, sometimes choosing one book over another is exactly as Ekong says," Molly defended me. "Not every work resonates with everyone."

"No, I meant my comment in a good way," Jack said.

"I know," Molly said. "But I'm saying it's not even a question of competence, but of taste, you know. He's not here to learn editing for the American market, but to understudy our operations and edit his anthology."

"Okay, noted," Jack said. "Ekong has raised an important issue, though—the flaws—but I truly believe they are very fixable. Trust me, Ekong, this could even be a learning curve for you when you see Molly's ideas on how to fix things. If all these other publishers want the book, it usually means they see a way around the weaknesses. Besides, no novel is perfect! Anyway, at least we have more diversity for you than usual in the novels we're discussing this week . . . ?"

"No, it's not about that," I pushed back politely, surprised to see him so vocal.

"I think Jack means this in the best possible way, you know," Bob clarified. "Personally, I'm glad we're considering minority works!"

"Yes, I truly understand what Ekong means," Jack continued in a tone that said otherwise.

"I like what Molly said about individual tastes," Emily said.

Angela raised her two hands and said: "Maybe Ekong's enthusiasm is a bit flat because he isn't acquainted with *our* publishing world and could use a bit of background: this author is an established author and did publish a part of this book in *The New Yorker*. Not *Atlantic Monthly*, not *Harper's*, not *Paris Review* . . . the freaking *New Yorker*! Maybe we don't know what you could compare *The New Yorker* to in your African publishing. Look, beyond the unbelievable storytelling in *Mistress*, once you publish there, you're bankable and, in terms of marketing and publicity—which is how Jack and I approach stuff—it makes our jobs easier. I think this is the author's best book, which is why there is such a buzz! So it's a big, big yes from my marketing team."

Though I knew of these magazines, I was shocked at the influence they wielded in these decisions. Nonetheless, I held a poker face and crossed my arms and thought about some of *The New Yorker* fiction online I had hated like shit. It was a magazine our growing noisy Nigerian literary tribe was killing each other to get into and bearing those who did eternal gratitude or grudge. Yet it was something our larger Nigerian society mistook for the *New York Times*, if it noticed at all. However, I felt my colleagues were doing everything to carry me along or, at least, to sincerely show me how they made their choices. I appreciated the attention they were lavishing on me, a Fellow.

"But I really understand you," Angela said to me. "What I'm saying is different from what Jack is saying."

"That's not how I meant it," Jack said in frustration, dividing and holding his red beard in each hand like two short tusks. "I didn't mean Ekong couldn't enjoy other writing. Anyway, never mind . . ."

"No, *I* understand you, Jack," I said, laying a hand flat on my chest.

Relieved, Jack leaned in to announce in a near-whisper: "I say we're even lucky we're considering this novel! Molly and Angela know how hard I've worked to convince my friend Chad Twiss— he's a super-agent—that we might be able to compete or even outbid the big houses on this particular one! The scouts say Random House's CEO can't stop talking about this book. If the author's editor and friend at Knopf hadn't died last year, we wouldn't even have this possibility. Molly would be a great editor for him. And just imagine how wonderful it would be if we took this one from the major houses!"

"By the way, Ekong, Chad has been to a few Nigerian book festivals," Angela said.

"Wow!" I exclaimed.

"He's really crazy about all this great literature pouring out from your country," she said. "He was so pissed about the embassy nonsense. You'll soon meet him, if you keep hanging around Jack, his pal."

"Well, ladies and gentlemen, please, don't let me slow you down from buying *Mistress*!" I said, to get attention away from my ignorance. "Even in the best of democracies, an eight-to-one vote is a landslide, no? Look, I'm just a bumbling Fellow." I hated to appear as the only stumbling block to their dream acquisition. "And, you know what, it's not as though I didn't like anything at all in the book," I said belatedly, gesticulating for effect. "I actually did. The love scenes were out of this world. I think they should be placed alongside the powerful sea and pirate passages." Folks giggled their agreement, as though in polite company it would be wrong to go into details of the sex passages.

"Well, I've already spoken to Liam about how important this one is," Molly confided, looking at Jack and Angela, like they three had been having private business meetings. "Liam—Ekong, Liam Sanders is our owner and CEO—is very sold on it. He'll support our going to the mid-six-to-seven figures. Yes, Jack is right. It would be a really huge statement that Andrew & Thompson is serious. We can't do it without committing to a big publicity and marketing budget . . . For now, let's just be cautiously optimistic. The bidding could get way out of our range. I know Knopf wants to keep him!"

"Molly, just being part of it is exciting, you know, but I was so thrilled by this novel!" Emily said, while Jack looked on as though he wanted to eat her lips. She went on to explain how this book touched her, not just because of all the great passages that we had read out to each other, but because her great-great-grandparents came from near that European sea, a place she had visited before. She said the setting was so powerful she had scanned some pages and sent them to her grandfather in Alabama. "I really hope we go for broke, because, for so long, we have been talking about repositioning ourselves, but never quite doing it."

We were like a country that was going to the soccer World Cup for the first time, where being in the same league with perennial winners was like winning itself. My deepest joy came from seeing an underdog go up against the big, established names. I loved the positive, bullish atmosphere, like a universal salary raise would soon be announced. When you are a minority, even being part of big battles matters, win or lose.

NEXT, WE UNCEREMONIOUSLY ELIMINATED *The Thunderous Sundays of Washtenaw County* before we got to *Children of Elijah Moses*, sponsored by Bob Hamm. But he fought in vain for this bakery race story. Jack and Angela eyed me warily as they attacked the book with unbelievable aggression. Though the previous night I had wanted to endorse *Children* and had concrete ideas on how to remedy the flaws, I did not jump to its defense because I did not believe Bob and I could convince the rest. But I was already mad at myself for not even praising the tantalizing aromas of *Children*'s bakery.

I reserved my energy for *Trails of Tuskegee*.

Now that I had a feel for how the meeting was going, I rehearsed my arguments silently. I knew I would be lining up behind Emily and Molly.

I googled the author of *Trails* and discovered she had never published in *The New Yorker* or anywhere, for that matter. This did not deter me. As our people say, the war that has a date should never overtake the cripple, meaning Jack and Angela's actions had forewarned me. If discussing *Mistress* had taught me anything, it was that Jack Cane and Angela Stevens were very powerful at Andrew & Thompson. But, seeing how slippery they were, I needed to figure out the best approach, especially with Jack, who seemed to think race stories should be my forte. I was a bit unsettled by his meeting persona, all devoid of his quiet subtle humor and deep kindness. This was not the colleague I had lunch with, the diplomat who understood how to ask sensitive questions about our Nigerian ethnic groups, the friend who often visited my cubicle, or the guy who wanted to lynch Lagoon Drinker. But, at this point, my heart was beating like a drum. My belief in *Trails* was such that if I needed to send word to or ask for a private meeting with the owner, Liam Sanders, I was going to do so.

Yet the gathering eyed me in a way that suggested I must have a bigger stake in *Children of Elijah Moses*, the race manuscript under consideration. I began to feel pressure and, slowly, my feeling of being the luckiest Fellow in the world began to wane. Then the tension spilled over into the room as Molly talked for a long time about the book, sometimes reading out a striking dialogue but skipping the words *nigger*, *chink*, and *wetback*, sometimes trying so hard to summarize passages they became incomprehensible. I supposed she fought to take the pressure off me. But then I felt my perception could have just been me living out my super-minority complex, something merely in my head. I felt so lost, so out of place, I looked down and began to crack my fingers. It was so strange that, suddenly, there were all these voices buzzing about in my head, as if I were a madman.

Would they have had a whole different or smoother conversation if they didn't need to use my face as the register of political correctness? said one voice.

I don't know, said another.

Shame on you for not speaking up for this book!

What if you lose out on Trails?

But what are you even doing at this table?

This last accusatory voice made me look up, to catch everyone staring at my fingers. I hid my hands under the table.

I myself disliked this Ekong Otis Udousoro, because he was uncomfortable in his own skin, like one long weekend of itches and welts and scratching had jinxed it. Then I worried over whether I had been actually cracking or scratching my fingers. Now Molly looked like someone who was afraid if she stopped talking, the silence could explode. It dawned on me that it must have been difficult for them, too, because this could have been the first time some of them were experiencing a Black presence at deliberations like this. To get everyone out of jail, as it were, I inhaled and raised my hand and Molly hushed:

"The humble opinion of a Fellow: I wouldn't publish this book. It's just too flat."

WE ALL BEGAN TO TALK at the same time about its demerits. It was like an extremely brutal MFA workshop without the teacher. And, this time, nobody accused me of not understanding the unique forces within their publishing industry.

The book was a dead rubber. Even the editor who championed it had gone back to extoling the powers of *Mistress*, as if to console himself. Thus, it came as comic relief when Angela said she really hoped we could outbid Random House for *Mistress*, just to get back at the managing director who fired her many moons ago. Short litanies of firings and migrations came tumbling out, some still bitter, some hilarious.

WHEN *TRAILS OF TUSKEGEE* came up, Molly said how much she loved it, that the humor kept her crying and laughing in equal measure. Like me, she swooned to the infectious hope the characters had in America, despite their ordeal. I was not surprised how pained she was about the discrimination, given her reaction to my embassy shit and family history. As she spoke, Emily jotted furiously on a pad. Jack watched Molly sympathetically. Angela folded her arms tightly like they were lashed with ropes, nodding the whole time.

Then, before anybody could look in my direction, Emily said that, having grown up only fifty miles away from Tuskegee, she could look at the manuscript through an intensely personal lens. Even her extended family had been sucked into the tragedy. She touched me most with her pained confession that, as an inquisitive kid, she had asked her parents about Tuskegee, and while they did not only deny that the Tuskegee events happened, they claimed that stories of violence during slavery were wholly invented by African Americans to demonize white folks, when they should express gratitude for whites saving them from Africa.

"I'm really, really in love with this child narrator, who eavesdrops into adult conversations," Emily said, her voice cracking. "This Black boy speaks for me, too, because, in my childhood I also overheard whispers about my grandpa's gay brother I never met. First, he was beaten up in 1952 for bringing syphilis back from Tuskegee to our white city. Then he was lynched for his love affair with a Black person. And, third, his body was burnt because his lover was a man. A relative outed him. Today, the more rights gay people have, the more divided my extended family is . . . I cried the days I misbehaved and my parents said my head was 'as ugly as a Tuskegee male' *n*-word, referring to the bulbous, ogre-shaped thing to which the experiment had altered the heads of Black men.

"My worst memory of childhood was the day I fought a Black girl in primary school in 1991 for accusing our government of this evil. She insisted she heard it from her parents, just like she heard from her grandparents about the mass lynchings of their distant relatives in Arkansas *like ornaments on Christmas trees*, an image she said her pastor used often. Our whole class started calling her 'Miss Christmas Ornaments' and threatening on the playground to lash her to a tree. She didn't change her story no matter how much we bullied her.

"Unfortunately, that one day at school, I totally lost it and punched and bit her when she swore it was the syphilis America gave to her Tuskegee auntie in the womb that led to her saber shins. Folks, I went to war even without knowing what *saber shin* was.

"Well, I never got the debriefing! Not even when my folks learned about the fight. Not from our white headmistress who suspended both of us, over the tears of the girl's parents begging the school to say at the least that Tuskegee happened. The only hint I got was from Father Schmitz in the confessional. 'My daughter, you're too young to understand America or this sort of original sin!' he'd said. 'Now, are you wholeheartedly sorry for the mortal sin of beginning the fight or not?'

"In college here in New York, I finally learned enough to research about slave plantations and found the sharecropper lynching photos. I called Father Schmitz to track down my old classmate in Alabama, and flew back to apologize to her not just for the fight but for calling her Miss Christmas Ornaments. Nobody understands the lingering guilt with which I listen to diversity stories these days—or how much this manuscript resonates with me. I'm sorry to be so personal!

"I'm sorry, this has been a long winding way to saying, naturally, once the author's agent, one of my best, Cecilia Myers, who knows a bit about my background, sent me this manuscript, I couldn't resist the sheer power of the story. The tone, the voice, the characters, the structure, the setups, the payoffs, everything! Like I told Molly and Jack last week, I think the flaws, like the underdevelopment of the white character, are totally fixable. He needs to engage his racist family and hint at his complexities, his righteous anger, and dreams for America. Cecilia is setting up calls so I can talk with the author this week, but so far she liked the suggestions I emailed to her.

"And, Ekong, I must say, like this white character, there are some of us in this company, or even in this room, who aren't finding it funny we were lied to as kids about slavery, or that our parents didn't plain know what to say—while Black kids grow up learning this history with their mother's milk!"

I put an arm around Emily's shoulder and gave her a side hug.

I raised my hand to speak and cleared my throat. But the image of Black kids breastfed on race atrocities nauseated me; it frothed to my throat and drowned my voice. I swallowed hard, strained and cracked my neck, yet gave up and signaled my support before dropping my head into the silence that had filled the room. The lessons of Emily's personalized history of America made me dizzy. It touched me that she had apologized to the Black girl, for I knew the pain of being bullied in school, of being called Son of Bloody Trousers, of being named after a family tragedy.

This was the most emotional editorial meeting in my life, including the painful ones on our Biafra project back home. And, from my colleagues' reactions, it was a fair guess nobody had ever been as confessional as Emily had been here. Yet, I was relieved that these white folks, not me, had made the most powerful case for the work. For the first time that day, the focus had completely shifted from me—from studying how this African was understanding fiction, from assessing whether I understood the white world enough to edit their stories.

JACK WAS THE FIRST to recover. He left and returned with Kleenex for Emily.

"Molly and Emily, I thank you for what you said!" Angela declared uneasily. "This is definitely a very moving book. To be honest, Emily, your very personal angle to the Tuskegee story has really made it relatable. I read somewhere someone said in apartheid South Africa that a country is like a zebra. Whether you shoot at the white or black stripes, the animal dies! Tuskegee haunts the collective soul of this nation, a story that needs to be told and retold."

Though I loved the zebra proverb, I refused to look at Angela because this did not sound like her at all. She and Jack could no longer deceive me.

"It has helped me see the book in a clearer light!" someone said.

"Oh Lord, Emily, I say it's a home run," another said.

"Emily, your story is as searing as the first time you shared it with me two years ago," Jack said, "though I didn't know it was this painful to you."

"Courage, Emily," Molly said, rubbing her palms together. "We've got a great chance at this. I'm sure you'll put a bit of your experience in the bid letter to assure the author he's in the hands of an editor who's emotionally in sync."

Jack and Angela exchanged quick glances.

"Please, I don't think I've had a chance to voice my opinion yet," Jack said, shifting uncomfortably. "I don't think we've discussed the bid yet."

"Okay, I'm sorry, I didn't mean to end the conversation," Molly said. "Of course you and Angela can add some thoughts about publicity and marketing to the bid letter, too, as usual. Please, go ahead, speak."

"I don't really know how to put this," Jack said, scratching his head.

"Just say you're playing the devil's advocate!" Angela prodded, chuckling.

He said: "Yeah, I wanted to say, with all due respect, *Trails* is still very far from the finished product. Actually, way further behind than *Mistress*."

"I didn't like the writing," Angela said, folding her arms. "It's too heavy-handed, too dependent on identity politics, and then the tone is all wrong, too comical in some places, too cloying in others. The personal story that Emily is telling, which has made us all cry, is 180 degrees different. That's not the book."

"I beg to disagree," Emily said like she wanted to cry.

"Emily, as I've told you before, I think what *you* have in mind may work better as memoir?" Jack said. "*Trails of Tuskegee* just doesn't resonate with me."

Angela agreed: "Emily, *you* could write this memoir—and, of course, Molly would be your editor, right, Molly?"

"It would be a really splendid book," Jack said.

"I think we should focus on the work in question," Molly said tersely.

"Anyway, when Emily spoke about Tuskegee," Angela continued, "it was so lucid, so painfully insightful, you know. Emily, you know already how much we're indebted to your knack for publishing the best multicultural voices. But I believe your writing would also go very deep. It would reach people who actually buy books. And it would also get our African American compatriots to also see how the unforgivable injustice done to them boomeranged on us, the so-called oppressors, and, maybe, ultimately, foster the kind of dialogue you and the author envision about raising kids in an increasingly diverse America. A memoir would also allow you to really authoritatively put forward the important points you made about challenging family and close friends about diversity. Lots of people need help and encouragement to take that very difficult but necessary step if we're to keep progressing.

"Emily, your voice would not only be relatable but would be more balanced, less sensational. I don't think our readers need to see images of weeping penis-less folks having sex. I'm not being prudish. I love the sex scenes in *Mistress*, but these are too extreme, gross. This book would be a tough sell."

"Yes, there are better ways to show how America has emasculated diversity," Jack said. "Beyond the difficulty in getting publicity, I just don't see the creativity in this book!"

※

As TENSION BUILT UP, Bob suggested we should take a break. But Angela turned sharply to challenge him like she wanted to head-butt him. Emily began to chew her nails. "Listen, am I the only one feeling a bit like there have been too many novels with a diversity agenda in the last few years?" Angela said.

"Market forces aren't respecters of diversity," Jack said. "We need to run this not as a charity but as a business."

Angela continued: "And, unlike Ekong's minorities, who, I hear, are yearning for dark war fiction like the unfortunate thing that happened to your family, here, in the United States, readers—those who actually buy books—are losing interest in these accusatory books about the sins of white people in America. And, luckily, we don't have these African tribal wars and corruption that rigs even the number of tribes so no one knows whether they even exist. Nobody knows why people in Africa are still waging these unending wars over land. Ekong, the truth is since the 1960s we've made undeniable progress in diversity and inclusion here—"

"Wait, Angela, this isn't about me or my father's rape!" I interjected, looking at her, then at Molly, who dropped her face into her hands for betraying my confidence about my family tragedy. "And I've never said my country was better than yours. Still, there's no need to trash my family . . . you don't understand what it means to be caught up in what you've rightly called, yes, *these unending* wars. And do you really need to remind me of my humiliation at the embassy?

"*Iya uwei*, I don't even know why you're picking on me. I've not uttered a single word—none—about *Trails of Tuskegee*."

"Ekong, I'm sorry," Bob said, and left the room as if to puke.

"No, *we* are all really sorry, Ekong!" another said, covering her face. "This. Is. Just. Not. Us."

Angela said, "Why is everyone acting as if I have a personal ax to grind with Ekong?"

"Angela, Angela, I just have to stop you right there!" Molly said, touching her arm, avoiding my face still. "We must keep this really professional."

"Ekong, I apologize if I said the wrong things," Angela said.

"It's okay," I said. "Anyway, Emily, I believe I can help you edit *Trails of Tuskegee*!"

"Ah . . . just hang on a sec," Jack said, pushing aside his notes, leaning into the table. "It could be tricky editing works from cultures you're not conversant with."

"Yes, you're totally right," I said, nodding.

He relaxed back into his chair and said, "Yeah, huge, huge cultural differences."

"But you guys have been editing African fiction, no?" I said as I felt the noose tightening around my neck again.

Silence.

Then Angela cleared her throat and said we needed to set priorities. Dodging my eyes, Jack said maybe *priority* was not even the right word. He said we really needed to be ready in case Liam said we did not have enough money to cover both wonderful books, which had already generated a lot of buzz in the industry. Molly said, well, Liam had promised to fund both, especially if we were all excited about them. But Angela looked Molly straight in the face and said when she spoke to Liam, her Harvard classmate, two days before, he was concerned about their cash flow. Molly did not like the fact that Angela had spoken to Liam, and flinched like she had been punched in the gut. When she tried to meet Angela's eyes without success, I felt we had lost the fight. Molly grumbled that Angela should have told her this when they did lunch the day before.

Angela said Liam himself was not very sure. Clearing her throat, she announced that we needed to be pragmatic. "Please, correct me if I'm wrong," she announced like an impartial elections official. "From our little conversation, *Mistress* got eight out of eight votes. If you factor in our Fellow's lukewarm appraisal, it's still eight-point-five out of nine. On the other hand, Jack seems to agree with me on *Trails*, so, that gets perhaps, what, seven out of nine? That puts it at number two, yes?" They went on to explain to me they were one of the houses that made these decisions by vote, while others gave their editors less freedom, with the publisher making all the final decisions. They tried to explain other models, but the whole atmosphere was too heavy for my heart.

I blamed myself for Jack and Angela's aggression toward me. I regretted saying anything at all about *Mistress*, though I did not know what I could have done differently about *Trails*. As they reopened the arguments about the strengths and weaknesses of the two works, I kept thinking of the words *relatable* and *resonate*.

When I sensed Jack watching me with the focus of a mind reader, I ignored him. I pretended to be watching Angela, whose face was quite angry at this point, only to discover she was watching Jack watch me. I refused to follow her eyes to Jack, to maintain my cover. I felt Michelle Obama was right when she said if you are not at the table, they are probably eating you. But, in my own case, even though I had made it to the table, Angela and Jack seemed bent on eating me alive.

Unlike with my Hell's Kitchen neighbors, I elected not to confront these two. I convinced myself they needed more time to adjust to my visibility. I prayed their madness would end with the meeting, returning us to the welcoming Andrew & Thompson I knew. Emily excused herself; she had a doctor's appointment and left. As the gathering went on to talk about Andrew & Thompson's other editorial concerns, the voices in my head would not let me listen.

Why is Jack taking this out on you, instead of Emily? said one.

Because you don't deserve even to sniff this table! said another.

But others appreciate you.

We're not so sure about Molly.

Give her another chance.

Just don't contact the owner behind her back like Angela did!

Next time, google those sharecropper lynching photos to shut her up.

Ekong, give us an anthology of Arabs crushing the balls of Black slaves for centuries because it's as bad as the lynching of Black men—

"Okay, ladies and gentlemen," Molly said, to close the meeting, "I shall present the reactions to the two books to Liam. Thanks!"

BACK IN MY CUBICLE, I was no longer the innocent who left Hell's Kitchen that morning. I was no longer the naïve person who confidently told Lagoon Drinker I would do anything to get the best out of my fellowship. I began to see that humility and friend-liness would not be enough at Andrew & Thompson. What did the momentous policy to publish a book by votes even mean, when one's race was not represented at the polls? I did not like this type of democracy, because this felt like a carefully orchestrated gerryman-dering, a deeply ingrained *wuru-wuru*. And how many publishers were Black at all those houses where publishers solely decided the fate of manuscripts? I was thoroughly scandalized by the whole envi-ronment and wondered what was going on in all these departmental meetings without minority presence.

When Jack and Angela left for an author reading, I was relieved they did not invite me along. Then I felt better seeing a text from Emily, apologizing for the meeting. "Please, forgive Molly and me for not defending you enough!" she wrote. But it also reminded me Molly herself had not said anything about her betrayal.

It was my most painful part of the day.

As others learned of our meeting, the office atmosphere festered with angry whispers against Jack and Angela. And though no one came to me, I was aware they were following me with eyes full of pity. I wanted them to speak to me, but at the same time I did not want them to speak to me. I did not want to listen to anyone. I worked hard on my war anthology, like I needed to flee to Nigeria after work. I buried myself in those stories of our tribalism.

And when work ended, I felt no relief in the streets, because, unlike the first day, my vision had refused to readjust to terra firma. No, my mind replayed the meeting nonstop. As I crossed Times Square, nothing could dilute my alienation. Even the sight of the high-rises repulsed me, for who knew how many white bubbles they protected?

When I called Father Kiobel and told him everything, he was shocked into speechlessness. But when I announced I was quit-ting, he began to ramble about how I must have an honest talk with Molly given all she had done for me, how I must remain strong to accomplish my mission in America. "Maybe she's just too crushed to immediately know how to react!" he said in a panicky, breathless voice. "From everything you've told me about her since you got there, I believe she's on your side. You don't know what she could be suffering from Angela and Jack! Didn't she share with you the ups and downs of her career? Didn't she cry over your father's murder? Please, be patient with her. Patience is a great thing in any culture."

He told me that though Molly's situation and his may have been totally different, he knew what it meant to struggle for decades and not know what to say about his childhood trauma in the Biafran War. "That reminds me: keep Emily in your thoughts, too, for sharing her childhood," he emphasized. "Spilling out her intestines like that must be a big moment for someone who has seen tons of painful manuscripts. As our people say, it is not a little disease that makes an old medicine man weep." He begged me to take solace in the fact that, in her brokenness, Emily did not only remember to text her apologies but also to intercede for Molly. He wanted me to let Emily know he was praying for her, because her childhood and Ujai's were basically two sides of the same coin.

He warned me I could not change the world alone.

"Father, I know you mean well," I said. "But are you trying to use Molly's negligence to excuse your silence over Biafra?"

"I'm sorry, no."

"It's not a matter of *sorrying* me."

"I don't want to remember this war or engage insinuations I myself was a bloodthirsty child soldier. Perhaps I shouldn't have vetoed your war memorial event.

"And, Ekong, please, you must also be careful with Usen, your childhood friend. The village knows already how disappointed he is in your American optimism. He's so angry you're the only Black person at your publisher's."

"I know, Father."

"He can't advise you right!"

THOUGH FATHER KIOBEL was not sounding like himself one bit, it was striking that Emily's powerful confessions had made him say the most conciliatory thing about the war that he had yet said to me. It would have been nicer, though, if he had spoken directly about my father's death, instead of referring only to the memorial.

When my phone beeped, I realized Emily had sent me eight manuscripts to read for the next editorial meeting in two weeks. I wandered the neighborhood, for I had no energy to go home to confront Jeff and Brad. Hell's Kitchen's Flea Market traders were noisily packing up their wares like Obo Annang traders when Molly called. She apologized she was stuck in back-to-back meetings and her phone needed to be recharged. Sobbing, she regretted sharing with Angela that I was thinking about writing an autobiography about my inherited trauma.

"Ekong, I'm sorry, I never expected her to use your war misfortune to humiliate you!" she lamented. "I just mentioned this briefly to her in one of our meetings knowing how much we both love memoirs. I'm glad you spoke up."

"No, thanks for stopping her," I said.

"Didn't do it soon enough! You know, Emily felt really supported by your presence. Your calm stopped her from walking out."

I felt better.

CHAPTER 8

Nigerian food.
Fulton Street. Brooklyn

THAT NIGHT, LYING THERE ON MY BED, I MISSED HOME. I missed Caro. I missed the tropical rains and the forever dampness of our September. I missed when the rains petered out in late October and the excitement and drumming in the buildup to our seasonal festivals and New Year celebrations. I missed the scent of the valley when the sun began to dry out the undergrowth, and the recession of the river and the communal work to clean the bleaches. I missed the changing of the water colors as the harmattan winds denuded even evergreen trees. I missed the sudden sharpened burnt smell of the queen-of-the-night flowers. I missed attending the Calabar Carnival with my extended family and friends and the unbelievable cuisines of the royal Efiks.

I missed the intervillage soccer matches, each tackle kicking up little puffs of harmattan dust, and the bragging rights that went into the New Year. Watching the global English Premier League on TV was not the same. And even if my team—Liverpool—won every day, it would never match the excitement of winning the village derbies, or the pain of such a defeat. Either way, the feeling lasted the whole year . . .

I woke up in a huff at two a.m., as though someone were knocking on my door. Groggily, I checked around. When I tripped on the recliner, two of Keith's dogs grumbled below. I could not sleep, because my body was slowly warming up, like I was being cooked. When sweat arrived, I removed my pajamas. Then my right nipple began to itch. But as soon as I grabbed it and pulled and twisted it like a beer top, it seemed to send a signal to the rest of its fighters to rise up in a mad ambush. I jumped out of bed again and started to scratch. I put on the lights, all the lights. The itches had spread, and my ribs looked like I had survived Biafran spray bullets. This time there was no warning, no slow ripening.

I sprayed the analgesic on my torso till it dripped into my pants, but it was of no use tonight. When my nails carved out jewels of streaked blood and the itches still did not abate, I resorted to slapping the spots. A good slap not only numbed the targeted itch but shook the whole system, as it were, took care of those itches I could not reach, and, I supposed, finally scared the old ones into submission. But, after four whacks to the stomach, I felt my intestines were moving, queasy.

I only knew I was moving all over the apartment, or, to be precise, standing in the restroom, because Keith's dogs grumbled. I sat very still on the toilet to placate them. Yet they would not let up. Frustrated, I flushed. The noise rumbled through the walls, soothing them. I tiptoed back to my bed and lay myself down gently.

THEN IT HIT ME the only people I knew who scratched or bore welts like these were AIDS patients in the hospice where Caro and I helped out. I did not want to think of this. When I closed my eyes, the flashing parking sign across the street was a strobe that went right into my brains. And even when I turned to face the wall, it continued to pulse on my eyeballs.

I got up again and set about an elaborate task of rubbing the anti-itch stuff all over my body, including the soles of my feet. Where I could see the welts, I stood dollops of the white ointment on them like the thick body paintings of *ekpo-ntokeyen* masqueraders. When I sprayed my back, everything was calm except that first gashed rogue itch that only the stairwell scratching had reached. It pursued me out into the stairwell wearing only a pair of boxers. I switched off the ceiling light and when nobody came out, I sat down and went to work.

Inside, I said to Caro, after pleasantries, I had rashes. She was quiet.

"Ekong Baby, *anyie* rashes *k'*America?" she said.

"Kind of."

"My husband, what do kind-of rashes look like? You done drink and fuck the white bitch finish! You couldn't even wait to land in America! *Aa-kung ajen iban mbakara ade!*"

"Listen, I've not even hugged her . . . !"

"For your information, last week they screened my blood at the hospice so I could donate. You're on your own."

"But I didn't say *you* gave me anything."

"So what else could you be saying?"

"I'm sorry if I sounded so—"

Jeff opened his door angrily, and even Caro could hear him stamping to switch the hallway light back on. She apologized that we had been too loud. She wondered whether Jeff would be angry with me in the morning. I said even if he was angry, he could not ask me to be quiet and I did not care. "Baby, it's okay, don't worry about him," I said. She whispered she hoped the itches were nothing but, perhaps, an allergic reaction to American food that soon I would feel better. We said a hurried goodbye.

AFRAID EMILY AND MOLLY would be downcast if I skipped work, I arrived wearing the biggest smile in NYC. I gave folks high fives and pumped hands.

When Jack came to the door of his office, looking very contrite, I took his hand and went inside. "Just to say, Ekong, I'm so sorry about yesterday," he said, offering me a seat. "There were things there we, no, I should never have said . . . I sounded like another person, racist and stupid and all. I should never have tried to hide under any *culture* bullshit. Last night, I really wished I had Father Kiobel's phone number. Given what you said at the Japanese buffet about how he smooths over these kinds of misunderstandings, I would've begged him to apologize to you on our behalf!" I embraced and thanked and urged him to put everything behind him. I let him know how much I appreciated his blood drive work at the Humane Society with Angela and Emily, because, in my heart, I understood that NYC minorities and the poor benefited the most from it. I did not believe anyone who invested that much in us was racist. I was a believer in action rather than words.

I went on to ask about the reading. He said it was wonderful. He promised to invite me along to the next reading, which he said would be in two weeks. He said Emily would not be at work today due to a bad cold. "I think she'd appreciate a text or something," he encouraged me.

By the water fountain, Angela was equally remorseful. "Look, Ekong, I apologize for my stupidity!" she whispered, grabbing my hands. "I apologize for insulting your family and continent, and I should never have belittled your embassy trauma. Listen, the word *racist* has been thrown around a lot, but I totally merited it yesterday. I sounded worse than Lagoon Drinker. I am sorry. And, for me, apologizing to you directly is more important than responding to the queries Jack and I rightly received."

"You're welcome . . . glad you brought this up," I stuttered. "We learn daily. I was just telling Jack let's put yesterday behind us, so it doesn't destroy the beautiful hospitality I've enjoyed here since I arrived."

Now Jack and a few people joined us, to chat. However, this time they were not asking polite questions about my background or bantering lighthearted stuff about their lives and the wonderful city. We were subdued, and even our laughter did not touch our hearts, as we say back home. And there was a distant echo of Emily's confessions as the conversation veered into who had minority neighbors growing up and who did not—or when and where they first learned about slavery, and how their parents and teachers presented things. The mob justice was understated, sophisticated, as though our colleagues were subtly rebuking Angela and Jack for whatever they said or did not say.

Jack and Angela silently and unusually looked down, neutered. They were miserable, their countenance bruised with sorrow. She held my hand for support. Because they had apologized, in solidarity I hung my head and kept silent, too.

"By the way, have you been to the Nigerian restaurant in Brooklyn yet?" Angela whispered, when the others were all gone.

"Nigerian . . . what?" I said, my heart fluttering.

"Nigerian food. Fulton Street. Brooklyn."

"I didn't even know of it!"

"The reviews say it's the best Nigerian restaurant in New York. Someone at the reading mentioned it, so naturally I thought of you. I think it's about time we took advantage of the wonders of the city. I'm going to beat Jack and Emily to sampling your dishes. Actually, my kid brother in Houston, Texas, is hitting Calabar Cuisine, a Nigerian restaurant, this weekend. I think he loves the photos of stewed beans and *afang* soup."

"Wow!"

The positive vibes had more than dialed back the tension; it had restored our usual amiable office environment. I needed this, especially since Hell's Kitchen was like a loaded gun to my head. "Hey, I love your stripes-of-the-zebra image!" I remarked, hugging her.

I met a little folded white piece of paper on my desk. It was unsigned and read: "Our business manager is on their case. He's also consulting our outside lawyer." I looked around but, unable to decipher the leaker, I trashed the note. Not knowing what official sanction was enough for their behavior, what stayed with me was our heartfelt reconciliation.

During lunch break, I found my way to a community CityMD in Hell's Kitchen for an HIV test. After filling out so many long forms like I wanted to buy a house, the wait was horrendous. The center was not even crowded, but the bureaucracy was as cumbersome as sharing the parts of a slaughtered cow according to blood lineage in the Ikot Ituno-Ekanem village square or in the Torah, too many workers milling around, taking care of too little.

When the nurse finally weighed me, I learned I had lost more than twelve pounds. My body had endured so much that the usually frightening sharp prick of the needle to take blood meant nothing. In fact, I was even giggling because, I thought, they were holding the needle like the Tuskegee experimenters in *Trails*. I had to tell them I was just nervous, though it would have been more correct to say I was thinking of how it must feel for the descendants of Tuskegee to visit hospitals—or whether it was possible for anybody, of any race whatsoever, to listen to Emily's childhood story and never have these thoughts cross their mind when visiting a health facility. On remembering that Tuskegee was in Alabama, where Keith's roots were, I thought of asking him about it. But I did not think we had yet developed the kind of relationship that would allow that sort of conversation.

The CityMD said the HIV result would be ready tomorrow, and they would call or text. If I was positive, I would have to come in for counseling and more paperwork, and since my Seven Corners international insurance plan did not cover stuff like this, I would have to pay out of pocket.

I asked whether, if I had HIV, I could embrace people. They said it would only be a problem if I was bleeding anywhere. On my way back, I texted Emily, but she called instead, to jubilantly tell me she had just had a lovely conversation with Cecilia, *Trails*' agent, and they were planning coffee together. I told her again how moved I was by her testimony, how Father Kiobel had promised to pray for her, and how her testimony had encouraged him to open up a tad about our war. She modestly said she was humbled her story had inspired someone. She repeated her desire to visit Ikot Ituno-Ekanem with Jack.

"Ekong, I'm glad you had so much fun at the reading yesterday," she said, giggling shyly.

"I didn't attend any reading!" I said.

"But Jack said the three of you were together." Lost, I stopped by a street corner, two blocks from our offices. "Perhaps I'm mixing things up . . . Anyway, they're attending another reading today."

"No, they're going in two weeks . . . he's just told me this in his office this freaking morning!"

"Actually, they're leaving in five minutes."

"Emily, are you sure?"

"Yes . . . why?"

I said goodbye and hurried back. I was eager to meet them, just to kill off the suspicion and anger that was teasing my imagination.

But, turning the block, I froze because I heard Jack's angry voice. He and Angela were standing on the curb, their backs to me. I hid behind a street vendor stand. Jack was shouting into his phone with one finger plugging his other ear, while Angela was having the laugh of her life, her tall imposing frame dancing. He was telling the caller about "our fucking African Fellow who's using diversity to twist. Every. Damn. Thing.

"Chad, we've already been put on probation, you know. I tried to call our outside legal counsel, but he wants everything written down, no phone calls, no meetings. Even Liam Sanders has bought into the bullshit. For the first time, he didn't return Angela's call either. She's really traumatized. We need to quit Andrew & Thompson. We need new jobs.

"Of course, Chad, I know we were never going to compete with the big houses. But we can't even seem to prioritize *Mistress* over, what . . . Yes, you told me you turned down that Tuskegee piece of shit last year . . . Yes, I remember you saying those atrocities didn't even happen. Personally, I believe they were exaggerated, cartoonish. I believe there are limits to fiction! Well, thanks for even submitting *Mistress* to us!

"You know that Nigerian fucker monopolized the whole damn meeting, passive-aggressively keeping people from saying what they thought. We couldn't breathe. You should've heard him defend his dysfunctional country. Whoever said Black people are ashamed of Black-on-Black violence or their shithole wars over land and oil? After the meeting, some of our colleagues attacked Angela and me like nasty dogs all the way to the reading yesterday. Again, this morning, they were still trying to guillotine us with guilt at the water fountain. It was funny Ekong himself spared us. He kept quiet and avoided their eyes and held Angela's hand, can you believe it? But, to be honest, that made us even more uncomfortable: the puppeteer controlled the situation with his silence, like when he refused to opine on that Tuskegee crap!

"Well, from his application for the Morrison Fellowship, I was quite confident he would be different—fresh, peaceful, logical, not resentful like African Americans. Liam wouldn't comment on any of this, but Angela thinks he accepted the jerk just so that Molly gets her checkmark—her virtual badge of virtue, so she can boast that she employed a person of color in publishing this year. I even helped with his visa through an acquaintance in our congressman's office. Huge mistake. I think we need to stop demonizing ICE or Lagoon Drinker—remember the Lagos consular officer?—for keeping some of these crazy assholes out of America . . . Yes, yes, you're right: we're making plans to quit. *We* have developed publishing, so I don't understand why *we* are being forced, blackmailed, to allow other races in—"

"Absolutely!" Angela shouted for the first time. "Can't work here anymore."

"Chad, since I told Ekong how Emily petitioned Yale and Columbia to establish his fucking Annang ancestry," Jack continued, "he's had the hots for her. You could see it in his deranged eyes! He even gave her a hug at the editorial meeting. Who does that? He almost kissed her. Maybe African editorial meetings are orgies . . . Emily has to be careful. And she was needlessly insensitive when she presented on *Trails*. She made it sound as though white folks were poisoning Black babies when she said they learned of the atrocities of racism from their mother's milk—"

"No, Jack, screw her irresponsible race imagery!" Angela said. "Just confront Ekong man-to-man to leave your babe alone, period!"

"Chad, Angela says I must confront him, period," Jack said. "Everybody knows he's already in Molly's panties! On conference call last night, she *educated* us for hours about diversity.

"Well, fortunately, knowing how much Ekong wants to cook for Emily and me, I urged Angela to learn to pronounce the names of a few Nigerian dishes from the internet. We needed to do something dramatic to reverse the lynching we knew was awaiting us . . . Chad, did you say *egusi* . . . *egusi* soup at the Nigerian book festivals looked like, what, vomit . . . ?"

I backed off, turned around, and scurried away.

I wanted to flee. Yet, since the whole thing felt like a dream, I wanted to confront them, at least, to authenticate it for me, to let it sink in.

I chose to run around the block, so I could approach them from the opposite direction, like some sort of new beginning, like I could go back to my first lovely days at Andrew & Thompson. It gave me time to think, the chilly fall wind hurting my eyes. I hated these two Americans—especially now that I realized that they hated me even more for bailing them out of the water fountain rebuke. Still, a part of me felt guilty I had invaded their very private moment, to ruin the fruits of our beautiful reconciliation. But then I got angry and ran faster, blaming myself for not cutting into the phone call to shame them.

ANGELA SAW ME FIRST. She smartened up and snatched the phone from Jack to end the call. She waved to me. I waved back.

"Hey, I told you in the morning our next reading would be in two weeks' time, right?" Jack said.

"Yes, indeed," I said, panting, holding my knees. They said they had to make an early dinner with a publicist friend from Little, Brown. "Oh, well, we'll still do Broadway together, Jack," I said.

"Absolutely," he said, looking away.

"And Angela, perhaps we could visit the Nigerian restaurant on Fulton Street," I said.

"Yeah, I'm sorry, my schedule has just become horrible right up to the holidays," she said, her gesticulation in full swing today, like that of a praying mantis.

I straightened up and said: "Your kid brother will be addicted to our dishes by then, ha!"

"Please, we're running late," she said. "That's why I disrupted Jack's important call."

I nodded and lumbered around Times Square to catch my breath, everything eerily clear in my head. I was a boast, a checkmark, a badge of virtue for my boss. But I was also hugely comforted that Molly had undertaken to try to "educate" Jack and Angela on my behalf.

The voices of the colleagues who berated Jack and Angela at the water fountain also strengthened my steps.

I thought about Toni Morrison, the name on my fellowship, the only African American editor I had read about. When I imagined that she worked in publishing forty years ago, I could only think of how alienating it could have been back then, or was I to believe publishing had gotten less diverse over time? What was it like for her to excel in that white space? Or, as an African American, was she more familiar, more prepared for the shock of this white space than I, an

African, would ever be? Or was it even more painful to her because of her close-up-and-personal experience of racism, something the depth of which I was only beginning to fathom? Today, my admiration for Morrison soared beyond her powerful books, beyond her indomitable courage, beyond her unforgettable quotes.

I googled current Black editors in American publishing and their profiles. I found a few; they were mostly young. Some of them hinted at the alienation of their workplaces. They did not elaborate. I did not blame them: in their shoes, if I wanted to progress in the system, I would be the same. My joy was that they all wore happy hopeful faces.

But by the time Emily phoned to say Jack said I declined to accompany him and Angela to the reading, it was as though I were listening to the Jack-Chad phone call afresh. My heartbeat was as fast as in that moment at the meeting when I knew I would have to fight Jack and Angela over *Trails*. My biggest worry now in New York was how to work with them—or even exist in the same building with them. And just thinking about it was more disconcerting, more frightening than what was happening to my skin.

THE FOLLOWING DAY, after checking my phone nonstop for a CityMD notification, I put up a brave front until I entered Molly's office. She herself seemed more exhausted than me. I was so guarded that she asked what was wrong. I avoided talking about itches.

When she said Angela and Jack told her they had apologized, I nodded absentmindedly and went on to ask what Liam thought about the two manuscripts. She said they did not want to prioritize one over the other but wanted us to pursue each manuscript as far as possible. "Ekong, I must say, I'm quite pleased with the speed with which he's making decisions and responding to my emails," she said. "By the way, our colleagues who overheard Jack and Angela's apologies yesterday were really moved by your graciousness! Thanks. But if anything comes up, honey, I need to know. I mean *anything*!"

"Thanks."

She said on behalf of her company she wanted me to know that Liam was completely mortified by what had happened. The company was ready to roll out sanctions without meeting with me, because they did not want me to relive the trauma. She held out her two hands like she was opening an invisible door: "We hope to be a publishing house that doesn't merely put out minority books but actually lets people of color into the intimate processes of shaping them. Ekong, our dream is to be a truly *world* brand. Personally, I'm really excited about this. Liam also hopes to get us into a bigger space so that someone like Emily can have an office of her own, you know."

I nodded.

I did not know how to tell her Angela and Jack had fooled everyone. It was no crime they no longer wanted to attend the readings with me—or eat my Nigerian food. More than anything else, I thought, my pride in our food had tied my tongue from bringing up these *street* gossips. I could just not bring myself to speak of *vomit* and our dishes in the same sentence. "Molly, all that's important to me is a conducive environment," I said. "You know, I need not be the friend of the Humane Society Two."

She leaned back and struggled with a nervous giggle. I could see her throat vibrating, pulsing, flushing up the noise, yet her face was frozen in misery like one with facial stroke. I was happy we could find any humor at all. The laugh returned some color to her face. When I lifted my gaze and our eyes locked, I smiled because I never wanted her to feel defeated.

Her honesty had entered my heart. Her fight against these two was now mine. I was ready to endure any humiliation to actualize *our* dream without even understanding American publishing. I was ready to be the experiment, the *badge of virtue*, in Jack's words.

"What's on your mind, Ekong?" she said.

"I was thinking . . . is it possible to meet the owner of Andrew &

Thompson?" I said. "Please, I hope you don't feel I'm leapfrogging over your head. I just want to thank him personally for having me here."

"I understand. But just to put it in context, nobody here has ever asked to meet him before. I hope you won't be too upset if Liam says no. He's a very nice but timid person."

"No, I won't take it personally."

"Right now I don't think he's in town. He has companies all over the place and is on the boards of lots of charities. Who knows, he might make an exception. I'll shoot him an email. Fingers crossed."

"Thanks."

Then she said her parents had just invited her home for the weekend and had suggested she bring me along. "It would mean so much to them to meet you, you know," she said. "You're smiling. Is that a yes?" I laughed soulfully. "Ekong, this is the first laugh I've heard from you since Tuesday, so this is good, yes? And, if you can't make it now, we can do it in the fall. Look, no parkway is more beautiful than our renowned Merritt Parkway in October!" But I had to claim I had other plans, because of my itches. I would not want a visitor scratching like mad in my house, and in any case I would be too restless waiting to hear from the CityMD.

THE CITYMD DID NOT CALL. I was so tense I could not edit a word.

By lunchtime, I was so restless I went to the nearest McDonald's and ate three Quarter Double Pounder combo meals with two vanilla Frosties and a Southwest Buttermilk Crispy Chicken Salad. When I was still not satisfied, I knew I was in trouble. I lost the desire to go to the square in the evening but instead went in the opposite direction, along the piers on Twelfth Avenue, saying my finger rosary, begging the Blessed Virgin to help me in my mission in NYC and to keep the Humane Society away from me. I wandered for miles before clambering up to my room, hoping the exhaustion would deepen my sleep.

Ke mmo-o? No chance.

Friday morning, I was so anxious of my test result, I cut work and told Molly and Emily I would be at the New York Public Library researching the war. Molly informed me we had lost out on *Mistress*. She said the only silver lining was that her friend and former colleague Paul Maher from Farrar, Straus and Giroux, where she had the best years of her career before Andrew & Thompson, would edit the book.

Worse, during my breakfast at Blue Fin, my right earlobe felt heavy. When I touched it, it was numb. I had never had a numb ear before. It began to feel warm. I touched it but the temperature was the same as my cheek's. But when the itch hit, I gently abandoned my eggs Benedict, barely touched, paid my bill, and left. An ear was not something you wanted to scratch at all. Touching it gingerly, I found the itch had birthed a welt. It was wet. If I did not touch it for a while, it felt like it was dripping, the itch spreading along with the moisture.

Back home, the mirrors revealed the thing was actually down in the middle of my ear. I pressed out some of the anti-itch ointment into a bowl and sprayed the anti-itch into it till a layer of foam stood on the ointment like on a mocha or beer, and, using my fingers, I mixed them together. I thought it would create an anti-itch overdose to completely douse the fire in my ear. But when I applied the concoction, the itch fought back, the discomfort consuming my whole head. So I applied it also to my neck, my face, and even mixed it into my crew cut like a relaxer.

When I wanted to put on my cologne because the new mix did not smell good, the voices in my head—which I had thought would disappear after Tuesday's traumatic meeting—said, *Ekong, what if the cologne actually weakens the powers of your concoction? Can't you afford to smell like shit for a day, to save your ear? Are you trying to bleach one ear? Mixing too many things may actually hurt your skin forever. As our people say, giving a monkey water is one thing. Getting the cup back is another.*

THE ICY FEEL OF THE CONCOCTION finally lessened my discomfort, thank God. But, unlike an ordinary itch, the thing started playing games with my mind. Sometimes a dulled pulse spread out into the whole ear, setting off distant bombs, and I got the impression my earlobe was mushrooming into a heavy lopsided thing that required me to hold my head in a certain way to strike a balance. Then I felt it was giving me a headache, but headaches did not feel like that, with a heaviness tiptoeing into my inner ear. I refused to touch the welt.

Then I got a real headache because I kept turning that ear downward and shaking my head, as though to expel water from the inner ear. After leaving a voice mail for the CityMD, I put a little plaster on it and lay down.

But when my phone beeped, it was a text from Jack saying he and Emily just wanted to say hello, because they were passing by the library on their way from lunch. I felt violated seeing his name on my phone. A searing, blinding rage slowly took over my whole body. I hated him so much it had totally anesthetized my itch.

When I did not answer, Emily called to say she was worried because Cecilia had not returned her calls, emails, or texts.

"What are we going to do now?" I exclaimed.

Sounding more and more perplexed, she said she did not know how to interpret Cecilia's behavior. I kept my anxieties to myself. Chad Twiss, the so-called super-agent, had already made a horrible impression on me. Now I asked myself: Was it better to reject the book outright like Chad had rejected *Trails of Tuskegee*, or to suddenly disappear on it like Cecilia had just done?

When Emily said she had heard about our Nigerian restaurant from Angela and suggested we should hit it the next day followed by *Newsies* on Broadway, I apologized that it was a bad weekend. I wished I could have told her her boyfriend was pure *afid-ebot*.

CHAPTER 9

Like the *tuke-tuke* buses of Benin City

AFTER LEAVING ANOTHER VOICE MAIL FOR THE CityMD that Saturday, I did not know what to do with myself. I could not eat. I was not even tempted to booze. When I made a decision to go to the Bronx, Usen gave me directions and asked what I wanted for dinner. "Stewed beans and boiled *Nigerian* yam!" I announced. They laughed at my emphasis on *Nigerian*, explaining, yes, they had exactly the kind of yam I needed.

After enacting the ritual of covering my body with my custom concoction, for whatever protection it was worth, I rode my first subway. I texted Caro that I was going to the Bronx just for information's sake; I knew she would not reply because of the war histories that stood between Usen's family and hers. The train was crowded, like everyone in Manhattan was escaping somewhere for the weekend. And then suddenly the train rode out of the underground and was on street level and then climbed onto the raised tracks. I looked out and smiled at the view before I knew I was smiling.

It was different from the Manhattan I knew. Here there were single-story houses instead of a forest of skyscrapers. The distinct structures of churches caught my attention, in contradistinction from the Actors' Chapel. My spirit opened up in ways that let me know I never realized how Manhattan had shuttered or shaped it. I felt freer, like I was slacking off all the humiliation of this week.

I saw a lot of people having fun down there, as the train scythed through neighborhoods. Some were barbecuing outside; some were playing baseball and soccer in parks and even in empty parking lots; some were returning from shopping, carrying heavy plastic bags; some were streaming into eateries and movie theaters. Each time the train stopped and the doors opened, my ears were pummeled by loud music. For me, already the Bronx was bass that thumped and changed your heartbeat like the *tuke-tuke* buses of Benin City. It was like one big endless neighborhood party. Apart from Bini and Urhobo and Isoko towns, I had never seen so many people moving about with so much swag. It was my abiding image of this borough.

I loved the Bronx.

The diversity of people was equally stunning as in Manhattan. But it was intense in a whole different way; the colorful tribes of America were more differentiated. Unlike in the mad rush of our Times Square, here you could see the patterns of color, and the overlap, the blur, was not as powerful. Where the intensity of Times Square was sometimes like a photo so zoomed in it lost focus, here, riding this train, I felt I could take in more, see the colors coming apart in the groups of people moving before me. And when I came into an open space, I looked around frenetically in every direction, to see as far as possible before the buildings blocked things out again. I would have loved to ask the Americans around me whether there was a word to aptly describe what I was seeing, some word that would describe this place and this place alone. But they all looked too serious, avoiding each other's eyes.

And then, precipitously, I began to see too much graffiti. I could not work out in my head how someone got to spray-painting that high wall or that bridge. And then it was weird that though the layout was more open than where I lived, there was so much trash on the streets. And, because of Molly's negative comments about the Bronx before I came to America, my mind could not abandon the fear of crime; the more we burrowed into the Bronx, the more I wondered about my safety. I studied the people around me more closely than I would in Manhattan, though I posted the coolest of demeanors, with my earphones blasting 2face, Omawumi, and BoA.

As the train began to empty out, I became afraid and moved to the end that was vacant. I texted my village people to tell them where I was, and they said I was on the right track. Of course, I did not tell them my feelings, good or bad, about their Bronx.

WHEN I STEPPED OUT of the train, a stuffy heat wanted to beat me back inside. I crossed two streets. Usen and family were in front of their building to receive me. Ujai spotted me first and sprinted forward, her flip-flops clapping behind her as she dodged this person or that group. She seemed to have run forever before flinging herself into my embrace.

"How are you, Ujai?" I said.

"I'm fine," she said. "But I've got three quick things to tell you."

"Hey, Miss America."

"Uncle, you're not listening."

"Okay, I'm listening."

"First off, you're my best uncle, okay?"

"Yay, thanks."

"Two, you don't smell good at all. You stink."

"I'm sorry, it's a medication cream."

"In America, we don't accept body odor. I think you should sue that pharmacy or hospital! And, three, you're not going back to *that* place with bad neighbors! You're going to work from here every morning."

"Yes, ma'am."

I started leading her toward the others.

"Daddy is so pissed you're the only Black person at your workplace," she said.

"I've got two dear friends," I said.

"What are their names?"

"Molly and Emily."

"Yay, Keith, Molly, and Emily are your new friends. But, Uncle, I believe folks from the same village should live together, especially in a foreign land. And I mean a real village, not East Village, which my parents love to visit in *your* Manhattan—where there are no fruit trees, no moon, no stars, no masqueraders, no village chief, no nothing . . . no, seriously, I want to bathe in that river in Ikot Ituno-Ekanem, which they're always talking about."

"These days kids learn in the swimming pools of Uyo."

"Nope, now that the Biafran War is over—as you said—I want to be right there when the river changes color. It sounds like so much fun running with your school friends after a soccer game, past the church, through the Stations of the Cross, then scrambling down the valley and splashing into our refreshing river. They talk about battling the raw force of the currents when they were my age. I want to swim at a tangent to make it to a targeted spot. I want to pick the cashew fruits myself from the slanted fields of the valley. I want to twist and pull and snap the nuts from the sweeter, softer, bigger end of the ripe fruits. I want to cut open the nutshell myself, even if the acid burns my fingers. Yep, I want to use it as a kid's tattoo, as Mommy and Daddy once did. I want the nuts that fresh, not the stuff Daddy buys from Aldi or Stop & Shop, all fried up or roasted with God knows what chemical on it. When the winds come through the valley in the late evenings, I want to stand on the lip of the valley to smell the jasmine from the queen-of-the-night trees. And I really, really want to learn how to stealthily shin up the mango trees without stirring up the wrath of tailor ants, and if I do, how to pinch my nostrils and use my arms to lock up my ears so they don't get in—how to endure without crashing to the ground—oh, they say if you call the names of the dead dogs in the valley, the valley will answer you . . ."

We cut short our chat so I could greet everyone. When Igwat, the toddler in the baby carriage, was not satisfied with a simple hug and started crying and reaching out, I threw him thrice into the air and then carried him back to the house.

It was a huge dull red-brick apartment building with tens of floors.

There were four identical buildings and, though they dominated the neighborhood, a poor man's skyline, they stood apart, wild intimidating territorial beasts. In my eyes they were the ugliest things I had ever seen, and even the doors were painted with the same dull brick color, as though to completely destroy your sense of beauty. The stuffy smell became worse than the reek of my concoction. It smelled like camel piss.

Anxious about how nasty the smell of Usen's place would be, how I would survive dinner, we rode the elevator up to the eleventh-floor apartment. Yet, when we stepped out, the first thing my eyes instinctively surveyed was the stairwell and what kind of banisters it had. They were newer, round, smooth, and without rust, definitely not the kind of thing that could aid your back when the devil struck.

WHEN OFONIME OPENED the door into their apartment, I was shocked at how beautiful it was. I felt like I had finally arrived in the American home of my dreams, what I had had in mind when I thought of living in Manhattan. This was a First World arrangement, and quickly I closed the door behind me, to banish the ugly exterior of the building from my mind. The air was fresh and clean, with a whiff of jasmine. The living room was bigger than I had imagined. I loved the seats and couch, the patterns on the marble floor, the rug, and the juxtaposition of colors. On the wall, the set of delicate *ekpo-ntokeyen* carved masks playing their bright colors against each other surprised me and took my mind right back to Ito Road in Ikot Ekpene, where this stuff was made.

I was jealous of their apartment.

"*'Jen* Annang, I knew you'd love my humble abode," Usen said, nudging me. "I may not live in the rich Bronx, but my place makes me rich!"

"*Gwoden*, you were right," I said, though I knew it would still be too crowded for me to live here. "You've set it up really well. Congrats! Caro would love your kitchen, too."

"Thanks," Ofonime said, and wanted to relieve me of Igwat, but the kid squealed and dug deeper into my rib cage.

"See, we all want you to stay," Ujai said.

My admiration for his home meant a lot to Usen. He told me it was the combination of the privileges of being a super and what the family had personally put into the place, with the permission of the landlord. He said he could not afford to come to America and live *ntere-ntere*, as we say. "Congrats, too, on your beautiful house in the village," he said, shaking my hand.

That was the day he opened up about the super business. That was when he explained that the rent stabilization law meant Lucci's rent had not increased more than two percent or so for all those years he had had my apartment. I learned how New York landlords in cahoots with supers schemed to get rid of tenants who had stayed *too long*, so that they could post a higher rent for the new ones. He warned me he could tell right away Lucci must be at loggerheads with the owner. He said the old man probably gave me many keys, the original one from the landlord and others he had put in—really to keep the landlord out. I remained silent because I trusted Lucci.

Soon Ofonime began to blend fresh Cameroon pepper and onions for the stew. I moved into the kitchen to get the fullness of the scent, a boost of smell therapy from another life. I offered to help but she said she had already poked and seasoned the fish steaks with a plaster of assorted spices before I arrived. As the black-eyed peas bubbled on the stove, their strong smell filled the apartment. Usen left to buy drinks, while Ujai dragged me to the balcony so we could wave to him on the ground. The leaves were a deep green, struggling under the pangs of the last throttles of summer. But the fields and parks were dry and a little brown from summer usage, like the fall was approaching the trees from the earth. When Usen crossed the road, he turned and looked up and waved at us. We waved back.

Seeing that Igwat had dozed off in my arms, Ujai took me to their bedroom to lay him in a cot. Before I knew it, she had sprayed her dad's cologne on me, laughing mischievously.

CHAPTER 10

It melted on my tongue like butter

THE SMELL OF THE BEANS WAS BROKEN, TEMPERED, WHEN the cook finally poured the blend into the hot palm oil to make the stew. By the time she stirred and the meek scent of boiled yam in the next pot rose to the fore, I became hungry and nostalgic. The yam was peeled and cut in low wide cylindricals. While downing a glass of cold water to settle the growls of my stomach, I got a text from Molly asking if I could accompany her Tuesday afternoon to an award ceremony, the Uramodese Prize. "It'll be fun!" she wrote.

I looked forward to meeting folks from other publishing houses, and the agents—the group that fascinated me the most, a group we did not yet have in Nigeria. So far, I knew of only the agent of *Trails*, Cecilia Myers, and Jack's friend, Chad Twiss. I was already angry I might meet Chad, but I wanted to personally let Cecilia know how much I loved the book she was championing. Silently, I swore to attend this function whether I heard from the CityMD or not. Even if the itches totally cut off my ears or disfigured my head and shins like those of the Tuskegee victims, there would be no stopping me. This prize event would make up for all the tours of New York Molly had promised me but had not yet acted on.

Better still, Molly sent another text saying Liam had just agreed to lunch on November 17, a week before Thanksgiving, if I was free. When I called her, she was euphoric that she was able to wrangle our lunch date. Of course I said I was free and told her to thank Liam for me.

In excitement, I spontaneously began to whistle "Ikworo Ino," an Annang folk song. But Ujai insisted I must sing it out so she and her mother could help with the chorus.

> *Ikworo ino o*
> *Ikworo ino*
> *Ikworo ino o*
> *Ikworo ino*
>
> *Iko Awasi anem akan ajen*
> *Ikworo ino*
> *Tutu ndikpa ndikpongke enye*
> *Ikworo ino*
>
> *Ikworo ino o*
> *Ikworo ino*
> *Ikworo ino o*
> *Ikworo ino*
>
> *Iko Awasi anem akan udia*
> *Ikworo ino . . .*

As I finished helping Ofonime slice up the mangoes and oranges for dessert, she tried to quietly resurrect her embassy abuses in Annang. But, once the daughter heard *embassy* and *visa*, she protested, "Nope, guys, no embassy or visa horror stories in any language, *mbok*! Tell me about the lady visa touts and our village masquer-aders. Or let's sing 'Ikworo Ino' again." We reached a compromise: I retold the story of the nice touts who gave me their pamphlet and showed her the moves of the embassy dancer who dressed like a masquerader.

ONCE USEN RETURNED and we sat down to eat, Ujai and I got our cans of Dr Pepper. Then Usen toasted me with red wine for being made the managing director of Mkpouto, before he and Ofonime set about mixing Guinness stout with palm wine. They told me this meal was the foretaste of my big Thanksgiving reception.

Ofonime apologized that the yam was a bit overcooked. But that was exactly how I liked it. Tender, it melted on my tongue like butter, not some Food Emporium thing masquerading as yam. In fact, it was like I had missed our yams for decades. Usen stood up to put on Uko Akpan Cultural Group, to move the celebration to another level altogether, and soon the musician's *nkwed* voice took to the air, the drumming guarded eminently by the pounding of the slit-log drum. The apartment's wraparound music system made it quite an experience, like we were in our village's masquerade square with its raised banks surrounded by palm trees, on the other side of the valley. It was so immediate, so real, a Mmanamo Festival day away from home. I felt homesick, as though, at any moment, the child masqueraders would jump out to seize the colorful masks from the wall and slip them on and explode in the somersault dance of *ekpo-ntokeyen*.

I was on my third helping—like I had a secret grudge to settle with Angela and Jack for insulting my food—when a fish bone slashed the tip of my left thumb. The cut was as clean as a surgeon's blade, and in no time an oval ball of bright blood grew on it, then exploded down my nail. I stoppered it with my fingers and held it away from the table as the others scrambled for their first-aid box. After the wound was bathed in iodine, the bleeding stopped. I insisted on covering it up with multiple wrappings of cotton bandage, and then my thumb looked like a drumstick. Usen said I had become a weakling since I had left Ikot Ituno-Ekanem; Ofonime asked whether the fish bone had also cut my ear, leading to my ministrations there; Ujai was laughing at me. But I did not want any open wound near my people, as the CityMD had advised. I put my injured hand on my lap and did not allow anyone to make contact with it, as we went on to talk about old times and carried the girl along as best as we could.

Ujai was dozing off. But, when the parents asked her to go get ready for bed, she quickly sat up and insisted she did not want to sleep before I left. She got up and started wriggling to the Annang beats. The father took one look at my full stomach and told his daughter I was spending the night. He handed Ofonime the toddler, who had just woken up, to feed. Ofonime plopped him back in Usen's lap, grumbling that the husband had done the same in my apartment and that some of our men were more rigid in America than back home. I avoided his embarrassed face as he fed the kid.

"Ekong, *ira ika-a* evening Mass in the African American parish," Ofonime said, forking another wedge of yam onto my plate, burying it under two scoops of beans, then fish, like a funny sandwich. "We've not been to the Black parish for a while now."

"Well, I'll be there to have my fill of Negro spirituals for the year!" Usen moaned.

"*Nside* Negro spirituals?" I asked.

"Heavy, ultra-sad songs about slavery!" she said. "It's like the African Americans have to steel their spirits every Sunday for one more week in slavery. Though we sing a few of them during Lent and Stations of the Cross in Ikot Ituno-Ekanem, these folks sing them all year around, all their lives."

"For us, it's an overdose," he said. "It kills off your week before it even begins. And, since we're not descendants of slaves, it gets to you after a while, *unwanga*? And then I really hate the side talk at the after-Mass coffee reception in the basement about *us* taking *their* jobs and college admission quotas and movie roles."

Ujai said she preferred to attend the Black church to any church Tuesday went to. "Uncle Ekong, he's too biased against African Americans, like a bigot," she whined. Usen reprimanded her that it was a slippery slope to insist on whom to worship with.

WHEN THE CHILDREN had gone to bed, we stayed up late to roll back the years, until the conversation got to how sixteen-year-old Usen stabbed our Biafran high school classmate who kept painting the Biafran flag in class in 1984, fourteen years after the war. Usen said uneasily: "Once my father told me how Biafra pinned Grandpa down and forced him to drink cow urine, I couldn't control myself the next time I saw the Igbo kid painting the flag." Ofonime quickly said he had since learned how to control his anger, rubbing his shoulder nervously. She said even Tuesday was very impressed that Usen was standing godfather to Biafran kids around the Bronx.

"I'm not sure our esteemed editor knows the whole story of what actually happened to Tuesday," Usen said, uncomfortably moving the conversation away from our high school days. "I mean during *that* more brutal 1968 second invasion of our minority lands."

"Yes, *sabo*, I don't know the full story," I told him.

"Six months after your dad's death—I'm sorry, Ekong . . . !" He paused, stood up to bring out a bottle of vodka, which he opened and poured into three glasses. I turned down the drink as they sipped it dry, like we drank our *kai kai* back home.

"Please, continue the story," I said.

"Are you sure?" Ofonime said uncomfortably. "This is why Usen and I and all people of goodwill have been patient with Father Kiobel for keeping mum about his war experience. Who can blame him for not wanting to revisit such a childhood? What if his childhood was worse than the part of Tuesday's we knew? I don't want to hear about wars tonight."

"Listen, *sabo*, it's okay to talk about my father," I said as she gulped her drink. But she shook her head and told her husband it was not right for them to betray Tuesday's confidence, to tell me what Biafra did to Tuesday in the valley. As he considered her point, she drank even more alcohol. Seeing how agitated she was, I told Usen to listen to her. Nobody knew what had transpired in the valley.

As Usen talked about his super work and Ofonime her school-
ing, what the village already knew of Tuesday's ordeal played in my
mind: the ten-year-old had to be hidden by his parents under the bed
days on end, to avoid Biafra recruiting him into the Biafran army
during the brutal second invasion of our land in 1968. Everybody
knew Tuesday's mother had to put cups of squeezed lime under the
bed for her only child to inhale, to avoid sneezing from the dust.

But one day Mrs. Ita had told their Igbo neighbors to go to hell
when they boasted they were the owners of Biafra. The quarrel
deteriorated when she lashed out that *"ewa annisi kpoi nyien, ekpe
aseata,* the dog that barks at me is usually devoured by the lion,"
meaning bigger bullies—the Yorubas and Hausa-Fulanis—were
coming for them. The neighbors tipped off Biafran patrols that the
Itas were hiding their son in the house.

One rainy afternoon, as Usen's father was visiting with Tuesday's
parents to play Ludo, the Biafran patrols arrived. The Itas refused to
hand over their only child. So the soldiers riddled the ceiling of the
living room with bullet holes, perhaps thinking Tuesday was hiding
up there. However, when they asked the stoic parents whether the
raindrops leaking into the living room looked like their son's blood
and then commanded them one last time to produce Tuesday or else
they would spray-bullet everywhere, she broke down. "Oh no, cry-
baby," the patrols mocked her. "Why don't you tell us why you're
going around calling Biafrans dogs and Nigerians lions?"

Tuesday himself had jumped out of hiding, throwing the soldiers
into guffaws. Usen's father said the boy's body was stiff like a rod
as he held on to his mother, his totally defiant and unblinking eyes
fixed on the soldiers' faces. "This naughty brat is even insulting us
with his eyes!" sneered one of the soldiers. His father covered Tuesday's eyes with his hands as the family huddled together and the
rain beat them like they were outside. Well, despite the parents begging the skinny thing to follow the soldiers, Tuesday was said to
have insisted he would rather die than join the Igbo-thing. But, with
the sass of folks who had already won the war, the soldiers ordered

Usen's father to leave as they dragged the seats to the corner, where they had not shredded the roof, to continue to play Ludo.

Nobody back home knew what happened after Usen's father had left the Itas'. The next thing the village remembered was Father Walsh quarreling with the Biafrans in the valley to spare the Itas' lives. And Tuesday's parents had died of starvation and disease before war's end. Tuesday himself had not visited home since 1975.

WHEN I WOKE UP on the air mattress in the living room, Ujai was waiting quietly on the couch, like a friendly dog. It was 9:43 a.m. Before I could say hello, she indicated she had something very important to tell me, springing to her full height, all nervous and stuttering, like she was forced to do an impromptu recitation. Ofonime said she had stopped her from waking me up at 7 a.m. when she got up.

The girl wanted me to follow her parents to her school during parents' week, because she had been boasting to her class about governors competing to build hospitals in our village. She thought hearing this from someone who had just arrived from there would boost her position. "You don't even know your so-called village!" she said they had told her, to shut her up. "It's not even on the internet."

I promptly agreed to go but told her I never said the governors were building hospitals in *our* village but in their separate states.

"You don't understand my school," she said, her large eyes dilating with fire.

"Okay, I shall explain everything to them."

"But if you change the story, they'll never believe me again, and then they'll call me *Real Miss Liar of New York*, and my friends would be *Team Liars* . . . Could you just say they built a hospital?"

"What about renovating Our Lady of Guadalupe High School, which is what Governor Akpabio actually did?"

"No, hospital . . . !"

"He built a clinic in the nearby village."

"It won't cut it. It's got to be Ikot Ituno-Ekanem. Okay, in place of clinic, we must say a small hospital. They used to tease me nonstop about wars in Africa, till one day I solved that problem by saying I'd just discovered only very noisy dogs died in Ikot Ituno-Ekanem's wars. When they didn't know what to say, because they couldn't find the place on the internet, I added that we buried them in the dog cemetery by the river in our beautiful valley! The bullies scrammed."

"Dog cemetery, huh?"

"Yes, they need to know we take good care of animals, dead or alive."

I nodded and kept quiet while her parents ignored us. They moved about the house talking in Annang, like people who had successfully passed on their problem to another person—parents on vacation. "Uncle, you have to always be ready, woke, for even your friends will make mistakes. Do you not push back at Andrew & Thompson?"

"Wow, you even know my publisher."

"Mr. Ekong O. Udousoro comma Andrew & Thompson and Co. comma Manhattan comma New York 10020. We're learning addresses in school, so Mommy used yours to help me in my homework. She says I personally write good letters, but I really love the group letter-writing challenge our class teacher assigns us. We've already written a really long and comforting letter to the uncle of one of our friends who was deported by ICE. Uncle, it's really difficult to write or edit as a group."

"Ha, your teacher is great!"

"She is, but we're woke because things are complex. As I said yesterday, *I* really know what's going on. See, Daddy and Mommy have already told me how to behave around the police: I shouldn't trust them but must *act* like I do. They tell me what to do in case of arrest or being shot. Yep, they say this every month, like a fire drill. But the whole thing is messed up big-time because our teacher insists we trust the cops. Me and my friends know what boxes to tick to pass our tests. We've seen stuff on TV."

"Oh, okay."

"I'm going to teach my bro everything as soon as he begins kindergarten, because they say Black men are targeted . . . When you sent my parents the cop selfie, they deleted it right away, afraid I might mistake cops for friends. I had wanted to give it to my Indian American classmates."

To have to learn so early on in life not to trust the police brought back Emily's painful imagery of African Americans learning of racism from the cradle. I sent my helpless eyes in search of the parents. They suddenly smarted up to warn her unapologetically never to copy me. They said they had managed to instill in her a sense of African pride. They said it was a different thing two years before when she cried daily from being bullied at school. "Look, the kids were vicious," they said. "Once she introduced herself as *African* and not *African American*, they resorted to Africa-this-Africa-that taunts to isolate her . . . and can you imagine some African American kids joined in?"

Bewildered, I got up, had a shower, and ate a brunch of leftover beans and *akamu* lightened with milk. When the itches hit, I visited the restroom three times in twenty minutes—flushing and washing my hands each time for cover. Usen said they had Imodium for bowel problems. I said, instead of the antidiarrheal, I needed to go home immediately. He pulled me aside to convince me to take the Imodium, arguing the subway ride was too long for a leaky ass, and that, by the way, too many stations had since changed their restrooms into storage spaces or newsstands, and that even the functioning ones might not be clean.

"Ekong, please, pace yourself," he said. "You've lost too much weight already and look shit-tired." I took the Imodium to placate him. I said goodbye to everyone with a one-handed hug because of my thumb, and, amid the children bawling, went home.

CHAPTER 11

We've got your back

ON MONDAY, WHEN THE CITYMD SAID I NEEDED TO come in, I left work like one going forth to see the hangman. In the consulting room, the nurse did not meet my eyes, as though I were a criminal. Then he offered me a seat with a gesture and left. The doctor came in and gave me something to sign and told me I was HIV-positive. I did not know what to say. She said it again and I nodded. But some man bashed in and dragged her away, without saying anything to me.

How would I break the news to Caro? Do that from here or wait till I get home? . . . The door swung open again, and they walked back in to say there was a mix-up.

"Mr. Udousoro, you have neither HIV nor AIDS," the man announced.

"What . . . you said I had w-what?" I stammered.

"Nothing. You're negative!" the doctor said, her eyes unshifting like she was watching an experiment in a petri dish. "There was a mistake."

I asked whether I needed a second test to confirm, offering my arm for another blood sample. They said it was not necessary. They said someone called me from the wrong list. "But do you know this *someone* who called me from the wrong list?" I asked.

"We should all be grateful we spotted it on time!" the doctor said, and showed me the result.

Seeing that I was never going to get an apology from these folks, in a flash I got off the seat and out of the room. I ripped through the cocoon on my thumb and tossed it in a trash can. Carefully, I took the plaster off my ear, too. It was like my life had been reset, given to me anew.

In the streets, I called Caro right away. But she did not answer, so I ran back inside and politely asked them for a signed and dated copy of the result, in case my wife wanted something concrete. It took an eternity to get even this. Since my stomach suddenly remembered to be hungry, I went out and bought a flatbread vegetarian Subway and Code Red Mountain Dew and went to eat at Starbucks. Bryan Adam's "Heaven" featuring Jason Aldean was playing.

Strolling back, I stopped at a liquor store to get a bottle of wine—because I just had to have a glass of wine, to mark the end of my fears, to celebrate my health. Then I came back to the CityMD and waited some more. When I got the result, signed and stamped, it was too late to return to work, so I strutted home, whistling under the gray skies. Though the temperature had dropped, I felt so warm inside. I was floating, my nose picking up the wonderful smells from Indian, Thai, and Dominican restaurants. I even stopped to watch construction work on Tenth Avenue, taking in the scene lazily, as drillers cut into concrete, sending up a cloud of dust, white and heavy.

I called the Bronx to thank the Umohs again for the weekend but could not reach them. I started returning the calls I had ignored from home. I shouted like they needed to hear me directly from across the Atlantic. I stamped my way to the piers, my screams sounding more distinct as the throng of people thinned, feeling more and more celebratory as I set eyes on the water. My homesickness pressed on my heart as though now I could see my callers waving to me from the beaches of Ibeno or Calabar or Lagos.

My spirit was brought down to earth when Tuesday Ita called to invite me and Usen's family to Sunday Mass and lunch somewhere in New Jersey. I promptly accepted—a chance to meet him long before Thanksgiving and to encourage him to bluntly capture his war woes in the foreword he had promised me on the speakerphone when Usen brought his family to Hell's Kitchen.

I RAN INTO MY TWO NEIGHBORS standing by their closed doors. Of course, my approach had silenced them, like they knew the devil's footsteps.

"Please, could we talk with you for a sec?" Brad said as I was opening my door. "Hey, we're talking to you, dude."

"Oh, me?" I said.

"Yeah, it won't take more than a minute, okay?" Jeff said.

I stopped, put down my wine, and stepped forward with folded arms.

They looked at each other awkwardly, before the white guy put on his glasses and introduced himself as Brad Parkes, adding that he was an unemployed engineer. The smaller man, Jeff Wengui, said he was an Iraq veteran and emphasized that he was an employed architect. The employment comments made all of us laugh, easing the tension, before I introduced myself and my fellowship. When they made no attempt to shake hands, I backed away to stand before my door, and folded my arms again.

"Ekong, do you have bedbugs in your apartment?" Jeff asked fearfully.

"Bedbugs?" I asked absentmindedly.

"Yes, bedbugs," he repeated.

"Wait . . . what?" I said, shaking my head, because we had learned in school that things like bedbugs and polio had been eradicated from America. There was silence, and I searched their faces to see whether they were angling to insult my continent like the Humane Society people at the publishing house.

Brad removed his glasses and said, "Yeah, the bugs, dude, the bugs. Hey, cut the crap. Do. You. Have. The. Shit. Or. Not?"

"No," I said ruefully, studying the ceiling's dirty bulb like I was in the wrong country. I expected them to say it was a joke, an icebreaker. I expected them to burst out laughing.

"No bites . . . itches?" Jeff said.

AND IT CLICKED.

"Folks, yes, yes, I have tons of *nnang ikuk*!" I exclaimed, dropping my hands. "*Iya uwei*, gentlemen, please, I'm sorry, I do have tons of bedbugs!"

"DON'T PANIC, MAN, we've got your back, okay?" Brad said, moving in to touch my shoulder. "We're full of the shit, too."

"I'm so sorry, Ekong," Jeff said, also coming closer. "And, please, keep your voice down. Brad's girlfriend is asleep inside."

"So you've not fucking seen the eggs, the babies, the parents, the grannies, huh?" Brad joked. "Well, it's the smell and the dead ones that gross me out."

Once he mentioned the smell, since I had not seen a single bug yet, all I could think of was the smells of my concoction. We laughed nervously and bared our arms to compare scabs and welts, as we were all hiding them in long sleeves. Of course, since they had lighter skin, their devastation looked worse. While Jeff was a worse scratcher than me and his skin was pitted, Brad said he did not have any bad itches yet, but his skin was like mottled pluots or dinosaur eggs. He was quite worried about Alejandra, a marine lawyer originally from Argentina. He bemoaned having to watch her scrape and fret. The whole thing simply sounded like tales from Nigerian prison yards. Though I was relieved to know what the actual problem was, the excitement over my test result had cushioned the impact. As our people say, an antelope that has just survived a lion cannot be rattled by a mouse.

They said the landlord was sending exterminators to our places a week from today but advised me in the meantime not to be in bed between ten p.m. and five a.m., to avoid the bugs' feeding hours. They praised me for not allowing bedbugs to derail "everything important" to me. When they glanced at each other, I asked them what they meant. They revealed that many a night they had seen me through the peepholes praying against the rails in "your solemn African religious ritual."

"Really touching devotion," Brad said.

I looked from one face to another.

"Wait, I don't understand you guys," I said.

"Oh no, we mean it in a good way," Jeff said, stepping back, alarmed.

"Tell me: Did you record my *solemn African religious ritual* session?"

"No," Brad said.

"Ekong, we have the utmost respect for your worship," Jeff said, like he wanted to cry, "which is why we never opened our doors, to avoid distracting you."

"What respect?" I said. "You're ridiculing me! You can't be talking respect when you hurt the feelings of my little niece in the stairwell late last month!"

"What . . . ?" Brad said.

"This shit has been going on in your country forever with Black folks!" I screamed. "At Andrew & Thompson, I'm suffering the same shit. At your embassies and airports, the same shit. I'm tired. And you ugly Chinese man, don't stand there looking all so innocent while China is shitting all over us back home . . . I think you in particular need to explain to me why you would break into tears just seeing Black people in this building. Why would the sight of a Black child break your heart?"

Brad stepped forward.

"Oh, Ekong, I think I remember the incident you're angry about," he said. "Parents and two kids? Keith filming them leaving? Look, we're sorry, for I don't even fucking know how I came across. Jeff was just bereaved . . ." He glanced at Jeff, who nodded permission to continue. "Yes, Jeff was crying because his brother had just died in a car accident. We're sorry."

"Oh, I'm sorry, too," I said.

"Thanks," Jeff said.

"I'm really sorry I misread the whole thing then!" I said. "Look, accept my deepest sympathy."

"I've no recollection of even meeting you guys then," he said.

I stepped forward and shook hands with them, because now I could understand how they came to hurt Ujai or misread my nightly back-scratching. And if they really avoided disrupting my *prayers* and now they voluntarily shared their ignorance, I thought I could drop my guard, too. They asked me to extend their apologies to Usen's family. Then Jeff shared a bit about the accident, the burial, and how he was coping.

"I'm sorry for accusing you of snooping on my prayers!" I said, and the kind of peace I had never enjoyed in Hell's Kitchen since I arrived coursed through my body. I told them about all the things I loved about their fabulous city. I told them how much I enjoyed Times Square, how Starbucks was my personal shrine of leisure.

But once I remembered my eavesdropping on Jack and Angela in the streets, the voices in my head urged caution and prudence. They reminded me that before Usen's visit or Jeff's bereavement, these same neighbors had never extended the least gesture of welcome such as would be expected when someone moves into your village anywhere in the world. Besides, I could not just discard Keith's sentiments; he knew them better. He had lived with them for a long time.

What to do?

Let's see how they relate with the African *henceforth*, I told myself. *Everybody deserves a second chance. Who knows, I might need them in this bedbug shit.*

BRAD'S DOOR OPENED and Alejandra poked out her head to invite him inside. When she smiled and said hello to me, I just nodded. I was relieved she did not join us, because her smile reminded me of Santa Judessa, the embassy Latina.

Yet her peek was enough for me to see that their apartment was completely different from mine. It was as stately as Usen's place, though much smaller. The floor was marble, and the windows and blinds were new. The painting looked professional like our house back home, no cracks or peeling. No pipes on the walls. No taped wires. I even noticed, for the first time, that Jeff and Brad's doors were different from mine. If I felt jealousy about the fact that Usen's apartment was First World while mine was Fifth or Sixth World, perhaps I could bear it because these were two apartments in two different buildings in two different boroughs. But I really felt angry and cheated that—in the same building, same damn floor—these differences existed. It was like my apartment could serve as a dumpster for my neighbors.

I was a strange victim of rent stabilization, though I loved the concept.

Jeff and I exchanged numbers, and he also gave me Brad's and the landlord's. I was grateful to him for telling me what to do before the exterminators came in a week's time. I was to put my beddings and all my clothes through the hottest of laundries; blast everything from bed to blinds to pots with anti-bedbug spray; and buy mattress and pillow covers from Rite Aid or Duane Reade. Finally, he warned me about furniture discarded on the streets, no matter how beautiful.

I could not call Usen, my super friend, for advice. He would be mad that I had even talked with Brad and Jeff. I called up Lucci, thinking it would be impolite to call the landlord directly. He sympathized with me, saying he would call Canepa shortly, yet he warned that New York landlords were the filth of the earth, with vicious lawyers sticking out their asses. "But listen, buddy, the worst is, if the best and the brightest enter the fray, as a Black man you could be home in a body bag!" he said, his voice surprisingly strong and steady. "My nephew who's a cop knows how horribly racist our NYPD is!"

I did not like how he quickly brought in race and cops. I shrugged and said the cop in my Times Square selfie was nice. He said I was naïve.

IN RITE AID, the Vietnamese American salesman said his neighbors used Hot Shot Bedbug & Flea Killer and showed it to me. On the can, there was a picture of an overturned and singed bedbug, helpless in the yellow flames of the spray. I grabbed five cans, like grenades. He said to pour liquid bleach all over the mattress, to drive them out of hiding, before spraying. I bought two bottles. They had run out of mattress covers, so he directed me to Bed Bath & Beyond by Columbus Circle, promising they would supply all my needs.

It was the biggest and most beautiful housewares store I had ever seen. But I felt dirty, like I was a distributor of unbelievable ill luck. There were many people buying pillowcases and bedsheets and bedcovers, as they must be doing daily, but, in my mind I could only see bedbug victims. I was staring at them, at their clothes, at their arms and legs for possible bites.

However, when a saleswoman smiled at me and I saw that there was no one around, I whispered my mission in her ear. She was an old African American lady. She nodded and simply led me to all the things I needed. I was relieved she did not even ask questions, for the shame of being infested did not leave me just because I thought the whole of America had bedbugs. I demanded anti-bedbug covers for the recliner, fridge, chandelier, bath, toilet, vacuum cleaner, etc. I needed to save my hide by all means. My heart sank when she quietly said those household items did not have covers. But I got white beddings to replace Lucci's colorful ones, so I could see the bugs, that is, if they survived my coming onslaught.

That evening, I overloaded my cart and laundry bag with dirty and clean clothes alike and went to coin laundry, as Jeff had advised. First, I stopped over at a dry cleaner's to hand over my suit, explained the circumstances, and promised a good tip. Thankful for the information, they quickly stuck my suit in a special container and closed it with a snap. At Clothespin Laundromat, I did my laundry twice, using the hottest options even with colored clothes. I set the dryer so hot some of my clothes shrank.

When I returned, I left everything outside my door and came in ready for battle. I doused my pillows and mattress in bleach, back and front and edges, before hitting them with spray. Next, I went after the woodwork around the bed. I pumped away excitedly, a cowboy firing from both hands. I folded the bed and sprayed the release holes. Then I mounted a thin straw on each nozzle, which allowed me to reach every spot. But I had forgotten about the pilot lights on the stove, so when I hit the stovetop, a huge red flame ballooned up, an enraged genie on four blue limbs reaching for the cans. I threw them away as I jumped back to save my face. The burned hairs on my arms drew a putrid odor. When I had been pummeled by a triple sneeze, I sprayed the chandelier, laptop case, and the three locks.

To avoid inhaling all the fumes, I went outside with my laptop case, and, afraid the harried bugs might travel into the laundry I had left outside my door, I decided to take it all with me to Starbucks. I wanted to let my bleached mattress and pillows dry, believing the spray would have killed every bug by the time I returned.

On the way, I called Caro: "Caro, baby, I have *nnang ikuk*."

"What?"

"Hey, you don't worry, for Ekong Baby has already nailed the little losers."

"Unfortunately for you, we all know Times Square, your neighborhood! *Abeg*, what would bedbugs be doing around that heaven? If the King Kong lady, as you said, could locate you, how would *nnang ikuk* survive such wizardry? My mother once used common camphor and *aran-ikang* to rid her home of bugs and then dried her whole bed in the sun. Are you saying there's no sun in New York?

Why not in DeWitt Clinton Park or Central Park? Just stick to the rashes stories, *mbok*. Why don't you just say you've been drinking and fucking?"

I parked the cart and told her I was vindicated by my test result. But she said if I were not drinking and fucking around, I would not have gone for a test. "Just come out with your hands raised and cut your losses," Caro said. "First, just *dey* help me understand what you were doing in a place called Bed Bath & Beyond a moment ago, as our credit card says. After bedding Molly and bathing together, what's left?"

"Please, just google Bed Bath & Beyond. Just google bedbugs in New York."

She started to cry and hung up.

I GOT A TEXT from Father Kiobel, telling me to keep away from booze. He informed me Caro also said I should not call her till further notice, though he himself had googled and understood what Bed Bath & Beyond was. He said ever since I told Caro of how Molly cried over my family war tragedy, she had not been the same.

When I plodded into the café, the crowd stared at my cart like the homeless had invaded. I was ashamed, because even I knew I was exhausted and sweaty from trekking all over the city and *weight lifting* the cart up and down the stairwell. Were my eyes red from all the fumes? Did I smell like camphor—the stink of the fumes mixed in with that of burned arm hair?

I asked for a slice of lemon cake and a venti Salted Caramel Mocha. I found some space to squat and prop up my laptop and cake. I googled *bedbug* and learned that *Cimex lectularius*, the species here, could survive for a year without food and that sometimes you may not feel the itch for several days, for they laced the bite with a numbing agent. This numbing business worried me.

I was distracted by the saleslady bringing me my order and napkins and apologies, hanging her head like someone who might lose her job. Sipping my mocha, I was relieved to read that bedbugs did not transmit any diseases and could only infest Keith's dogs if the levels of infestation are high. I nodded slowly when I saw that light-headedness, loss of balance, weight loss, high blood pressure, and fever were some of the complications that could worsen or result from infestations. But when I beheld the Wikipedia picture of a white man's back ravaged by bugs like spray bullets or like Jeff's arms, it nauseated me.

I trashed my cake and went to the square. When I caught myself scratching my stomach, bathed in all these flashing lights, it was like I had been caught red-handed, outed—or as though Lady King Kong would beam my shame and everyone would go, yes, it must have been that crazy thermos food. I stormed home to dress my bed in the new sheets and bedcover. Yet everything still smelled like old urine because of the bleach.

CHAPTER 12

I'd give anything to participate in a Jewish liturgy

I WOKE UP THRILLED TO ATTEND THE URAMODESE PRIZE ceremony. After breakfast, I got into a very special moss *senator* outfit Caro got her childhood friend, the fashion designer Ejiro Amos Tafiri, to craft for me. This would have been another great occasion to don my formal Annang attire. But the last time I had worn it to go to St. Patrick's Cathedral, the steep stairwell had made it impossible. My morning got better when I received a text from Brad and Alejandra and Jeff asking to take me out to dinner. We chose Friday, though they sounded like they wanted to hang out right away.

Full of energy and purpose, I threw on my winter jacket, scarf, and cap, and zipped downstairs, whistling folk songs like "Ikworo Ino" all the way to work. In the office, I toiled on the twentieth anthology story, "Divide and Rule Among the Minorities of Biafra." I immediately hated this title because it sounded more like an essay than a piece of fiction. It was a story about a girl's rape by a Biafran patrol. But it was not particularly well written.

In an introductory note, the author, an Ibibio engineer in Dakar, Senegal, included the following important lines, which I considered priceless in any conversation about the war and minorities:

Of course, most of us minorities have said General Philip Effiong—the Biafran leader's No 2 and a minority of Ibibio

stock—was a sell-out, a traitor, a quisling and so on . . . but
we would never put Chinua Achebe in any of these categories.
We insist Achebe truly and innocently believed in his Biafran
cause, no matter how tribe-centric he's come off in There Was
a Country.

I ground my teeth as I wondered if I should suggest that the author
of this novella do some fictionalization to make General Effiong look
like a saint—the way Achebe himself had deodorized Ojukwu, the
Biafran leader, in his memoir. But I could not manage it. Then I
became angry I had even considered this.

Someone arrived at my cubicle with a box of books, gifts from
Angela. But, unlike what Molly gave me, these were all books by
Black authors. To play along, I gave the dude a quick side hug and
asked him unfailingly to relay the same to her. After editing the
novella title down to "Divide and Rule," I fired Angela a thank-you
email praising the book covers.

I was very relieved when Emily texted from a café in Tribeca to
say that Cecilia Myers had assured her she was the perfect editor
for the book. She had thanked Emily for the "most touching bid letter she had ever received, which really moved the author." She had
also made Emily understand that though there was a lot of interest in the book, she was the author's first choice. I was hooked. I
wished Emily would take me along the next time she went for coffee
with an agent.

I began to dream that perhaps Liam would add the money we had
saved by losing *Mistress* to that we were offering for *Trails*, so we
could stay in competition. Father Kiobel, who had been using the
story of Emily's confessions to preach inter-ethnic reconciliation at
Our Lady of Guadalupe, said he would pray for the project.

When I lifted my head to see the Humane Society Two whispering at the water fountain like they were plotting a terror attack, I
suggested "The Divided Bubble" as the new title for the novella. But
the thing was simply not publishable. In my gut, I understood the

author's burning need to mention the dozens of ethnic groups that made up Biafra. I felt his pain for all the invisible tiny groups fighting to be seen. My mind returned many times to my struggles at the embassy to prove the existence of the Annangs. But the piece was too chaotic and confusing. The author had failed in creating a gripping fictional narration. Finally, I threw out the novella and sent the author a rejection email.

I walked into the hallway to call Lucci to ensure my apartment was on the exterminator's list. I left a voice mail, and he texted to assure me. I thanked him.

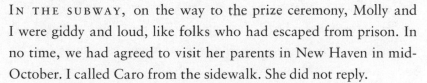

IN THE SUBWAY, on the way to the prize ceremony, Molly and I were giddy and loud, like folks who had escaped from prison. In no time, we had agreed to visit her parents in New Haven in mid-October. I called Caro from the sidewalk. She did not reply.

West Houston Street, though calmer than Times Square, looked older and used up to me. I was not even tempted by its Starbucks. It seemed in the wrong place. Our destination was a renovated beer hall, whose front wall looked unkempt and its façade dirtied by streaks of rust and grime. It reminded me of the front gate of Mapo Hall in Ibadan. Immediately I decided I would never visit this part of New York again. I thanked my ancestors I did not get all dressed up in my precious Annang outfit for this kind of environment. It was even too ugly for the moss *senator* attire I was wearing.

But inside we met an even more jubilant prize crowd than ourselves. Unlike my workplace, it was incredibly diverse. It was like someone had just cordoned off a part of Times Square and shipped it here, except that it was all so formal. Someone was pounding Sam Smith on a piano in a corner. The names and pictures of the nominees and past winners and the Uramodese plaque were continually flashing on screens on the walls. The stage was lit to perfection. Acquaintances and old friends greeted each other, while caterers served wine and finger food. Molly nursed a glass of red wine, but I was so happy to be here I did not want even water. She introduced me to fellow editors, agents, journalists, bookstore owners, critics, authors, publishers, translators, sponsors, special guests, and, of course, the prize nominees, resplendent and nervous in equal measure.

B U T   T H E   B U Z Z was about the two manuscripts that had turned Andrew & Thompson upside down. Everyone was talking about the agents and authors and, in the case of *Mistress*, its new editor, as though we had gathered to hand them the prizes.

One of the caterers, a big Black guy, kept staring at me, after I had declined his offering of appetizers twice. Fair-skinned, he had ceramic braces and a head of cornrows. His uniform had two Jewish tzitzits. Studying his dark elbows and knuckles, I suspected he had bleached his body, though not so badly as the dancing guy at the embassy. His accent left no one in doubt he was African American from the South. Each time he came around, I avoided him. Why was he not staring at other Black folks? Was it my *senator* outfit or accent?

Next, Molly introduced me to Paul Maher, a short lively guy, the editor of *Mistress*. He kissed her lightly on the lips. She hugged him. We shook hands. She congratulated him on winning the auction. I could see they still held each other in great esteem from their time together at FSG. "Emily is the most sensitive of editors, and an even better human being!" Paul said. And though I tried to smile like Molly, I could not process my feelings: it was as if *his* book had set me up for all the evil that had befallen me since that editorial meeting.

"I hope you're liking New York," Paul said cheerily, rearranging his bow tie. "Molly and Emily are so happy to have you here, after all the visa bullshit." Then he whispered in my ear: "It's too bad your lovely colleague, Emily, is still dating Jack . . ."

"Oh, you know Jack?" I said.

"Yap, but that's a tale for another day. I must say, though, I really love his absolute commitment to the Manhattan animal shelters and blood banks, you know."

"Well, as the Egyptians say, a beautiful thing is never perfect."

He told me he had been to literary festivals in Nigeria thrice, and in fact had been all over Africa, most times getting his visas on arrival. "No one had ever made me feel like a criminal or prostitute or pimp," he said. "Molly told me what you went through at the Lagos embassy. And how they let that starving small boy pee on himself." The people around us squirmed in anger and embarrassment. Ashamed of being pitied, I changed the subject to compliment him on *Mistress*.

To allow others do the same, Molly nervously guided me toward a man standing alone in a corner. My elation dissipated once she introduced him as "Chad, Jack's friend, another regular at the Nigerian book festivals." Suddenly all the glitter and prized smiles and sharp dressing around me seemed empty. He was short and rotund and completely bald. His thick round glasses were a shade smaller and magnified his lifeless brown eyes, the two handles biting into his bloated face. His tie was badly done like a machete dangling from his neck. He was supremely calm, though periodically his eyes livened up, restless, scanning any new person who came through the door.

Our handshake was limp, in some sort of mutual antipathy. I guessed we knew too much about each other. I stood right before him, knowing, certainly, this was not the agent I wanted to ask to explain what agents do—or the one Molly should suggest for me, if I wrote my memoir.

My deepest desire now was to hack and puke all over him, from head to toe, for comparing our *egusi*—the most popular West African condiment—to vomit. I wished I could ban him from setting foot again in Africa. I wished I could grab the PA and shout at him, to let everyone know he did not believe America infected Tuskegee with syphilis. But my lips were actually pursed, locked against releasing a word, as the memory of his long phone call with Jack turned my stomach and reproduced too much salty saliva for my mouth.

Molly stepped in to offer a million congratulations to Chad over *Mistress*. "Jack says you guys are really into *Trails of Tuskegee*!" he responded scornfully. "As you know, I turned it down last year. It's not just that it doesn't resonate with me. There's something wrong with the structure. It can never be fixed!" She laughed it off and tried to ignite a conversation the idiot had no interest in, till she herself recoiled and dragged me away to our seats.

"Ekong, by the way, if Cecilia comes, please just let her know how much you love the manuscript," Molly said. "Talk up how you and Emily first encountered the Tuskegee story from very different parts of the world, what this means to the fight against racism in the international community, how emotional you were after Emily praised it at the editorial meeting, how we would be a great home for the book and the author's career."

"Will do," I said.

"But, hey, you should've just said 'Big congratulations to you, Chad!' We all try to get along around here, okay? We're small. We're like an invisible minority tribe: we eat the humble pie."

"I'm sorry . . . Molly, are there Black agents? Just curious."

"Met one in my whole career."

"Okay."

"You can say she looks like an orphan or alien, a hidden blemish on an immensely white beast. But Cecilia isn't Black."

"Agents are mysterious animals to me. I don't even know what to compare them to in Nigeria. I want to say the capricious housing agents of Kaduna, but, at least, when they get you the house, they are gone from your life. Let's just say I prefer Cecilia to Chad."

"Don't we all! I hate to say this: if Chad Twiss agented *Trails*, it would've been sold along with *Mistress*. Now that the applause for *Trails* gets only louder, Satan alone can read Chad's mind. Who knows why he's watching the door? He's so slippery, a complete cutthroat of a guy. Not that he cares, but you won't find a single fellow agent greeting him!"

AS THE PRESIDENT of the Uramodese Awards, Dr. Marcus Zapata, an elegant Latino American, welcomed the audience, tension spread in the hall. The nominees, their agents, and their editors sat like statues, knowing the winners would be announced soon.

In a powerful speech full of anecdotes from his birthplace in northern Colombia, he expressed the power of stories to change minds and shape our world, and most importantly what it had meant to him to be elected the president of the prize. His little Colombian village invited him home to celebrate as though he had won a huge new literary honor for his country of prizewinners and original literary voices. "The atmosphere was that of a victory parade after winning a mini–Copa América," he said. "For them, one of theirs had finally gotten into a position whence he could influence the very processes of rewarding great literature! Colombians were no longer just prizewinners but kingmakers. And where else in the world is this even possible except in America!"

The hall rose to applaud. I hugged Molly. When he expressed a deep hunger for diversity in every aspect of publishing, the positive energy was so palpable that people like Molly and Paul lifted their ovation by continually standing up, like at a political rally. The feel in the hall was like the folks in Oedipus's town pining for the solution to the riddle of the Sphynx. "More and more, we're celebrating the diversity of books and authors!" he had said. "But how do we make publishing itself as diverse as this crowd or this blessed capital of publishing? We must never rest or forget that, like in the larger society, anti-diversity forces can roar back to squash our little visibility." This drew the biggest applause, and even my nemesis of a waiter, now standing by the far wall, was banging his empty trays like cymbals. Chad, too, was cheering and nodding, though his eyes were still on the door.

Next, Dr. Zapata introduced and thanked the prize judges, again a diverse group, who went onto the stage to introduce the finalists in each category and praise their works. The hall erupted as the judges announced each winner and Zapata presented the citations.

MOLLY HAD DISAPPEARED into the evening with Paul without inviting me. But what could I do? I lined up to compliment Dr. Zapata on his speech and the wonderful Colombian soccer tradition. When I said I could not forget how Colombia beat Argentina 5–0 in the lead-up to the USA 1994 World Cup and the national party that followed it, he guffawed and winked and gave me a fist bump, like an old acquaintance. I laughed louder when he said Nigerians and Colombians should have a competition over who had the crazier post-match celebrations. He was so warm that my prejudice against Latino people, rooted in my visa interview with Santa Judessa, melted away.

Then, seeing the Black server was still monitoring me, I decided to reach out, to ask for a glass of Coke. "Your accent tells me I'm from your part of the world!" he responded. I looked at him a second time. He had his hands in his pockets, a bench separating us.

"I'm a proud Biafran!" he said.

"*Ntere* . . . and you think I'm a *proud* what?" I said in total shock.

"Nah, you Nigerians don't understand. My granddad came to Mississippi in 1965, before the war, when he was *still* a Nigerian like you, before we became Biafrans. My pops was born here. He and my granddad have never visited Africa. But my granddad has been to Israel five times, because we Biafrans are Jews."

"And you? Will you visit Africa?"

"Oh nah, never! I said I'm Biafran, not African. Our real ancestral land is in the Middle East. You know, we Jews by blood. Some Igbos say the Jews originated from Biafra itself. But since we Black, maybe somebody is fuckin' with our history, as usual."

"I admire these strings you're wearing . . . By the way, Ekong is my name—" I reached out for a handshake, but he shrugged and kept his hands in his pockets. I ended up holding and admiring the tzitzits, saying, "Mr. Biafra, it's like holding what Abraham, our Father of Faith, wore!

"I'd really love to be inside the synagogue, you know. I'd give anything to participate in a Jewish liturgy . . ."

"I don't give a damn about synagogues. I go to a Catholic church. I'm tellin' you."

"Well, I'm Catholic, too, but from minority Biafra."

"What the fuck, my granddad says *our* minorities betrayed Biafra . . . anyway, nobody does Roman Catholicism like us. You know, we are Jews by blood. But once we settle in Israel, then we'll return to save all of y'all from that Dark Continent. Tel Aviv will soon issue all thirty million Igbos Israeli passports!"

"Did you ever ask the Ethiopian Jews, airlifted with such fanfare to Israel, whether they feel accepted?"

"Grandpa says the Blessed Virgin Mary has appeared to many in Onitsha with the message that the Israelis shall finally accept us in 2025. And to step shit up, to be more visible to Israel, Grandpa also says that in Onita . . . no . . . Olinishashajota, our people are already flockin' to embrace Judaism—"

"Onitsha!"

"Whatever. But, please, listen, my bad for sticking my nose in your shit: I overheard you tellin' the bow-tie white guy you're homesick. *Homesick* for Africa? For real, man? Let me break it down for you. You managed to escape from that zoo called Nigeria, right, you managed to secure a visa, and now you tryna go back? What are you really missin'? Should I lend you, Mr. Minority, my Igbo or Biafran brains? Shit, you know what, we probably shouldn't be kickin' it, for real. I detest unreasonable people!"

I walked out on him.

CHAPTER 13

Make your prayer sessions longer

JEFF'S TEXT SAID MY APARTMENT WAS NOT ON THE exterminator's list. Lucci declined my call. I left a voice mail threatening to contact the landlord myself. Suddenly Lucci phoned. I did not pick up because it was too noisy on Forty-Second Street. He texted me not to call Canepa before we talked. I texted to say I agreed. Yet he kept calling, as if to make sure I had no time to dial the man. When I answered, after apologizing he had been distracted by an important phone call from his cop nephew, he said it was illegal to go straight to the owner. He warned I did not understand New York enough to start fighting landlords or calling city hall. He said since my rent was less than half the market price, I should hire my exterminators, and finally that the landlord could evict me and none of my so-called neighbors would harbor me. "Hey, I take you in, out of the kindness of my heart," he sobbed, "and now you want to hand Canepa the bullet for my execution? If not for Saint Joseph, the patron saint of tenants, the man would've finished me off."

"I just don't want another bite in this apartment. That's all."

"Don't trash-talk my apartment as though you live in a castle in Africa. You Nigerians are the most ungrateful people on earth! I hope you pay for special cleaners to exterminate the stink of your African food."

I laughed because I thought he was joking.

"Sir, you were supposed to call Tony Canepa yesterday, no?"

"Where did that come from?"

"Where did what come from?"

"I mean, I never said such a thing."

"No, Mr. Lucci, you did, and today you even texted I was on the list!"

"I meant the list of my squatters who pay promptly."

"Really?"

"Look, I may be eighty years old, but I remember everything I've ever told you, from the first phone call. Yesterday, I even clarified the landlord isn't my friend-friend. Now, if you don't believe the bit about the reputation of our cops, just ask the next Black American you meet. My nephew knows what he knows about our police departments. I swear by my wife's cancer, I never ever said I would call Canepa . . ."

I took the phone off my right ear, where I once had the little plaster, and looked at the screen incredulously. It was misty because my ear was sweating. Did the bedbug bite affect something inside my ear? I felt inside the ear for a new outgrowth. I put down the phone, pressed down my nostrils and pinched my lips and blew out my cheeks to pop my ears. Nothing happened. I was fine.

"You can't just lie about something we talked about for two long days," he bellowed. "You can't bring your Nigerian four-one-nine scammer mentality here. Worse, you're making me doubt my memory like I have Alzheimer's."

I felt this was a dangerous situation, not just because of my guilt from his weeping, but from the acute feeling that New York was affecting *my* memory, too. His culture-shock comment underlined this feeling. To reorient myself, I started thinking about my conversations with random people, like the African American at Bed Bath & Beyond, Paul Maher . . . "I swear I shall never call the landlord or tell anybody," I said, capitulating. "And I solemnly promise to hire a firm."

I ran into Keith Jim-Stehr outside our block. I apologized for causing his dogs sleepless nights. But he said he had been worried that I myself looked sleep-starved. Clearly, he wanted to catch up; however, I told him I needed to get to my apartment to make a quick call to Usen.

Before seeking Usen's advice about the bugs, first I told him about Jeff's bereavement and apologies for being rude. He was very quiet and cold, before asking whether I was now friends with Jeff and Brad. Before I could answer, he put the call on speaker and said he was terribly disappointed and warned me never to tell him anything about Hell's Kitchen again.

"Usen is also angry you called him *saboteur* Saturday night!" Ofonime said.

"I thought we could still playfully call ourselves this like in high school," I said.

"That was then," he said.

"Okay, I shall never even use the word *sabo* or *sabotage* near you again," I said.

I was still assuring Usen I would never use Biafra to mock him, especially given what the patrols did to my family; I was still telling him how much I enjoyed their home when he screamed at his daughter to go stand in the corner. She shouted she wanted Ofonime to ask me about my thumb and ear. "If you say *kpim*, I swear, Ekong will never visit your school!" Usen chided her. He rejected my apology, insisting I only brought up his stabbing of the boy to tell his wife he had a murderous temper. "Since you ignored every advice to marry Caro," he said, "whose granddad gleefully fought for Biafra and even sabotaged your dad's burial, you've become insensitive." They would not believe I did not really discuss the war with my wife.

When Usen said he had reported me to Tuesday Ita, I realized I was being invited to a Biafra peace summit in New Jersey on Sunday. I could now understand why Tuesday was so tense the day before when he extended the invitation. But I believed the little I knew of Tuesday's war travails had given him the moral capital to settle any war disputes and being older than us also meant he could shut Usen up.

After the phone call, I felt too weak to go down to eat. Bedbugs and Biafra had joined forces to dissipate my great experience of Usen's home and of the literary awards. To forget everything, I tried to sleep right away. Yet when I stretched out on my bed, the urine-bleach stink was stronger than the night before. I endured. I thought about the smell of my concoction. But now I had two distinct smells in my head.

I got up and perfumed the whole bed and lay down again. Yet I could still smell the two smells within the perfume. I opened a bottle of wine and downed three glasses in trembling swigs. My gut bloated with hunger and jealousy and guilt for wanting to kiss Molly lightly on the lips like Paul. I dressed again and blundered out to look for something to eat.

Jeff was also going downstairs, carrying two bloated black trash bags. They were full of noisy empty cans, and I needed nobody to tell me these were used anti-bedbug sprays. I helped him with one bag.

"Two hours ago, I left Canepa a voice mail on your behalf, so that he could make arrangements to cover at least our three apartments on Monday," he said after we had fed the bags to the dumpsters.

"Wait, wait, *iya uwei*, who sent you to do this?" I said.

He offered me a cigarette. I said I did not smoke. "I've got your back, Ekong. We needed to move quick, man. This is New York!" Terrified, I told him he should never have called the landlord, that I had just assured Lucci *I* would personally handle things. Jeff said he was sorry in the tone of a non-apology apology, stroking his hungry goatee.

He told me hiring a firm could not solve my problem—or our problem, for that matter—as this mess was better cleaned up with all apartments at the same time, or the bugs could crawl from one apartment to another. "You want to foot the expensive bill while he's making a ton of money off you? You know he's paying just the pittance fixed by rent stabilization?" he said. "Lucci, that bastard, was never going to call the landlord! You're an illegal subletee."

"I'm illegal . . . what?"

"Not *illegal immigrant*, just illegal squatter. It means Lucci didn't get permission to squat you. If he did, the law says he should charge the subletee only ten percent more than the rent and that *everything* must go to the landlord . . ." My head spun and I leaned against the wall of the building.

The word *illegal* clanged around in my brain.

Lighting another cigarette, Jeff assured me he did not mention my name in the voice mail for the landlord but only my address and apartment number and had insisted Lucci had asked him, his neighbor, to call.

"So I am illegal. Do you think the landlord would call the police to arrest me?"

"No."

"Lucci?"

"Nope. But two years ago there was someone he paraded around as an undercover cop. I think he only uses the guy to gather dirt on the landlord for possible blackmail and court battles. Organized racketeers are all over this city. I'm just being straight up with you. Listen, the man is so fake that sweet-old-man portrait on your bookshelf isn't his real photo! He's a fifty-year-old giant of a scumbag with a nose bigger than Texas."

My knees hurt and I slid into a squat against the wall. I was breathless.

"Ekong, Lucci has got this long, complicated feud with the landlord. These two Italian Americans have been at each other's throats forever. Someone said they both trace their roots to Palermo, where they have all this Mafia shit. My advice? Pay him his shit and don't think about it." He blew a torrent of smoke down to my face till I sneezed mightily and stood up and staggered.

"By the way, Ekong, did you sleep better last night? We all heard you spraying, blasting, rummaging in there like a bison."

"I slept well. Thanks."

"Ha, it's a mere cease-fire. And you probably flushed them all out to our end . . ."

"Oh, I didn't mean to do that." I held his arms pleadingly.

"Brad and Alejandra and I understand. We're holding off from spraying our entire apartments so that the bugs won't crawl back to yours. We only spray our beddings so they can't get into our sprayed zone around the bed. Yet, last night, each time I closed my eyes I could see them scurrying away like they were being hampered by an invisible electric barbed wire. The thing will take over your mind, like racism, if you're not careful! The shit is bad. Bill Clinton had the shit. Victoria Secret had the shit. I'm going to buy a plastic bedcover, to seal in the reek.

"But I think you're the luckiest man in Manhattan: When you pray by the stairwell, your face is absolute peace. My advice? Make your prayer sessions longer!"

AFTER GRABBING A STALE HAMBURGER, I was so down I bought more wine, using cash to conceal my vice from Caro. As soon as I returned, I yanked Lucci's fake picture from the shelf. I spat on his calm smiling gentle face and smashed it under the bath.

From what Jeff was saying, it was going to take communal efforts and sacrifices to save our hides from those bugs. It was like some of our ethnic clashes which had roots in comic or forgettable events, like two people from different ethnic groups having a disagreement in the open market over, say, palm oil or *akara*. And then before you knew it, the two groups were at each other's throats. And then someone was killed and then properties razed in retaliation. And then other groups took sides and then peace meetings were brokered, which calmed or did not calm everyone. And then some youths ambushed the other ethnic group to avenge the dead, and then chaos broke out again.

CHAPTER 14

I've totally lost interest in Argentine soccer

FRIDAY EVENING, ALEJANDRA LEDESMA AND BRAD Parkes and I left for a dinner in Chelsea. Jeff could not make it for some work reason.

On the way to the subway, I expected them to ask politically correct questions about my background like my office folks had done. So, though we were full of laughter, I was nervous inside, plotting my responses. I decided to tell them of my embassy mess but would cut out the fight to prove our Annangs' existence, to avoid shame. But then I was already upset from the tiring mental edits, like carrying garbage I could not dispose of. But instead my neighbors talked about *The Americans* and *Brooklyn Nine-Nine* and *Motown: the Musical*. I complimented them on their matching fashionable J.Crew boots and said I must get them for me and Caro.

My spirit finally totally relaxed when Alejandra brought up soccer. We went back and forth about the games Argentina, her country of birth, had played against Nigeria. She told me how sad she was when Nigeria beat Argentina in the final of Atlanta '96, to take the gold. She confessed her only real pain, though, was that things were so tense that night in Buenos Aires, the capital of Argentina, that in some quarters Black immigrants were apprehensive, for it was like the whole Black world had defeated Argentina. Brad reminded her that since Argentines had been mocking the Brazilians, their archrivals, for losing the semifinal to us a few days earlier, after Argentina lost, a Brazilian was killed in a bar in Buenos Aires for laughing at his hosts.

Argentina's racist history has ensured there were no Blacks on their national soccer team, but I held back from mentioning that. I did not know how Alejandra would react; I wanted us to have a good evening out.

So I just told them Nigeria had been so happy, the government declared a public holiday to celebrate our gold, that we celebrated like our twenty-two players had taken twenty-two golds at separate individual events. I told them Diego Maradona, Gabriel Batistuta, and Fernando Redondo remained my soccer heroes, especially Maradona for single-handedly destroying England, our colonial masters, in Mexico '86. I told them soccer was the only thing that united our country. She told us soccer was an endless incurable fever in Argentina, every loss a national crisis. What pained her was that so many of her compatriots sadly took particular umbrage at losing to an *African* country at an Olympic final. She said, for example, where she grew up, losing to Ecuador, whose team was predominantly Black, was bad enough, but losing to Blacks *living* in Africa was unthinkable. She said she was praying for her hometown from NYC during the 2008 Beijing Olympics soccer final because she did not know what they would have done if Argentina had lost again to Nigeria.

As we sat down in the train, I congratulated her belatedly, though we ourselves were still smarting from that loss. Brad said if Argentina and Nigeria met in the next World Cup in Russia, the three of us must be there to watch.

"But, guys, look, I've totally lost interest in Argentine soccer till we're able to have Blacks on our national team," Alejandra lamented as I turned sharply to stare at her. "Yes, yes, Ekong, your reaction tells me you already know of our sordid race history." She admitted it was a crime Argentina went from enslaving their Black population to sending their Black brothers en masse to be killed in their wars. She spoke about covert genocide against the Blacks by the government of Domingo Sarmiento. I pursed my lips when she said that even war widows were disappearing from home.

She was quite emotional that these systematic atrocities meant postwar gender imbalance in the Black communities had forced the women to procreate with white men, leading to mulattos—a slow *bleaching* of the population! I was not surprised when she added that lack of opportunities for Blacks resulted in squalid conditions and death from cholera or that, at the end of the day, many fled north to Brazil and other places.

"Gentlemen, my dear Argentina went even further than this, so we don't have to face race issues like America! My great-great-grandfather was a general in the Argentine army, so we have crazy stories of what policies guided the deployment of Blacks in the Argentina-Paraguay wars.

"Worse, I grew up hearing my grandfather tell me snidely how hard he worked to help hide Nazi fugitives, making them fake IDs. He converted from Catholicism to Pentecostalism to, as he said, 'improve my personal holiness.' Before he died, he requested the swastika be carved inside his coffin, under the cover so he could contemplate it forever! Now you know why I skip family reunions and refuse to watch our national team even though I miss Argentina like crazy. I miss the food, the *carbonada*, the *asado*—"

"Sorry to interrupt, but I wish I could taste this food, Alejandra!" I said.

"I miss our beautiful seasons and traditions," she said. "I miss dressing up in my most gorgeous summer clothes for the Christmas Eve Mass, followed by the huge raucous eleven p.m. meal that ushers our extended family into Christmas. I miss our end-of-the-year summer season and will never get used to America's winter Christmas! But now visiting my town is all so complicated for me. Four years ago, I disrupted a Christmas gathering conversation which was blatantly racist, and they all shouted at me like I was an outcast, a New York smart aleck. It didn't end well. Someday I'm going to write the autobiography of my childhood.

"I'm no longer a child, so I don't have to fly back to listen to some relative at these gatherings praise the *valor* of our ancestors or visit their gravesides. How do I relate to these folks who honored Grandpa's anti-Semitic wishes . . . ?"

"It's okay, baby," Brad said, grabbing her hand and kissing her head.

"Courage!" I said.

"Ekong, Brad has his war woes, too."

"Yeah, I, too, don't go home for Thanksgiving," Brad said. "Will tell you why someday."

I could see that NYC had changed Alejandra's life. In her story, I could hear echoes of Emily Noah's journey, especially the way the city had remolded their worldviews. I was touched to learn that Alejandra was already having the kind of difficult family conversation Emily had brought up when she praised *Trails*. Yet the image of the swastika inside the coffin had cut deep into my mind. I did not know how angry I was till I felt a stiffening in my right foot, a longing to kick her grandpa's corpse till it rolled out of the casket and was buried in the naked humility of mere earth, our common home. A numbness began to climb my leg. I resisted the temptation to ask Alejandra if the burial pastor knew of this swastika. I was afraid a yes might spoil my dinner.

My mind was numb. It simply refused to consider the fate of the Black Argentine soldiers and their survivors. I was too ashamed.

WHEN WE GOT DOWN TO CHELSEA, my mood lifted. Brad told me this was the Lower East Side. Though it was almost night, it was more scenic than Hell's Kitchen, the Bronx, and the awards ceremony neighborhood. The cobbled streets were narrower, and the architecture, by and large, looked Georgian and Greek Revival. I thought the folks looked calmer than the crowds in Times Square. The cobbles even brought a measure of tenderness to our strides, forcing us to look at the ground, like everyone was discovering the place anew. Restaurants had fronts all made of windows to allow you to see everyone having fun inside. You could even hear the talk and laughter from the curb.

In this strange sort of intimacy, my nostrils picked up on food scents again, despite the deadening effect of fermented bleach. The strong smell of vindaloo washed over me, then of barbecue, then of oregano, then of saffron, dark and sweet. Then all of them at the same time. But a little warm wind diluted and then swept everything away. And even this smell of nothing was pleasant because it cleansed my memory, too. It reminded me of what it once meant to smell nothing. It endeared me to Chelsea. Brad and Alejandra pointed in one direction and talked excitedly about something called the High Line and how cool and crowded it was on weekends. Though I could see fun-seekers moving as though they were floating on air, my focus was on my food aromas of Chelsea. I smiled to myself and tilted my nostrils upward like I wanted to inhale the entire neighborhood's freshness, till, subtly, the scent of newly baked bread nibbled at me.

There must be a bakery nearby. The scent changed into that of cinnamon cookies and then of burnt chocolate. It was such wonderful novelty, and I allowed my nostrils to be teased. It reminded me of the smells of the bakery in *Children of Elijah Moses*, the manuscript I sacrificed for *Trails* at the editorial meeting.

IN THE BEAUTIFUL RESTAURANT, my companions insisted I must sit on a particular chair and promised to explain later. I drank Sprite as Brad and Alejandra enjoyed their glasses of Riesling. We asked for appetizers of sticky baked chicken wings and fried calamari and onion rings. I asked for sirloin steak, rare, while Alejandra wanted a buffalo burger and crinkle-cut fries and Brad cedar plank salmon, medium, with mashed potatoes and Brussels sprouts.

Alejandra excused herself and went to the restroom.

When she returned and the drinks, water, and bread arrived, like my village folks in the Bronx my friends toasted the Toni Morrison Fellowship that brought me to Andrew & Thompson. They toasted me for acclimatizing so fast to NYC. But then, lowering their voices and leaning very close to me, as though they wanted to kiss either of my cheeks simultaneously, they whispered, *To your first weeks of gallant bedbug survival!* This took me completely unawares, sending all of us into fits of laughter. I almost splashed my Sprite.

Their faces brewed with even more mischief when they abruptly stopped laughing, putting on poker faces. When I hooted even louder, they came back in with guffaws. I could not remember when I ever laughed like that. Other diners wondered what we were celebrating. A waitress and waiter offered to sing for us if we were celebrating a birthday or anniversary celebration. We shook our heads and said we could not share our joy with the world.

When we recovered, I hugged them and held on to Alejandra a bit longer. I thanked her for what she had shared about her childhood and family and background.

I declined Lucci's four calls as we ripped into the calamari and onion rings and deboned the chicken wings. They asked whether I was hearing from home and whether I would ever consider relocating to NYC. They asked me about the state of publishing in Nigeria. They asked what I thought of the Bronx. I asked them how they became friends, what countries or U.S. states they had visited, and told them how much I wanted to see the rest of the country.

As we settled into our entrées, my neighbors became curious about what sort of food we ate in Africa. I told them it was so diverse I could only actually talk about the dishes from *my* part of Nigeria. I explained this without feeling any pressure.

I loved their company.

I told them all I could about our dishes. To bring it back home, I announced there was a Nigerian restaurant in Brooklyn. In the little silence that followed, I said I even had some of our foodstuff and did cook. More silence. I concentrated on the sirloin steak and sprouts because their indifference did not worry me. And I did not push the matter by inviting them to a meal. Foreign taste has to be learned at an indi-vidual pace, I reasoned, unless it is forced upon you by travel or famine.

But each time they brought up a new subject or ordered more drinks, I started giggling like they were going to surprise me with another badass toast.

"So, what are you doing tonight?" Brad asked.

"After this, we mean," Alejandra said, forking the last piece of salmon from Brad's plate.

"Nothing," I said. "Maybe work?"

"Come on, man, you've got the whole weekend," he said.

"Ekong, we were thinking of catching a late movie," she said.

"Absolutely, I'm coming!" I said, almost choking on my soda.

"Fucking perfect," he said, giving me a fist bump. "We're trying to decide between two movies, *Split* and *Suicide Squad*. Great reviews. You make the choice."

I chose *Suicide Squad* without waiting for them to say what they were about. I liked Brad and Alejandra's spontaneous spirit. I also felt they had so enjoyed our outing they were finding a way to pro-long it. It was an evening to remember. Chelsea was my best part of NYC so far, because of how they made me feel.

We had no interest in dessert, but they were in no hurry to leave. So I asked Brad what his war story was. Alejandra quickly ordered for three cups of coffee. When the waiter placed our cups before us, Alejandra rubbed Brad's back.

"Vietnam," Brad said stoically, his hands clasped in front of him like in prayer, as the waiter poured our coffee. "The Vietnam War has fucking shredded my extended family to this day. My cousin commit-ted suicide in the rice paddies of Vietnam upon learning my grandma was protesting the war in Union Square. My grandpa's brother never returned from the fucking Korean War . . ." Alejandra nudged Brad to drink his coffee. His trembling fingers betrayed his pain.

Brad said, "Well, the point was that I never go to my extended family at Thanksgiving any longer, because it always turns into a big argument between the hawks and the doves, warmongers and peaceniks. It never fucking changes." But, like Alejandra, he had remained quite nostalgic for the celebrations during his childhood. I reached across the table to hold his hands and said I knew what it meant for the two wars that happened long before he was born to still be raging within this tough-talking New Yorker.

Brad looked away and pulled his hands back and folded his arms. Alejandra said he found it difficult discussing wars. We finished our coffees.

BUT MY NEW FRIENDS were not done with surprising me on this magical night.

The bill came with pictures of our faces during the toasts—including our biggest laughs when we toasted our survival of the bedbugs. Apparently, when Alejandra claimed to use the restroom at the beginning, she had gone to finalize plans for the restaurant staff to secretly take photos of us during the toasts, having put me on the seat with optimal view. "You guys are too mischievous!" I said as we roared again with laughter.

The waiters cheered that they had gotten the shots right. They forwarded them to our email addresses. Alejandra emailed them to Jeff—who she said played a role in organizing this surprise. When I called to thank him for a memorable evening, he joked they should frame *the* photo and hang it in my apartment, an elixir, a bronze serpent, for the days when the bugs would roar back or brook no relief. "Jeff's got the worst mouth in Manhattan!" Alejandra warned me, as we left for the movie theater. "Hey, listen, we believe he's the only one who knows the secret of avoiding the bugs. But he won't say, maintaining the *secret* is not useful. We just want to know what it is."

I did not know why Jeff would hide something like that from them. But I promised I would try my best to get the information.

IN THE MORNING, I rode the E to Queens to buy Nigerian foodstuff. I spent the afternoon cooking *abak-atama* soup and steaming wraps of corned beef *moi moi*, boiled-egg *moi moi*, and sardine *moi moi*. And with all the sweet thick Starbucks drinks I was consuming, I prepared even more *etidot* soup—which was what my grandma had used to control her diabetes. After serving the soups into small plastic containers and stacking everything up in the freezer, I went to spoil myself in Starbucks.

Later I saw Jeff Wengui smoking and pacing up and down our block. He told me he heard we had a blast, from the dinner in Chelsea to the movies. We posed for a bunch of selfies with mischievous faces, trying to mimic the Chelsea photos.

"Next time you must be there," I said, sipping my tea.

Jeff paused and hesitated and looked down. "Ekong, do you think you civilians can talk about wars? I really love Brad, but I avoid talking war shit with him or anyone. Sometimes he wants to ask questions about Iraq, but I never want to remember that place, you know. His father was deployed there during the First Iraq War in 1991, when Brad was only four. He saw him return in a wheelchair and die a year later. I think it still hurts him bad."

"Courage, my friend, courage."

Already, in a short while, we had traveled a long way from those early days of silent confrontations. Listening to Jeff, I felt even closer to Brad. It was even more profound, more intimate, that I did not get the entire story from Brad himself, but from Jeff, his friend, who struggled to share even while nursing his own war demons. I could not thank my ancestors enough for the warm blanket of intimacy that was wrapping itself around my new small community.

Jeff cleared his throat. "I googled your fellowship. I know you're working on the long effects of the Biafran War." He stalled and threw away his cigarette and put his hands in his pockets and looked down. I felt bad, like I was forcing him to remember Iraq. I adopted his silence and moved beside him, shoulder to shoulder, facing the street, facing a line of mounds of sealed transparent bags standing on the curb like badly spaced flower shrubs. I stared at these bags as though I could see the bedbugs inside.

The wind came in, big and strong. It skimmed the sealed plastic and drew a muffled whistle. I knew this was not the time to ask Jeff for his bedbugs secret.

✕

JEFF QUIETLY SAID he was offended by my comments about the Chinese on Monday. I apologized and said the Chinese were also creating jobs. I tried not to be judgmental because now I was talking to a friend. I swallowed my venom because maybe I should say Jeff—away from Brad and Alejandra—was more expressive, vulnerable.

He asked whether the Chinese treated our people better than the Americans. I pretended I did not understand his question, but it did unsettle me a bit. I did not like these comparisons. And since he was Chinese American, with a foot in both camps, I could never win. Talking colonialism, any type, simply exhausted me. It gave me no joy to compare our torrid procession of colonial masters, white, Black, or Asian.

"But, Ekong, do you think the Chinese in Nigeria today could possibly treat your minority peoples worse than the Biafrans?" he said abruptly, glancing at me.

It felt like he was turning the screw on me. I turned and faced him. My mind dwelled on the African immigrants who were being beaten and locked up in freezing immigration centers by the Chinese authorities in Zhangzhou. I was angry and ashamed because in Nigeria our police protected the Chinese like white people.

"Well, Jeff, it's difficult to make these comparisons," I managed to say.

"Hey, you're dodging!" he said folding his arms.

"I can honestly say it's easier to get a Chinese visa than an American or European one. Chinese consular officers don't belittle us even though China doesn't believe in human rights. But, you know, China has been known to do very nasty things to its own citizens! I'm saying it's just difficult to judge or compare Igbo colonialism in a three-year war fifty years ago to what a real superpower like China is doing right now in peacetime. For example, I don't know why China is bringing fake drugs into Africa, or sponsoring killings in the gold mines of Ghana and Congo . . ."

He stepped back, lit a new cigarette, and puffed and blew into the wall. I threw my cold Starbucks tea into a trash can and searched his face, as he pulled at his goatee, his eyes searching the skies. He was not the unfeeling tease the others knew him to be, or the distant Chinese I saw in our streets back home.

"Jeff, you're uncomfortable with Asians being seen as racist?" I said, shoving him away playfully. "Alejandra and Brad really give you a hard time over this, am I right?"

"Yes."

"Well, I say hire the Biafrans to help you with worldwide victim propaganda!"

"Not funny, man. I've done everything for America, my country . . . almost dying in Iraq. Yet sometimes you live with this doubt about whether you're American enough. Whether you belong. Some days, this insecurity frightens you more than facing enemy bullets in Iraq."

"Be strong."

"Don't get me wrong. Brad and Alejandra are wonderful friends. See how far they went to welcome you to Hell's Kitchen? See how they refused to spray their apartment, to keep you safe? We're fine. We make mistakes, we apologize to each other. I'm sorry you misunderstood us the day my brother died. Been here five years. We've grown in talking deep stuff. But you're so right: anyone who is a minority just has to be strong and hopeful."

I MET KEITH on the landing of the second floor, on his way out. He looked really sharp. But he was not his usual self; he was looking daggers at me. I quickly complimented his clothes. He said he was going to a dinner and a Broadway show.

I appreciated when he straight-up told me he was worried for me, because, these days, I seemed to be having a lot of fun with the white and Chinese and Latino folks of Hell's Kitchen, with everyone but him. He told me I was always in a hurry around him. "Ekong, the other evening," he said, "you literally ran away, claiming you needed to call the Bronx, and yet seconds later I saw you lugging down Jeff's garbage, like a slave. I just wanted to tell you how confused I am. And I wanted to tell you my brother did the Ancestry .com and 23andme.com stuff and said we have genes from sixteen African countries. None was Nigeria, which is where I really want to go. I mean, I really love what your little niece said the other day about your village in Nigeria . . . you Africans don't understand the nightmare of the strange longing for *home* some of us suffer in this country."

"I would just pick a place to visit," I said when I got a chance. "I mean, you can still come to Nigeria."

"But I just wish I knew my ancestors' true ethnic group! You understand how you really, really want to belong?"

"I do."

"No, you don't . . . you're spending way too much time with our neighbors! You've forgotten I was right behind you that day, recording everything. *Everything.* On this same damn stairwell. Jeff couldn't even afford to look up, like Black people were dirt. Should I forward the clip to you, to refresh your memory? Do you know how traumatizing this could be for that girl? Come on, nigger, don't tell me what lies and spin they fed you with! You have no damn clue what it means to be a minority because you're all Black in your country."

Though I knew he did not understand our tribalism issues, of course I also knew I did not have his same gut understanding of his racism issues. But I did not want to be impoverished by our joint ignorance, to allow it to define my budding relationships, to block me from the growth that could only come from relating with sundry people, the kind of diversity only cosmopolitan NYC offered.

I had chosen to remain positive.

I could never let anyone, not Usen, not Keith, decide whom I should befriend based on the racial or tribal or gender histories of our broken world. I had not come all the way from Ikot Ituno-Ekanem to enlist in entrenched racial divisions in NYC. Besides, I had just been humbled by the confessions of the war woes of my neighbors and their families, of their direct or passed-on traumas of all kinds of wars. So far, I had succeeded in limiting my malice to the Humane Society Two at work, instead of blanketing the whole place with it. And who was I even to think that I, Ekong Otis Udousoro, did not harbor any shred of distrust or discrimination, of any kind, in my thought or action?

Well, since Keith had stood his ground, I apologized and confessed that bugs had united me with the neighbors. But he stepped away from me in worse horror than when he saw the cop selfie. I told him even if the exterminators did not succeed on Monday, Jeff might know the secret to save my ass from bedbugs. "Oh no, be warned," Keith said. "Chinks will never help you! Chinks betrayed the civil rights movements, not just by not joining us to ask for those rights, but by cornering the benefits once we succeeded. Anyway, your friends had the bugs two years ago. They'll have them again next year! I've never had them—not once. Maybe when you take care of other people's precious dogs, you're a bit more responsible, cleaner. I think this cleanliness is also part of why the landlord respects me . . ."

When the pets whined upstairs like I was hurting Keith, he dropped his voice, excused himself, and bounced downstairs. While I clomped up the stairwell, certain in my research that bugs had nothing to do with dirt, I abhorred what was happening to my relationship with Keith and Usen, my two Black anchors in NYC.

CHAPTER 15

Ikud, the tortoise, knows how to embrace his wife

I HAD JUST FINISHED A CUP OF TEA AND A WRAP OF *moi moi* for breakfast when Ofonime called. First, she apologized for "everything" and said she had to back her husband for peace's sake. "Ekong, please, just accept your relative in New Jersey as you see him!" she said portentously. When I saw she was not ready to say more, I said I understood everything, to get her off the phone.

On the long train ride into New Jersey, I read the last chapters of *Thumbtack in My Shoe*, the last of the eight manuscripts for the next editorial meeting. It was sponsored by Bob Hamm.

The book was set in Trinidad and Tobago, and I wished it would never finish, because I was in love with the first-person point of view of the eighty-year-old protagonist. The story began when the doctor told him he had one more week to live: it was a reflection on his life as a cook in different households. In spite of the brutal racism he had suffered all his life both from white and Asian families, his portraits of Caribbean food and beautiful beaches and the Main Ridge Forest Reserve were as nostalgic as Ujai's longing for the fresh fruits and the scenic valley of Ikot Ituno-Ekanem, or as evocative as the descriptions of the lush beaches and hilly islands of *Mistress of the Sea*. However, what made the book most memorable was its unique exploration of "Black shame," that the old man's last employer, a Black family, had been the most abusive.

I sent a quick email to Bob, to let him know how much I loved this book and how much it reminded me of my own Biafran shame. I was reflecting on the Biafran reconciliation meeting that awaited me in New Jersey when I got a despondent text from Emily. Jack had told her Chad Twiss had indeed seduced the author of *Trails of Tuskegee*. Chad had not only promised to get him enough money to buy a house and send his kids to college—things the author had discussed with Cecilia Myers. No, he talked up a big movie option and simultaneous six-figure publishing deals around the world. He had fixed the auction for Wednesday.

I called Emily when I changed over to a bus. I did not know what to say, except to feel bad for Cecilia and Emily, who first believed in the book. But Emily said if I must tell Father Kiobel, I must let him know that losing the book was not a big deal to her. "He thinks too highly of the publishing industry, ha," she said, and laughed.

My head throbbed with images of Chad shitting on *Trails of Tuskegee* behind the author's back yet pocketing his fat percentage.

WHEN I ALIGHTED in a little picturesque city in New Jersey, it was as chilly as yesterday. But I was dressed like these Americans around me, in jeans and a shirt and a gray I ♥ NY sweatshirt. Looking around, I noticed most of the Blacks who had traveled with me moved in one direction. And most whites moved in the other.

I studied my map app twice, yet it still asked me to move in the *white* direction. After a brisk twenty-five-minute walk, I spotted Tuesday's church, its tall gold-plated cross cutting into the blue clear skies, a heavenly lightning rod. I put my map away and followed the cross like the Star of David. Sometimes it was obliterated by thick foliage and other buildings, but it had entered my heart. I knew where I was going. The houses here were more spread out on the streets than in the Bronx, with their well-kept lawns and flowers and hedges. The meadows bore a hint of fall, a fire approaching the leaves.

I waved confidently to folks on their porches or lawns playing and barbecuing, but I got nothing back. But, unlike in Chelsea, I did not like the smell of this American barbecue. It smelled of lighter fluid and chemicals of instant charcoal. A Black man drove out of his garage. I stopped and waved with two hands. But even through the windshield I could see that the shock on his face from seeing another Black ass was more exaggerated than a face carved on a watermelon. When he drove by, he stuck out his hand and gave me the middle finger salute.

My faith had landed me in a strange world.

When the traffic increased on the road, I knew the early Mass had just ended. Of those departing on foot, nobody looked me in the face, and a few crossed over to the other side. As they say, if folks leaving the shrine do not answer to your greetings, maybe the oracle itself is deaf. I called Tuesday to say I was three minutes away. He said I should wait in front of the church, for he was in a quick meeting in the basement. "Please, no worries, take as much time as possible," I responded in an attempt to be as pleasant as Ofonime suggested.

The fields on both sides of the church were marked by life-sized Stations of the Cross, like the ones of Our Lady of Guadalupe, and as I drew near to this beautiful church, the smell of incense hit me. The individual Stations were linked with a winding path of non-motorized tarmac, while ours back in Ikot Ituno-Ekanem was paved with lose pebbles. I could have stared at the fields forever, for, in all my stay in America, nothing had reminded me more of home.

A white priest was outside greeting his white flock and hugging crying babies and gracing selfies like Father Kiobel. Though he also had the Ogoni priest's height and carriage, his Father-Duffy-of-Times-Square face was dulled by a mustache that ate up his upper lip. His simple vestments were nothing compared to Father Kiobel's embroidery and frills that drove parishioners to complain that the man could not stop buying clothes. I could hear the ushers encouraging people to stop by the basement for coffee and doughnuts, just the way their Ikot Ituno-Ekanem counterparts of yore invited people after Sunday Mass to the sharing of sweet palm wine, something so sweet even children could sample it. I went and stood near this priest, waiting for him to finish with the family he was greeting so I could say hello. They called him Father Orrin, and he seemed to know each person's name and what they did last week and the week before and whose cousin missed Mass.

Yet, each time a family went away and I got my smile ready and stepped forward, he grabbed the next family and next woman and next man and next child, or even the next tree. It was like there was a bone in his neck that prevented him from turning in my direction, much less seeing me. But I told myself perhaps there was an invisible line Father Orrin was attending to, something I could not work out, a Catholic protocol the Irish missionaries forgot to teach Nigeria. I waited patiently, hoping that at the end of *the* line, my elephantine patience would get me somewhere, that I would be *seen*.

But, just when the line had ended and there was a huge opening and I moved in, the priest exploded in a laugh. When I also smiled, he pointed behind me, to someone else who had not even seen him. "Mary, Mary, my friend!" he called out.

She was an old frail woman in a wheelchair. Her nails were long and curved and were painted in mixed colors, futuristic talons. She was wrapped up in blanket, her sharp mouth meticulously painted in red like an American white ibis. Her face only gave you peace when she smiled. When she spoke in a little grating voice, she moved her hands like Angela Stevens. Now the priest took off toward her in such a great hurry that the back hem of his chasuble bucked and expanded behind him, riding the light wind, the tail of a bird.

I shrugged and continued to give him the benefit of the doubt. Maybe he was greeting only worshippers leaving the church, maybe he knew I had not said hello to Jesus yet and so he was reluctant to supplant the Most High. Then I felt stupid, like folks were staring at me for doing something bad, and when I looked around they actually were staring at me, though I could not catch their eyes. Even if I turned abruptly, their eyes were already elsewhere, including those of teenagers. If this was what Tuesday was enduring every Sunday, I encouraged myself, then I must submit my soul for his sake.

The only people who gave the game away were the little children, who slowly came close to gawk at me. I appreciated their openness, their honesty. It confirmed I was reading the alienation right. But, I did not believe they could not have seen Black people before, or been in school with some, or been to Times Square and seen its daily global carnival, for that matter. No, I believed their problem was that *I* was out of place, like a pagan statue roaming through their holy premises: I had shown up at the wrong shrine, my blackness falling, as it were, like a shadow, a stain on it. Their innocence reminded me of the stories of Emily and Alejandra's childhoods.

SUDDENLY SOMEONE WAS HAILING my name and walking toward me. I turned around. But I was so shocked I could not tell who he was. The children greeted him, "Dr. Hughes, Dr. Hughes!"

I stepped back when he stopped before me.

He was a white man—totally *white, mbakara, onyibo.* If this was Tuesday Ita, he had completely bleached off his Black skin. While some of the people wore a tan, Tuesday's skin was already an irreversible lily whiteness of a sunless dead of winter. The whitening job was so good, so thorough, I would never have suspected anything if I knew nothing about him. He was nothing near the photos of his earlier years in America, which I had seen in Ikot Ituno-Ekanem, or of his relatives. Unlike the quack bleaching of the embassy dancer or the Biafran waiter at the prize ceremony, Tuesday's knuckles were as light as Brad or Alejandra's. All I could think of was the frightening transformation of Gregor Samsa into a giant bug in *The Metamorphosis.*

Though I was appalled, like Gregor's relatives, I pretended not to notice his change. Such was the depth of my betrayal.

"Call me Hughes and nothing else, please!" he emphasized to break the awkward silence.

"Hughes, *amesiere!*" I greeted him, just to be doubly sure, and put out a hand.

"*Asiere nde*," he said, grabbing it. "Welcome to America and thanks for coming out to your brother's end. *Irung-o?*"

"*Mmode* . . . everybody is fine. It's really my pleasure. I've been hearing of you since I was a kid! I know you don't like to be complimented for all your charity back home, but the village really wanted me to thank you in person . . ."

"*Ikud*, the tortoise, knows how to embrace his wife, as our ancestors say. You never forget your people no matter where you are."

"*Gwoden Annang, agwo uko!*" I began to hail him with Annang traditional praises and proverbs.

"*Se-nyien do-ng*," he responded timidly.

"*Gwoden Annang, agwo esit mbom!*"

He raised his hand to stop me, shaking his head, looking away.

"*Ekong, aa-gwoden Annang, agwo Ifiok, aninge inua iko!*" he said, taking over the praising, beaming.

"*Nsinam ikpa ekpe?*" I responded, relieved.

"*Unyie agwo ade mfon emama o!*"

"Anesthesiologist *ajid, irung anyie inyang enyie ubom.*"

"*Aa-gwoden Itiaba.*"

I offered him a little bow with a two-handed rigorous handshake. "*Mmo ntom, mbo-om* . . . after all these years, you speak *iko* Annang better than some of us back home!"

"*Sosongo.*"

"Hughes, your church and city are beautiful!"

"Thanks, *da* Ekong."

Then I thought, oh no, this man must have a skin disease. Nobody with such a clear pride and grasp of our culture and language would destroy his skin like this. Besides, I doubted any bleaching could have succeeded so thoroughly. Then I felt bad I had prejudged him. I tried to pay attention to other aspects of his appearance. He was clean-shaven and in a black suit, black shoes, white shirt, and red tie. He wore a black bowler hat, the type the minorities of the Niger Delta call "resource control," because this was how our politicians fighting for oil ownership in the national assembly dressed. But the headgear did not stop me from seeing that he was bald or had shaved his hair.

He led me to the front of the church, where a few people now greeted me, and even shook hands with me, seemingly emboldened that one of them had taken the risk. I could not imagine they knew he was once Black—or, should I say, was now still Black? Had this *whiteness* been part of him all along?

The fact that I did not even know how to phrase the question in my heart meant that, as strange as it sounded, I felt more at ease with these other white folks than with my village man, because I thought I knew what or who they were. But while Tuesday's accent was exactly like theirs, mine seemed to alienate me or increased the distance between how they saw him and me. When I had to repeat things twice or thrice for *clarity*, Tuesday did not speak up or "translate," as though it would be a crime for him to claim an understanding of my accent.

I felt lost.

"Ekong, just to let you know, there are Black folks in our city though they don't come to our church," he confided in me when they were gone, avoiding my eyes.

"Yes, I saw them on the train and bus," I said.

"I used to attend their parish, you know. But many of them thought they must remind me *we* Africans sold them into slavery four hundred years ago. But, somehow, they just fail to understand that *I* am not—that *we* are not—descendants of slaves!"

"Is it that bad?"

"*Mmayin*, I swear, they really rub it in. Africa this, Africa that."

"That's awful! But it would seem you traded in a four-hundred-year itch for the forever itch of racism? So they need visas to worship with you, then? I do hope you didn't say all of this descendant-of-slaves stuff to their faces."

"Hey, I had to at some point, to breathe! I had to tell them I'm an *African*, always . . . not Negro today, tomorrow Afro-American, next week Black American, next month African American, and now just Black or something called 'Black with capital *B*'? Except a few people like Usen and Ofonime—who still stop by their churches— Africans would rather go to hell than worship with African Americans. Well, since I changed a few *things* about my life and relocated to this side of the city, I've had peace. Look, I'm done with all this multicultural diversity shit."

I wanted to say I was sorry about his skin and even more sorry about his trauma in the war. But, afraid this might embarrass him, I swallowed the idea. I realized he was still avoiding eye contact no matter what I did to warm up the chat, so I reached out for a belated embrace. It startled him. But he accepted it awkwardly, holding me off, giving me two back slaps that felt more like something designed to shock my body from bedbug itches than to welcome me to the Eucharist.

I held on to him till his body softened and I could feel his breathing. I did this for my own good, too, I must say, because I wanted him to feel I had accepted him. I held him till our necks jerked back like two snakes and our eyes finally met.

USEN AND HIS FAMILY arrived in their beige Audi sedan, a gift from his brother in Burkina Faso. To get to the parking lot, Usen drove so close to us I could pick out the Liverpool FC decal on the lower corner of the car's back window, even as I juggled my attention between the car and Father Orrin, who was still lost in a conversation with Mary. After finding space in the crowded parking lot, they stepped out. Ujai had spotted me immediately and wanted to dash hither, but I could see Usen stare her down.

They were all in ravishing traditional Annang attire, over black turtlenecks and other layers to beat the chill. Ujai was dressed in the same style and colors as her mother. In her double-layer *wrappa* and aqua-blue lace blouse and shiny black heels and outrageous head-gear, *afong-iwuo*, or what the Yorubas call *gele*, the girl walked gracefully with her parents, continually searching my face and their faces, hindered as much by the tension between me and her dad as by her *wrappa*. I could tell immediately that she had not stood with her legs apart, like the embassy Muslim lady, to tie her *wrappa*, hence her constricted stride.

The guys, Usen and the toddler son, were decked out in long-sleeved white shirts whose tails flew over their single-layer *ofong-isin iden*, or *usowo or* male *wrappa*, and flat-sole black shoes. Each man's *wrappa* was gathered to the right side of the waist in a big knot, skewing the shape of the shirt. Their black hats matched their shoes, though they were different from Tuesday's.

Of course, all eyes were on them, but I thought they were so colorful that the gaze was more benevolent, kinder, than what had been lashed on me. Even the priest had stopped the chat with Mary, to *see* and *notice* the newest visitors who seemed to be straight from Africa. And the children now clapped and cheered like the day my food was raised up and celebrated in Times Square. There were phone cameras flashing.

Unyoked from the punishing attention, I felt like jumping and hailing them, too. I silently cursed our stairwell for making it impossible for me to ever celebrate my outfit in America. When my eyes met Tuesday's, he was fighting like mad to maintain his disguise, to hold in his ringing laugh, covering his mouth like Lagoon Drinker. When I pushed away his hand from his mouth, he joked that I should yodel their arrival like the women did for important visitors back home. I said *he* should do it, so I could see whether he still remembered how. But he straightened up to join the white people clapping for them.

When they came to a stop where we were, more people gathered around to welcome them. Ofonime hugged me and Tuesday, but between Usen and myself there was a needless nervous *Biafran* energy, which could neither be diffused by the sacredness of the locale nor the buzz occasioned by their arrival. As the whites receded,

Ofonime, chatty and affable, did her best to paper over things. Ujai, already looking so grumpy and bored, found a way to give me a good hug and ask about Keith, Molly, and Emily. "Uncle Ekong, unlike in the Bronx, you smell really great today!" she whispered. But she refused to hug Tuesday till her father intervened.

We all beamed with smiles when Father Orrin ghosted in from behind to greet us. A crescendo of noise struck up as the whole premises acknowledged his arrival. He gave the African family a quick handshake and then plucked the toddler from the mother. Father Orrin still did not welcome or *see* me, even though I was the only person who greeted him by name. He hoisted Igwat in the air, and the collective excitement peaked and broke into an open cheer at his big long wet kiss on Igwat's forehead with the kisser's eyes closed.

As he returned the kid decisively to a startled Usen, not Ofonime, the priest told Tuesday, "Good job, good job!" for making us welcome. Tuesday nodded and executed a deep bow but did not introduce us as *his* people. I thought his estimation before Father Orrin, as a parishioner who could manage international chaos, could have only grown.

When the priest left, Usen, who had seen him snub me, glared and nodded maliciously, like God was already punishing me for my iniquities. "When you understand America, you shall be noticed!" he gibed. Tuesday tried to cover for Father Orrin, saying he must have thought I was an African American from across town, because I was not in our traditional wear. He blamed himself for forgetting to give me the dress code. I hated his little speech, though I smiled to hide my alienation.

Was he happy, then, that a disease had made him acceptable here, unlike the rest of us healthy Blacks? Had the disease affected his brain? I began to think of Tuesday as one of those Blacks who hate their color. But then again, I backpedaled, because I did not want to judge him. So many things in this country were taking me out of my depth.

Moreover, when I remembered that at the award event I myself had mistaken the Biafran waiter for an African American—because of his accent and dressing—I shrugged and blew out my cheeks in shame. Dealing with this white Annang brother was already more daunting than discussing race with Jeff Wengui.

I was tired.

it was an excellent Caucasian look glowing in a sheen of oil, even though the man's head was anything but smooth, with the kinds of little hills and valleys that tested the genius of barbers.

BUT UJAI, who had been following my eyes, stuck her mouth in my ear and whispered in disgust: "Uncle, he used to be a Black man with black hair till two years ago, when he moved to this city. He went and bleached everything away! Everything. Completely, *uked-uked*."

"Oh no, girl, *iya uwei*!" I said, pulling both of us back as though to hide our whispers in the deeper murmurs of folks still greeting each other outside. The shock was such that my knees slipped from the kneeler and both of us fumbled till we grabbed on to the pew. While Tuesday remained buried in prayer, her parents glanced back. I signaled we were fine. I closed my eyes. I did not want to see Tuesday for a while. Yet I could not bolt from him. My stomach turned. My groin gave me the false signal of needing to pee. My chest tightened. I sweated in my palms like at the embassy.

"But, Uncle Ekong, it is true," she said, scudding closer.

"Okay."

"He just showed up in the Bronx one day like snow in summer. I thought he was one of those Halloween vector ghost characters, the ones in chains. He blamed it on the Biafran War. He mumbled something about always feeling white *inside* since Father Walsh saved him. He said this was how he wanted to celebrate the fiftieth anniversary of the start of the war. But Daddy said he was talking BS, *nnisime*, and vomited a ton of swear words on him and pushed him out into the stairwell. Neighbors came out. Like Igwat, Mommy just wept and sat on the floor and shuffled her feet till Daddy changed his mind and Uncle Hughes himself stopped sobbing. It was not funny. You can ask Daddy, your BFF."

"No, no, I believe you."

"Because these white people don't even know he's Black. That's why they're only staring at us. But *you* know he's really Black, right? Mommy said you've never seen him before?"

"Okay."

She touched my arm.

"No, Uncle, please, could you stop praying for a sec and open your eyes and tell me you really understand things?"

"Of course, baby, I do."

"I've something very important to tell you, when you open your eyes . . . If we don't talk now, then when?"

Shaking my head, I felt my eyeballs gently with my sweaty fingers like they had sand under their lids. In my shoes, my socks felt like they were dripping with warm water. "My dear, you know, let's talk after Mass, please?"

"But I just don't want you guys to bring *him* to my school!"

My eyes popped open.

"Ujai, who said he was coming?"

"Well, Daddy really wants him there and I just don't know why. You must totally *sabo* your BFF and Uncle Hughes's plans. I know they hate that war word."

"Ah, stop, wait—ah, maybe I should ask why *you* don't want him."

"Listen, my classmates remember him as a Black man! They'll call him Mr. Gross and, worse, they can start calling me things like *Niece of Mr. Gross* or *Niece of Reverse Oreo*! My friends would be called the *Real Friends of the Niece of Reverse Oreo of New Jersey*. And how would I even explain it to all my minority friends?"

"Have you expressed this to Daddy?"

"He got really mad at me."

"Mommy?"

"Daddy doesn't listen to her. He keeps telling me, 'Young girl, you don't know what Uncle Hughes suffered in the war as a child.' Uncle Ekong, did they leave him alone to bury the dogs? Is that what Father Walsh saved him from? Are all our war victims bleaching into white fifty years later? I just deserve to know. After all, you're talking about *my* village, you know."

"What did your parents say?"

"They say he buried no nothing!"

"Good."

"But I overheard Mommy telling someone on the phone that Uncle Hughes himself said he began craving to be a white man because of Biafran patrols . . . Uncle, I just don't understand why Uncle Hughes hates his real color while he's helping lots of our Black orphans and women. I think they'd reject his help if they knew his new color. Please, tell me: Are my parents playing with my mind? Are my grandparents really still Black?"

"Honey, they're telling you the truth."

Ujai's consternation cut deep into my heart. She had thrown up so many questions about Tuesday. I did not want to dwell on any of them or on the part of his story I did not know. Because, even if I did, whom could I ask? This was not the space to have a good conversation with Ujai. I tried to hide my anger at our Annang white man; I stared at the ceiling to avoid his shiny head.

"Daddy also says he doesn't want me to get away with racism, to judge anyone by their skin color," Ujai whispered.

"Okay," I said.

"I think only you, his BFF, can convince him. I'm not a bad person. I'm not racist. I just want you to come alone and really finally explain Africa to my schoolmates . . . Uncle Ekong, do you remember our conversation last Sunday about governors building hospitals in our village?"

"I do."

"Well, I've really, really thought about it. Here's the plan: When you visit our school, just skip that altogether, even if my schoolmates ask you. But, if you can just let them know that people don't die in our wars, that will be perfect, magical. As long as they don't find Ikot Ituno-Ekanem on the internet, we're good! And just *sadly* say we 'kill *really* evil dogs who cause wars,' though. You must include *sadly* and *really evil* so those who have pets won't be offended. Uncle, you have to do things exactly right in my school; otherwise, you'll mess up my entire life!"

"But Uncle Hughes can do things right, too."

"Nope, his situation is really, really complicated. They could also ask him when he visited Nigeria last, and do you know how much they'd mock me on the playground if he admitted that he hasn't been home since 1975? He said this three years ago! Whoever stays away from *home* for that long, if not serving a jail sentence?"

"Yeah, it's complicated."

"Worse, Uncle Hughes also blabbed too much about our food, even when I'd coached him, like we're doing now, not to mention food. The bullies said our food smells like shit and looks like diarrhea and locked me up in the toilet. Daddy said to ignore them so they don't know how much it hurts . . ."

"I, too, can't stand any food insults! So, no food talk, period."

"Please, please, one last thing? You're not allowed to mention embassies."

"Deal."

※

AS THE SACRISTAN LIT the altar candles, Igwat suddenly started to bawl. The choir intoned the entrance hymn, accompanied by an organ, guitars, percussion, and cymbals. Usen carried the boy, and we rose as one and sang from the songbooks.

Just as Usen had managed to placate his son and another child took over behind us, an usher sidled up to us. She was college-age. She was in the most casual of moods and reached across Usen to greet her fellow white person warmly, without saying a thing to the rest of us. Then she turned to Usen and asked us to move to the column of outer pews, pointing somewhere near one of the side chapels or under the fixed scolding downward stare of the window saints.

Usen looked at her and then at Tuesday and then furtively around the singing church. He leaned toward the usher like he did not hear her well. She offered to lead us to the new place.

"*Iyo o*, we're not leaving," Usen whispered, shrugging.

"Oh no, we're not asking you to leave," she said, her face pained by being misunderstood. "We would never do that."

"So what's the problem, then?" Usen said.

"Please, we're just humbly asking you to move away from this central position because your child is really disturbing everyone."

Tuesday turned to Usen and said, "It's not a good idea to hold up Mass . . ."

"Well, you move yourself over, white man!" Usen said. "But for me and the other true children of Ikot Ituno-Ekanem, we shall serve the Lord right here. Usher, why don't you go move other families whose babies are crying right now? Because my toddler is now quiet."

"Young lady, I don't know why you're singling us out!" I added.

"Sir, we don't have any racial agenda," she said, her eyes searching around exasperatedly, like a single cop in need of reinforcement.

"Ekong, I'll handle it," Usen said. "You don't understand America."

The choir continued to sing. Everybody was now gawking at us, craning and asking what was going on, their murmur eating away the fine edges of the beautiful singing, like a sudden background noise messing up an important phone call.

By the time five male ushers appeared, genuflected as one, and turned to us, while Usen avoided my eyes, my heart was pounding. I knew the number five was not coincidence but to handle each Black person here, including the toddler. A queasy feeling vacuumed my stomach. And, with everything I knew about Usen, I was sure, sooner or later, he would explode.

"Hey, it's a win-win situation if you and your folks just scud over there," the lead usher said brightly. "Liturgy is about helping everyone pray."

"I see," Usen said, moving the dialogue from the realm of speech into that of action by sitting down. We all sat with him, while Tuesday remained standing.

"This is not the place nor time for a Black protest sit-in!" another usher said like he was going to take over negotiations. The leader admonished him for saying "Black protest." But the guy still stared at me as though I—this dangerous African American—had engineered this. Like the ill-dressed wedding guest in the Bible, I feared they would flush me out first.

OFONIME WHISPERED TO USEN to relent, but he wiped his ears with both hands like a cloud of gnats was trying to perch there. She became really restless when I, too, refused to meet her eyes. She pulled out her phone and started to record the proceedings, to the discomfiture of the ushers.

Ujai leaned on me, placing her head on my shoulder snuggly. Her headgear came off, landed on the pew and tumbled to the wooden floor and rolled under a kneeler. I picked it up and set it next to her, while the ushers followed my movement closely. Ujai stood up and grabbed and untied the headgear and straightened and rolled it into a long band of cloth. She tied it around her stomach. She was ready for a fight; this was how the women of Ikot Ituno-Ekanem, especially Awire Womenfolk, showed they would not back down. She kept searching my face, her lips trembling like the embassy boy's who urinated on himself. I held my breath and looked at the ceiling, because I did not know what to tell her. In America, I was getting increasingly unable to articulate the fissures between the races to myself, much less to others.

But suddenly, undaunted, Ujai bent down to remove her heels. She set them on the pew, spikes up. She stood like Tuesday and had one hand on the spikes, her eyes fixed solely on her brother, as if God had created her for the sole purpose of protecting him. She was sweating, her upper teeth biting down on her lip, defiant, like she wanted to bite someone. Her breath could not enter her stomach anymore, as we say in Annangland. Even her toes on the kneeler were bunched up like folded fists. I pulled her close to me till she sat down and lay her head on my shoulder. I untied the cloth around her stomach so she could breathe easy. I held her hand and told her everything would be fine, till she let go of the shoe.

"Please, go and tell the priest to begin Mass!" Usen said.

"This is sabotage," the usher said.

Sabotage hit Usen like a bullet. He jerked and then steadied himself in the pew, his elbows out like he was on some throne.

"Who's fucking saying this Mass?" Usen roared over the choir.

"Father Orrin, Father Orrin," the ushers whispered, stepping back.

"*Efiig ijire nyine* . . . may hernia swell your testicles!" Usen said, cussing them both in Annang and English.

The choir hushed.

The church went totally silent as he stood down.

ON REALIZING HIS MOUTH hung open, Usen himself used his two palms, one against each cheek, to shut it, the very effort making his eyes pop. Then the church slowly released its breath in mutters, then in consumed consternation, then uproar. But we remained still, and nobody looked backward, except Usen's wife, who continued to record everything. However, the people I could see in my peripheral vision seemed to be pelting *me* with glares, like *I* had said the *f*-word or forced Usen to.

Embarrassed, Usen said: "Okay, I need to go to confess to Father Orrin right now, so I can worship in spirit and in truth!" But the ushers blocked and locked him into the pews. A big gasp echoed through the church. I placed both hands on Usen's shoulders, to steady him. I filled his ears with pleas in Annang to stay put.

"Listen, guys, Father Orrin is my confessor," Tuesday finally intervened, scratching his head. "I believe *I* should meet him on behalf of our African guests. You're just doing your job, ushers, and our visitor is really sorry to detonate the *f*-word in church."

This made the ushers feel better.

My intestines settled as the lady usher led him to the sacristy while the rest stood guard over us. Some parishioners also trooped out to the sacristy, including Mary, Father Orrin's friend, whose tiny scratchy voice harassed ushers to push her there. "We must deal with this evil delay right away!" she said in a screech worse than a baby's cry. Ujai plugged her ears with her fingers. She turned and knelt on the pew, her back to the altar, to watch the chaos. Yet now we also deciphered that some were going to the sacristy to support us, because they had announced their intention quite loudly. We were relieved to know we had had such silent support all along. It gave us the grace not just to stop being ashamed of ourselves but to look at each other again.

MOLLY CALLED. "They're shitting all over us!" I whispered into the phone. She pleaded for me to step outside so we could talk. I said it might be dangerous for a Black person to be outside. She began to text in full sentences as though to underline the seriousness of the situation: "This sounds like some really racist poisonous shit. I don't even know what took you to Jersey. Anyway, Ekong, just to be sure: did you pick up anything that doesn't belong to you . . . ?"

"No, Molly," I texted back.

"What about hugging or chatting up the women?"

"I touched no one, not even men. But, just hearing from you strengthens me in ways you'd never know!"

"You know what, let me come get you! Where are you? If you don't know the address, just text the name of the church and priest and I'll google."

"Please, don't bother."

"No, wait, I'm going to call the cops . . . !"

"We'll work it out. Aren't we all Catholics?"

Ujai wanted to use the restroom. Ofonime asked her to put her shoes back on and went with her. They were accompanied by an usher, who reminded them to genuflect before leaving the Sacred Presence. It was the first time I saw an usher guarding the church toilet.

"Ekong, like at that editorial meeting, don't accept any bullshit!" Molly wrote. "And, please, keep me informed."

In my heart, I wanted her here. It would be nice to be in the company of a white person we could relate with, as opposed to Tuesday Ita. Then I could begin the serious conversation about how inappropriate were her two questions about theft and sexual harassment.

"FATHER ORRIN HAS DECIDED you must stay exactly where you are, whether the child cries or not," the lady usher said, with Tuesday nodding beside her. "But, most importantly, all of us ushers owe you an apology. You deserve better . . . please, Father would love to meet you in a private sacristy reception after Mass, to personally apologize."

"God bless you!" Usen quickly accepted, standing up to shake hands with her. Tuesday beckoned the rest of the ushers to come shake Usen's hand, too. When they left, Tuesday confirmed it was the parishioners who crashed the sacristy summit who made the difference. By the time Ujai and Ofonime returned and the choir restarted the opening hymn with real gusto, the prayerful atmosphere was totally restored. When my eyes met Usen's, we winked and nodded.

We had made our Biafran peace.

After Father Orrin and his procession arrived to begin the Mass, he apologized profusely for the delay and praised Tuesday as an embodiment of the Beatitudes. The congregation thunderously applauded Tuesday, who turned around and waved and bowed and distributed eye contact, like Communion, to everybody.

And then, with a wide smile, Father Orrin welcomed us and asked the people to also applaud us. But, apart from a few people who responded and pounded their pews like there was no tomorrow, the response was muted, like the applause of fingerless lepers. What pleased our hearts was Mary's high-decibel joyous laugh riding it like a rock guitarist's experimentation. It confirmed she was in our corner. We waved into the air without looking back.

Nervous, the priest fidgeted with his mustache and tried again to rally their spirits for worship: "My friends in the Lord, we're most happy to have our colorfully dressed visitors today, because, as Hughes Ita said in the sacristy, these are the people we've been helping in Africa." Now true applause rang out. "In fact, our association with them started during the Biafran War in the late sixties." A bigger applause. "Our older parishioners will remember all the prayers and relief materials we shipped to them through Catholic Charities and the Red Cross." There was great jubilation, as old people suddenly remembered our war and told the younger people of the posters of Biafran starvation.

Father Orrin paused to encourage the chatter. The atmosphere was so charged that I thought, if not for the sacredness of the space and liturgical restraint, they would have swamped us with hugs. Some surged forward to fill up the three empty pews behind us, and a few reached out and rubbed Ujai's back, saying sweet things to Usen's family. I was ignored, I guessed, for leeching onto the Umohs.

They could never *relate* to my presence.

"So, my dear parishioners, here we have before us the Biafrans, the children and grandchildren of the survivors of genocide," the priest continued. "It's very important to emphasize here that they're neither Yorubas nor Hausa-Fulanis, who did everything to steal their oil and coastlines! So, please, let's really welcome the Biafrans—in their magnificent tribal attire. Without the Quaker oats and Incolac dried milk you generously sent them, they would've been starved to death. But man shall not live by bread alone: you also saved their culture from extinction because of the T-shirts and khakis you donated during the war, till they could resume making these beautiful native costumes." He paused and pointed at me, as though to confirm my suspicion: "As we also welcome the African American friend behind them."

My face dropped as all the attention strangled me. I studied my jeans and sweatshirt.

"Though we always give to the needy," the priest had continued, "Muslims, Hindus, pagans, you name it, during that war the Igbos or Biafrans were eighty percent Catholic. Their Muslim compatriots slaughtered them for believing in the Mystery of the Trinity, the supreme model of diversity, and in the Communion of Saints. In the mere three years of its existence, Biafra, also known as Igboland, was already the most peaceful and homogeneous and educated and democratic nation in Africa. Their enemies fought a religious war within a war, a jihad against our august guests.

"My dear parishioners, as many of you know, I also have a huge personal and emotional reason for learning these details, something I'll explain to our guests in our sacristy reception after Mass. I feel very close to Biafra because my grandfather's cousin, from the Liberties in Dublin in Ireland, a missionary, is buried in a church cemetery in Onitcalasha in Biafra, thanks to malaria . . ."

"Onitsha, Onitsha!" we shouted gleefully, like I had corrected the Biafran waiter.

"Thanks, sorry, Onitsha!" Father corrected himself, bowing to us. "Next year, many of us from my extended family in the U.S. and Ireland and Australia are making a pilgrimage to his grave and to nearby churches, to enjoy the beautiful African liturgical dances. We want to experience their Thanksgiving Masses—nothing to do with eating turkey but celebrating and thanking the Lord! We want to be in that throng, dancing, yodeling, marching toward the altar. Nobody does Roman Catholicism like these Biafrans!"

HE COMPLAINED, though, that what really galled even the Most High was the fact that we Biafrans were trying too hard to be called Jews—despite all the Catholic Church did for us before, during, and after the war, and all the Irish priests and nuns who lost their lives gifting us the faith. "Why do they think joining the religion of those who killed Jesus would endear them to the world?" he said. "Why do they think dressing in Orthodox Jewish attire is more spiritual than the habits our Irish monks and nuns brought them? To be fair, perhaps, these Biafrans have developed these complicated needs because of all they suffered. But, after all said and done, these Biafrans—the best and the brightest of their continent—are still so oppressed their governors are elected by other tribes. If they plan to build hospitals, they receive death threats. They can't even fix school roofs, pay salaries, clear garbage in their counties. They'll be killed if they don't embezzle the money and share with the chieftains of these spiteful tribes . . ."

As the church boiled with anger, Usen wanted to charge up to the altar to let Father Orrin know that "*k'enye atuum ewio* and bullshit and *nnisime*" because we were neither Biafrans nor Igbos. "And who fed him this pap about Biafran politicians being better than everyone else?" he fumed. The wife begged him in Annang to take a cue from Tuesday, who did not react. Tuesday begged for patience, promising to correct the priest later. He said his only spin in the sacristy was saying we chose to be here because New Jersey churches were some of the greatest donors to our country, to win more people to our side in case Father asked them to vote to decide whether we stayed or not.

"You need the patience of an elephant to correct war history," Tuesday whispered. "As they say, the centipede might have a hundred legs, but he cannot outrun a human being. Look, Americans can't handle your entire history and diversity in one lump. They don't even know where Nigeria is—just as you never knew much about Americans before you came, right? So no need to look down on us!"

Ujai said it was really important that Father Orrin say both in the bulletin and in church that only very evil dogs were killed in Ikot Ituno-Ekanem, not people. Tuesday said she was right. "Girl, why don't you just shut up like a good Ikot Ituno-Ekanem kid while adults sort out this mess?" Usen scolded her. I grabbed her hand, explaining that Daddy was upset, but he insisted she was being disrespectful.

"Maybe we should leave?" Ofonime said. "Now that Father Orrin has introduced us as Jews or fake Jews, insisting we killed Christ, how safe are we?"

"We'll set things right in the sacristy," Tuesday said, touching the couple. But, like me, Usen said he was not going to receive Communion while Ofonime and Ujai said they would. Ofonime also added that, well, to educate these Catholics, the Vatican would have to buy spots on Fox News and Rush Limbaugh radio.

FATHER ORRIN WAS a better homilist than Father Kiobel, which meant he was really good. Toward the end, he caught everyone by surprise by asking the children to stand up. He said pointedly, "Our eternal homework is to love our complex world, befriending people of all colors and orientations." They stood up and repeated this after him like in a catechism class. Tuesday was very proud of his church. We all poured our hearts into the comfort of the priest's familiar chanting of the Fourth Eucharist Prayer, and then Usen and I watched others receive Communion.

After Mass, many welcomed us outside with selfies as if we had just arrived. The old people were emotional about the memories of our war. But when we tried to say we were not Biafrans, they became very confused, as though they had sent the relief stuff to the wrong place. So we gave up and thanked them for everything and told them some family stories of how their charity and novenas kept us alive. They thanked us and condemned the "needless squabble over seats." And, for the first time, *I* felt they had finally received me like the rest. When I revealed I was not African American, everyone laughed nervously, bemoaning the folly of prejudice and discrimination. More people joined our group, because we were loud and fun.

Usen apologized for the *f*-word.

"Oh no, a more appropriate *f*-word usage and timing and place would be hard to find!" someone joked.

"And if you didn't make a scene, none of us would've suspected the ushers were harassing you under God's very nose," another said.

"Look, we've already told Father Orrin there'll be a complaint made to Bishop Salomone about his comments on Judaism," someone said. "The bishop can't tolerate this shit. He is conscious of social issues."

"We look forward to seeing you next Sunday," Mary hollered, rolling in and shaking hands with us. When Tuesday said he always loved her laugh and praised her role in the sacristy, she laughed even more. She revealed she herself had told Father Orrin on my arrival—having watched him snub me continually—that he must allow me to stay for Mass.

We could not join them in the basement for refreshments because of our sacristy reception. A man brought us coffee in Styrofoam cups. A lady took orange juice and pastries to Ujai and a bunch of kids in the field. They were noisily playing among the Stations and admiring her outfit.

I texted Molly our change of fortunes.

No reply.

CHAPTER 17

My son is playing with you

CLIMBING THE STEEP STEPS TO THE SACRISTY FELT LIKE a trip to heaven. It was a big room with lots of vestments, sacramentals, sacred vessels, and unburned incense; it smelled exactly like ours back home. There were two inner doors. The one into the main church was wide open, and the one to his private quarters was closed, with RECTORY written on it. Atop this doorpost was a portrait of the diocese's chief shepherd, with BISHOP RAY SALOMONE written under it. He was a serious-looking man with a tan complexion, short hair, sharp cheekbones, thin lips, and square glasses. This face told me if the parishioners really dragged Father Orrin to his court, it would be serious *wahala*.

But as Father Orrin shook our hands and smiled and asked our names, I prayed the parishioners would not tell the bishop. People give bad first impressions all the time, I told myself. In fact, my heart swelled with the memories of my Hell's Kitchen neighbors taking me to Chelsea, to reset the bad beginning we had had. It was great to have such beautiful recollections to lean on.

And, looking at Tuesday's face, you just knew this reception meant more to him than to us, that his hope that his church was getting our visit right was being realized. Father Orrin himself was upbeat, though he was drained and tired. Now, just in his sweat-soaked Roman collar, his carriage could not be more like Father

Kiobel's. He said he still had to take Communion to the prisoners at a nearby prison before coming back to celebrate the evening Mass. He tried to learn our names and temporarily carried the little boy. He asked whether we needed water. We said no and thanked him for the refreshments outside.

"Okay, first things first," he said as he closed the church doors. "Please, does anyone still want to go to confession? I'm sorry we couldn't do it before Mass. When you, Ekong and Usen, didn't come to Communion, I felt bad."

"Oh no, Father," Usen said, "I just wanted to have a chance to report the ushers to you. That's all."

"Dr. Hughes, do you want to go to confession for messing up our minority story, ha?" I joked, and everyone laughed. "On a more serious note, Father Orrin, you would never know what this private reception means to all of us . . . even this toddler will remember your humanity when he grows up. Thank you."

"We're grateful," Usen said, as I grabbed the priest in a two-handed handshake.

"You're welcome," Father said, blushing, then blowing out his cheeks. "And thanks, too, for being so forgiving of the ushers . . ."

"We always knew they were a bit overzealous," Ofonime said, making everyone laugh again. "By the way, your fellow Irishman, our late Father Gary Walsh, also came from the Liberties in Dublin, though he was buried back in Ireland."

"Wow, small world!" Father Orrin exclaimed.

"He was immense for us," Usen said. "Schools, hospitals, lots of family visits. He loved our cultures and masqueraders and Awire Womenfolk. He risked everything to protect us in the war. Anyway, we really loved the choir here. And you chanted the Eucharistic Prayer just like our priests back home. Ujai shall remember the befriend-all-people homework forever!"

"I appreciate the compliments," he said, touching Ujai's headtie fondly.

Tuesday thanked him for the elaborate introduction of Biafra, before setting about to correct him. He took up the Jewish comments first: He reminded the priest of Pope Benedict's books emphasizing that the Romans killed Jesus, not the Jews. He also insisted the Pope had done away with Limbo, where dead unbaptized babies and Jewish souls had previously been waylaid, unable in our dogma to enter paradise. Father pushed back angrily that the Pope had no authority to destroy Limbo, otherwise we should also do away with infant baptism. He quickly ended the conversation, saying he was squeezed for time. But Tuesday tried to say that, though our die-hard northern Nigerian Muslims had their bullshit and blood thirstiness even in peacetime, they were not responsible for Igbo or Biafran politicians' malfeasance. But the priest again cut him short. "Okay, I'm sorry I got your war details wrong," he said. "I, too, come from a long line of soldiers and the pain of war. Please, I meant no disrespect." Then, after thanking Tuesday for escorting us to the sacristy, he asked him and Ujai to leave while he spoke to *the Biafrans*. Seeing that we were stuck with the Biafran label, we abandoned altogether that fight to establish our minority identity.

I told Father immediately I was also African, not African American. He was so shocked he laughed. To be doubly sure, he asked whether the Biafrans knew me. They nodded as I spoke Annang with them, to back up my ancestry claims. But Tuesday was silent as though he had never heard of the language before.

"Well, Ekong, you can stay, but it's good you spoke up," Father said. "Because I was going to ask you to step out also . . . and then have a whole different conference with you alone." Ofonime, who was wedging her son astride on her right hip, asked whether she should hand him over to Tuesday. The priest said Igwat could stay. We waited for Tuesday to say he was one of us, since his entire body language wanted this. He kept mute till Ujai dragged him outside. The priest quietly closed the door and apologized that there were no seats.

"We're okay standing," Usen said, searching our faces for consen-

sus. "If our priest who's already stood through two Masses is standing, we, too, can . . . Yes, niggers?"

We nodded.

"Sir, please, don't call anyone the *n*-word in my sacristy, okay?"
Father cautioned. "You may be using it as some in-group thing, but
it doesn't sit well with me."

"I'm sorry," Usen said with a little penitential bow, his enthusiasm
curtailed.

"We're sorry," Ofonime said.

"That's okay," the white American said. "I think we should go
right into what I want to tell you, why I invited you. What I'm going
to say is not out of malice but after prayerful reflection. After weigh-
ing every angle of the key issues here."

"Okay," Usen said.

We nodded, moving closer.

"You have really caused us a lot of pain today!" he said frankly,
stepping back. "And I wanted to let you know you won't be coming back here. Since your clothing shows you've come from afar, I
needed to be gentle and sensitive. But even before Mass, I'd been
wracking my brain for the best way and place to let you understand
we're not open to outsiders."

"Oh . . . okay," Usen said absentmindedly, cracking his fingers.

"Thanks, then, for your understanding," he said, relieved, a shy
smile almost crossing his face. "You have saved our community from
future stress. You're the real salt of the earth!"

"You're welcome, Father, and thanks, also, for your candor," I
said when the other two went quiet.

"You guys are Liverpool fans, too, huh?" Father said lightheartedly.

"How did you know that?" I said, laughing.

"The decal on your car!" he said. "I'm a fan, too."

"You are?" Ofonime said, finding her voice.

"You bet," he said. "We're not doing very well this year . . . Anyway,
you guys have a nice day, then!"

"You'll never walk alone," I said, proclaiming our club's motto.

"Never!" he responded.

But when he opened the door to let us out, we did not move. He closed it again and came back into our midst. He looked at us. We looked at him.

He laughed, a shocked laugh, and smoothed his mustache with both hands. Then he showed us the door again. We took our eyes off him to search each other's faces. Everyone looked serious for a while, as I tried to decide whom to compare the priest to between Jack and Angela. But it was not comparable, because the Humane Society Two, at least, did not know I had busted their secret phone conversation. Father's banishment was as blatant as it was unbelievable. We shrugged and collapsed in fits of laughter, covering our mouths with our hands. It was what Chief Zebrudaya, the TV comic who retaught postwar Nigeria how to laugh at each other's tribal foibles, called "Laughter of Ridiculous."

"MY BIAFRAN FRIENDS, maybe a little background would help," he said gently, nudging Usen, who was still smiling. "The last time we had this kind of division in this parish was during the Vietnam War . . . Today, I humbly ask you in the name of God not to show up here again, please. I understand your hesitation and shock, mind you. I wish to God I didn't have to say this. But we need to prepare our folks slowly towards becoming the kind of church *you* have in mind.

"There's an African American Roman Catholic parish on the other side of town, on Lincoln and King Boulevard. While our diocese is closing down parishes for lack of membership, funds, and priests, I want you to know that Bishop Salomone has really bent over backwards to keep our Black church running. We pay their utility bills. We buy them bread and wine for the Eucharist. We give them everything, so it's not like we're redlining them. You guys will fit into that equally beautiful church—"

"Listen, we were never going to return anyway!" I interrupted him angrily. "If you noticed, two of us, Usen and I, avoided your poisoned chalice, excuse the pun."

"Fair enough, fair enough, then why didn't you leave when I sent the ushers to move you?" he said, and I replied by telling him he must be from Argentina, because they were the ones capable of this kind of racial cleansing and anti-Semitism. He said, well, he was just pointing out the Biafran obsession with Judaism and nothing more. Ofonime said we owed the Jews everything because the Holy Family and huge chunks of our religion came from them. "I just wonder why you even bothered to stay when I sent the lady usher to move you!" Father Orrin snapped. "Listen, I don't want to talk about the Jews or why the Church is trying to destroy our beautiful theology of Limbo to favor killers of the Savior of the World!"

"We're sorry, Father," Ofonime said, stepping back.

"*Nkudo ujo nsio o*," I said.

"I assume that means, 'Have a nice week!'" he said, and reached out for a handshake like a man who had just negotiated a difficult cease-fire. The hand hung in the air till the toddler grabbed two of his fingers and babbled and smiled.

All this while, Usen had gone unusually quiet. He seemed to be staring at the sadist, but instead was focusing on the wall behind him, his hands behind him, cuffed by shock. The posture tightened his shirt around his torso, his big funny stomach throbbing with his deep breaths. He looked like a man who had abandoned the fight to prove that he was a minority in our homeland and now equally had no energy to begin this arduous push to elevate us to the status of humans. I was afraid Usen could explode in uncontrollable anger as he struggled with the invisibility the priest was dissolving us into, a fight I had waged ever since I arrived on these premises.

I was numb. This was beyond gerrymandering.

"BUT ARE YOU HONESTLY banning us?" Ofonime said, kissing her son's forehead.

"I wouldn't put it that way," Father said, looking from face to face. "Dear Biafran Nigerian Roman Catholics, the Lord has many rooms and tables in his house to accommodate everyone. You guys aren't Black Americans, so I don't expect nonsensical fights."

"My son is playing with you, not fighting," Ofonime said, her voice cracking. "Just tell us, today, what our crime is . . . *us*!"

"Again, it's not about you," he said, releasing his fingers gently from Igwat. "Just that if you return, then the next week more Blacks will be here, and our church will be even more divided."

"We're sorry my husband said the *f*-word in church," she said. "He's sorry. My son is sorry. My daughter is sorry. Even Ekong is sorry for the poison-chalice insult! Father. We. Are. Your. Children."

He said we must then accept his judgment, his eyes clouded with tears of being misunderstood. Pleading he was almost late to his prison ministry, he said honesty demanded he acknowledge the white man, Dr. Hughes Ita, who accompanied us throughout our visit. He said even if we were fighting racism, like Dr. King, it would be nice to appreciate the whites who stood with us. As he began to switch off the lights, he said if we religious people were going to be the salt of the earth, we needed to begin by learning how to see people and issues, not colors and mirages.

This sudden change of lighting focused Usen's eyes. As they squinted and followed the priest around the room like a double-barrel gun tracking a target, infused by a sudden strength, I seized my childhood friend and dragged him out the door. By the time we stumbled to the bottom of the steps outside the church, I myself was sweating and dizzy, my chest hurting. A certain darkness descended on my vision. Still, I held Usen tight. His wife shook her head and abandoned the toddler in the field to contend with her husband, as if he were the most vulnerable child. Together, we pulled him behind the building, to nurse him back to sanity.

"Yeah, '*jen Annang, jen-eka*, hold yourself together," I pleaded. "You told me, on my second day here, I couldn't fight everything."

I secured him in a tight chokehold, like those days of our childhood when we wrestled on the narrow beach of our river in moonlight dripping with fireflies, or the day I knocked the knife out of his hands before he could stab our Biafran classmate the second time. Now, like a lullaby, I hummed "Ikworo Ino" straight into his skull, to remind him of home. I told him the fact that racism had stolen our universal Church from us did not mean it could steal our God from us. But I could not break the tension in his body. When he wanted to overpower me and fight for his church, his wife panicked, jumped in, and snatched Usen from me. She shook him like the leaves of a tree caught in a bad wind. And then she slapped him, a hard forehand across the face. Like good CPR, it jolted him out of the dangerous befuddlement that had masked his anger.

Ofonime and I were startled by the sound of a rectory window snapping shut. We looked up in time to catch the shocked gnarled expression on Father Orrin's face—before he moved away with his phone and drew the red blinds. Ofonime and I exchanged glances. "Listen, Ekong, we must leave here fast before Father panics and calls the cops to stop this *nonsensical fight*!" she railed as Usen's body finally relaxed.

He wanted to sit on the grass to recover, but we dragged him away like he was a soldier being evacuated from incoming fire by his colleagues. When he exhaled and shook the stupor from his head and smoothed his clothes and asked where the children were, I released him guardedly. Ofonime said he must look for them himself. He scanned the area to discover Ujai by Tuesday's Maserati, entertaining him and other children with spirited dance moves like the embassy boy on his way to Montana. Finding only Igwat's cap where Ofonime had put him down, we scurried around to the front of the sacristy. We saw him crouching and prattling and pounding on the cement with an open palm, having toddled across the field and crawled back up the steps to the locked door.

Usen yanked him away like from the lip of a cliff.

WHEN WE RESURFACED in front of the church, our supporters walked toward us with their children. The smiles were genuine and fresh like the rising sun. It was good to see them. Their presence allowed us to breathe, to be. They strengthened our spirits. They were not in a hurry. It was like we had known them all our lives. Indeed, these friends did constitute the true Eucharist for us today, the Word made flesh. We chatted about all manner of stuff. But seeing how excited they were that their priest had given us this long audience on a busy Sunday, we were too ashamed to tell the truth. It would be too much for them. Sometimes there are things you cannot even tell friends, I consoled myself. So we made do with small talk and told them about the beauty and diversity in our church back home.

It was going to be a tense goodbye. Yet, for me, it was in the midst of these friends that my heart thawed and the sacristy events began to hit home. I fought back tears and looked around the premises like it was my last visit to any church.

Then, in belated shock, I followed Usen's lead because, ironically, he was managing things better now. His embrace of the parishioners was tight, his eyes almost teary, a man saying goodbye to the best of comrades-in-arms. We copied him to the letter while the exuberance of the children saying goodbye to one another in the little Annang Ujai had taught them lightened the mood. Ofonime took more selfies of our embraces. Then Mary assured us again that, despite our beautiful sacristy reception, she would still personally lead a delegation to Bishop Salomone the following morning just for the record.

A POLICE CAR DROVE into the near-empty church premises as Father Orrin himself was heading out to the prison waving to us. We all waved back. He gave the cops a thumbs-up when they turned toward the back of the church where Ofonime had just slapped Usen.

They revved the car around the tight place like the criminals were hidden in the wind or under some rock. Then, they began to radio God knows where. A second car arrived, the officers in it consulted with the others, and then the second car left. Then the first car drove by our happy crowd, the officers staring at us like we were a strange movie. There were two cops, one Arab American, the other white. Not knowing what to do, they drove into the field and parked among the Stations of the Cross, in between "Simon of Cyrene Helps Jesus Carry the Cross" and "Veronica Wipes the Face of Jesus." From there, they kept a steady eye on us.

We joined Tuesday in the parking lot. Soon, with the number of white people on the property reduced to just him, the cops stepped out and leaned on their car, to make themselves more visible, to protect him. Now, each time Tuesday asked in Annang what had happened in the sacristy, Usen sniped that we no longer understood him. Finally, Usen told him we were too tired to eat the lunch he had offered to buy for us, and his tone warned us not to contradict him.

CHAPTER 18

Ujai, *agwo nwuaan Annang, agwo uko*

U SEN AND OFONIME DECIDED TO DROP ME AT THE TRAIN
station. I was in the backseat with the kids. Ofonime drove, because
she seemed the least disturbed of the two of them. Usen sat beside
her. We were all quiet, enjoying the music from a soft rock station.
The afternoon sun was out and had burned up the morning chill.
Though my stomach was totally empty, I was not hungry. I was
dizzy but not tired. Ofonime wound down our windows, and the
soft warm air filled the car, as if to remind us of what it meant to
breathe the air of freedom.

I had peace for the first time since I'd left home that morning. I
was also brought back to earth by a text from Alejandra suggesting I
leave my spare keys with Brad that night so he could let in the exterminators the next day.

B UT AS SOON AS I arranged Igwat's head in his car seat, for he had
fallen asleep, Ofonime calmly announced in Annang that the patrol
car from the church was trailing us. We did not look back. We did
not want Ujai to know. Ofonime rolled up the windows, monitored
the police in the rearview mirror, and set our car to cruise control to
be sure we were driving within the speed limit. Other cars overtook

us. To say we were afraid was an understatement. I called Caro, but her phone was switched off.

When Ujai complained that we had not said when we would return to Tuesday's church, Ofonime said they would have to go to the African American Mass in the Bronx first, to reconnect with long-lost friends. She dug out three Negro spiritual CDs from the glove compartment and stuck them in the player. Ujai lashed onto that first clear voice asking whether we were there when they crucified the Lord; she sang and hummed like she needed to practice for the trip to the African American church. The music filled me like nothing had before. It dragged my floating anxiety about the police car down like lead and anchored me back in my being. Then it became too heavy and began to crush me. The music smelled of bruises. It smelled of blood. It smelled of burst blisters. It smelled of iron, rusted and heated, pounded through flesh. It smelled of bones, exposed and cracked and snapped. I had never been so scared in my life.

It was my unending day in the life of *this* African American.

And, perhaps for the first time, I viscerally glimpsed the bottomless melancholy in African American spirituality. White and Black American Catholics were singing from two different songbooks, as it were. And, for me, it was not even about completely understanding Black American issues or white American issues, for that I could never do. It was just the pain of being profiled daily like you were in minority Biafra, just the pain of knowing Biafra tracked Papa's coffin from the sacristy to the grave. To avoid a total meltdown, I refused to think of Keith, the only Black American I knew, especially our last chat about how *some days* gave him this nightmarish longing to escape to Africa.

I regretted my decision to stay on in America after that editorial meeting and street phone call I had overheard. I saw these as a foreshadowing of our Calvary today. If I had left then, I would never have visited the Bronx. We would not have fought over Biafra today, nor would I have had to smell New Jersey.

THE PATROL CAR PARKED behind us at the train station. It was a small park full of evergreen trees, and we were not far from the platform, yet with these guys around the platform felt like a thousand miles away. Ofonime kept the car running and the windows rolled up. We were all singing now like Meshach, Shadrack, and Abednego in Nebuchadnezzar's fiery furnace.

The police officers got out of their car. We dodged their eyes and pretended we had never seen them before. But when one of them, the white cop, bent down and yanked up the leg of his trousers to scratch his calf, Ujai stopped singing and pointed and said she knew him from church. I beat down her hand and said it was impolite to point at people. She wanted to say why she thought he was scratching, but the parents said they did not want her to talk about him at all, that she should keep singing because Saint Cecilia said those who sing pray twice.

Then the Arab American cop pulled out a pair of black gloves and slid them on and flexed his fingers like someone who was ready to commit a crime. He looked at us like we were dirt before taking a black mask from his pocket and pulling it on. Then he climbed the stairs and disappeared onto the train platform. I was so freaked out knowing he was on the platform, it seemed I was watching this happen to another person, in one of those distant stories we used to hear in school about American cops and African Americans.

As Ujai continued to watch the scratcher cop with consummate sympathy and we feared she might catch on to why they were trailing us, we debated in Annang whether they should drive me straight back to Hell's Kitchen. But these cops looked like folks who would follow you even to the real Hell. I was afraid of getting on the train and said perhaps we should call Tuesday. Ofonime said the man would only make us feel worse by doubting us or blaming the whole thing on African Americans. "Ekong, there are just too many of Tuesday Itas who got to America and became whiter than white folks!" Usen said sourly. They rejected my suggestion that we should get out of the car to explain to the cops we had not been fighting under the priest's window.

"Baby, you remember all our monthly lessons about the police?" Usen asked Ujai in an eerily peaceful voice, as though it belonged entirely to another. "Like not staring or pointing, so they don't think it's a gun?"

"Yes, Daddy," Ujai said.

"What do you do with your bro if things get bad?" the mother added, joining in the covert preparation of the daughter in case the police did us in.

"Yep . . . love him forever, Mommy," Ujai said, snapping back into her seat. "Oops—I'm not staring at the cop anymore. I'm sorry."

"That's okay, dear," Ofonime said.

"You know we have always and shall always love you whether we're here or not, right?" Usen said.

"I love you, too!" Ujai said.

"And, look, even if we don't take you to the village or die today, you must find your way there when you grow up," Ofonime said. "Ikot Ituno-Ekanem loves you . . . can never stop loving you. The earth, the river, the meadows, the masqueraders, Our Lady of Guadalupe, Awire Womenfolk, everything."

"Yep, Mommy."

"If you call my name in the valley, the valley will always answer you," Usen said. "If you call Mommy and Uncle Ekong, it will answer you then, too. If you call the dogs of war from their cemetery, same thing. When you grow up, the village will tell you their names and stories.

"And you must greet everyone, especially Auntie Caro, whom you must tell everything you saw in this parking lot today. You must remain very close to her, going forward. You also know, when we came out of the sacristy, we were very pleased to see you chatting away with Uncle Hughes. He cares about us, you know, no matter his color. He loves you and your bro. We love and trust him, too, now and when we get to heaven. Next time you see him, you must also tell him and even other cops these were the same cops you saw in church . . . but, whatever happens today, never forget Father Orrin's befriend-all-people homework!"

"Yeah, 'To love our complex world, befriending people of all colors and orientations,'" the girl recited. "Me and my new friends call it *The Father Orrin Pledge*. Uncle Hughes made us cram it when you were in the sacristy."

"Good, you must keep those friendships, no matter what happens here today," Usen said. "They're innocent children like you."

"Yeah, they're so cool and fun," she said. "You know, we kids really talked. We've decided to all sit together next time right there in the front pews! I really love them! They really understood when I told them I was afraid the ushers would hurt Igwat."

"We love the way you love them . . . never forget that!" Ofonime said.

"Yes, you're a good child," I said.

"When are we going back?" Ujai said.

Silence.

Usen said: "And, of course, you and your bro shall always be the good kids of Ikot Ituno-Ekanem, okay . . . ?"

"Yay!" Ujai said, and kissed his head. "Hey, people, everything is fine now. But where's the masked cop?"

"Ujai, *agwo nwuaan Annang, agwo uko!*" I began, singing her praises to distract her.

"*Se-nyien do-ng!*" she responded, gurgling with laughter.

"*Nniruok-nniruok abaikpa Annang!*"

"Ah . . . *mbok* wait . . . Daddy, what shall I respond?"

"Say *nniruok*, say amen, say *anyedede*," he said.

"Uncle, could you sing my praises again?" the girl said.

"*Abaikpa oniong m'ifiok!*" I said.

"*Nniruok!*" she responded, dancing in her seat.

"*Nniruok-nniruok mbobo ati-Annang!*"

"*Ami ndem o . . . ?* Mommy, does that work?"

I hushed as I saw her mother's face rain down tears in the rearview mirror. To hide it from Ujai, I stretched and turned away the mirror.

WHEN THE TRAIN ARRIVED, I got out of the car.

The cop in the patrol car stepped out, too, and yawned like he wanted to swallow me.

I leaned back inside the car to kiss Ujai and Igwat each on the forehead. She pulled up and whispered, "Please, no cop selfies, okay?" I nodded. Usen got out, too, to replace me in the back with the children in case the cops continued to trail them. I wanted to say how much I loved him, to thank him for our childhood, how much his words to his daughter had calmed me. I wanted to hug him. But we were both too tense, because we both knew it was not over yet. We could not even look each other in the eye. Shame and fear had estranged us, denying us the dignity of saying a simple goodbye.

Ofonime rolled down the window and increased the stereo's volume, like a dirge accompanying me to my noose. As her daughter told her not to cry because I was returning to Manhattan, not Nigeria, I walked stiffly across the parking lot and joined others going up the stairs to the platform.

I saw the cop from the back; he was leaning on a metal post, one hand on his handgun, the other jangling his cuffs. I walked past him like I did not see him, putting both hands behind me to show I was unarmed.

But I felt he was following me. I steeled myself so that I did not look back or run toward the train. When I got on it, I slipped from coach to coach till I got to a crowded one at the end of the platform. I found a seat and lowered myself into it and put my hands in between my legs and looked down. When the driver announced a few minutes' delay, my mind raced. I thought they wanted to search for me. I tried to figure out what it meant to hear yourself being shot, or how long it took for the pain to hit, if you did not die right away. Then, again to show I was unarmed, I brought out my hands and put them on my chest in the mea culpa position . . .

The train doors snapped shut, and I exhaled and rubbed my palms together and opened my eyes. I took the risk and raised my head slowly to look out the window in the hope of catching a glimpse of the Audi. Yet the cop was standing there, outside, facing me; he had indeed followed me. His hands were still on the handgun and cuffs, his legs parted. The eye holes on his mask accentuated his hard stare.

When our eyes locked, he nodded and turned away.

AS WE ROLLED AWAY, I called up Usen but could not get through. His line was busy. I called twice more, same thing. I felt like I wanted to stop the train to go see what the cops were doing to my people. I blamed myself for leaving, when there might have been safety in numbers. And how would I explain my callousness to Ikot Ituno-Ekanem? I called Caro thrice, but her phone was still switched off. Molly, too, did not respond. Ofonime, nothing. I went back to calling Usen until he sent a text complaining *my* line was busy, diverting his calls to voice mail.

"Are you OK in the train?" he texted.

"YES," I wrote back. "Are they gone? Where are you guys?"

But my outgoing texts hung. I stared at my phone as my fingers began to tremble. I copied-and-pasted the texts. Same thing. I sent another: "I can't forgive myself for putting you all through this." I turned off the phone and restarted; it seemed to take years to reboot. I put it down to a bad network connection. I looked out the window, but the sight of trees flying past me made me woozy.

When the phone rang, I jumped from my seat. Usen told me the patrol car was truly gone and they were safe.

I breathed easy.

THAT NIGHT, in my apartment, as phone calls came in from Ikot Ituno-Ekanem, I knew Usen and Ofonime had been talking to our families. And, of course, our village had as many versions of what had happened as there were palm trees in my grandfather's plantation. I tried to play down the whole thing, though, just because I was not in the mood to talk. I was also more worried about the news stirring the whole village awake late at night.

I was abysmally lonely, lost.

When Father Kiobel called to sympathize, I thanked him and told him to return to bed. "But, did my brother priest actually banish you?" he asked sadly, and added that Ujai's grandmothers and Two-Scabbard, the youth leader, who escorted them to the rectory, were quite disturbed. I confirmed it happened but that he should tell them we were all okay. He told me he tried to reach Caro but could not. I called her again, but it went straight into voice mail. I texted and gave up, and once I called my family and in-laws, whom I also could not reach, I switched off the phone altogether in frustration.

I met Keith downstairs on my way to Academy Records to buy my first stack of Negro spiritual CDs. I blindsided him with a big hug. When he said I was trembling and asked whether I had a fever, I said I was just homesick and tired. I disappeared before he could see my pain. I bought hard Liquor. After I got the CDs, I avoided Hibernia Bar so I would not transfer my aggression to its manager, who had not banished me from his business, even though bedbugs had driven me to actual antisocial behavior. I also avoided the street of my Actors' Chapel. Tonight, even the spectacularly lit spires of St. Patrick's Cathedral had lost their magic.

CHAPTER 19

The frenzied imagination of an old man

When Alejandra Ledesma pounded on my door in the morning, I was still drunk. At first I thought it was Molly, because I was afraid something really evil had befallen her, to stop her from returning my calls. I knew she was the only person who could truly understand what had happened to me yesterday. Advising me to be as bullheaded in the church as at the editorial meeting meant she had a grasp of the broader context of my racial anguish in America.

Alejandra reminded me to hand in my keys for the super, her boyfriend. I did. She said we were all looking forward to sleeping on fresh bedding tonight. She was already dressed for work but was oozing with the patient excitement of Ikot Ituno-Ekanem's town crier of yore trying to ensure that everyone showed up for the difficult coordinated business of cleaning up the village river and trimming the bushes around the beach.

But when I imagined masked people in yellow industrial overalls, gloves, goggles, and pressurized tanks blasting everything, I thought, *What food would be fit for consumption after that?* How did I know they would not spray inside the freezer or oven? I got rid of my frozen *moi moi* and *etidot* and *atama* soups. I emptied the pantry of everything, including my *garri* and *poundo* flours. I trashed even my sodas and bottled water. But when I got to my big Ziploc bag of *ujajak*, out of sentimental reasons I decided to smell the spice before disposing of it. Its aroma quickly told me I must keep my favorite Annang soup spice. I layered it in four other Ziploc bags and hid in between clothes in my suitcase in the living room and locked it.

I had no appetite and went earlier than usual to Andrew & Thompson. It was my most depressing Monday morning. I was not myself. I could have been sleepwalking. And I hated the fact that I was going to shadow the marketing department, Angela's domain, this week.

But seeing a handwritten note by Molly on my desk—apologizing for not responding to my texts, calls, and emails and asking to see me—boosted my spirits, like my drunkenness had deserted me.

I could see the light in her office under her door, though the whole place was quiet and dimly lit. This meant she had come in early. I thought it also meant she wanted to see me soonest. There was no other person around. My heart was beating. We could have a little private time, I thought. I fantasized about telepathy and Paul's light kiss. My fingers tingled, and my toes felt stretched. I was going to tell her not just everything that happened yesterday but how every twist compounded my feelings. I knew only she could begin to let me see light in this darkness. I looked at her handwriting again. It was neat and shy, more personal than all the texts she had sent me. I folded it as gently as a man trying to pick up a just-laid egg whose shell was yet to harden. I put it in my drawer.

I picked up on her perfume. But, to protect her, I went into the restroom to quickly study my bedbug scars. The scars were not that bad. I was sure by the time I told her everything there would be more hugs and tears in that office, like when I told her about my father's rape and disappearance, and after everything I would gently sit her down and let her know I did not appreciate how her desire to rescue me from church quickly slipped into racist stereotypes— questions about whether I stole or whether I sexually harassed their white women.

I believed she would apologize profusely, because many well-meaning folks who wanted to obliterate racism from the earth did not know they had a bit of it within them, a blind spot, a conditioning over time. I did not think one mistake like this made her a racist. I believed also it would embolden her dream to fight racism.

I was already thinking about how we would plan our trip to New Haven in four days' time, when my penis went rogue, shooting up in an erection, arching my zipper like a bow. It was like it had been taken over by my inebriation. Now I tucked in my shirt properly, straightened my trousers with two little kicks, and made sure I was presentable even from the back. I wiped my shoes with a swath of toilet roll so that they would shine in her office. I moved my belt's pin one notch deeper, to give my waistline that tight snug look and my butt its true sharp muscular sculpt. "Today *na* today," I whistled.

Yet, as I walked in, Molly cringed, her face drained of color. She sat like a statue. When we shook hands, she did so from behind her desk, giving me only a few fingers, like she was holding something in her palm.

"Listen, Ekong," she said icily, "Greg Lucci is terrified you're bent on helping the landlord cancel his lease because of 'a little incidence of bedbugs,' as he put it."

I was so shocked the booze cleared from my head. My erection collapsed.

"Hey, good morning, Molly—"

"The thing is, I myself have a huge, huge aversion to crawling things, a bad phobia!" she interrupted me, folding her arms. "I'm disappointed you didn't tell me you had bedbugs! Good morning."

"I'm really sorry. I can see the phobia on your face. Normally you would've offered me a seat."

She told me she was sure I understood why we did not need to sit down today and why we needed to postpone the trip to New Haven till things improved. I said I understood. "But I can assure you," I swore, "I've already fixed my really, really 'little incidence of bugs.'

And the exterminator will treat the whole floor, if not the entire building, this afternoon!" I promised I would be the last person to jeopardize Lucci's lease, knowing it was her connection that got me the apartment. She said he was afraid I might turn him in since I was not returning his calls or texts.

She studied my face carefully as a warm sweat covered my butt. She was unusually frightened, her eyes were reading my every movement, and her fears had eaten up all rational spaces in her mind.

I knew immediately this was not the time to bring up her racist questions.

"Ekong, just for your information, you know, Lucci has this stupid perception that African bugs must be many times more vicious than ours," she said with anger toward Lucci. "I've already seriously warned him off such bullshit!" I laughed and responded it was the frenzied imagination of an old man at work and added that my neighbors—except the African American—all had the bugs before my arrival. Now she apologized for her discomfort, explaining she had never been around infested folks and had not slept all night. I apologized, too, I was just a poor confused immigrant who knew neither NYC culture nor the etiquette of infestations. I explained that even Mr. Lucci said New Yorkers had gotten used to bugs.

Finally, I braced myself and rubbed my palms and asked whether I should still show up for work, given her phobia. She said yes, but my hand movements only seemed to scare her more, like I was reacting to an itch or trying to disguise scratching.

※

IN MY CUBICLE, I put my head on my desk. I had a headache. I felt so embarrassed for those few minutes of drunken lust for Molly. I could hear my broken heartbeat against the desk, and a cold sweat glued my cheek to the wood laminate. I was a busted soul. I was sadder than last night.

I was angry. I wanted to strangle Gregory Lucci. What worse

calamity could he bring upon me than to destroy my professional and personal friendship with Molly?

After an hour, Emily woke me up to say she was leaving for a vacation in Europe. She had dyed her hair black and white, instead of the spiky multicolor style she had been wearing. She said she was going to be doing a lot of pleasure reading and waved Anthony Grooms's *Bombingham* excitedly in my face. She said it was a great American take on racism/tribalism and the Vietnam War, how African American soldiers went to fight for freedom, something they did not have at home. "You know the protagonist is from 'sweet home, Alabama'!" Emily said. "Birmingham, actually. Just two hours from Tuskegee. Groom's portrait of 'Bama is genius. The book was a *Washington Post* Notable Book of the Year." As I escorted Emily downstairs, I told her I loved the book cover and would read it on my flight back to Nigeria.

She assured me I would be fine at the editorial meeting the next day. But on my return, I found a note on my desk with a NYTimes link: https://www.nytimes.com/2014/03/16/realestate/when-bedbugs-bite .html?hp&_r=0.

WORD WAS OUT.

It was a story of a Park Slope, New York, mother who fought bugs for a year while the housing authorities dallied and her two little children were bitten blue-black. I shivered when I imagined Ujai and Igwat being caught in this situation. The lady was saying she could not afford the cost of private extermination and was asking the *New York Times* whether to sue the authorities or the neighbor from whose apartment the menace spread. When the paper advised her to get rid of the pest first, it sounded like that old clichéd chicken-and-egg circular argument. I was thankful for the link, for I thought someone was sympathizing with me.

Yet, when I looked up, I caught a few people ducking my eyes. I could feel the tension. It had flattened our usually bubbly Monday morning. Like the day of the editorial meeting, nobody stopped by my cubicle. Nobody said zip to me.

My phone or laptop beeped with email. It was the marketing department announcing the afternoon meeting had been postponed, because "three key people could not make it . . ." I stretched in my chair and looked at the ceiling and stifled a laugh as I tried to figure out who these three people were. Who was Angela trying to deceive? So, was I now three people rolled into one, like a trinity of bad omens covering the Andrew & Thompson universe?

I stood up and walked the place like a man deep in meditation, like one inspecting the ruins of his once-priceless estate. But I was able to account for everyone in their offices or cubicles—except Molly, who had closed her door for the first time since I had arrived. Phobia or not, closing that door transformed my sadness and alienation into anger and despondency.

Then Angela and Jack really got under my skin. I was approaching them in the hallway, to ask her what the marketing department needed me to do; I heard them talking about death before they changed the subject and walked away. Were they talking about their death from bugs? Were they talking about mine? I texted Molly twice to thank her for sharing her phobia with me. She did not reply, though my phone showed *delivered*. If she had even acknowledged my texts with a simple "Tx," I was going to beg her not to mention Lucci's special African-bug fear to our colleagues, as belated as that was. I just wanted to be accused of having the same bedbugs as the rest of NYC. Any other thing was going to make me feel I now had six eyes and twelve limbs, being "three key people."

I was beginning to think Molly might even cancel my meeting with Liam Sanders when Bob Hamm, the sponsor of *Thumbtack*, enveloped me in a big embrace. "Please accept my bedbug sympathies!" he whispered. "How overwhelming all this must be in a new city." I thanked him; his kindness confirmed I was reading things correctly. Jeff was right: the mental effects of being infested could steal your mind.

CARO'S TEXT ASKING WHETHER this was the right time to call brought me down to earth. It filled me with so much guilt.

The long text said she was sorry about New Jersey, and sorry to have gone silent, but she had developed malaria. Her phone had been dead all yesterday because there was no electricity in the whole state and a fuel shortage had ensured she could not run our generator. She said she had gone to spend the night with an auntie in Ekparakwa, which was why Father Kiobel could not reach her. I was very ashamed of those wild thirty seconds I lusted for Molly in the restroom. I swore never to drink again in America.

I went into the hallway to sit on the floor with my back to the wall like a beggar, to ask how Caro was treating her malaria. Then I told her the full story of New Jersey, closing my eyes like I was not worthy to hear her voice.

"Listen, dear, you must stay on, even though, in your position, I would scram home immediately," she said, sobbing.

"I still *dey* shock o . . ."

"But *ana* finish the anthology! It's a must."

"I know I don't deserve you."

"Don't think like that. Please, be careful you don't transfer your anger to your workplace. Because if this *arusat akeme ee*-happen *ke* church, why do you think *ke* Andrew & Thompson can't call cops on you? How are we even sure the cops aren't still tracking you like the King Kong lady?"

"It's scary, right?"

"Keep a low profile, okay, and avoid even jaywalking. Absolutely no drinking!"

"Will do."

She told me the youths were gearing up to protest our New Jersey shit in a way the international media could not ignore, to send a strong message to America. She prayed it did not lead to our white parishioners being abducted or killed the way Biafran soldiers had killed Italian oil workers in 1969, to make a point to the world. I tried to lighten the mood by talking about my editing progress and sharing Dr. Zapata's uplifting speech. However, when she asked of Lucci and I dismissed him as a skilled racketeer, she did not buy it. She said I was spiking her malarial headache by tarring an old man who did everything to welcome me. Afraid of losing the fragile trust we were rebuilding, I changed the topic to our families, Nigeria's scarcity of gas, power cuts, new hip-hop hits.

KEITH HAD JUST MESSAGED me to know how I was doing, when Brad called to say the exterminators would come on Thursday instead of today. "We just have to call fucking city hall, if the landlord hangs us out to dry on Thursday!" he thundered. "I'm going to handle this like a fucking full-time job."

That night, Molly's replies came in. They were meaningless at this point. Keith's dogs were purring with so much happiness they were almost singing. It was as though the noise were coming from the holes in my floor. I drank myself to stupor while listening to "Hold On," the Negro Spiritual, my misery and shame centering mainly on those moments before my meeting with Molly. In all that had happened to me in America, this was my own personal failure. But drinking and listening to this song was like mixing two opposing elements in an experiment—a new kind of concoction to rinse my soul of my New York woes. It would have been better to separate the music from the booze, or to have no booze, but I could not help myself.

Jeff knocked on my door. He was drunk and had a bottle of gin and had pulled a chair from his apartment onto the landing. He wanted me to pull out my chair, too, so we could drink together. But I declined and thanked him all the same. "Listen, my mattress smells like shit because of the bleach!" he slurred. "I must buy a plastic bed-cover to keep the reek off my nostrils."

"What's your bedbugs secret?" I asked.

"I thought I had a secret but, fuck, nothing is working."

"Okay, what did you try?"

"Not good for your health. Just tell Brad and Alejandra it's not good for health."

He shook his head and put down his chair on my threshold and kept drinking. Usen called twice. To hide my own drunkenness, I texted I would call him later. Then, gently, I unsat Jeff and moved him and his chair back into his apartment.

CHAPTER 20

The Handmaid Sisters
of the Child Jesus

THE BREAKFAST CROWD IN BLUE FIN WAS AS DIVERSE AS
usual. But today I counted minorities, something I never did before
New Jersey.

Confirming Caro's fears, Father Kiobel said the youths were
mobilizing neighboring villages to "call white America's bluff." He
said all types of angry *ekpo* masqueraders were already roaming the
place night and day with machetes drawn, that the echoes of their
nonstop drumming alone had denied everyone sleep. The priest was
ashamed the youths were demanding, in the language of diplomatic
row, for him to enact "equal and mutual and reciprocal" banishment
of our white parishioners, for peace to reign. The elders were saying
the last time the masqueraders were this wild was when they forced
the bishops to transfer the pedophile Father McQuinn to Igboland in
1975, arguing the Igbos deserved someone like this for running a war
that raped our young boys. To boot, the powerful Awire Womenfolk
had also rolled out their womenfolk to emphasize the seriousness of
the unrest, these women who once told the Biafran commanders to
turn their Igbo nuns into comfort girls instead of raping our women.
Today they were threatening to protest stark-naked against America.

The pain of Sunday returned to me when Father Kiobel explained
that though he and the village chiefs had informed our crazy Nige-

rian police of the degenerating security situation, the cops themselves were complaining they, too, were tired of these nasty stories of their American colleagues terrorizing Blacks while they in Nigeria prioritized the protection of white people and institutions like the embassies. He had suspended Holy Communion classes altogether because he could not explain the absence of white kids to their Black, Asian, and Latino friends. He knew the rioters would never differentiate between white Americans and other whites, just as American cops did not differentiate between us and African Americans.

TO DEFUSE THE WORST crisis of his priesthood, Father Kiobel was planning an emergency Nigerian Thanksgiving Mass on our behalf on Sunday, to let everyone know, first, we were alive and well, and second, to give the true account of what had happened in New Jersey. Unlike in America, our Thanksgiving meant dancing up the altar with family and friends, to celebrate special events and having the priest say a blessing. He would highlight the people who stormed the sacristy in our favor, mobbed us after Mass, and received us after our ban. The stories making the rounds did not include these, because Usen and Ofonime had forgotten to mention them in those first frenetic calls as they raced home from the train station. Now, no matter how many times they said good people had supported us, folks felt he, Father Kiobel, had asked them to embellish for the sake of peace. Worse, the youths had sworn they would only back down if the Mass was named "Call White America's Bluff Thanksgiving Mass."

When I begged him to compromise, he went on to say he needed images to go with his social media explanations and pleas. He was glad our Bronx folks had sent great selfies of white New Jersey Catholics embracing us. "The pictures are to be enlarged and placed all over the church like holy pictures," he explained. "Ofonime also sent me a recording of your harassment by the ushers—I'm inviting our parish council to watch it, to help present a strict chronology of events." Lamenting that Ofonime had edited out Tuesday from this video because he did not want Ikot Ituno-Ekanem to see his new skin, he asked whether I could contribute any photos.

I gambled and sent shots of our Chelsea "bedbug-toast" cheers, for, after all, Alejandra and Brad were lapsed Catholics. Father Kiobel exclaimed these were the best photos of racial harmony and inclusive Church of the lot. He was sure these would excite the children the most, as Christianity had no holy pictures of saints or angels having fun or being mischievous, and would have pride of place in the sanctuary, like the Paschal candle. His chuckle was like lightning in a darkened sky. The fact that they were images of Black, white, and Latino people meant more to him than the New Jersey black and white shots. So, I added the Jeff-and-I selfies; after all, Jeff also had wanted to be at my Chelsea reception. I also sent the Native American cop–*mmun-edia* selfie.

"This last one is the key to convincing even our cops that their American colleagues aren't all rotten!" he exclaimed. "I'm making copies of this for the police stations right away, to encourage them to step up security." I suggested since the Native Americans are minorities like us, he must do better than Father Orrin by properly introducing them and talking up their brave struggles for their lands and resources and respect.

However, I was most consoled to hear that this morning our Ikot Ituno-Ekanem American parishioners were outraged by Father Orrin's actions. Encouraged by Father Kiobel, they had rallied and put forward two volunteers to give a speech after Communion on Sunday, to denounce him. It was really sobering that some of these white folks then refused evacuation orders from the joint forces of the CIA, Russian GRU, European Union, and Chinese security agencies. Father Kiobel told me we must act fast because this singular act of solidarity was what was actually keeping the lid on this explosive situation.

"But I doubt you can tell the whole truth about New Jersey!" I demurred.

"Why?" he said.

"How are you going to present the way Father Orrin confused us for the Igbos?"

"I'll completely skip that."

"Hell, no. Everything suggests we must tell the whole truth about Biafra!"

"The big crowd on Sunday will come to hear how to tackle racism in America. If they realize our foolish war, in the first place, swam the oceans and forced Tuesday to invite you guys to New Jersey, we're done. Do we want New Jersey to lead to another civil war?"

"Just tell the truth!"

"Like you, the Bronx insists we must mention Biafra. And Tuesday would rather I talked about Biafra's rape-as-weapon-of-war all day than utter a word about racism! He even calls me a coward for letting the youths label the coming Thanksgiving Mass 'Call White America's Bluff.' I told him it was insane to think that just because he has *become* white there's nothing like racism . . . Are you saying I should talk about rape big-time in our Holy Communion classes of eight-year-olds? Look, I don't want to end up quarreling with you also. It's a pity you've decided to attack me on a day like this."

"Father, let me be even more candid with you: you should just admit you're *Biafran* or, well, as Tuesday said, a coward."

"It's bullshit to call folks names without even knowing their story."

"At least you can tell the congregation what you think of Achebe's book! And if you really call me your friend, why the hell can't you write the foreword for my anthology? After New Jersey, I'm dead-set against asking Tuesday. And, please, stop idolizing Emily Noah if you can't face your own childhood. If you spray-bulleted folks during the war, say it. Own it with your chest, as we say back home. Why can't you return to the villages you terrorized and apologize?"

He was *akwuog* angry. And he seldom got angry. Since I had never heard him describe anything as bullshit before, I surmised things were really tense back home. I left him alone to do what he could. I felt bad New Jersey had pushed me over the edge.

THE ATMOSPHERE AT WORK was like yesterday's. Molly's door was still closed. Fighting resentment, I waved to and maintained eye contact with folks who cared to look at me. I went straight to the restroom to check my clothes for bugs. I did it again and again, for I was restless.

But, in my cubicle, I quickly noticed little white powder traces on the blue-black carpet. Though I stared at them for a while, they did not bother me then, even when more powder spilled out from the eyes of the electrical socket in the wall, like dry tears, as I plugged my laptop cord. "Maybe the powder was there yesterday," I spoke to myself. "But since my mind had crashed, how was I to notice? Did I even plug in my laptop yesterday?" I went about my business, for if the powder truly bothered me, whom could I ask? With Emily in Europe, who really wanted to see me in their cubicle or office or sacristy?

When I met Molly in the hallway, we said hi and did small talk. She looked exhausted and said she had been working all night to meet deadlines for two of her authors. But the whole conversation was hollow, different, needless. We were like two new arm-amputees who had to suddenly adjust to not shaking hands with each other. Her apologies for the long delay in replying to my texts were off-putting, worse than if she had said nothing. Fear she might have spread Lucci's superbug nonsense spiked my disappointment.

"How's Hell's Kitchen?" she belatedly asked.

"Good, really good," I said.

"Good, good."

"Good, good, good."

I WAS TOO ASHAMED of my bedbug issues to attend the editorial meeting that morning. If Molly was this uncomfortable around me and Emily was on her European vacation, who exactly was going to appreciate my presence there? What if no one really wanted to sit near me? Why should I subject myself to this torture for one hour? I emailed Bob Hamm, the guy who embraced me the day before, asking for his advice; he replied that, given my fears, it was actually best to just email my reports to everyone. "Ekong, you know, after our shameful last meeting," he said, "I can't put it past my colleagues to embarrass you. We're fucked up. I know how much you love my *Thumbtack in My Shoe*, but protect yourself, my brother."

I sent in my reports, strongly recommending *Thumbtack*, and left for Starbucks to read. But, unlike before, I waited for the elevator alone, feeling watched. In the café, I went straight to the restroom. With my little mirror, I studied my clothes carefully to make sure they did not harbor any surprises. Then I took them off completely, including my socks and boxers. I searched the seams and pockets and hems until an impatient customer pounded on the door.

That afternoon, I went to McDonald's. And while I was standing in line to order, I caught myself counting the minorities in line. Then I saw Jack and another colleague. The next moment, they were gone. I felt bad because I was not even going to greet or sit near them. When I scanned the nearby streets, I saw them scuttling empty-handed toward a Burger King, looking over their shoulders. I did not feel like eating at McDonald's anymore. I grabbed the food and strolled over to Rockefeller Center. I leaned on the half wall overlooking Prometheus and the empty ice rink and had my lunch. I found solace watching all those foreign flags lapping up the gentle winds. I texted Father Kiobel my apologies for my outburst.

Back at work, I made efforts to engage people again, in case they were reacting to my negative body language. I stopped by their cubicles, as I used to. But they were all too busy and if I leaned too close, their faces screwed up in horror. I put on my earphones to listen to MI Abaga's "Beef" and lingered by the water fountain. I ended up staring at Matisse's *The Moroccans* on the wall. For the first time, I noticed even the minority figures in the painting were all turning their backs to me or looking away or faceless.

When suddenly I was awash in anger as if I were in a flash flood, I decided to take my campaign to Jack's office, to confront him once and for all. He was making a phone call by the window. A flicker of sourness crossed his face. As he told the caller he needed to go because he had an emergency, I closed the door and slid into a chair.

"Have you heard from Emily?" he said chattily, standing behind his desk, faking a smile.

"No," I said, crossing my legs.

"She's really enjoying *Bombingham*, which I hear you'll read on your flight home! By the way, your lovely and insightful report on *Thumbtack in My Shoe* carried the day. And, wow, Emily's report on *Thumbtack*, which I'm sure you've seen, was exactly like yours! I just never knew about Black people being ashamed to talk about the dysfunction in Black countries for fear of white stereotyping. Oh, this is so, so sad, you know.

"You know, I've been thinking about this all afternoon. I really understand. It's a double whammy for you guys. In the first place, our white colonialism messed up your Black countries by forcing all these different tribes together within artificial nation-states and our greed populated the Caribbean with Black slaves. And now you suffer the fear we'll turn around to mock and stereotype Black-on-Black violence . . ."

"Jack, do you have any phobia for crawling things?"

"No."

"Jack, Jack, please, make yourself comfortable. It's your office. I really need to talk with you."

He perched on his seat uncomfortably, arms folded.

"Crawling things, crawling things?" he said. "Two years ago Molly told me she had a very bad phobia of insects. If you have any insect infestations, I'm sure Molly would ask you to stay home till things cleared. Oh my God, Ekong, I think you're in the wrong office!" He then relaxed and stroked his beard and winked at me.

"Didn't Molly tell you I'm crawling with bedbugs?" I said.

"No way . . . oh oh, wait," he said.

He pushed back his chair, his fingers trembling. For me, Molly's stock had also rebounded once Jack confirmed she actually had a phobia. And I was more than intrigued to learn our colleagues had kept news of my bugs from the two racists.

Now I watched him closely as he babbled that nobody told him and Angela anything about me anymore. Goose bumps had emerged on his arms like stretch marks; his face had become redder than his beard and he could not look me in the eye, as though I were one giant bug. I was upset he was more afraid of these tiny reclusive insects than all the armed conflicts in our entire developing world. Was he no longer the guy who was fascinated by African "shithole wars over land and oil" and how we could never solve our problems, big or small? I did not want to shout at him like I had at Father Kiobel that morning. I just wished to hell, though, I could eavesdrop into how Jack would narrate this conversation to Chad or Angela.

"Jack—?" I said.

"I'm here, I'm here," he said, relieved I spoke.

"Excellent, excellent, this cold war between us ends today. I mean, after avoiding me in McDonald's, what are you going to do with my fucking Black presence and Black smell in Andrew & Thompson? As our people say, the bird that flies from the earth to the termite hill is still on the earth."

"I don't think I understand this proverb."

"Then come closer, if you don't mind my Black smell. We need a heart-to-heart chat about your racism."

"No, you're being unfair. I've always been open to diversity."

"Call it what you want . . . good. First, could you relay my nigger compliments to Chad Twiss for finally raiding *Trails of Tuskegee*?"

"Hey, wait a sec, Chad is a true believer in diverse voices!" He sat up like he had finally found the opening to counterpunch. "He told me how delighted he was to meet you. I think he would be the perfect agent for your memoir—he's already intrigued by the war, from his visits to Nigeria. Please, don't be offended, but the kind of tragedy your family went through would make great reading in any part of the world. And, yes, he can get you a huge advance. Ekong, I think you're mistaking his outstanding understanding of market forces and agenting for racism. He's got tons of minority authors!"

"Excellent, excellent . . . listen, just tell Chad *egusi* soup does not look like vomit."

"What?"

"And *you*, too, should never repeat stuff like this. We're not vomit eaters."

"I never insult international dishes. And being against identity politics doesn't make me a racist!"

"Well, streets have ears. Be very careful where you spew your damn racist phone rants with Chad. You were standing with Angela on Lexington, who laughed like a robot, the same damn morning you both claimed to apologize to me. Then you lied you weren't attending any reading, to avoid me. You also told Chad I was fucking Molly . . . ?" He grunted and fell back into his seat as his memories caught up with him. He had both hands on his head, his eyes blinking like a Christmas tree.

I stood up and waved in his face to refocus his mind: "Please, put yourself in my position. If someone treated you like this, no, if someone went to all that trouble to hurt you, to belittle your race and competence, then fake an apology, then spat in your food, how would you feel? Dude, how's quitting Andrew & Thompson, as you and Angela swore to do in that street phone call, going to cure your racism, oh, anti-identity politics? I don't care what you think about my friendship with Emily, my sister from another mother. Finally, Jack Cane, soul mate of Chad Twiss, it's your bounden duty to inform her of that racist phone call and of your plans to confront me man-to-man for lusting after her, ha! You must tell her this before she returns from Europe. Or I shall!"

✗

VISITING OTHERS' SPACES also did clarify an aspect of the carpet powder mystery.

Only my cubicle and Emily's, the nearest cubicle to mine, had it. But her dose was like an afterthought.

I refused to be worried, still, and blamed it on the night cleaners. *Okay, you're overthinking things,* I countered the voices in my head. *If you're telling me they want to convince me they're using some powder shit to tell me this is a white space, why does Emily's have it, too? All right, even if she's tainted by weeping over Tuskegee, fuck, what do you want me to do? I'm not going to spend my precious time figuring out the perpetrator. And I shall not suspect or condemn everyone. What are these harmless traces of powder compared to New Jersey?*

Yet, all day, I was suspicious of being shunned by Angela's department. Did she meet with her marketing staff without this Black ass? When was the rescheduled meeting that was canceled because of that "personal crisis?" Were they waiting till next week, to shunt me to another department?

Usen texted me at 2:47 p.m. to ask where I was watching the midweek European soccer matches, which had just started. I said I was too busy. He said, well, he was coming into Manhattan on Thursday and invited me to watch a soccer match in a sports bar.

By work's end, I could not point to one major thing I had accomplished. After picking up a few things from the Food Emporium, I saw Jeff on Forty-Ninth Street and waved to him. He was in high spirits, going off to shave and scrape his flat head. "You fucker, I hope you didn't steal my chair last night, for your own sake!" he hollered.

"Jeff, are you still drunk?" I gave him a thumbs-up.

"No, Ekong, you were the bombed one. Well, how are you enjoy-ing my chair?"

"What chair?"

"Ha, did you take it to Africa?"

"Fuck you!"

UPSTAIRS, THE FIRST THING I noticed was Jeff's lovely piece of furniture standing in my living room, one leg stuck in the broken floor. But all my chairs were also there. The whole thing looked like voodoo, so I called Jeff immediately. He said I actually joined him the previous night to drink by the stairwell and explained that at the end I wanted to borrow his beautiful chair because I complained I was tired of Greg Lucci's old ugly worn stuff. "Ekong, you said you were homesick because mine reminded you of home," he said. "So I let you have it . . . Listen, save your ass and spray that shit and keep it till after extermination!"

That was how I knew I had been totally drunk.

I hated what was happening to me.

In frustration, I grabbed the anti-bedbug spray and hit his vintage chair at close quarters till it was completely wet and the liquid came streaking down its beautiful legs. I turned the chair upside down and sprayed all over its gray soft-clothed butt. Sometimes I put the noz-zle directly on the cloth and pushed in and sprayed, overdosing it as though to compensate for its long hours in my home. Then I dropped and kicked the can away in shame and anger. It landed on the door of the fridge, but before it hit the floor and found its way into the bath, the dogs were up in arms. I flushed to calm them and walked around the apartment till my mind was spray-bulleted by details of New Jersey, till I began to think of how Father Orrin could have seen the Liverpool decal hidden, as it were, at the very bottom of the rear windshield of the Audi.

From where he stood when Usen drove in, he could not have spotted it, period. In his busy Sunday routine, did he send *his* people to spy on the car then . . . ?

Caro's texts liberated my mind from New Jersey. She told me Father Kiobel said not to worry about my outburst. She also said the priest had been thinking a lot about Emily and her Black Alabama primary school mate and Biafra. "You must thank Emily for me when she returns from vacation!" she said. "I can't go into details now."

I was happy to hear Father Kiobel had picked Caro herself and Usen's father to read at Mass on Sunday. The cop selfie had surely returned the Nigerian police to their beats, and Sister Augustina Ngwu of the Handmaid Sisters of the Child Jesus, recruited by Father Kiobel, had convinced the Awire Womenfolk to suspend their nude march. However, we were happiest that sharing our pictures on Our Lady of Guadalupe's WhatsApp portal had brought some solace to the white parishioners. Indeed, they had teamed up with our New Jersey friends, who had just learned the truth about our sacristy reception, and had already had a Skype meeting with Bishop Salomone.

CHAPTER 21

Screw you all

SADLY, THURSDAY WAS NOT WHAT WE HAD EXPECTED IN Hell's Kitchen. At two p.m., Brad Parkes texted me at Andrew & Thompson to say, instead of exterminators, the landlord had sent in a private inspector.

Since I had never heard of "bedbug inspectors" before, initially I thought their job was to count the bites and scars on the bodies of victims and report to the government. So I texted Brad that I did not fancy strangers poring over my hide and lied that my welts had healed. "Nobody is taking my photo!" I wrote. "I'm no poster child of bugs, period." Once he reassured me the inspection had to do solely with our apartments, I told him I would call him back from downstairs, as I was already planning to meet up with Usen in a sports bar. I did not care that more white powder poured out from the socket when I unplugged my laptop cord.

But, as I hurried out, Angela Stevens, who was also leaving her office, seemed to panic and rushed back inside her office like she wanted to scream. She banged and locked her door. Someone laughed, but when I turned, she hushed like an interrupted alarm. Bob Hamm cleared his throat to get my attention. He gave me two thumbs-ups. "*I want to eat this egusi soup!*" he whispered fondly and loudly, which made everyone laugh and clap and relax. I smiled and gave him a kiss in the air for letting me know that Angela was apparently running from the kind of *egusi* visit I had paid Jack.

Outside, I felt worse when I called Brad back and he said my apartment had not been inspected because it was not on the list, even when Brad told the inspector "the tenant" had informed the landlord and reeled out the date and time Jeff made the call. The inspector insisted Canepa had specifically told him not even to speak with me. So Brad himself then had phoned the landlord but was told Lucci needed to have called directly.

I apologized for all the pain I had caused them, saying I was ready to cope without fumigation. But Brad asked whether coping meant getting totally drunk like Jeff and I were Monday night. "If I didn't fucking come out to ask Jeff to allow you to have his chair," he said, "you'd still be screaming at him now!" He warned that public drinking was a crime that could invalidate my visa, and ICE could either deport me in short order or put me in a detention center for years.

When Brad and I invited Jeff and Alejandra to a conference call, our tone was surprisingly good, almost humorous, different from the shame and anger I felt. We pondered calling the city bedbug hotline but decided against it because the city would still send their inspectors first. Brad and Alejandra proposed we approached Keith to place a call to the landlord, his friend, on our behalf. They said the landlord was always using the African American as an example of a model tenant. "But how do we get Keith interested since we don't talk to him, duh?" Jeff said. "Personally, I can't stand his arrogance!" Brad asked whether I could approach my fellow Black man. I said no, without giving reasons; I had not yet recovered from Keith's accusations of selling out.

Next Jeff ran his big mouth, declining to join the delegation. He still had some ill feelings about "Blacks in this country" refusing to side with Asian Americans in the late 1960s on the issue of affirmative action and quotas. He said Blacks refused to back them because they claimed Asians first snubbed Black marches. "God knows how long Black folks are going to blame their failure on others!" he grumbled. These comments rankled. He spoke as if he could not see I was Black; it would have hurt less if he said *African Americans*, instead of *Blacks in this country*.

"Please, could I advise you guys to drink less?" Alejandra said suddenly.

"Gosh, you sound like our father!" Jeff said.

"We need to protect Ekong's fucking visa," Brad said. "I've already told him."

"Okay, that makes sense," Jeff said. "I didn't even think of that." There was silence.

But when I said I needed to go, Jeff exploded: "Ekong, why didn't you tell them you were already drunk when I knocked on your door?" Though I apologized, Jeff accused us of backbiting and ambush.

"This is really, really fucking Biafran shit!" Brad said.

"No, Brad, don't go there!" I said.

"Exactly my point," Brad said. "Of course, it's no longer funny on our floor . . . I say it's a wonderful adjective. A state of complex dysfunctional self-sabotaging fucking reality. Ekong and Jeff, I'm also fucking begging you not to turn our stairwell into a bar ever again! This isn't acceptable in America."

"Brad, how insensitive of you to insist on using *Biafran*!" Alejandra said. "Ekong, I'm totally on your side on this!"

"Screw you all!" Jeff said, and hung up.

I WAS STRUCK BY the gold and green motif of the front of the Australian Bar & Restaurant & Lounge on Thirty-Eighth Street, where Usen and I were supposed to meet, some color in a dull midtown street. But the dullness could have been in my mind, because any place that was not as intense as Times Square no longer excited me. The colors reminded me of the Australian national soccer team, the Socceroos. We had always thought they had mistaken soccer for rugby, until Harry Kewell pulled on our Liverpool jersey and Mark Viduka and Tim Cahill lit up the English Premiership.

The presence of two Black patrons comforted me, and hearing

some of the workers speak their Australian English with accents heavier than a stutter felt like I had run all the way to Australia to escape my woes. Usen said I should order, as he was running late, yet I went into the restroom to check for bugs on my clothes.

In the opening exchanges of the Liverpool match on TV, I could see this was going to bore me to death. I studied the menu, their grilled Kangaroo entrée offering me the distraction I needed from the fight with my neighbors. I thought this sort of steak would have gone down well with one or two great Australian beers at the bar: Coopers Sparkling Ale, Foster's Oil Can, James Boag's Premium, etc. But the fear of ICE bundling me back to Nigeria blocked any temptation. I asked the waiter whether they served specialties like the kangaroo pouch, that thing the animal carries the young in. I was craving something really unusual because I was disoriented. Startled, the guy said no, that they only had kangaroo skewers and steak. I ordered something called "Kangaroo Loin dish" well done.

Usen was so passive-aggressive when he arrived that he refused to hug me. "I hate how the Australian Embassy is also shitting on Nigerians!" he sneered, his eyes counting the colored customers. "Anyway, Ekong, Google says Australia has treated the Aborigines worse!" I said if we used these criteria, we would not eat any Western or even Asian food. I urged him to take solace in Australia's reparation program for the Aborigines. He shook his head and ordered salad and a James Boag's.

He said Ofonime was right in insisting he must meet with me, because my eyes were swollen like I had not slept since Sunday. He said I was losing weight. "God bless her!" I said. "The good news is I'm having a private lunch with our boss on November seventeenth, just a month from now!"

"Wow."

"*Anyedede*."

MY LUNCH ARRIVED as we watched the boring Liverpool game, the kind of midfield quagmire that would produce no goal even if it went on for a year. The food was a sizzling, glorious pan-seared fare with smoked cheddar gratin, buttered green beans, and a cherry-red wine glaze. It smelled great, and I wished I could hold this smell forever in my mind. It was like the night my nostrils filtered a procession of novel food smells in Chelsea. I descended on the food as soon as the waiter assured me the "red wine glaze" had no power to intoxicate.

The meat's flavor was really stubborn, strong, gamier than buffalo, yet more tender than I knew how to describe. I finished a container of black pepper on it. My pleasure buds were in a crisis! On any other day, I would not have been able to taste even the pepper, because I would be thinking of that funny pouch and powerful tail and sturdy hind legs that align with the ground like the legs of a rocking chair. But I was on an adventure to escape my desolation. Even as I ate, I was strangely pining for kangaroo skewers marinated with Cameroon pepper and *ujajak* and *ata*, because our native tastes are deeper in our psyche than we would ever understand. And I thought, among our Annang soups, the gaminess of kangaroo could only be paired with the assertiveness of *atama*.

Knowing that I was not an adventurous eater, Usen stared at me like I was someone who had completely lost his bearings abroad. "Boy, you're changing so fast!" he scolded me, and pulled away his seat. "If you stay longer, you might go on to 'burn up' your body like Tuesday." I shrugged and ate my kangaroo. I could tolerate his insults as long as he did not attempt to shame the Australian waiters. Having become quite sensitive about our food, I hated to see anyone humiliate another on this score. So when Usen's order arrived, I dropped my cutlery and got ready to shut him up. But he respectfully got the waiter to assure him his seasonal quinoa salad had no kangaroo meat.

I only figured out Usen's passive aggression when he complained I had not returned his calls since Monday. I said that at least I had replied to his texts. "'Jen Annang, you sent me a text meant for someone else!" he scolded me. I apologized for how he felt, too embarrassed to ask what I said in the text, tired of the unending consequences of my drunkenness.

HE THOUGHT IT WAS FUNNY Father Kiobel had called him to get a picture of the Liverpool decal on their Audi, to aid in retelling our story, because village Liverpool fans had accused the priest, a Manchester United fan, of scapegoating their club. In their letter to the church and police, they asked to attend the Mass "in a big way, to launder the image of our dear Liverpool from the odium Father Orrin, the evil fan, had poured on it worldwide."

Usen compared this to wartime soccer obsession. He told me a story Tuesday had just heard from an Annang friend in Texas: In late October 1968, the Biafrans in Ikot Ekpene had suddenly agreed to a cease-fire and even suggested a friendly match[*] in honor of the Olympic Games going on in Mexico. The traumatized and starved folks had trooped to the stadium to cheer and dance like this foolish civil war between Nigeria and Biafra had ended. They chanted, "One Country United We Stand" the whole match. I was already laughing when I heard that a sprightly dressed Father Tom Flannery, twenty-six, a giant of a man, was the special guest of honor. He rode his Honda in from Port Harcourt Diocese and distributed little Olympic flags to the children before kickoff.

Team Biafra, the home team, made Team Nigeria welcome by volunteering to play shirtless to distinguish the teams, since both could not wear the national jerseys. And Biafra started the stronger side, scoring first via a sweet bicycle kick from the edge of the penalty box. Stung, the Nigerians threw everything at them, peppering the Biafran goal with shots—not knowing they had walked into a trap.

---

[*] See Brigadier General Godwin Alabi-Isama's *The Tragedy of Victory: On-the-Spot Account of the Nigeria-Biafra War in the Atlantic Theatre* (Spectrum Books, 2013), although some of the spectators who went to the stadium that day have funnier versions.

The Biafrans went defensive, enacting a low block and sandbagging the Nigerians. By the time a Nigerian player bundled in the equalizer from a goal-mouth scramble, his team was already exhausted. The Biafrans staged a loud quarrel among themselves and even with their coach. The Nigerians mocked them and swiftly doubled their tally, leading 2–1 by halftime.

But the crowd was still singing and the Irish priest was still sipping palm wine and playing yo-yo with the children, when the Biafrans sprang a well-coordinated attack to recapture Ikot Ekpene. The Nigerian army and the spectators fled, scattering toward Ukana and Ikot Atasung and Ikpe Annang Junction—which Biafra had changed to Umuakpara Junction. The priest lost his Honda and yo-yo.

It was the first time Usen or I would ever laugh over any account of the war. And that was certainly a more interesting match than what brought us here. I told Usen, well, today our national preoccupation with soccer had reached another level altogether. I recounted how, during a Nigeria–England match at the 2002 Japan–Korea World Cup, a certain part of Lagos had suffered the usual power cuts and how Lagosians marched upon the local power station to murder the manager. But by the time I told him how, in 2008, after the European Champions League final in Russia between Chelsea and Manchester United, the fans had clashed all over Nigeria, leaving more than fifty people dead, Usen had lost his laugh.

Now he called up our mutual friends in Nigeria to say he was happy our Liverpool fans would protest against New Jersey at our Mass. Everyone was optimistic the American speeches would go well, because Father had assembled a committee, including Caro, to show them how to dress in our Annang traditional attire, how to walk up to the podium remorsefully and respectfully. Not to show up in T-shirts and shorts and flip-flops as usual, just because it was the tropics. Not to impolitely stick their hands in their pockets while addressing the people, as they did even while receiving Communion on the tongue. We quickly sent a joint text to Father Kiobel to remind him to drill the Americans on our local eye contact etiquette, the very reverse of their expectations at the embassy: they must look down as a show of humility on arrival and during the speeches.

"USEN, DO YOU FEEL BAD we didn't tell our New Jersey friends what happened in that sacristy?" I asked as soon as the horrible TV match ended.

"Not at all," he said.

"I do."

"But if you'd picked up your stupid phone Monday night, I was going to update you on their visit to Bishop Salomone's court! He got my phone number from Tuesday and called right away, full of apologies and all."

"*Iko irien?*"

"Yes, he even called again after dinner because Ujai was in school in the morning. That was when I kept calling you, leaving long voice mails and texts! Well, he also wanted to visit our home—and yours—to hear us out. To spend the day with us. But, look, I have no interest in any of this drama. I refused to give Bishop Salomone my address. I politely thanked the chief shepherd and assured him we had put everything behind us, because he'd already suspended Father Orrin based on what he said about the Jews, which everyone heard. A probe is under way, but it's useless because the ushers have refused to say the priest sent them to move us and the children are buzzing he taught them the Father Orrin Pledge . . . Nobody can make me revisit that whole sacristy stuff with anyone, not even God!"

Usen asked the waiter for two shots of vodka. When I declined, he downed both, cleared his throat, and continued. He said it was not about the bishop, whom Tuesday described as kind, soft-spoken, but that since Sunday, his head had been playing Negro spiritual medleys nonstop. He was afraid that, at the end of the day, the Church would figure out a way to blame us, the victims.

I disagreed and blamed him for not giving my number to the bishop. But he reminded me of how the bishop of Ikot Ituno-

Ekanem in 1975 had punished the whole of Our Lady of Guadalupe for the *sins* of those who went to listen to pagan masqueraders sing of "Father McQuinn raping the altar boys like he had three dicks." He rehashed the legendary standoff between our villages and the bishop, how the *ekpoakpara* masqueraders—our native investigative cult—outed McQuinn but protected the names of the minors, how the bishop ignored the reports, how most Catholics shunned McQuinn's Communion plate, how the police refused to step in, how the bishop finally had to evacuate the white man to Igboland when the main *ekpo* threatened to "abduct and machete his trinity penises down to one, like normal humans." Some say the bishop was not really afraid of his castration, but of the threats of the women of Awire Womenfolk. They had vowed to invoke the Defecation Curse on Our Lady of Guadalupe: women from nearby villages were to shit all over the church and Stations of the Cross. This was no small thing, for no premises ever recovered from this curse.

I insisted I was impressed by Bishop Salomone's moves so far and begged Usen to give him a chance. I reminded Usen of how he himself took the lead in helping us manage the emotional goodbye in New Jersey and how he equally edified us by telling Ujai how to live if we did not make it out of the train station. I pleaded we could not afford to be too extreme or negative, since we already had friends in that church, folks who were fighting on our behalf. But Usen revealed that even his parents and our village chief had just warned against releasing our addresses to Bishop Salomone, afraid he would forward them to the American police. "Ekong, like many African Americans, our confidence in the system is shot," he explained. "What's the use of a bishop's visit, if we couldn't open our hearts to receive him?" He said he and the wife had never felt so homesick; they wished they could be at the Thanksgiving Mass in Ikot Ituno-Ekanem.

But, according to Tuesday, there was fresh *wahala* in that parish: the new priest had quickly posted on the church doors that Christians owed more than a debt of gratitude to Jews. The poster was shredded overnight.

subway conductor, who finally caught on to my game and fiercely stared back. I did not care and only gave up when a cop strolled into view, his gloved hand on his firearm, like the Arab American New Jersey cop. Though this guy was shorter, his gait was exactly like that scum's. And when he turned in my direction, though he wore no mask, his eyes were stern and unblinking.

I found refuge in the nearest Starbucks. I downed two bottles of water because I was sweating, and read my emails, which I had not done since Tuesday. But the one from Angela, which had come in yesterday, caught my attention. The marketing department meeting had been rescheduled for tomorrow afternoon. Worse, I was quite embarrassed to discover, on rereading Monday's postponement email, that it had said something completely different. It did not say "three key people could not make it because of a sudden problem" but "three key outside analysts could not make it because of a sudden passing of one of them." I read it six times, but it said the same thing, and six times I replayed my phobia conversation with Molly, my *egusi* visit with Jack, my crippling suspicion of everything.

Slowly, I realized I had gotten so many things mixed up, like I had been drunk the whole week. I was ashamed I might have misread the office atmosphere. My head voices disappeared.

CHAPTER 22

The breakup hurt

Friday morning, I ran into Jack, who had cut work since Tuesday. He could neither meet my eyes nor share some crazy laughter with Angela. He had lost his swagger, and, like me, he seemed to have lost weight, too, and his new clean shave and haircut only deepened my suspicion. Angela herself was always cocooned in the company of other people, as though she expected me to attack her. When we could not avoid each other, no matter my smiles, her greetings sounded more formal than an embassy announcement.

That was when I finally decided I could never work with these two.

I deadpanned and continued my parade of friendliness, and even shook hands with the person who had laughed yesterday when Angela ran into her office. Then I knocked on Molly's door lightly because it was open a crack. When she said hello, I peeped inside to say a bright good morning. She responded with a nice smile. Although the day had just begun, I wished her a great weekend and left.

"Ekong, could you come in a sec?" she called after me. "Please, we need to talk about New Jersey!"

I stepped back inside and closed the door, almost leaning on it, because I suspected she was not ready for any serious conversation. "Molly, New Jersey is old boring stuff, like two years ago!"

She hesitated. Given Jack's testimony to her phobia, I could not but conclude she had wanted to say something about bedbugs. Now even her not offering me a seat finally showed me we were still not ready for New Jersey; such a conversation needed a good level of comfort. I could not risk the fragile thing we were negotiating now. I could not endure any more misunderstandings in NYC.

"Could we talk next week, please?" I said. "Too many things on my mind today. But I'm also really wondering whether it wouldn't be better to meet Liam with you . . ."

"I think you would be great in a one-on-one."

"Okay."

"Or is there some reason you're concerned about it? What's on your mind?"

She studied my face. Yet I could not tell the white woman my fears since we had not discussed New Jersey. I simply said it would just be nice to go together.

In truth, I worried I might be walking into another well-choreographed private sacristy reception, while Molly, like our church friends, would be waiting innocently and expectantly outside to celebrate the outcome. What would being banished from Andrew & Thompson or from the whole American publishing industry feel like? I did not want to put myself in a situation where I retched my New Jersey bile on Liam. And, *Awasi mbok*, where were the expats in the Nigerian publishing industry who would take the kind of risk the brave American oil workers were taking this Sunday across the ocean, to defend my humanity?

"Molly, maybe we should cancel the lunch altogether," I said, studying my shoes.

She rose and came around her desk.

"Ekong, it's just lunch," she said.

"I know," I said.

"Liam asked after you two days ago—he can't wait to meet you. What I told him about your boldness at that first editorial meeting really impressed him! Even when I told him you had a bug infestation—I hope you're okay I extended this little courtesy to him—he shrugged it off, saying he himself had spent a fortune on bugs in his penthouse four years ago."

"I already feel better!"

"I knew you would. Well, your comments have got him thinking about the heights minorities have to climb to be seen. To exist. The whole thing blew his mind."

She said his new agenda would be figuring out whether his charities were actually reaching minorities or had been hijacked by the biggest ethnic groups, something he never thought about before. Molly believed my assessment of things would be a great blessing to his understanding. "I think, too, the kind of stuff the Uramodese president talked about has to be sensitively reinforced often and in different contexts," she argued. "Ultimately, to be honest, our industry will only diversify if the boards and owners want it. Liam is on our side."

"Okay, there's another thing. I'm also just realizing rotating to work with other departments won't be as useful to me back home as staying with editorial. I've learned so much already since I got here!"

"That's okay. Just send the others a note. I'm sure they'll understand. Again, don't forget: if *anyone* makes you feel uncomfortable, I need to know!"

I was convinced Molly did not know about my visit to Jack's office. But, most of all, I was relieved I had gotten my sorry ass out of having to deal with the Humane Society Two at such close quarters.

THERE WAS A LITTLE PILE of books, gifts, at the entrance to my cubicle—this time on the floor, not on the desk. Whoever brought them must have waited until I was in Molly's office. Was it the same person who had leaked the sanctions against the Humane Society Two? Was this similar to sending war victims relief materials, folks you never wanted to meet?

However, when I bent down to pick them up, I noticed that the white traces on the carpet had actually increased from yesterday's. No, I refused to touch the books.

I went immediately to inspect Emily's space, but her white powder was gone. I stood there trying to figure out whether I was seeing right, or, more complicated still, whether I was remembering right. When I bent down to study her electric sockets, there was nothing. But I smelled a whiff of alcohol on her desk and chair. I thought, perhaps, the cleaners were boozing in her cubicle the night before.

I inspected my desk and chair and shelves very carefully. No white stuff. And none on the books. I refused to set down my bag. I refused to plug in my laptop cord. I refused to sit down. Though I knew I was paranoid, today I refused to overlook it. No, I stared at the powder till all my fears about New Jersey, all my fears about Andrew & Thompson, wracked me.

I needed to sort out this powder shit.

I went down into the streets in search of the nearest Starbucks for a strong drink. They said I needed something called Doubleshot on Ice, and when it arrived, the strong icy coffee scent hit my nostrils like snuff. It was just what I needed. In the transparent cup, the color looked sinister, like mixed paint. I protested that I had never taken iced coffee or tea before. They explained it had no hot version. I slipped the drink into a paper jacket, to spare my fingers the cold. By the time I stepped outside, closed my eyes, and took one hesitant sip, the fog in my head had cleared. Though the ice numbed my tongue, I felt like jumping. When I could finally taste the shit, the caffeine had kicked in.

In my cubicle, I took a big gulp again and again. Then I took a deep breath, knelt down to really study the powder traces. I wanted to make sure the chaos in my head no longer affected my judgment of objective reality. And though the beams of the overhead lights were at their fullest, I switched on my phone flashlight, like a mechanic monkeying around the tightest crannies of an engine. I could spot at least four new layers of the powder. I reckoned these signified the four days since I spotted this on Tuesday.

Slowly and tentatively, I touched it with the tip of my right index finger. Rubbing the finger against my thumb, I could feel it was grainy, like some kind of salt. I smelled it. It was odorless. When I tried again, I sneezed and hit my head under the desk. I gave up and plugged in my laptop cord and stood up and put away the books. I sat down and kept my feet away from the powder as I started to edit my stories. But my mind was on the mystery under my desk, like it was going to crawl over my shoes and spread out and grow like bubble bath and fill up my cubicle, to suffocate me.

I did not tell Caro for fear she would think this white stuff was a tracking device from the New Jersey cops. Yet I wished its existence were a figment of my imagination, another mangled understanding of the wordings of some memo. To focus, I sipped the drink and swallowed four ice cubes. Yet, instead of getting used to it, my mouth felt dry and a heavy thirst taped my tongue. I began to sweat, something I never experienced with hot coffee. And the sweat seemed to come out all at once, soaking my shirt, the type of abrupt cold sweat our people call *ikpo ekpo*. My nose ran and my eyes shone like they would never know sleep again. When I sneezed again, I dropped the drink into the trash can.

I did not believe this powder was to protect them from my bedbugs, because it was not like anything we were using in Hell's Kitchen. Then I worried this powder could have been programmed to grow, spread all on its own. Then I worried about the fact that it had made me sneeze.

I went to lunch alone at Ruby Tuesday, from which I emailed Angela and Jack to cancel my presence at their meeting. When I returned to my cubicle, I saw that Lucci had called five times. Patiently, I sat through the long voice mails, each the kind of ramble you knew only ended because the caller ran out of recording time. I felt violated as he asked about my village population, my cousins' occupations, the architecture, age and price of our home, how many relatives I lost in the war. His inquiries were as random as the American visa interview questions. His voice now felt as though he was an audio version of the carpet powder, another addition to the Humane Society Two.

When I sneezed again, I lost focus.

Who told you to smell this poisonous powder? a voice whispered.

And twice or thrice? another said.

After that sneeze, if I were you, I would see a doc ASAP!

What if Liam ordered this powder like Father Orrin ordered you to be moved?

You're taking Molly's word on Liam without discussing New Jersey?

Just cancel the fucking lunch.

You see why Usen doesn't want the bishop's ass in his home?

Ha, poor you, the powder can only increase on Monday!

I was sickened by that last but new sarcastic voice that had already pushed my anguish into the following week. My weekend felt crapped upon by this mind-leap, destroyed.

That afternoon, I sprinkled water on the powder, just enough to soak through. My thinking was that when it dried up, it would cake over, making it easier for me to better judge on Monday how much of a new dose was being poured.

LATER, ALEJANDRA TEXTED to say Brad's plans to recruit Keith had ended in a nasty confrontation between the two men. She blamed me for not approaching the Black man myself. She accused me and Jeff of voting along color lines against Brad, with whom she said spent the whole of Monday night washing off our drunken puke dripping down the stairwell. "Ekong, I think we need some space!" she announced, to end our friendship. I was too dejected to reply. Instinctively, I called Jeff. But after two rings, I hung up, remembering he, too, was already angry with us.

The breakup hurt.

To deal with the pain, I took a walk into the city, going as far as the New York Times Building and UN Building. I got some perspective on my way back: I could never forget that their blessed Chelsea pictures and selfies had already saved our villages from certain riots and would set the tone for our Thanksgiving Mass in two days' time. I tried to see our friendship as a wonderful dream I did not want to end, but it did anyway.

CHAPTER 23

America was meaningless

IT WAS A STEADY WINDLESS SATURDAY NOON WHEN I RAN into Keith pacing the sidewalk in front of our building. In white Crocs and a long blue Portuguese flannel nightshirt over a red T-shirt, he looked like a man who was sleepwalking. I was trying to decide whether to greet him or not, when he suddenly swooshed away from the building, unwittingly coming toward me. My heart began to beat fast. When he saw me, he waved and called out to me. He stopped before me, yet he could not look me in the eye and had his hands behind him, to discourage a handshake, I supposed. His cologne so filled the air I thought it might attract bees.

Thinking he was going to talk about the clash with Brad, I spoke first: "I'm sorry, I heard you guys had a bit of a confrontation."

"I don't want to talk about your friends, please, okay?" he said, still looking away.

Still standing there on the sidewalk, I reached out for a handshake, to invite him further into my space. But, instead of moving, he stretched and bent forward and released one hand to offer the lightest of fist bumps.

I saw progress.

He hesitated, but just as I opened my mouth to compliment the weather, he burst out:

"Look, Ekong, I've got the bugs!"

"Welcome to New York, my village," I said.

"Could you stop sounding like that embassy lunatic you told me about, Lagoon Drinker? You keep downplaying this stuff."

"Then maybe I'm more of a New York toughie than you."

"Come on, man, stop . . ."

"Listen, without humor, you can't deal with this shit. So smarten up and tell me when you discovered you're the newest *carrier* in town."

"This morning. This freaking morning, and I called the landlord right away. Though I have no itches, my thighs, my back, my arms are fried. My ass has been ripped in shreds, dripping liquid like I need a diaper. If I don't wear cologne, I smell like the egg yolk of a farm-raised chicken . . . !"

"Hey, dude, calm down."

"Don't tell me to calm down, because I just need to know what to tell my school principal on Monday. No school wants this shit on its profile."

I advised him to buckle up because these little fuckers were already winning. I told him he might struggle with light-headedness and insomnia. "Keith, hey, I would've taken you out to eat, to really welcome you to the club, like the fancy dinner Brad, Alejandra, and Jeff organized for me, if you don't mind me bringing their asses into this, our little midday tell-all," I said. "However, in your case, the restaurant tables or spoons aren't long enough to maintain this *distance*, you know." He was laughing now, and for the first time that afternoon he lifted his eyes to behold my face. He was less sad, less embarrassed, less frightened, less alone. He said he had showered five times already but still felt dirty.

"Bro, were you able to get *the* secret from Jeff?" he asked.

"All he told me was that the secret is not healthy," I said. "I don't think he would ever say."

"Then what're all the cozy chats in the stairwell about? I warned you, chinks won't help you!"

BURSTS OF WIND BEGAN to come in from the river, whipping the streets. The trees shook till the leaves abandoned the branches and rode the currents. On earth, each frenetic gust pressed on the piles of garbage and the plastic-wrapped furniture till you could see the shapes of wing chairs and love seats carved momentarily in sharp relief.

After I relayed to him the instructions I got from Jeff when my neighbors first revealed I had bedbugs, Keith demanded in a rather curious way, "Is this how they do it in Asia, then?"

"Do I look Asian to you?" I said.

"Why do you Africans always act like *we*, African Americans, are stupid and clueless? . . . I've placed an expedited order for a snazzy electronic bedbug detector. Expensive but great reviews."

I ignored the taunt on Africans and went on to tell him about the bedbug inspectors. Suddenly he got back his confidence: he warned me to keep away from Lucci. Keith was furious the guy had rented so many places in this city a quarter of a century ago. "His fellow Sicilian, the landlord, says the crook has got an empire of illegal sublets!" he said. But then he asked me to just play along with Lucci, for I would not be able to get rid of him. He said if I did not cooperate, Lucci would harass me with phone calls or visits. He reminded me he had my spare keys and knew I was a lame duck, for I had signed no papers and was an alien. I said Lucci was already leaving me endless voice mails full of random personal questions. He said the rogue was building my profile so if the landlord dragged him to court for illegally squatting, he could at least tell the judge I was his dearest internet friend whom he invited to New York, to garner publishing experience from his friend's niece. He said, to save his lease, he could marshal these intimate details, including my grandma's maiden name and the shape of her tombstone. Lucci was desperate, he confided, because mine was the last of the six apartments he once had on the block. "Organized racketeering is a big

problem here, man!" he said. "You Africans need to stop romanti-
cizing America."

I did not like this revelation about how Lucci was mining my personal details. By the time Keith said Lucci was only fifty years old
but always talked like he was eighty, Canepa's age, I was weak. I
remembered his myriad practiced laughs and cries and coughs. I
felt like someone was in the process of stealing my identity. When
I remembered he had already extracted information when I arrived,
about my wife and our desire not to have children, I felt like one who
suddenly realized he had been duped all his life. I needed to lie down.
I needed to go upstairs while my legs could still carry me.

Completely agitated and forgetting Keith himself was still adjust-
ing to being around *carriers*, I stepped forward. But he glared at me
and backed off as though I had come too close, as though I were
going to worsen his bedbug woes. "Stop right there, you African
nigger!" he warned.

"What?"

"You heard me!"

I lost it and exploded, asking him what "you African nigger" was
doing in that sentence. "And you get this right," I shouted. "We ain't
no descendants of slaves. There's just nothing like *African nigger* but
just *nigger* and that is *you* guys, period. I'm tired of this Africa-this,
Africa-that shit. You sound like a certain Angela Stevens at Andrew
& Thompson. Didn't history tell you Benin City in Nigeria was the
grandest medieval city, the first city on earth without crime, before
Britain and Canada massacred its citizenry, looted its arts, and razed
it in 1897? Did they not tell you that city's moat was once longer than
the Great Wall of China? You sound like all your Lagos embassy
folks, paid to invent a thousand ways to insult us. *Ino-mkpo*, just get
African out of African American. What's even African about you if
you hate our asses so much?"

I drenched him with all my frustration in America, telling him it
was cowards and unpredictable and useless folks like him that we
Africans sold to slavery, not counting the good folks white people

kidnapped on their own, burning down kingdoms that did not cooperate. I blasted him that people like him had put this idea of being
superior to Africans in the heads of their primary school kids like
Ujai. I laced my tirade with endless Annang profanities.

When I spat on the ground between us to underline my irrita-
tion at our mutual misunderstandings, it jolted him. He blinked and
stepped back. I stepped forward and spat again. He turned around
and walked toward Times Square. I trailed him, but he kept his cool
with hands in his pockets, like I was berating someone else ahead of
him. I let him go when I saw two NYPD officers at the intersection
of Fiftieth and Eighth.

I WAS STILL FUMING when I got to my apartment. But by this
time I was fuming at myself, for saying more to Keith than I needed
to, or was true. I had gone too far with the whole thing about who
was sold into slavery. The truth was if the African Americans had
a bit of support in America, who was to say they would not have
flourished like white folks of Australia—those real descendants of
die-hard death-row white criminals shipped there by Britain?

Standing there by my window, I hated the fact that I had sounded
more bitter about my African American brethren than Tuesday
Ita, and more discriminatory than the Humane Society Two. I held
myself totally responsible for this second breakup. I had let myself
down, beginning to join the ranks of those I hated—the sadists. I
could see the faces of the good embassy touts, disappointed in what
I had become in America. I could also see the bad touts pelting me
with stones, saying all my precious relationships with my neighbors
were a lie. It was not just the Black American I had lost. America was
meaningless. I could not live with anyone.

I, the immigrant, had also become the problem. I felt I could never
snap out of it, that things could only get worse. I felt like I had lost
my entire balanced feel to life, like a man who was either screaming

or whispering when he simply wanted to talk. These days, life came to me in frightening exaggerations.

I was sinking. Fast.

To cut the dread growing in my head, I splashed cold water on my face and began to drink, mixing Azteca de Oro brandy and Stolichnaya Elit vodka. I was angry with Jeff's chair, for it reminded me of the friendships I had won and lost in America. I covered the chair with Lucci's navy-blue bedsheet and dragged and deposited it near the door like a blindfolded prisoner awaiting execution. I walked around the apartment gulping and reciting Mohammed Dib, the Algerian poet, like a new rosary:

I was then still sustained by some kind of hope,
but hope so enclosed in inaccessible places
that I now hesitate to call it hope.
A stone had been dropped into an abyss
and I listened to its interminable fall.
I was that stone
and the hope
I clung to was that I would never reach the bottom.

CHAPTER 24

"Call White America's Bluff" Thanksgiving Mass

DEPRESSED AND SLEEP-STARVED AND COLD, I WAITED outside Starbucks till it opened. Since I could not shake the thoughts that Lucci could invade my apartment, I had carried some of my important things like my passport and some clothes in my computer bag. And yet, I could not really concentrate. I left the café twice to check up on the apartment, the first time cleaning up and restoring Lucci's photo to the shelf. I searched the streets for someone with a huge nose, fitting Jeff's description of Lucci.

It was nine a.m. New York time, three p.m. Nigerian time, when my phone started to ring. I knew the long Sunday "Call White America's Bluff" Thanksgiving Mass was over. It was a six-hour celebration. As soon as the first callers said it was a great occasion and that my wife read well, I congratulated them. But, given my deepening woes in Hell's Kitchen, it was as though taking in too much good news would weaken my guard, exposing me to Lucci's torment. I could not reach Caro.

My friends apologized that they could not send videos because the internet was slow. I perused all the photos and text descriptions of the bustling crowds that had come to protest American racism on this hot sunny day. They overflowed the church into the fields, swamping the life-sized Stations of the Cross, down to the edge of the valley and the adjacent school. There was a group of Liverpool fans in their red colors; they carried a large banner with the message: NOT IN OUR NAME: KICK FATHER ORRIN OUT.

I was equally captivated by pictures of people perching atop the Stations of the Cross to get a better view of things, like concert-goers, especially the shot of Gabriel, or Two-Scabbard, the youth leader, who had asked me to speak at the canceled memorial. Today, he dared to sit atop the Twelfth Station, the Crucifixion. He had climbed the cross higher than Jesus. In fact, he was sitting on the horizontal beam, on Christ's shoulders, the Lord's head in between his thighs, his feet dangling, tapping the Lord's torso, his two scab-barded machetes slung across his bare sweating body. He wore dark glasses and a face paint of charcoal, like the war dancers of Tungbo, Sagbama, at their October 22 annual festival celebrating their liber-ation from Biafra. WE MUST TALK BIAFRA! was written on his chest. It was as though he had gone up there either to cut Jesus's body loose from suffering, or to behead him. The only reason folks did not haul him down or stone him for blaspheming this most sacred of sacra-mentals was because this was an extraordinary gathering: we were totally fed up with racism and American police brutality.

Then my friends sent me pictures of our white parishioners arriv-ing in a police-protected convoy. When they and their children stepped out, all of them were dressed like Usen's family in New Jer-sey and hung their heads in humility. With the photos of the crowd applauding, I could imagine the valley clapping back. The Awire Womenfolk, camped out in a field, yodeled and gyrated and beat their *nkwong*, as though they were accepting the initiation request of our white guests into their association.

I could not resist calling up Two-Scabbard, who told me that once inside the church, the tension was such that the speeches could not wait till after Communion. So the Americans had gotten up from their usual front pews and quickly denounced Father Orrin and the American police, surprising everyone with striking proverbs. They blamed the major religions for not doing enough to stamp out all kinds of discrim-ination. They apologized for slavery. They praised Father Kiobel for saving our villages from doom. "Hearing of our white wickedness in New Jersey, how could we abandon you in Ikot Ituno-Ekanem?" one of the white speakers said rhetorically, and pointed to our enlarged Chelsea and New Jersey photos and the Indian American cop selfie, posted everywhere. "As your ancestors say, both God and *utere*, the vulture, cannot reject the corpse. How could we allow the CIA and MI6 to cart us to *safety* in Europe or America when you've received us with open arms all these years? As your ancestors say, when palm oil touches one finger, it touches all. You've never harassed our children for crying during Mass or for using the restroom. Please, then, accept our humble gesture of standing here today, to cry together for the damage racism has perpetrated on our dear Church, the Body of Christ. We want to assure you that Bishop Salomone of New Jersey also believes we've made the right decision to stay on. In the last week, we've Skyped with him daily. He sends his apologies and has already personally notified Pope Francis of, not just the criminality of banning Black folks from a Catholic church, but of the mortal sin and deep wound this inflicts on the Body of Christ . . . we hope you'll forgive us today. We also want to apologize for all our expatriates who quickly fled and abandoned and betrayed you once this crisis broke. As the ancestors say, some flies go to cover the wound, others go eat it. It's important that we stick together, hand in hand, through this, as racism flares back up in America. We're also grateful to Father Kiobel for his guidance in the past week."

Then Two-Scabbard said the Americans got emotional when they read out the Annang praises I used to distract Ujai at the train station. Though their accented Annang led to sobs and muffled laughs in equal measure in the congregation, it must have reminded our old people of Father Walsh's broken Annang. And anything, anybody, that reminded us of our wartime pastor was a god.

Other villagers who called wondered, though, why our New Jersey host, Tuesday Ita, was not in the pictures and wanted me to confirm the rumors of his new color. They said his phone was switched off. I did not reply. I equally ignored those who wanted to know whether the Native American cop really tasted our *mmun-edia*.

They said the most emotional part of the Mass was when Father Kiobel, after accepting the American apologies on behalf of the people, said almost in tears that Mary's poster reminded him of his late mother. Nobody had ever seen him that emotional before. He had even opened up about his personal experience of the prewar genocide in northern Nigeria. When he could not continue, everyone had clapped and assured him he was really their priest now, for hurting more than he was able to say from this war, like them.

Excited that Father Kiobel had brought up Biafra, I ran out of Starbucks to scream into the phone for more details. My fellow villagers pleaded that I should wait for the video clip, for the experience could not be summarized. Instead, they spent time regaling me with stories of dancing and singing in and out of the church after the American apologies. Mercifully, that night the internet finally allowed Caro to forward the clips to me. She said she herself was jealous of Father Kiobel's ability to tell his own story. Knowing Biafra was a no-go area for us, I said nothing.

One of the videos began with our tense priest pacing the sanctuary of the packed church. This rough week had taken a toll on him; he looked different and ragged because he had neither shaven nor scraped his head. His round babyish face was lined with misery, and he had lost weight, too, like that of a long-suffering refugee. Of course, given his obsession with clothes, we all knew he had bought brand-new vestments for this occasion. But today I loved the deliberate nattiness to his dressing. As he pointed repeatedly at Mary, in the poster-sized photo from New Jersey as he said she reminded him of his mother, his wrists were adorned with beautiful blue-white tzitzit bracelets with golden menorah clips. I loved the Jewish touch, a counterpunch to the anti-Semitic rhetoric in New Jersey.

"PRAISE BE TO JESUS!" Father Kiobel exclaimed in the video.

"Honor to Mary, the Mother of God!" responded the church crowd.

"My dear friends, I thank you for the welcome and applause for our American speakers! Their refusal to abandon us is a rare gift to all of us. In their words and presence, we also hear the goodwill of our friends in that New Jersey church.

"On a personal note, I must say, our people in New York—the very victims of such orchestrated racial profiling—have asked me to use this occasion to also talk about our ethnic issues, in keeping with the spirit of today's Mass. Please, allow me to personalize this spirit by confiding in you that this old white woman in the wheelchair, Mary of New Jersey"—he stopped momentarily in front her group picture—"who led the protest to Bishop Salomone—has reminded me of my late mother like nobody else in the last fifty years. I also want to use this chance to apologize to all of you who believe I'm suppressing conversation about what happened to us all fifty years ago."

Applause.

"When the genocide broke out in July 1966, a year before the Biafran War, my family was living in northern Nigeria, near Marna Market in Sokoto, precisely. I was ten years old and in primary four. I can never forget the sight of Hausa-Fulani mobs sweeping through the neighborhood. Daddy was one of the thirty-five thousand victims.

"He had locked us inside and blocked the front door of our home where we were hiding with our Igbo neighbors, who had run to us for refuge because Barisua, my thirteen-year-old elder brother, was best friends with Arinze, their son. We all barricaded ourselves in Barisua's room. While the Igbo boy was a clown with big ears, the Ogoni boy, my brother, was serious-minded, his sharp eyes giving him a tense look. Yet, they wore the same haircuts and had received First Holy Communion together. Because they were tall muscular things, their soccer coach had picked them for the two-pronged attack in their high school team, despite being in mere form two. Since I was a quiet brooding child, the only time I spoke with Arinze was when he cajoled me into mock wrestling during his sleepovers in Barisua's room.

"Now, Daddy could have tried to tell the mob we weren't Igbo or spoken to them in their Hausa language. But he also realized he couldn't get the Igbos with him off the hook, and I don't think he could live with himself if they died and we lived. We could hear Daddy begging loudly for our lives against the backdrop of chants that the coup was an Igbo coup, since it spared all the Igbo leaders, who were as corrupt as the leaders from other ethnic groups, who were assassinated. When someone smashed our window, Arinze's dad started to cry and moved to take his family outside, to spare us. Mommy, Barisua, and I held and corralled them in. Daddy was saying, "You cannot continue to kill the Igbos—" when his voice disappeared. We knew they'd killed him because the mob cheered. We let go of the Igbo family. Barisua pinched his own left arm till it bled. Arinze shat in his red shorts.

"By the time the mob destroyed the front door and the metal protector behind it and got into our living room, the Hausa-Fulani business partners of Arinze's parents had arrived to rescue us. We were one plywood door from death. I was watching everything through the keyhole when the sharp smell of blood made me vomit and sit on the floor.

"Thus, my last memories of Daddy weren't of his body, but of his voice. Then of his blood on the machetes and crowbars and Korans of the attackers bursting into our living room. Though Mommy and Arinze's parents didn't allow us children to see the corpse, they'd gone outside, where she knelt by it to soak her most expensive headtie with his blood and roll and tie it up in a bag with camphor, to bring home to Ogoniland on the Atlantic or wherever we would be killed.

"Our rescuers evacuated us from the semi-desert—Igbo and Ogoni alike. They hid us till they could figure out a way to relay us city by city, village by village, forest by forest, for months, our version of the underground railroad. They took huge risks, for even the Nigerian army and police were intercepting and killing refugees. After six hundred and sixty miles of trekking and busing southeast, we arrived at Arinze's ancestral village near Onitsha. Everyone celebrated our arrival, and their priest praised Daddy's martyrdom daily at Mass . . ."

The camera showed Father Kiobel holding back tears and apologizing that he could not continue. The Igbos and minorities clapped and embraced, and shouted we really needed a Biafran War memorial Mass. The PA announced that this was the first time Biafra was mentioned in a multi-ethnic gathering without violence.

The valley agreed.

I COULD NOT CALL Father Kiobel immediately because the violent death of his dad reminded me of mine. I felt closer to the priest, as though a veil had been removed from his face. I battled my tears as I tried to imagine what it must have meant for him to actually hear his dad being killed, how the Good Samaritans could have disposed of the body, how he accompanied his mom and the blood-soaked headtie and Arinze's family in that long treacherous Sokoto-Onitsha refugee march-cum-burial procession. And, seeing his emotional state, I decided right away it would be insensitive to ask him of the connection between his mother and Mary of New Jersey.

When I finally did phone Father Kiobel that night, he had been waiting anxiously for me. "Ekong, I'm so sorry I couldn't tell you I was going to bring up Biafra, in case I couldn't," he said, and finally broke down and wept like he needed to drain himself of fifty years' worth of tears. He said the silence he broke that Sunday began with the abrupt silencing of his father's pleas for the Igbo family. He thanked me for pushing him to speak up.

I was pleased the war was finally thawing in his heart, beginning to water our multi-ethnic dialogue in ways only he—who was loved by all—could manage. And to hear our war story being proclaimed fearlessly in this international gathering, to hear it cascade down from the sanctuary and echo in the valley, had the weight of an Eighth Sacrament. It was the first time our minorities were getting a detailed account from someone in authority of our 1966 genocide, instead of the Igbo versions.

When he stopped sobbing and said he hoped by the time of the memorial Mass to mark the beginning of the war the following year, at least the anthology might be some guide to our people's journey to peace, I could not have thought of a greater endorsement of my project. It seemed it was worth the wait. I was also happy to hear Two-Scabbard—on behalf of the youths—had asked him to quietly inform the foreign parishioners they would no longer be entitled to the front pews. The youths had decided that henceforth, they must sit wherever they found space, or stand outside.

"*Mbok*, Ekong, you'll help the parish organize a memorial as inclusive as today's celebration next year, in July," Father Kiobel appealed. "Two-Scabbard has already suggested you as the natural chair of such a planning committee."

"I shall accept only on one condition," I said. "We must include Caro's story—the murder of her grandpa—in our reconciliation plans."

"Absolutely. As you know, Caro has always found it easy to confide in me about her Biafran history. This was how I became close to you two. Actually, on Tuesday, to calm her, I had confided in her I'd bring up Biafra. So, yes, we'll prepare our parish, to avoid another civil war."

"We have to hit the right note. Your speech today was the first and major step."

I was so proud I had made that spontaneous decision five days before to challenge him on Biafra. His sharing of his Biafran story was my first unqualified success in America. It was totally unexpected. I had rescued something from the ashes of New Jersey.

CHAPTER 25

Bless her heart

AFTER SMELLING THE ALCOHOL ON EMILY'S DESK, I WAS kneeling under mine, staring at where the caked white powder had been, when Emily and Jack's laughs distracted me. I did not jump out to welcome her back from Europe, because I did not know what the asshole had told her. It was not also the right atmosphere to relay Caro's compliments.

I continued with my inspection. The week-old hardened layered stuff was scraped off, but there were new traces in other parts of the cubicle. They looked fresh, like sprinkles of new snow. But it was good for my mind; I finally felt I was reading this powder stuff right: it was not a figment of my imagination. I took many pictures of the spots. When I pulled my chair out, I hesitated to sit because I noticed a smudge of the powder on it. Still, I brushed it off and steeled my back and lowered myself mightily and defiantly into it with a grunt.

As I was putting away my passport and a few folded clothes in a drawer in case Lucci "visited" my apartment, Emily burst in to hug me from behind. She was full of happiness. She sounded refreshed and said she and Jack and Paul Maher had had dinner the previous night in Soho, where Paul told them how happy he had been to make my acquaintance and how much he enjoyed the Uramodese Prize president's powerful speech. "By the way, Jack and I had a deep,

deep chat in his office," I said, and waited eagerly for her to signal to me they had discussed his racism.

She never did.

The more dramatic she was about her trip, the more silence froze the rest of the office. Everyone was hard at work. I decided not to bring up the truth about Jack with Emily now, for it would have been a cruel blow to the benefits of her trip. "Ekong, Angela says Liam is really excited about your lunch!" she announced. "You Nigerians have balls. It should be great for both of you, my two fav peeps." A few people looked up with shock or jealousy on their faces.

As Emily began to ask me what I was doing with my passport and a bloated bag in my office, Molly came out, tense as *ekpan*. I greeted her but she avoided my eyes. Emily hugged her and relayed Paul's greetings as they went in and closed the door. For the first time that day, our colleagues relaxed and spoke to each other or sipped coffee. Some kept glancing at Molly's door like a bomb could explode behind it. Angela and another person laughed and left altogether.

EMILY EMERGED CRYING and trembling. Her face was crimson red, and she was sweating *ikpo ekpo*. She told me she had been fired.

"And, you know what, it doesn't matter," she said.

"*Iyo*, Andrew & Thompson can't fire you!" I said, standing up. "Molly did this to you . . . ?"

"No."

"I mean, why?"

"She's crying, too. You don't understand. It's really nothing to be upset about."

I walked into her cubicle and offered her Kleenex.

"Is it the Black book of Tuskegee?" I asked. "Are they punishing you for spotlighting the racism of your Alabama childhood?"

"No, no . . . diversity issues didn't get me fired! I would've told you straight up. In our business, anybody can be fired. It's not personal. Molly says Andrew & Thompson can't sustain my salary. So, yes, yeah, money fired me. I'm okay, I'm totally okay. It's my second layoff. Gosh, I'm so embarrassed. What do I tell my authors? I'm sorry to cause a scene. Please, Ekong, go back to work."

I tried to get her to sit down, but she could not. I phoned Jack, who was outside. He was in shock. Two people, who stopped over and spoke in nervous whispers, could not look into our eyes. When Jack arrived and raised his voice to protest Emily's firing, they disappeared like *ifot*. When I realized our colleagues had known what was coming to Emily, Andrew & Thompson felt like a crab basket. When I suspected Angela also had known without telling Jack, it felt worse.

Then, before Jack could stop Emily, she ran back into Molly's office and banged on the door. A few more people left. The whole development began to hit home when Jack brought a box and a trash bag and started clearing her stuff. When he continually smiled at me and stroked his chin, I knew he was posturing as a good company guy, despite his anger. The bastard even began to fill my ears with his weekend. Well, on a day like this, I could not help but oblige. "Could I beg you not to tell Emily about my reckless private-comic phone call to Chad yet?" he whispered. "She's already in pain. Let's give her a week to recover, okay? Please?"

I nodded because, even for me, the timing of the firing was brutal. And I was not distracted by his "private-comic" phrasing of his racist shit, because I was beginning to understand that New Yorkers spoke in codes about racism. I never wanted to adjust to this culture. Anyway, to see my friend at her happiest and then, shortly, at her saddest only reminded me of Molly's own tales of layoffs and headhunting. Though later Emily was calmer when she called from home and promised to stay in touch, I felt like I was cut off from the last white person who truly understood my anguish about race. My knack for losing my Hell's Kitchen friends had followed me to the workplace.

Caro was mad about Emily's firing, like she wanted me to return home that minute. Father Kiobel was so depressed he asked a torrent of incoherent questions. "What exactly is this carpet powder?" he kept asking, no matter how many times I said it did not matter. "Is there carpet powder or no carpet powder? Would you stop saying Emily is fired? Are you sure she's not poached by those who bought *Trails of Tuskegee*? Why do our police prioritize the safety of white folks over our people? Ekong, are you sure you're not drunk? Why does world security mean white security? If you're really, really sure the white powder is in your cubicle alone, why not call nine-one-one? What if Liam Sanders doesn't want to talk about it at your lunch?"

It was as if he had lost Emily, the guardian angel of his turbulent retracing of his war-torn refugee childhood. I assured him I would keep in touch with her.

WORK WAS QUITE DIFFICULT for me that week. I kept my anger about Emily Noah's dismissal to myself. I did not talk much to my colleagues. And I was also lucky Jack was doing everything to avoid me. I greeted Molly as casually as possible, for after all, our relationship had not really recovered since she revealed her phobia for crawling things.

The next Monday I heard the exterminators were coming. I wanted everything to be sanitized. But since my relationships in Hell's Kitchen had evaporated, I had no one to leave my keys with. To give the workers access, I did not lock my door but simply closed it. I was not too worried about theft or Lucci's invasion because I was still carrying my vital documents around.

At work, Molly nervously invited me to her office. She was in a purple shirt, ash pants, and black shoes, Lenten colors, as though to mourn the departure of Emily. She looked exhausted like she had had no weekend, and without makeup her freckles burned deep. "Please, have a seat," she said, beckoning me to the chair in front of her desk. I did not know whether to call this progress or not, because of the way Keith had come close to me two Saturdays ago, only to profoundly insult me. I perched on the chair without my back touching it. My hands were hanging straight down, and my knees were trembling with anger as I poured out my disappointment over Emily. I told her how foolish, how humiliated Emily looked when she emerged from her firing to realize everyone already knew of her shit.

"Let me begin, first, by saying I'm so sorry Emily is no longer with us," Molly said. "I understand how much this has hit you, and I didn't know word got out, okay? This has been really difficult for everyone. Very difficult. As Paul told you at the prize event, I pulled every string to get Emily here. So, I'm not only sad as in sad. I'm wracked with guilt. I'm sure she'll find another job soon."

"I'm not blaming you, though. Emily did say you yourself were crying, too."

"Bless her heart."

"Molly, you'll need another Emily for your dreams here! Maybe I'm paranoid, but to be honest, I hope *they* don't fire you before then . . . to totally end the test run of Black presence here. Because, if you didn't leak the news of the layoff, then the tentacles of evil must be longer than one victim! I'm saying if Angela could keep that away from Jack, you need to watch your back, please."

"Ekong, I could quit Andrew & Thompson myself, you know."

"*Nse nkpo?* If you leave, isn't that like losing Emily twice? And where would Liam Sanders get another Molly Simmons to fight racism here? I say buckle up to fight, in case whiteness pushes back like Dr. Zapata said."

"Well, let's not dwell on this depressing stuff." She stood up and excused herself to leave the room. "Ekong, could I get you some water? Coffee?"

"Water."

When she returned, she did not wait to set the two paper cups on the desk, before launching into the subject of New Jersey. It took me unawares. I finished the water in one swig to quench the fire that wanted to erupt again in my heart. She did not mince words in condemning the New Jersey incident as the worst case of racism whose victim she personally knew. Her tired eyes lit up in pain like they were going to burn down the rest of her face.

"Worse, my two questions to you in that church were racist, too!" she said inconsolably, dropping her head, bracing like I was going to scream at her. "Oh Lord, I feel like going to confession!"

"Calm down first."

"You're just being nice to me."

I reminded her of how she almost ran over to the same New Jersey to rescue me from "some really racist poisonous shit." I reminded her of how she wanted to call the police.

However, I advised her, if she was talking Catholic confession, she herself needed the consciousness of her wrongdoing at the moment of sin for it to be a mortal sin, a crime unmitigated by ignorance. "But who runs these confessionals, anyway?" I continued, fighting to calm her. "What if you don't get the help you need there? Do you have the right confessor to educate you on racism? There's a world of difference between a Father Orrin and a Father Walsh/Father Kiobel/Father Schmitz. Some of these confessionals are mere spiritual death traps!"

"But, in your heart of hearts, Ekong, do you think I'm a racist?" she said bluntly, lifting her face.

"I'm glad you yourself have brought up these two questions you texted me that day. I've been thinking of how to broach the subject, seeing your commitment to uplifting minorities and the immeasurable support you've given me even before I got here . . ."

"Look I'm so sorry I ever sent those texts."

"I accept your apologies, my friend. Yes, they were racist, but I believe you made a mistake. I haven't known you long enough to even situate it in your character. Character maketh a person. And folks make mistakes."

"I sincerely apologize. I swear I've never asked any Black person those questions before, and I've had tons of Black friends. I've always seen myself as someone who puts everything into leveling the field for all. But now, I guess, I am one of Dr King's *white moderates*!"

"No, no, no."

Tears came down her face. I said nothing but pushed her Kleenex pack and water closer to her. It was still fresh in my mind how moving to shake hands with Keith two Saturdays ago had led to unpalatable consequences. People need space to grow. "I wish I could tell you why carrying these stereotypes is particularly shameful for me!" she said. "I wish I could share my very complex childhood with you." I told her she was putting too much pressure on herself. When she continued to cry, I told her I myself was also learning to navigate the discrimination issues of our world. I recounted my disgraceful spitting before Keith. But she shook her head and wept more and said I was comparing apples and oranges. She said I did not understand white fragility.

"How come you're not scared of my infestation today?" I said when she got a hold of herself. "Is your shrink that good?"

"He's good, but I think it came down to wanting to talk to you. You have no idea how embarrassed I am that I couldn't listen to you that Monday. And let me tell you what is even sadder: how frightened I've been this could blow up and Andrew & Thompson would see I'm not even qualified to be talking diversity. I just wanted to lay everything before you. It shouldn't be about how to protect my image or interest. I've already messed up. I'm sorry hiding my bullshit only makes it worse."

She said she needed to do more than write a long angry letter to the embassy to prove I existed or scream at JFK immigration to process me in. "I thought I needed to change publishing," she said. "But now I see *I* am also publishing . . . I'm so lost."

At her prompting, I began to lay out our New Jersey mess. But by the time I got to the usher asking us to move, she was already disoriented, looking like she wanted to puke. She blurted out that she was ashamed of her color. I said I was ashamed I was religious. I adjudged she had suffered enough already from Emily's departure. I felt an obligation to save her from the full wrath of our pain, though this in itself hurt, like forcing down a vomit. I edited out Tuesday Ita's whiteness and reduced the sacristy episode to "Father banished us from his church." When she sobbed, I cut out the police shit.

"I'm so sorry about Father Orrin," she said. "And, fuck, *I* should never have asked those questions."

"Put those behind you, please."

"Not when I sounded like Jack and Angela or even Lagoon Drinker."

"You know, we don't even need to be perfect to fight for others. My only worry is, with your polling system of picking books here, where are you going to get the votes to publish fresh, unapologetically Black books? What if the best you could do for this world, which literature seeks to improve, is to *stay* right here? To push that door open?"

WHEN I RETURNED to Hell's Kitchen, I was in a panic.

My door—which I had left unlocked—was locked. I tried the handle multiple times, like I had memory problems. I believed Lucci had finally come to lock me out or reoccupy his apartment. So, after a while, I knocked gently, because I did not want to startle him by using my keys. And who knew what could happen if I walked into an ambush from his crazy cop nephew? I looked into the peephole as though I could see through from outside. I was consoled that my passport and a few clothes were in my cubicle at work. Then I tapped the door some more, before I went to stand by the stairwell to google possible hotels to spend the night.

But then I noticed a brown envelope by my threshold. Picking it up, I realized it was from Alejandra. She had left my spare keys, wrapped in a note that said Brad had to lock up my apartment when the landlord stoutly refused to touch it and Keith's. It clicked immediately that my neighbors still had my spare keys. I turned around to stare at their door, the keys and note pressed to my heart. The knowledge that they still had my back comforted me.

I sent a thank-you text and lingered in the stairwell. But neither of them came out.

I COULD NOT FIGURE OUT why Keith was excluded, as he was a tenant in good standing, a friend of Canepa's. Well, whether I liked it or not, Keith was more than my racial ally. I went to look down the stairwell at Keith's landing. Yet the silence only seemed to grow. Was he home? Did he know already his place had been skipped? The best thing would have been to call him, to surprise him with kindness as Alejandra and Brad had just done for me, or even to look for him and apologize as Emily did with her primary school victim. But I lacked the courage even to forgive myself.

Not even the voices in my head knew what to name the angst between Keith and myself. It was not racism. It was not tribalism. As my friend Okey Ndibe, the Igbo writer of *Never Look an American in the Eye* fame, liked to say: "Ekong, I know what I have with the Yorubas or Hausa-Fulanis or you minorities, and I know what I have with other races. But this other thing between us and our Black American brethren is nameless, unsayable. It's so shameful, I guess, no one is brave enough to name it . . . but we must name it before white people name it for us!"

Once inside, after reading Molly's long text thanking me for our conversation, I called the Bronx. Usen said everyone except Igwat was recovering from the flu. I wanted to visit, but he said no, to save me from infection.

"Before we forget, Ujai's classroom visit is the Friday after Thanksgiving weekend," Ofonime said when Usen had put the phone on speaker.

"Great, I've got weeks to plan."

"You better!" Ofonime said. "Because she'll stop calling you *uncle* if she can't show you off."

"Well, we've also acceded to Ujai's wish not to have Tuesday at school," Usen said. "Smart girl, she worked it out in her head and came telling us that though she's trying to accept Tuesday, she thought since you're only here briefly, you should be given the honor to come alone this time, and meanwhile we should strongly suggest to Tuesday to suspend his bleaching, to get back his Black skin, so he can visit the school in the future. When we agreed, she was relieved. It was like she was coaching us on what to say, how to manage the living confusion that is Tuesday Ita. He gets so defensive about these matters that he's sworn never to forgive Father Kiobel for insulting his white skin."

Ofonime said she was just tired of dealing with Tuesday because he had become too angry and unreasonable and was accusing all of us for telling people back home he had become white. Afraid Tuesday may call to blast me, she wanted her husband to tell me what had really happened the day the Biafran patrols went to Tuesday's house to conscript him as a child soldier. "Ekong, I just want you to understand him, if he calls you," she pleaded.

Her husband agreed with her. "But Ujai says she even asked you, Ekong, in church to beg me not to invite the guy to her school," he said. I explained I did not know what to do, as I myself was still struggling to accept him. They said he was upset with the calls from home to quit Father Orrin's church. He was mad with Nigerian newspapers and bloggers pestering him for interviews.

CHAPTER 26

Punishment of an unpatriotic un-Biafran Biafran

As I heard the clinks of glasses, I knew Ofonime and Usen were serving themselves vodka, to tell me the story. "Ekong," Usen said, after ensuring Ujai had gone to bed, "Tuesday told me when I got to America, long before he became white, that he'd refused to follow the soldiers who tried to conscript him because he wanted his parents, at least, to know his real grave, to bury his real body.

"I'm sorry, nobody wanted to be disappeared like Tuesday's two uncles and your father. And, as you know, child soldiers weren't coming back from the forests where Biafra, this Igbo-thing, had sent them to spy on the Nigerian army. And the stories of the torture of child soldiers who ran AWOL but were recaptured and raped had frightened everyone. Tuesday just wanted Father Walsh to anoint his real corpse and bless his grave—a real interment, at least!"

"I totally agree!" I blurted out as Usen paused to sip his drink. "I would equally have done everything to avoid the shit memories of my father's trousers burial. Then the bullies wouldn't have called me *Ajen Arukpo ofong-ukod*, Child of Bloody Trousers, in school!"

Usen went on to say he learned from Tuesday that, when the soldiers left, one angry one had stayed behind like a bad ghost. He tore Tuesday from his parents and dragged him behind the house to rape him till his eyes softened and rained tears. To stop the bleeding, the soldier had plastered his anus with wet sand, packing it in with his rifle barrel. That was when Tuesday's mother herself fainted, thinking the soldier was playing Russian roulette with her son's organs. Next, the soldier came inside and trashed the pots and saucepans by using them to wash his dick and rifle.

For days, Father Walsh had visited the boy with the Eucharist in a worn golden pyx in a frayed green leather case. Since the Nigerian air force had bombed out the nearest hospital, Tuesday continued to bloat from his inability to go to the toilet. He twitched at the sound of every distant bomb.

No one knew what to do till one drizzly night when Tuesday began to pant. When the *ukebe*, enema, of crushed okra his mother performed on him did not relieve him, his father laid him on the floor, gagged him, and climbed on his son's stomach like that of a drowning victim. He heaved till Tuesday defecated and tore off the gag and screamed till the soldiers ran over from our primary school barracks. In no time, they had secured the house and were already dragging the family toward the valley. Tuesday's mother led the way while his father followed, carrying Tuesday piggyback, while Tuesday was still bleeding and bleating, a boy wailing his own dirge.

But Father Walsh, alerted by Usen's father, his sacristan, had run after them from the rectory. He was in full black vestments, barefoot, complete with a metal Mass box, ready to celebrate the ancient Liturgy of Excommunication at the execution site against the soldiers, ready to blow out their baptismal candles if Biafra did not back down. Stumbling down the muddy slope of the valley, he startled them in a torrent of full-throated Irish-English-accented cusses. That night, the valley echoed his pain so clearly that the surrounding villages, which had learned to sleep despite the shelling of Aba by Nigerian forces, stayed up in a vigil.

I descended on my brandy as Usen said the priest swore he was tired of our so-called *sabos* being disappeared across the Igbo-Annang border. Of having to say our burial Masses using pants and shoes and shirts in place of bodies. Of not waiting for the Canon Law–sanctioned seven years before doing the requiem for the missing or disappeared, because even God knew the Igbo border was a point of no return. His voice was hoarse and defiant and sick, ripping through that wet valley, denouncing our Igbo colonization. But Tuesday had told Usen the soldiers had retorted that Black-on-Black colonization was better than what his white people had given us, that God had decreed that everyone must bow to Ojukwu, King of Biafra, instead of Elizabeth II, Queen of England.

The standoff on our river's narrow beach was so intense that some villagers had even blamed Usen's father for bringing the priest in; they feared Biafra might kill him to increase our terror. Father Walsh had called the soldiers by name, warning that it was one thing for them to come crying to his confessional for forgiveness—blaming their spray-bulleting on fear and anger over supposed minority betrayal, or direct orders from above—and quite another to kill members of his flock, fellow Catholics, against the direct intervention of the confessor.

Father Walsh explained that, just as no one could force the Igbos to love Nigeria, and just as no one could force Black people to love white folks, their colonizers, the Igbos could not force Biafra down our throats. He said Ojukwu should listen to the outspoken Jaja Wachuku, his fellow Igbo and first speaker of the House of Assembly, who was dead-set against using child soldiers. He said his fellow Irish priests and nuns in Igboland had told him even the Igbos were beginning to hide their boys, too, because they could see this was not the Biafra Ojukwu had promised the world.

"Now, why isn't it fucking enough you gobshites have already performed your specialty on Tuesday?" Usen mimicked Father Walsh's Irish-accented screams as Biafra refused to back down. "May you anus busters burn in the hottest part of hell, beyond the Four Last Things' recall! How does Tuesday ever recover from this? And does the punishment for unplugging their son's ass, for reversing the punishment of an unpatriotic un-Biafran Biafran child have to be death to child and parents? How much fucking pain must one family endure? Can you even imagine the pain of Mrs. Udousoro, whose husband you disappeared last year? Oh Laudy Daw, how many examples do you need to set of so-called *sabos* in this very valley, how many graves, before you realize these tactics are about as much use as a back pocket in a shirt . . . ! Okay, go ahead, kill us all."

"TUESDAY SAYS HE FUCKING started craving to be a white man that night!" Ofonime jumped in, her voice full of anger. "I don't think he has ever recovered from what his fellow Blacks did to him. He's so ashamed of folks back home knowing his new color . . . !"

"Baby, you're jumping ahead of the story," Usen said.

"I'm sorry," she said.

"Ekong, Tuesday told me the soldiers only relented and left the valley when the white man swore if they killed anyone, he would scoop the blood to say Mass as a curse on the soldiers."

But the villages were still on edge: without the *sabos* or priest returning or hearing gunshots, who could tell whether maybe the family was drowned? Usen's father had hid behind the wet ixora hedges near the rectory all night, awaiting the return of the priest. He told Usen, as the soldiers finally emerged with their flashlights to announce their return, they fired into the skies in front of the church. Yet the echoes were completely different from when they executed *sabos* in the valley. Nobody was deceived; the last thing everyone heard had been, *Okay, go ahead, kill us all.*

Meanwhile in the valley, with a flashlight, the priest and Tuesday's parents had washed the boy in the river and discarded his soiled clothes. From the Mass box, Father Walsh poured wine on the Purificator and Corporal, which he used to wipe the boy's ass. The parents moved away, protesting the sacrilege of turning sacred linens into toilet paper. But he calmed them down and pressed on, the scent from wildflowers as thick as burned incense. He took off his vestments and wrapped them around the shivering Tuesday before feeding him with the bread, both consecrated and unconsecrated. And, after the boy had finished drinking from the water cruet, he laid him down with the box as pillow. When Tuesday still trembled, the old man laced his feet together with the stole and amice.

"I liked how, In the morning, the villages scrambled for the least painful way to haul Tuesday out of the valley," Ofonime said as her husband paused to pour himself more drink. "They decided on *ikat-ebot*, goat cage, padded with *ekpat isighe*, burlap sacks . . ."

There was a knock on my door. I excused myself and told the Bronx I would be back shortly. I opened the door abruptly—only to be startled by Keith Jim-Stehr's presence.

It was like seeing a ghost.

I switched on the chandelier, to see properly, and backed inside and simultaneously apologized that I could not invite him in for obvious reasons. "Though I'm already infested, I understand," he said, nodding. He looked comfortable, while my heart raced with guilt as I tried to quickly forget the trauma of Tuesday Ita so I could attend to Keith. I poured a whole glass of brandy into my throat to steady my nerves.

He was in a black suit, light blue shirt, and loosened red tie. We had nothing to say to each other. We did not shake hands. He looked tired, his eyes beset with sorrow, just as I might have looked to him. I returned to lean on the doorpost. We were both looking at the floor. Though his cologne was in the air, all I could think of was *the yolk of a farm-raised chicken*, which was what he said his trashed body smelled like.

New York City had beaten the hell out of us.

"Look, Ekong, let's forget our disagreement for a moment, so we can really talk," he said, clearing his throat.

"You're very gracious . . . thanks," I said, straightening up. "Keith, talking is good, talking is really good, bro."

"Yes."

"No, I'm sorry for my outburst and attack! I didn't have to say that about slaves and your ancestors—*our* ancestors—and the word *nigger.* Thanks for keeping your calm. And I didn't even have the courage to apologize, you know."

"I guess we can't resolve four-hundred-year-old bad blood by screaming at each other on the streets."

"I know."

"Bro, how was your day?"

"So-so."

"Mine, too."

He suggested I come outside and close my door. I apologized to the Umohs, who were relieved I needed to attend to Keith and not Brad and Jeff. I said a quick goodbye before Keith and I settled into our positions on either side of my door. He told me he had a good chat with Brad the night before. But, of course, this afternoon he felt humiliated by his friend the landlord. While the exterminators were buzzing all over the place, he had tried to reach Canepa, to include his place, without success. Later, the workers said the landlord had called them, instead, to say Keith had reported the case *too late* to make the list. Now Keith moaned that he had paid a dog shelter to house his brood for two days for nothing.

"ACTUALLY, EKONG," he said after a pause, "part of why I knocked on your door was to inform you I had called the city's bed-bug hotline to report your place is also infested."

I moved away from him.

"Why entangle me with your government when you damn well know I'm in this apartment illegally?" I said.

"Legit or not, we're a sanctuary city, for Christ's sake. They just want you to call. To ensure the place isn't overrun by bugs or rats or bullying landlords. Please, I had to act for the sake of my schoolkids, call it a sense of civic duty. But the city is complaining of a week's backlog. They'll come next Monday. I thought Jeff said he clarified things when you panicked because he called the landlord on your behalf the week of the Chelsea dinner—"

"Wait, does it mean you also spoke with Jeff?"

"Oh yeah, we bumped into each other Saturday night on my way to sheltering the dogs so the exterminators could spray. He was leaving to squat with friends because he couldn't sleep. But, hold on a sec, you got a problem with me talking with Jeff?"

"No, not at all."

"By the way, I don't think this guy has any *secret* solution anywhere! He said to tell you the plastic bedcover he bought only made the bed feel like a sack of bay leaves. He'd rather die of the bedbug reek!"

I asked if he could call the city back to say he mistakenly mentioned my name. I came to understudy publishing, not city hall bureaucracy. If the city punished Canepa, he was likely to react, either hitting me directly or taking it out on Lucci, who would still torture me. Then he swore the city was not going to come after me for not calling them. He said even Brad, Jeff, and Alejandra, whose names he also mentioned to the city, had refused to oblige. They told Keith they needed a week or two to see whether today's extermination worked. I said it was an *afid-ito* hotline if their reaction time was a week, backlog or no backlog.

THOUGH I WAS HAPPY to make up with Keith, the following day, Father Kiobel and I cried for Tuesday, because we could only imagine the trauma that finally threw him into this abyss of whiteness. I thought of calling Tuesday, but I did not know what to say. I assured the Bronx I would be gentle with him if he himself called to accuse me of "exposing" him back home. Then I thought, perhaps, people like him would benefit from the theme of "Black Shame" in the manuscript *Thumbtack in my Shoe*.

CHAPTER 27

If she hears you quarrel with your BFF, she'll be gloomy

Yet, on the night of October 20, I had no doubt that I had finally come face-to-face with my executioners and sadists when I felt something burrowing in between my butt and the white sheets. It was a week after Keith had hired an expensive firm with sniffer dogs to solve his problem—and only God knew how they did it.

I leaped for the lights and straightened the sheets, to search. Searching my bed, I discovered a splatter of bright blood near a burst bug, the carcass the size of the smallest dark crushed grape. I believed I had popped it when I jumped. It had a wild pungent smell worse than that of the fireflies I caught as a child, and the amount of blood was far more than what six mosquitoes could have drawn. It seeped through to the mattress cover. I saw another fresh accident site with even more blood. I started feeling my buttocks, a blind, unconscious search. Nothing. When something moved on the mattress in the periphery of my sight, I smacked at it but missed. It leaped up like a ball on a trampoline and landed. It feigned death, before plodding off. It was dark brown, its flat, encrusted top bent by a swollen, distended tummy. There was no time to take a shoe to it, so I attacked it with the tip of my forefinger. It was soft, initially resisting like a balloon. It pushed back. I persisted till it burst. The dark heavy blood did not splash but stood like a dollop on my sheet, a mound over the carcass, some settling in the whorls of my fingerprint like dye. My suspicion was this guy had sucked me last night or the night before, hence the coagulated blood. The smell was worse.

I ripped off my sheets, only to see two flat hungry ones, apple seeds, scurrying in opposite directions as though they were paid to confuse me. I went after the one which climbed over my pillow, snatching it with my fingertips. But it was so flat I did not feel I had caught it, so when I opened my fingers it dropped and disappeared into the woodwork around my bed. The other had vanished, too. I was tempted to take a crowbar to the whole bedframe and heap the splinters by the sidewalk.

It was bizarre sitting there, staring at my bloody fingers. I was surprised at how calm I was, till I remembered the itch would come. I thought about the anesthesia they had injected into me, to take that amount of blood, at different places without my knowledge. Was it yellow? Was it white? Black? Red? Was it colorless? Now the delayed panic hit me, and I started searching my body as though I had a hundred hidden unfeeling bites. I went and opened the window for fresh air as the real stink of the bugs made me want to retch. The voices were back in my head, saying, *In how many places were you bitten?*

Three.

No, twenty.

And how many days before the itches?

Four days?

SOMETHING CLIMBED OVER MY FOOT. I bent down immediately, and against the dark wooden floor it was almost whitish and transparent, with a dark spot in its middle, like the intestines of a baby termite. Transfixed, I watched it carefully as it heaved up its head like in a push-up and twisted up its head to stare me down. It was a defiant confrontational pose. Then it moved its head from side to side and then began to work its mandibles in a show of force, moving its retractable proboscis in and out, a dragon warning me of the fire in its belly. I panicked and jumped and stamped the baby bug with both feet four times but regretted this immediately because the dogs sent up an unbelievable din. When three flushes only made the pets progressively more manic and the blood from my hands stained the handle, I tiptoed away, trembling like one lost in the *Hammer House of Horror* series we watched on Usen's father's TV as kids.

I could deal with the welts and wounds. I could deal with the itches and scratches. I could even deal with the flat, fast, hungry bugs or the lazy engorged creatures, little mobile beans. But experiencing that see-through baby of theirs freaked me out. But, above all, I brimmed over with the dread that they were going to suckle on me till they matured and darkened and burst. I went back into the restroom to use my two mirrors to inspect my naked butt. I could not see a thing. No blood idling around a needle's prick, no little swelling, no enlarged sweat pore. These guys were clean, professional suckers! I was still trying to put my fear of the delayed itches into words when a rash of goose bumps began to pock my buttocks, small lighter mounds with a stiff strand of hair atop each, a Black soursop skin. When I touched my butt, it was cold and rubbery and numbed. How was I to know these were not the slow risings of the bites into visibility? I panicked and scrambled and dropped my little mirror.

It was time to abandon the apartment.

It was time to confide in Usen, no matter the cost. I put on my pajamas and came to stand in the middle of the living room, and on the fifth ring he answered his phone. "What's up, *da*?" he said from sleep. "Ekong, nobody calls nobody at two-thirty a.m. in America!"

"I'm sorry, my brother, I get *wahala*."

"Calm down, make it snappy. *Ade* weekday, for Christ's sake."

"*Nnang ikuk.*"

"What? *Akwa Awasi, no!*"

"It's bad, it's bad."

He told me to take it easy and started to laugh, a dry disconnected distant dreamy thing, and told me an Annang man was not supposed to be that afraid. "Please, let me move in with you," I said. "I know you'd never ask for it, but I shall pay you even more than I'm doing in Manhattan. *Mbok*, I've suffered silently for too long. And the bloodstains on my fingers right now smell worse than fireflies, and you knew how much I hated that smell as a kid. I shall be there by eight a.m."

THERE WAS SILENCE before he erupted in an angry, fully awake whisper: "So *you* brought this shit then to my home!"

"No, I didn't," I said.

"Well, since you slept over, we've not had peace."

"Ah no . . . *iyo*, but it wasn't me."

He became angrier as he told me Ujai was the worst hit. He said she started scratching after my visit. He blamed me for her cutting school, for their lying that the family had flu today, cold tomorrow, cough next week. He said Igwat now slept in a special plastic contraption they carpentered for him, to save his skin.

My night got worse.

Guilt sat on me like on Judas Iscariot. I felt like a man who had destroyed the only refuge he had. My grief reached another level altogether from the Monday my workplace knew of my infestation. Usen said I should pray he did not have to replace their furniture, threatening my family would have to return the piece of land his grandfather gave us before the war. He started telling me the number of New Yorkers who had fled from their homes because of bugs. I apologized again and again for visiting them. I explained I thought I had been itching because of a blood infection, which was why I bandaged my thumb heavily, to protect everyone.

On the speakerphone, Ofonime reminded him it was *ubiomikpe* in our culture to shout at someone at night, and in the background Igwat began to squeal. She begged Usen to be sensitive to me and reminded him my grandpa took over her father's cousin's tuition after Biafran patrols disappeared her father. "Sensitive, my ass!" he stopped her, screaming louder than the child. "Let's not becloud things with our Biafra bullshit and his coward grandpa. Ofonime, you sent me to comfort Ekong in the Australian restaurant. Knowing what we had here and feeling bad we didn't warn him in New Jersey, I even refused to hug him, to protect him . . . Why didn't he say *he* already had the shit? Ever since he started planning to visit America, he's never been sensitive to us.

"Now that Ujai has not seen any new bites for days, why should I allow this Hell's Kitchen super-carrier to relocate here? We must guard against re-infestation!"

Once it dawned on me my lodgings appeal was a direct danger to the children, I withdrew it and apologized and asked them to go back to bed. Ofonime ignored me and asked her husband how he knew they themselves did not give me the bugs during the visit or Mass or at the train station. "Please, perhaps Ekong could stay with us if he abandoned everything in Hell's Kitchen and subjected himself to *the* crazy bath we've been talking about?" she said.

"Even if he abandoned his Black skin totally like Tuesday Ita, I cannot let him jeopardize my kids' safety," Usen shouted.

"If you don't lower your voice, you'll wake our daughter up," she said. "And if she hears you quarrel with your BFF, she'll be gloomy for a week."

"I don't care!" he insisted.

I apologized to Ofonime and hung up.

WHEN I HAD GATHERED my spirits, I texted to praise Usen for prioritizing the children's safety. I begged them to share this *crazy bath* stuff with me. They thanked me for being understanding but ignored my request. When I pushed—like Jeff Wengui—they pointedly said it was not good for my health. They let me know they were no longer fighting, which gladdened my heart.

I washed my hands in warm water and soap, to banish the bedbug reek. I folded up my bed, like I would never sleep in it again. Then I sat on the recliner, my head filled with recollections of the two kids and mom in the *Times* article who were roasted for a year while the housing board ignored them. I was so angry I decided to risk everything to fight my infestation.

It was 3:14 a.m.

I called the landlord direct and left him a long stern voice mail, saying he should know he was also punishing the good tenants by avoiding my place. I also said I considered it cruel for one old man to torture another with a broken floor and bad windows. "Do you, Tony Canepa, live in such a rat hole with your family?" I sneered. "Have your grandchildren been bitten by bugs before? It's beyond inhuman to bully Greg Lucci into using his tears to blackmail me daily. I'm not afraid of your mafia shit! Now, listen up and move your ass: if you know the *secret* of dealing with this bug shit, justice demands you share it with me, ASAP." I left him my name, address, and phone numbers. And I told him in no uncertain terms I was Lucci's illegal subletee.

Just as I was ready to fight alongside Molly even without understanding American publishing, I was ready to fight this stuff even though I did not understand NYC housing laws. I was ready for whatever the combined forces of Greg Lucci, his so-called nephew cop, and the landlord would throw at my foreign Black ass. After all, my Seven Corners insurance covered shipment of my corpse back home—strangled or poisoned or spray-bulleted, like Amadou Diallo was in 1999.

I went to sleep on the recliner because I could not trust my bed anymore. Though I was exhausted, I could not sleep immediately. The recliner was uncomfortable and angry thoughts about Canepa and Lucci and American police filled my mind. *Why would Lucci keep throwing his nephew cop in my face?* I pondered. I wished he knew that our people could also avenge American police brutality against Black people by going after white Americans in African countries. I wished he knew Father Kiobel had just miraculously stopped our people from certain reprisal violence from consuming our white parishioners.

CHAPTER 28

I Wish I's in Heaven
Sitting Down

AT NOON, USEN SAID HIS LANDLORD HAD ORDERED THE extermination of his entire building. In excitement, I buzzed into Molly's office to declare I would meet with Liam Sanders alone. "How should I dress?" I asked. She said he did not care but that everyone loved my moss *senator* outfit at the prize ceremony, or I could wear a jacket. Then she said Jack had resigned to protest Emily's humiliation and had taken up a job at the Chad Twiss Agency.

I was happy the *ata-ufud ata-ufud* of a man was gone.

It was like a needle had been pulled from my ass. I did not acknowledge his departure when Emily, who had heard of Molly's summary version of New Jersey, called to sympathize. With her, I was able to share everything, including the happy reports of the Thanksgiving Mass.

After watching the video clips with Jack, she called to ask more questions about the sacristy, the masked cop tracking me through the coaches, how I coped that whole week, and what I thought of Usen's refusal to allow Bishop Salomone to visit them. Finally, she said, "Well, since New Jersey has already unfortunately happened, please tell Father Kiobel that, I, too, am touched by his bravery and tears and inclusion of Caro's family in the memorial. And, Ekong, take heart, too, for Father's story must remind you of your dad's."

"Yes, it's united us."

"Hey, Jack and I think this war memorial may be the best time to visit Ikot Ituno-Ekanem."

"Jack really thinks that? Unbelievable!"

"But I also want to thank you for the race chat with Molly, phobia or not. After her racist questions, she was crushed. I thought she'd quit her job. Telling her humans don't need to be perfect to fight for others . . . you taught her the importance of self-acceptance. Without this kind of self-examination, we can never acknowledge the hidden slippery racism of supposedly woke liberal America. I'm heartbroken way too many of us are like this. Ekong, I can't thank you enough for the enlightenment you've brought to me and your graciousness around Andrew & Thompson.

"This is also why your Bronx folks' parting words to Ujai at that train station broke me down. They reminded me of *Trails of Tuskegee*'s characters' hope in America even as their hell raged. It reminded me of my African American classmate's faithfulness to her story of sharecroppers' lynching no matter how much we bullied her. Listen, Usen and Ofonime's ability to reach instinctively for love, to make that decision in such a hate-charged train station, will stay with me forever!

AS SHE BEGAN TO TALK about my visit to Jack's office, I sat up, hoping he had confessed his racism and that perhaps she was going to pour out the grief of discovering her very lover was another Father Orrin. But she said Jack wanted us to pick a day for Broadway, because the dancing urchins in *Newsies* could remind me of the street children of northern Nigeria.

Finally, when I found my voice, I suggested mid-December for Broadway, to buy time to figure out how to publicly confront someone as slimy as Jack. When I hung up, I hated how he had conveniently swept his racism under our Nigerian shit. As the Annangs say, Jack was not the kind of bird to track on a rainy day. But my biggest worry was this could rupture my friendship with Emily. Could I handle the aftermath? Was it better to have a dear friend who could not spot the toxic racism in her lover or not to have a friend at all?

No, I must confront her! I swore silently to myself. Caro said I could not return home without this conversation with Emily. She said anybody who could forgive Molly for firing her deserved my honesty no matter what. She said I must confront Jack and Emily in mid-December during our Broadway outing. Father Kiobel said the trick was getting Emily to our memorial event without her boyfriend who called our food vomit.

I could not yet tell Emily that we were humiliated by Jack seeing our Thanksgiving clips. We could imagine him watching our people and silently cursing them while she wept. We could imagine him siding with Father Orrin and his minions, the way he came around to backing Lagoon Drinker. "I can imagine his disdain at my mere suggestion that Mary and Mommy had anything in common!" Father lamented.

THE FOLLOWING DAY, I got two emails from the Bekwarra family. The first said the old man got his visa and would be in New York the following week. I immediately sent my congratulations and sympathized with all their stress. I called Ofonime three times to share the good news. My calls did not go through. My texts failed as well. I tried Usen. Same thing. "But I'm no longer asking for accommodation!" I gasped when I realized they had blocked my number. I sent an email. Ofonime replied that they would be in touch shortly.

Ominous.

The second Bekwarra email started off as a general thank-you to all "who prayed and supported our old infirm dad through his America visa ordeal." But there was a special appreciation reserved for the big clerics of our area "for weeks of dry fasting during our struggle with the forces of Satan at the American embassy and for all your Visa Condolence Visits."

But I sat up when the email went on to solicit even more prayers for all visa interview victims, especially a certain "Montana-bound student who was shipped back to Nigeria from Salt Lake City International Airport and banned from America for five years and is now in a makeshift refugee clinic in Makurdi. His right leg has been cut off, the stump heavily bandaged." I googled the story quickly, for something would have to be seriously wrong for people across the country to know of this bleached embassy Tiv dancer guy—or was it another person altogether?

However, sadly his internet photos confirmed it was our beloved dancer. He had flunked his point-of-entry interview on his way to Montana; the news story said the Salt Lake City immigration officers had canceled his visa and deported him because he could not prove he would return to Nigeria after college; the boy insisted in the same article that in Utah he had not even been allowed to speak, as the immigration folks were shouting at him like exorcists. During the appeal in Lagos, according to the dancer, the consular lady kept saying, "Excellent, excellent!" but, in the end, denied him all the same.

After he returned to his minority village, the killer Fulani herdsmen, this fourth most deadly terrorist group in the world had descended, killing and maiming to grab the land. But the Buhari government had taken the side of the terrorists by simply moving survivors like the Tiv dancer into refugee camps and warning them to either share their lands with the terrorists or be killed. Next, the government attacked Bishop Matthew Kukah, Senator Shehu Sani, Rinu Oduala, Obadia Mailafia, and David Hundeyin for speaking up.[*]

---

[*] For more about the Buhari administration's "Your Blood or Your Land" policy, see https://www.hart-uk.org/wp-content/uploads/2019/12/Nigeria-Visit-Final-Report _Nov-2019-1-1.pdf. Also read the Fulani Farooq Kperogi's "Buhari Is Actively Instigating a Civil War" at https://www.herald.ng/sunday-igboho-buhari-is -actively-instigating-a-civil-war-by-farooq-kperogi/.

WHEN MY PHONE RANG that night as I strolled near Madame Tussauds, it was the last person I expected, Tuesday Ita—this Annang whose head was bumpier than NYC sidewalks. I was afraid he was calling to scold me for supposedly exposing his acquired whiteness back home. I wanted to sympathize with his rape and ordeal in the valley, but I knew the Umohs did not want him to know they had told me. I tried to tell Tuesday of the dancer's fate, but he simply said he was tired of Nigeria's dysfunction and started talking about the Umohs. He apologized on Usen's behalf for screaming at me the night he said I could not take refuge in his home. I told him I was not angry and was even ashamed I could have endangered the children.

"Thanks, Hughes, and good night, *asiere*!" I said to dismiss him.

"No, please, we have a little favor to ask," he said.

"And who's this *we*?"

"Look, your little friend Ujai is in trouble."

"What?"

I stopped by the curb to listen properly.

"Even the grandparents hope you cooperate . . . Ujai was awake and heard every insult Usen hurled at you and Ofonime."

"*Iya uwei!*"

He said she had been crying for days now about my banishment from their home. And then she was blaming her parents, also, for not allowing the bishop to visit, when the catechism said good Catholics obeyed their bishops. But having heard from Usen of my disappointment over the bishop not calling me, Tuesday complained the man of God had refused to call him, too. "The bishop was more interested in diversity," he grumbled. "America has lost its mind to this diversity shit. This must explain why Usen says your CEO takes you out to lunch weekly!"

When I ignored him and pointedly asked whether Ujai was okay, he said he had expected me with my literary acumen to sympathize with his freedom to change his skin color. He blamed us for supposedly blowing our one visit to his church out of proportion—something that should have passed for a little cross-cultural *dialogue*. He refused to believe the cops had followed us to the train station. He said if Father Orrin were the racist we had painted him to be, he would have handed over the tape of our fight behind the church to the police. Tuesday said he only supported the priest's suspension for the anti-Semitic remarks.

Then he blamed Father Kiobel for spreading the news of his color change. "Since Father Kiobel thinks he can turn me into a laughingstock back home, I'm going to sabotage his Biafran memorial plans!" he said menacingly. "Wait till the folks I've paid finish digging out his past. They've already figured out why the Ogoni bastard is obsessed with new clothes!"

I implored Tuesday to allow Father Kiobel to finish the story of his refugee flight from northern Nigeria himself. I promised to ensure the memorial centered on tribalism, which he, Tuesday, believed was our biggest threat. "Please, we'll officially invite you, Hughes," I said. "You can even send a letter to be read out in church. Providence has given us this chance to reconcile our peoples."

"Part of the memorial, possibly a Mass, should be by the river," he said. "Usen said he told you of my near-execution by that river."

"I'm really sorry about what Biafra did to you. Yes, I appreciate this input. God bless you. There'll definitely be a ceremony in the valley . . . but, Hughes, hey, you're pulling my leg about Ujai, right?"

He laughed portentously and said that ever since Ujai saw a pack of baby bedbugs coming down the leg of her bed days after the New Jersey incident, she had not been the same girl. Her dreams had been violent and loud. The teachers were worried about her frequent absences. And now she was insisting she wanted to see "Best Uncle" even if I had all the bugs in the world.

"Oh, now I get it: that's why they've blocked my number, right?" I said.

"Yes, yes, that evening of your call, Ujai saw new bites . . . I'm actually sent to tell you they've even deleted your numbers *ke* America and *ke* Nigeria, to prove to Ujai you're truly gone," he said.

"Gone where?"

"Luckily, we've convinced her you were quarreling with Usen from Ikot Ituno-Ekanem—where American immigration had suddenly deported you!"

"Me?"

"You were *deported* five days ago, turned in by those neighbors of yours. Isn't it better for Ujai *ee*-continue *ee*-hate immigration than for you to re-infest their home?"

He said, to meet Ujai halfway about Bishop Salomone, her parents had put the bishop on speakerphone yesterday evening. Nobody talked about Father Orrin, except when Ujai herself asked whether the bishop was as good in his homilies and recited the Father Orrin Pledge for him. When the bishop laughed a deep bubbly funny laugh, she said she could not reconcile the laugh with his serious sacristy portrait, which led to more laughs. They all bantered about the bishop's parents and friends and childhood, his favorite NFL and NBA teams and stuff. Now Tuesday praised the bishop for gracefully handling Usen's insulting questions, like whether the cleric had ever visited the homes of his Black congregants. Bishop Salomone said no but that he would be honored to begin with their family. Tuesday thought the bishop's honesty had finally convinced the Umohs to assure him of a future invite. And, at least, Ujai was relieved she was not living with evil Catholics.

"Don't worry, I shall replace you at her school presentation!" he announced.

"*Iyo-ng*, no way!" I said, gutted.

"But you're already back in Nigeria, get it? Her class was quite excited to see me three years ago. Listen, her extended family has already told her they've seen you back home. The whole village has protested your deportation. You know, Ujai's mind is fragile . . . Listen, I would never have lied to the girl. I would have handled this differently. But where we are now, *abeg*, *mbok*, we need your cooperation."

AFTER WE HUNG UP, while I was still typing an email to Ofonime to ascertain the truth, Tuesday sent a short video. It was of my Bronx family in their living room. Ujai was weeping while her father scolded her for doubting I was gone. Her mother stood behind her, sobbing and dabbing the girl's forehead.

Usen had no shirt on, and the video caught his profile, and it was as though the insects had exclusively feasted on his big hard stomach. The scars were whitish and sandy, as if the man had lain on the beach. In the background, the plaintive voice and sonorous guitar of R. L. Burnside was weeping the Negro spiritual "I Wish I's in Heaven Sitting Down." Over this, Ujai's voice, sharp and fiery, pushed back. She was not only crying because of how I was tied up and deported by ICE and how I could never visit them again, but for what might happen to her brother if the bugs finally got to him.[*] I knew right away they wanted me to know they had a real housing crisis, not some gimmick to stop my visit.

Ujai insisted she wanted my Nigerian address so she and her friends could write me. "Uncle Ekong just deserves to know how sad and ashamed me and my friends are of our shitty immigration!" she screamed. "Mommy, you can't suddenly forget how they terrorized you in the embassy." Her parents ignored her. She began to cry. I deleted the rest of the video; I could not keep watching how our evil was boomeranging on our kids. If I could not handle the sight of one baby bug, what was the pack of baby bugs Ujai saw doing to her friable mind? And if Ofonime, who could not stand immigration at all, could stoop to use the same agency to deceive her daughter, it meant her own helplessness was worse than that of the Park Slope mother whom the *New York Times* said fought bugs for a

---

[*] See https://www.nytimes.com/2018/04/04/us/california-bedbug-lawsuit.html.

year while the housing authorities dawdled. I remembered Ujai saying clearly in church, "Uncle, you have to do and say things right in our school; otherwise, you'll mess up my entire life!" And here I was doing exactly that, being the architect of her worst misfortune, even without stepping into her school.

I mourned for her American childhood.

I mourned for the home she thought she had in Nigeria.

Her childhood was definitely different from mine, different from Keith's, different from the Biafran waiter's, different from Tuesday's and from what Father Kiobel was only beginning to reveal about his. It was different from Alejandra's or Emily's, or that of the girl Emily beat up in Alabama, different from that of her age mates forced into child marriages across northern Nigeria.

Ujai was our Black diaspora burning at both ends.

CHAPTER 29

I love quad biking on the beaches of Swakopmund

FOUR DAYS AFTER I BLOODIED MY SHEETS WITH BUG carcasses, the powder was gone from my cubicle. It was unbelievable, though my body ached from sleeping in the recliner.

I checked myself to make sure I was at the right cubicle. Then I squatted and crawled and studied the place, like I wanted to undo every thread in the carpet, to ensure I was seeing well. Though I could now smell a whiff of alcohol on my desk, I felt free. *The cleaners can drink all they want at my desk and Emily's!* I said silently to myself. I felt good. I felt safe. This was when I realized how much this shit had crippled my spirit. When I sat down, I still kept checking under my desk. Then I stood up and plugged and unplugged my cord in all the sockets, in case something fell out. Nothing. I visited others' cubicles to see whether the powder had relocated thither. Nope.

Trying to get used to its absence took a bit of time, I must say. By lunchtime, I had made a short video of the entire carpet and dated it. The sense of violation was gone. And all day, I played the music of Flavour featuring Semah and felt like doing cartwheels on the streets of New York.

BUT THAT AFTERNOON, Caro told me Our Lady of Guadalupe had started a novena for Ujai because her parents sent word she was losing her mind. She would see a shrink if prayers failed. Nobody told Ikot Ituno-Ekanem she was suffering from bedbugs, for none would show up for prayers; it would become a village joke. "What's important is that our child is suffering," Father Kiobel told me solemnly. I texted Tuesday to pass on the word to her parents that I, too, would do a private novena in solidarity. I went straight from watching soccer at the Australian restaurant to the Actors' Chapel for evening Mass.

Of course, it felt totally strange to be in church again in America. I swallowed my anger continually like saliva and shuddered at every turn. Nothing else could have dragged me back except the guilt of Ujai's trauma. Having lit a votive candle, I sat in the last pew and said the novena. I avoided looking at the sacristy door. When the priest started Mass, to control my anger at his New Jersey colleague, I double-dosed on my prayers by saying the rosary. I dug in and persevered throughout.

THAT NIGHT, I sat down to edit another novella in the anthology, "Biafra in Rome." It was about the spray-bulleting of ten Italian oil workers by Biafran commandos in May 1969—which effectively ended the Biafran War.* The author was an Igbo woman married to an Italian in Rome; she had said in her cover letter that she was moved to write the story because her cleaner had called her *terrorista biafrana* the day she fired her. The novella was written from the point of view of Italians who were infuriated by General Ojukwu's broadcast saying that he had killed their compatriots to raise

---

*Read Roy Doron's "Biafra and the Agip Oil Workers: Ransoming and the Modern Nation State in Perspective" in *African Economic History*, 2014.

the consciousness of white folks, "the owners of the world," to the slaughter of the Igbos by Nigeria.

It was our worst Italian summer since WWII. By the time we understood that once the so-called saboteurs were taken they never returned, Europe had forgotten about her dead and went on her knees to beg Ojukwu for mercy. We feared for the 18 European oil workers, including Italians, Biafra had also abducted and put on death row on charges of sabotage. As our grandpa said, "No Black man has ever held us by our balls like this!"

We couldn't understand why this new newest Black Catholic country would treat us, the owners of the Vatican, like trash. And the longer the Mafia bosses met in Palermo, the more powerless we felt. We started wearing black when our military failed to come up with a rescue plan, and rumors said intelligence from Britain, Biafra's colonial masters, said Ojukwu was so irrational he'd kill the prisoners if Western countries even dreamed of a rescue. Another said once France, which had openly supported Biafra, and Russia and China declared their helplessness and urged caution, our Italian government had turned to the Vatican, to pressure the Irish missionaries in Biafra to convince Ojukwu, a devout Catholic, not to kill the prisoners. Some Israelis who were interested in helping Biafra in exchange for oil—and because the Igbos said they were Black Jews—now hesitated. And we heard American politicians who had hitherto been neutral hated Biafra.

Worse, after learning of the heartbreak of Chinua Achebe, the Biafran War envoy, as he futilely pleaded with his mad leader to free our brethren, Italy collapsed in rare national depression . . .

With dark humor, "Biafra in Rome" went on to say how the condemnation of the fate of these European oil workers on the U.S.

Senate floor quickly turned America against Biafra. It detailed how
the Pope's personal letter to Ojukwu, a devout Catholic, helped in
the release of the death row inmates, and how the world decided it
had seen enough of Igbo "self-determination." It was quite painful
reading how the Nigerian forces, armed with this diplomatic victory,
went in for the kill, again massacring Igbos, the center of Biafran
support, and shooting down Red Cross planes, as Ojukwu fled into
exile in Côte d'Ivoire in January 1970. The story ended with the
revenge of Italy, when it dumped nuclear waste in Koko in defunct
Biafra in 1988, eighteen years after the war, an hour's drive from the
site of its citizens' massacre.

DESPITE MY LOVE FOR these "international" details, I quickly
decided to throw out "Biafra in Rome," because it was too dense and
lacked a believable Italian voice. I began to email the author, urging
her to write, instead, a creative nonfiction essay about her relationship with her cleaner and what the *"terrorista biafrana"* insult did
to her war memories . . .

Lucci called to berate me for contacting the landlord about my
bedbug issues. I was afraid the two enemies had united to attack me.
I decided to confront this pig, as I'd confronted Jack in his office. I
ran downstairs and stood in front of our block, where I could yell
as I liked into the phone. Lucci said the landlord had promised to
send an inspector next week. But I was not in any mood for games
and said, "Damn it, tell that hyena American landlord it can't wait
till next week! How many fucking inspections does the scrooge
need to know we're the Ground Zero of *Cimex lectularius* . . . ? I'm
hanging up."

"What happened to the gentle, sympathetic African I met in late
August, who promised to handle the bugs himself?"

"I'm going to sue your ass for my rent! I've figured out your housing laws. You're a heartless shameless racketeer!"

That silenced him.

"Good. Since we now understand each other," I said, pressing my advantage, "never ever call my number again. I owe you nothing. I wish I could tell you how beautiful my house in Ikot Ituno-Ekanem is, how much it's a step down to be living in this unelevatored trash can."

"Well, I really hate to have to do this," he said, exhaling noisily, clapping twice. "But I want you out of my *trash can* by tomorrow night because I'm moving back in!

"And, remember, you've been known to eat at Blue Fin and really love Father Duffy Square in Times Square. You shop at the Food Emporium. Folks have even seen you some nights at the piers praying your stupid finger rosary—and they didn't mistake you for a Muslim and push you into the water! You're in love with Starbucks, and your church of choice is the Actors' Chapel, after initially trying out St. Patrick's Cathedral. You've visited the Bronx once, at least . . . you want to mess with me? Listen, I don't think you have a gut appreciation of what it means to trace my bloodline to Sicily. Ekong, you've already fumbled twice: One, contacting the landlord, my enemy. But since you were nice to me in the beginning, I let it slide. Two, you made Molly think I'm a racist, according to her uncle. I want you out of my space tomorrow!"

"Ye-yes, sir," I stammered, my head throbbing with the threat of being pushed over the pier. He said I must be standing outside, because the background to my phone was too noisy, and he commanded me to get inside to avoid the cold. "Okay, sir, I pro-promise never to call Tony Canepa again!"

"Why should I believe you this time?"

"I swear by the Blessed Sacrament!"

"Bullshit, just get out of my pied-à-terre. If you Africans poured half the sulfur you pour on white folks onto your tribal leaders, maybe your multi-ethnic countries would meet their potential. I know what I'm talking about—I've been to festivals in Senegal, and I love quad biking on the beaches of Swakopmund in Namibia."

Consumed by the image of being pushed from the pier, I dashed inside. He paused to say he knew I was inside now. I feared if they saw my finger rosary that meant they really came close. Or were they using binoculars on me? Was I followed every time I went out? Was it one person or a group?

✂

A WHITE MAN THREATENED to drown me.

I was tormented by the fact that Black subjugation was accomplished by the unbelievable magnification of terror across racial lines—in the blood-soaked voyages across the Atlantic, this very ocean which separated New York from Ikot Ituno-Ekanem, these voyages which shall always cast a shadow on any Black person, irrespective of whether they still called Africa home or had bloodied their knuckles and heads for four hundred years on the iron door of America's heart.

If Lucci's words pierced my heart—I who had a home to return to in Nigeria, an extended family, an ethnic group, a language, a culture, an ancestral land—I could only imagine what it would do to African Americans. What would it take for America to finally process African Americans into *citizens*? I could hear the echoes of the stamps of my visa denials by Santa Judessa and Lagoon Drinker.

Where would Keith Jim-Stehr go after four hundred years?

I knew neither Brad nor Emily nor Molly nor Paul would ever *deport* Keith. I could imagine, too, how these comments would boil the blood of those Americans who recently risked their lives to console our Ikot Ituno-Ekanem with the true message of Christ, these folks who had even made us believe we could risk reconciliation within Biafra.

"Mr. Lucci, listen, I'm sorry for ignoring all your phone calls," I said in an attempt to get him to rescind the eviction order.

"You made me look really stupid!"

"I really apologize for insulting you. I should never have threatened to sue you. I don't know what got into me. I feel really bad . . . since you asked in your voice mails how many relatives I lost in the war, well, my family really suffered—"

"Please, please, your old friend's heart can't handle too much pain today! Okey dokey, you can stay on in the apartment. Apology accepted. Just be nice, okey dokey?"

He began to cough like his lungs were on fire. I apologized endlessly for causing him so much stress, till he hung up.

CHAPTER 30

Canepa's lawyers had sent me a strongly worded letter

THE FOLLOWING SATURDAY, BRAD, ALEJANDRA, KEITH, and I rode the C back from getting our chemicals from Washington Heights, because the bugs had migrated back to their fumigated apartments. Keith came anyway, though his apartment had been safe since he had hired the expensive firm and sniffer dogs.

Our interminable affliction, which brought us together in the first place, had finally sent us on a group outing. We were as animated as boarding students going home on vacation, because finally we had got all the authentic chemicals. We laughed triumphantly and continually. Brad and Alejandra looked honestly funny; their beautiful J.Crew boots were now shapeless and lopsided due to PackTiting—something they said had to do with using heat to rid an object of bedbugs. But I became more determined to buy the shoes for Caro and myself, because no shoes were meant to be cooked like that. We laughed at the pest control guy in Washington Heights, who swore we all had the wrong mattress covers because the right ones should have "anti-bedbug certified" written on them. He sold us his.

Outside the subway station, when I kept ignoring Lucci's renewed calls, Alejandra winked and said finally I had a secret lover and had lost my gentleman's status in her eyes. I said it was Lucci, who wanted to checkmate Canepa, whose lawyers had sent me a strongly worded letter two days before. It ordered me to pay rent straight to their client, beginning with December's. The lawyers had warned me how "aliens" could be criminally prosecuted under New York housing laws, how I might never be able to leave America because of the slow case. They had mined my particulars from my angry voice mail to the landlord; the copy of the letter for Lucci had also come to my mailbox. On the phone, Lucci had said I must trash the letter but should not offer the landlord any information as it was a final stratagem to cancel my apartment's lease. Lucci also insisted that, on this important matter of forking out another December rent, *his* lawyer had counseled I should write the landlord's lawyers promising to pay after Christmas when I would already have arrived in Nigeria.

Alejandra suggested I should write a nice appeal letter straight to the landlord, not the lawyers, during Thanksgiving week. She said, if I was Catholic, she would advise me to say so in the letter. Keith said, as a former friend of Canepa's, he believed mentioning soccer would be equally effective, that Canepa attended every World Cup with his family, that he came to America at age nine and his beloved Palermo soccer club and Mafia violence was how he remembered his Italian childhood. He said while he did not know how I could phrase all of this in the letter, I should not be surprised if he knew more about Nigerian soccer than me. Alejandra said I should just say that as a child I rooted for the Italian national team when they won the World Cup in Spain in 1982, that it was my first-ever World Cup and I loved Paulo Rossi's goals and Dino Zoff's goalkeeping heroics. Jeff and Brad said to include rent receipts, and that, most importantly, I would leave before Christmas.

On reaching home, I quickly got the stuff ready in a big brown envelope. Yet I had no guts to mail it to the landlord, because I was afraid Lucci was monitoring my movements. I hid it deep in my suitcase like I never wanted to remember it.

THAT EVENING, I was caught off guard when the landlord him-self called. His voice tight and guarded, he had gone straight to the point: his inspectors would finally come on Monday. I got off my recliner, my knees unfeeling.

"Good . . . g-g-good evening, Mr. Canepa!" I greeted him first, stammering, balling my fingers.

"You heard what I said about inspectors, right?" he barked.

"I did. But, permit me to begin by thanking you for calling back though I'm an illegal occupant of your property. God bless you for your patience."

"No, wait, did you *not* get my lawyers' letters to you and Greg Lucci?"

"I got them, sir, and forwarded his."

"Otherwise, we can't be having this conversation!"

"Please, I just want to say I'm sorry for all the pain I've caused you, my landlord. The truth is I didn't even know I was illegal. So I'm in a state of total shock and confusion right now, as any three-month visitor to a strange country who receives a letter like this would."

"Okay."

"And, cross my heart, I shouldn't have shouted at you in my voice mail!"

"I think so, too."

"Well, since August I've been here on a fellowship at Andrew & Thompson."

"Yes, I know of Andrew & Thompson . . . Go on."

"I am sorry, too, for berating you about the *bedbug secret*!"

"What bedbug secret?"

"I thought I said something like that in my voice mail that night."

"No, I listened to it again five minutes ago."

"My bad, then."

"Listen, I have to call up more tenants and subletees elsewhere, hopefully legal ones."

"I promise you I shall return to Nigeria shortly before Christmas. Please, I'd be grateful if you could call your esteemed lawyers off my ass. It would really be sad if a little feud with your fellow Sicilian-American Catholic affected this innocent Annang-Nigerian Catholic!"

"But Lucci, in response to my voice mail, said you're his bosom friend, that you met in a vacation on the beaches of Swakopmund in Namibia."

"Really?"

"Well, he knows an awful lot about your life, your decision not to have children, how I must not disturb you because you're really traumatized writing a memoir at Andrew & Thompson about the Biafran War. In five voice mails, he went on and on about how, unlike African Americans, you so gently helped him understand his racist blind spots. When you first arrived, you said the rosary together on the pier and attended Mass together—"

"Please, permit me to interrupt you! As the ancestors say, I disrupt the words from your mouth, not your heart."

"Spare me the proverbs, will you? What's the date on your return ticket?"

"December twentieth."

"But are you truly writing about the war?"

"Yes, I'm editing a war anthology, sir."

He was quiet.

I assured him I did not even need the inspectors anymore. This was because we were so positive about annihilating the bugs the following day, Sunday, given the fury with which we were going to deploy the new chemicals. And I did not believe his inspectors would find anything on Monday. After I had said all the sweet Italian soccer stuff Alejandra had suggested, after I had explained I had already paid December rent as deposit to Lucci, the landlord cleared his throat and said if I left before January, he would waive my rent. He said, though he disbelieved everything Lucci said, he was cutting me slack, for he himself remembered the devastating posters of the Biafran War. I thanked him and said goodbye, but he asked if I could come downstairs.

"I'm already under your window!" he announced tautly as my heart skipped. "Ekong, it would be nice to conclude our little agreement with a handshake." I went to look down the window, only to see a fat old man waving to me. He was in a milk-white suit and matching shoes and a shiny yellow newsboy cap. I could not tell whether he was sitting or standing. From this height, he looked like an egg sunny-side up on the curb. Afraid he might ask for proof of my paid rent in order to implicate Lucci, I decided to lie that I had paid cash. For my safety, I studied the street carefully before going down.

Standing up delicately from a folding cane seat, Tony Canepa wobbled politely up to me. He was a bulky man with soft features and his jowls sagged like his face was just hanging on to his quick large eyes. He looked really familiar, but I could not place him. I blurted out that I might have met him before. He shook his head slowly like it might fall off his neck and offered a trembling two-handed handshake. As he struggled for words, his eyes blinked as though he had forgotten something precious. I steadied him. Looking him in the face, I reassured him I would leave before Christmas.

He cleared his throat and explained he actually wanted to meet me because I said I was sorry. He said he was touched, for New Yorkers never apologized to him, no matter how much they abused his properties or left nasty voice mails. He moaned that relatives in his beloved Palermo had revealed Lucci's grandfather was an inveterate soccer ticket racketeer, just like his progeny. "Please, my brother, pray that soon Saint Joseph, the patron saint of landlords, will take Lucci off my property and out of my life," he said, his eyes closed. Though everyone had said he was a talker, I knew he had to be really frustrated with Greg Lucci to pour all this out to a total stranger.

"THERE ARE PEOPLE NICKNAMED Zoff and Rossi in your village?" the landlord said, lightening up, going back to what I had told him earlier on.

"Absolutely, sir," I said as I helped him settle back onto his cane seat.

"Good. Let me tell you the story of how your Nigerian soccer team converted my grandkids to ardent soccer buffs at the 1998 World Cup in Nantes, France—"

"Nigeria vs. Spain. Everything stood still in Nigeria. No traffic, nothing."

"Yes, yes, the Spanish supporters, in their red and white, were already triumphal in their drumming and dancing. But your Nigerian fan club was unyielding. Your diaspora people flew in from all over the world! In green and white, they filled the atmosphere with singing and drumming and trumpeting; they gyrated and danced as though they were going to spill onto the pitch."

"Sir, there's nothing like the World Cup."

"And I've always loved how your team gels, despite its diversity, all the divisions back home. Suddenly there's no tribe, no religion, nothing but possibilities! Someday I shall tell you how I came to know a bit about your country. I'm just happy Spain has since let Blacks into its team, unlike Argentina!"

"Who'll save the country of my beloved Pope Francis and Maradona?"

"Ekong, it still hurts I didn't see Spain's second goal against Nigeria live two minutes into the second half. I was jostling back from buying hot dogs, burgers, and drinks, since my American grandchildren hated *les galette-saucisses*. Worse, the ecstasy of the Spanish fans knocked most of the food on the floor. The kids took one look at my face and knew I wasn't going back."

"Spain two, Nigeria one . . . *na shakara*."

"For the next twenty-six minutes, the game hung in a balance.

Spain missed their chances and Nigeria dug in. To beat back the tension rising from the pitch like a fog, everyone, except my disgruntled grandkids, exploded into mammoth waves as spectators rose and hollered. Finally, the Spaniards succumbed to pressure, peeing on themselves, conceding an own goal from a fluke shot by Garba Lawal. Nigeria two, Spain two!"

Tony Canepa bolted up and folded his chair to really dramatize things, as his voice rose above the evening traffic and a film of tears lit up his eyes. When he took off his yellow cap and smiled and laughed, I knew immediately he was the old man in the portrait on my shelf, a portrait Lucci had once made me believe was his, a portrait I had smashed under the bath.

Now I masked my shock at Lucci's lie in big laughter, clapping as Canepa recounted how some Nigerians had completely stopped watching the match and were lost in a colorful dance. I laughed even more when he attempted to mimic our fans' *asa-asara* dance, the kind of display TV cameras never picked up, because the match itself was too riveting—blink-and-you-miss stuff. "But Ekong, the world can never forget that twenty-five-yard half-volley thunderbolt from Oliseh," Canepa said, giving the air an uppercut. "That rocket graced the post and bulged the onion bag. You guys sank the Spanish armada and took the lead for the first time, twelve minutes from the final whistle. Nigeria three, Spain two."

I told him how that goal stole my mind and I suddenly found myself seated silently on the beer-wet floor under the bar table drinking palm wine in celebration, how I couldn't see the TV screens but just the legs of the chanting crowd hopping like in slow motion. I was feeling the underside of the table with my palms like one who had finally touched the sky but was still singing, "Higher and higher." He recounted how the swashbuckling Jay-Jay Okocha orchestrated our team's new self-confidence, opening up spaces for us to shine, how we played like a powerful intricate machine made up of 250 or 500 parts representing our ethnic groups. "I told you I know a bit about your country and war!" he hollered, holding my shoulders.

"We all sang the referee's name, imploring him to remain fair till the end, because too many Black teams never get their dues even in soccer! One day, FIFA shall regret fining and shaming Black players who protest racism from the fans directed at them on the pitch by walking off!"

"Ha, you said it, boss, you s-a-i-d it!" I agreed, shaking his hand, bowing.

"My grandkids were shivering, chewing their nails, stamping their feet, cussing, irrevocably falling in love with the beautiful game before the final whistle . . . Ekong, I need to run. Are you sure you don't want exterminators?"

"I'm positive."

"Listen, if you want to hang around to experience American Christmas, that's fine. But I know by New Year you'll be watching European soccer under some bar table back home, ha. Because in January my lawyers shall throw the kitchen sink at your *friend*. I must upgrade the apartment and rent it to a new tenant!"

After Canepa had gifted me with a bottle of wine from his car and left, I called up Lucci to say I had promised the landlord I would take care of the bugs. He was quiet. "Did you give him the rent details?" he barked. I said no. To assure him I had not broken my promise to protect his lease, I explained that his enemy had called me, not vice versa. He relented and chuckled when I assured him even Nigerian housing judges would not rule against bosom friends like us.

THE NEXT DAY, Keith was already hard at work when I returned Jeff's chair. The Asian American burst out laughing, because no one wanted to remember how it got into my apartment. It was like very serious spring cleaning. Personally, I spent a long time unscrewing the panels from all electrical outlets and joints, which the Washington Heights pest control guy emphasized were the main conduit for bugs traveling in between apartments and buildings. I let my boom box do its thing, thumping out Angelique Kidjo's "Conga Habenera" and Bez Idakula's "Say."

But, as I sprayed the JT Eaton Kills Bedbugs white powder through its long nozzle, as directed, into the now-exposed sockets and boxes and joints, it dawned on me this was the *same* powder on my office carpet. I stopped because my hands shook, and I sat on the floor. The fact that I had always suspected the office thing was made specifically for me did not ease the shock.

I played with the powder a bit, fingering it, smelling it, basically reenacting that day I knelt in my cubicle to study it. Now, when I sneezed, a procession of diverse feelings went through me. At first it felt like someone had bugged my cubicle. I was angry. Then I felt violated, as though I should have been told. I was disappointed. It did not matter who did this, though my mind blamed it on the Humane Society Two.

When I called him, Father Kiobel wanted to laugh but could not. "Ekong, I must tell you this," he said. "Of all your American troubles, nothing has scared me like you breathing this carpet powder stuff day in, day out. I had hoped you were hallucinating about it. But when it disappeared from your cubicle, it started appearing in my dreams! I just pray Ujai doesn't need a shrink . . . it's not looking good." I pleaded, if it came to that, he must let her parents know I was ready to pay for her mental health costs.

I went back to work as though my zeal could heal her: I screwed the panels back on and powdered the backs of the fridge, stove, microwave, TV, even the grille of the AC, which had been turned off earlier in the fall. After replacing the mattress cover, I exploded in one last long blitz, spraying everything in the apartment with JT Eaton Kills Bedbugs Plus and Steri-Fab. The alcohol in the latter made me sneeze again, and I knew right away this was the mystery alcohol on my desk and Emily's. At the end, I vacuumed the place to destroy the eggs even though I did not still know what they looked like. Since I had no PackTite to bake the books Andrew & Thompson had given me, I used the powder to draw a thick ring on the floor around the bookshelf. Carefully, to save the books—or to trap them, if the bugs were already there—I employed water to cement and set the edges of the ring, so the heat vent would not blow it away.

Finally, I took everything again to the laundromat. Brad and Keith were playing Scrabble, swigging big cans of cold beer dressed up in brown bags. Brad was telling Keith about the soldiers in his family. I silently retreated to the doorway, glad Keith was listening to him. But when Brad saw me, he started laughing that Alejandra had overheard me and the landlord talking soccer.

"Hey, the joy of finally becoming a *legal* subletee!" I said.

"It's fucking sweet to have you in New York, you know!" Brad said.

"Not fair, you guys should've invited me along to this laundromat World Cup," I said.

"Come on," Keith said. "We didn't think you could ever finish unscrewing your Twentieth World electrical outlets today."

When I stretched and began to tell them how much my back ached, how my chest was pounded by sneezes, Keith nudged me to keep it low. After I stuffed my load in the machines, we went outside, where I finally thanked Brad for washing my vomit off the stairwell. The November skies were cheerless, and the black birds of New York had taken to them as though their mirth alone could poke holes in the bleakness to let a late afternoon sunshine drip down. It did not bother us much, because we believed the sun was up there anyway and, if it were not, we had imbued a long drab day with the energy of spring.

CHAPTER 31

The eye must learn to behold the sun

TUESDAY AFTER THE WAR ON BEDBUGS, I RETURNED TO my bed from the recliner like one forced to visit the site of his horrible accident as a confidence boost.

Later that day in the office, when Molly summoned me, I saw stacks of familiar books on the floor. Isidore Okpewho's *The Last Duty*, Noo Saro-Wiwa's *Looking for Transwonderland*, J. P. Clark's *Song of a Goat* and *The Casualties*, Lindsay Barrett's *A Memory of Rivers*, Igoni Barrett's *Blackass*, Max Siollun's *Oil, Politics and Violence*, Helon Habila's *Oil on Water*, Tanuri Ojaide's *The Beauty I Have Seen*, Fola Olewole's *Reluctant Rebel*, Odia Ofeimun's *The Poet Lied*, Ben Okri's *The Famished Road*—all quickly caught my eye. I immediately squatted to admire the covers. It was like I was in a bookstore dedicated to Niger Delta issues.

"Ordered them as holiday gifts for friends," she said impatiently.

"Wow!" I said.

"Ekong, I'm so sorry to tell you this, but Liam has canceled your lunch meeting."

I rose from my seat.

"Oh no . . . wait," I said.

"Yeah, rather unfortunate," she said.

"Any reason?"

"Ekong, his email said he had a scheduling conflict."

I shrugged and lowered myself onto the couch.

"That's okay, I can wait," I said.

"No, no, there are some crazy politics going on here. He didn't offer to reschedule." She read out the complimentary parts of Liam's email, I supposed to soften the blow: *Molly, we're very honored to have provided Ekong with the space to work on such an important project! I know you're really impressed by his gifts and graciousness and industry and boldness. His presence has been great for Andrew & Thompson. Please, let him know that, like you, I look forward to more collaboration with Mkpouto Books.*

I was going to ask Molly to thank him for me, but she shifted angrily in her chair. "I'm so disappointed because I got you all psyched up," she said, her freckles redder than beets. According to her, Paul said Chad said Angela said Liam was backing out because he was afraid I would bring up Emily's firing. Angela had accused me of being so angry I had shouted that Liam was an "incurable racist." She was also telling folks I had threatened to beat up Jack over *egusi*, how she found him quite shaken when she responded to his SOS right after my visit to Jack's office, how scared she was I might similarly invade her office.

Though I could see how all of these lies could scare Liam off, I was humiliated. Suddenly his sweet letter felt bitter, like untreated *etidot*. There was no need to say anything, though, because Molly was even more upset. I held on to my knees and breathed slowly. As they say, if you have nothing else to hold on to, your knees are always there. I could never get used to how the crazy politics of Andrew & Thompson always left me exposed as a minority. The head voices, these stupid noises that emanated from these same offices, taunted me for not listening to their cancel-the-fucking-lunch advice when I canceled the marketing and publicity rotations.

For the first time, I googled Liam. I wanted an image to which to direct my anger. His photos showed a tall lean modest man, almost shy of the camera. He wore a smile behind dark glasses in all of them, which seemed to fence him off from my bitterness, while he enjoyed the privilege of peering at every pore on my face.

Knowing Angela Stevens could deceive even Satan, I swallowed hard. I tried to imagine what I could have advised Liam Sanders, my fellow bedbug victim and diversity advocate, at lunch beyond sharing my American experience: Would I have said: "I honestly urge you to go ahead and visit your foreign charities, the soup kitchens of India and fishing villages of Togo and the *banlieues* of Belgium, wherever. Periodically, too, I urge you to do a spell or two of voluntary community service on Indian reservations and former slave plantations across this beautiful country. Because, if humane people like you or corporate boards who have sunk untold wealth into creating these important literary companies did not feel comfortable around people of color, or POCs, how could you open the doors of your precious businesses to us? Mary of New Jersey went against her bosom friend and pastor. Are you ready to fire your Harvard classmate Angela to have Andrew & Thompson run right? Like Alejandra Ledesma, my Latina neighbor, would you sacrifice the comfort of extended family to change the toxic conversation about minorities . . . ?"

"Don't worry about Liam," Molly said, like she was reading my mind. "Our colleagues know better than to pay attention to Angela." And though she added that some of them had confirmed Jack was in distress after my visit to his office, he himself preferred to talk about the shoddy way Emily was axed. And he was still trying to recruit volunteers for animal shelters across the city. Molly also said the grapevine said Jack actually resigned because he thought Angela had leaked to me his "private-comic" phone call with Chad.

"God bless our colleagues, *mbok*!" I said.

"Amen."

"And *diong a*-Jack-*am* as well, but *k'ukpok utong*!"

"That must be a blessing, too. Of course, I knew you never

called Liam racist because of the very sensitive way you handled my issues. You know, we'll have a diversity training workshop in mid-December, to really sit together to thrash stuff out."

I almost shouted this was bullshit. What was the point of running a diversity workshop for all these intelligent white people, instead of simply hiring minorities? My disappointment stirred in me a distant echo of Father Orrin pleading he needed time to prepare his church "slowly towards becoming the kind of Church *you* have in mind." It baffled me that publishing houses, these shrines where literature is manufactured, celebrated, and worshipped, was leaving itself so open to ridicule from other industries which had diversified long ago. I thought we were too smart for this kind of shit.

TODAY, MY PATIENCE SAVED ME from expressing my anger because Molly herself had always been honest with me. I cleared my throat and bitterly laid out my story, from the Humane Society Two's fake apologies to Jack's "private-comic" phone call to the urge to puke on Chad to my visit to Jack's office. When I finished, Molly, who had since sunk into her seat and clasped her fingers as if in prayer, was tense. "Lord . . . what you've described here, ah, disturbs me," she stuttered, mopping sweat from her brows, looking around disgustedly like she was sitting in a dump. "I think . . . I'm truly depressed this is happening under my watch. Please, um, if I may ask, how did Emily react when you told her?"

"I'm still working out how to tell her. When *ekpa-mkpud*, the gnat, comes from the sky, the eye must learn to behold the sun. But, you know, they're planning to visit Ikot Ituno-Ekanem."

"Ugh, no! Emily just has to hear the things you've just shared."

"Now, Molly, listen!" I stood up and leaned onto her desk with my two palms flat on it and calmly spoke my mind. "Scrap this diversity training shit! You know, in my research I've discovered that minority

authors and editors like Kacen Callender, Preeta Samarasan, Rox-
ane Gay, and Vanessa Willoughby have been lamenting the lack of
a 'diversity agenda' in publishing for donkey years . . . It really hurts
that now *you* can't even hear us.

"Okay, my supervisor, tell me, after this training, on whom are
you white folks going to practice? The Yorubas, the owners of Lagos,
say you cannot shave a man's head in his absence. Or, how long is
Andrew & Thompson going to use me, the naïve Fellow, as a guinea
pig to help you grow your humanity? Where are the minorities you
promised to bring in, to make this really a world brand? Have we all
forgotten Dr. Zapata's speech?

"Being the only Black person here is too much pressure. It would
kill me at that diversity training. How am I even sure you won't
bring in an all-white cast of facilitators to run the fucking shit for
you white folks, the owners of publishing? Are they, too, going to
use me as an example or ask for my experience here or simply feel
sorry for me? I never want you guys coding and mouthing *identity
politics, multicultural books, diversity plans*, etc., when I know you
are damn well talking about me and racism and Black books. It's
like being forced to smile over your pain in a torture chamber, to
shoulder the added burden of denying your experience. And all the
while, Angela would be sitting there, gesticulating and asking her
little cute questions? How do I not publicly shame her for lying to
Liam Sanders . . . ? Please, could you delay this diversity training till
after I leave?"

I said the only bits of consolation left for me in America were finishing the anthology, brainstorming from afar on the Biafran memorial event, and confronting Emily about Jack. Beaten, Molly worried
I might leave the next day. I said I wished I could, to escape their
ruinous white bubble politics. I told her even their shadows were
white at Andrew & Thompson, something that could happen to me
if I stayed longer. I said she could not be happy that Angela still
worked there.

AFTER MY NOVENA PRAYERS in the Actors' Chapel, I called Tuesday to find out how Ujai was doing. But he was in a bad mood: he blamed me for the calls he was getting from Ikot Ituno-Ekanem begging him to change his color back to Black. I told him I had not discussed his color with them. When he revealed he even heard all my evil whispers to Ujai in church, I said I never disparaged him. "Do you seriously think I'd allow you and Father Kiobel to celebrate this memorial with such hate in your hearts?" he threatened. "And then you want to rehabilitate Caro's *Biafran* family?"

I said I was sorry for his rape and near-execution in the valley. "Having heard your entire story, I'd never judge you for changing your color," I sympathized. "But, please, do nothing to thwart our desire to reconcile our peoples back home."

I explained why he needed to give peace a chance and gently reminded him I, too, was a victim of Caro's grandpa's spying on Papa's burial Mass, which was so traumatic Mama almost miscarried me. I begged him to allow my wife some closure and not punish her forever for being born into the wrong family. I said if he foiled our plans, his new color would totally galvanize our people against him, that they would shift all the pain of colonialism and racism to him, from the scramble and partitioning of Africa in the 1800s, which resulted in bundling all these disparate rivaling African ethnic groups together, to the neocolonial exploitation of our natural resources, to France's insistence that Francophone countries must pay colonial tax forever for the civilization they brought Africa. "Please, Hughes, my brother, the current political climate would not allow Ikot Ituno-Ekanem to hear your pain," I concluded.

But again he changed the topic: he became suspicious that, now that Father Kiobel had begun to share his war stories, I was going to ask the priest, not him, for the foreword to my anthology. He hung up and blocked my number.

I emailed the Bronx for an update on Ujai's health and to ask them to prevail on Tuesday not to sabotage our memorial plans. They did not reply.

TWO DAYS LATER, everybody's itches were totally gone in Hell's Kitchen.

I trashed my bottles of Advil and bleach and sprays. I did not have to visit the restroom at work or restaurants to inspect my clothes anymore. And to be free of my jury of head voices litigating every difficult moment was to be free from a bit of the burden of that meeting whence they originated. It did not bother me that, though my cubicle powder had disappeared, I still felt monitored, watched. I smiled as I sneezed from the alcohol on my desk, for the cleaners, I supposed, were swiping it with Steri-Fab.

Bob Hamm got fired next. I would miss him for the abiding memories of him almost vomiting at that editorial meeting, of him hugging me to steady my spirit that drunken Monday, of him making everyone laugh and relax the day after the *egusi* visit to Jack's office. He thanked me for my report on *Thumbtack* and said he hoped he would have another chance to publish the author at his next job, if he could find one. As for Angela, whenever she came close for a chit-chat, I secretly recorded it on my phone.

Yesterday, after the editorial meeting, by the water fountain, Angela confided in me in tearful joy that Andrew & Thompson had accepted her proposal for a diversity workshop. I replied in Annang.

I EXTENDED THIS SAME nonchalant attitude to Usen when he phoned ten days before Thanksgiving, from a restricted number. He said though once I was *deported* he had canceled my Thanksgiving reception party, he was not having any get-together whatsoever because his family was exhausted. I thanked him all the same because I knew he feared I might gate-crash.

But I jumped up and clapped and raised my fisted hands like Fela

Kuti during his performances when Usen confirmed the children were now sleeping well, for his building truly got fumigated. I said the curse I had brought upon them had finally been broken, a world of guilt off my shoulders. I exploded in the singing of "Ntiboribo-o." Usen sang the response.

> *Ntiboribo-o*
>> *Oho oho*
> *Ntiboribo-o*
>> *Oho oho*

> *Ekiwo iboko bedbugs*
> *Yak iboko, iboko, iboko ammo*
> *Yak iboko*

> *Ntiboribo-o*
>> *Oho oho*
> *Ntiboribo*
>> *Oho oho*

> *Ekiw'idem osong Ujai m'Igwat*
> *Yak osong, osong, osong ammo . . .*

We only stopped because Usen was laughing too much, all choking and gooey with nostalgia. He said, just like "Ikworo Ino," which I used to placate his madness in New Jersey, he had not heard the folk song since our childhood.

Then he said Bishop Salomone had decided to send Father Orrin to Nigeria and Israel after his suspension, to learn how to live with Blacks and Jews. I doubted these foreign "immersion tours" were enough or appropriate, but Usen sounded conciliatory. He regretted that the bishop only had the anti-Semitic comments Father Orrin had made at Mass as evidence of his crime. "Well, Usen, tell him to send the racist to Black America, not Nigeria!" I said. "I suggest the other side of his own town—or Tuskegee, Alabama. Before then, he shouldn't even be allowed to visit the grave of his missionary relative in Onitsha. Tell him visiting us doesn't prepare him to live with his African American brethren."

"That reminds me," Usen said, "we've finally decided to hang out with the bishop in a Harlem Starbucks after Christmas! Your friend Ujai cannot wait to actually see him laugh that deep funny laugh. If that *coffee* goes well, we shall bring Bishop Salomone home. Look, we admire his patience and care; he's proven he's the good shepherd who wouldn't rest till all the sheep are back in the fold. But we're breaking him in slowly, so he doesn't arrive in our home like a field trip to Exotica! It would still hurt even if he himself wasn't aware of his body language. If I sound crazy, it means you don't understand the minefield race has become in America."

Next, Usen whispered conspiratorially that Tuesday's supporters had indeed dug up Father Kiobel's war childhood, especially how he came to obsess about clothes. "This shit really sucks," I screamed. "Tuesday is paying people to discredit the priest."

"Blame Father Kiobel, too!" Usen said.

"Why?"

"I mean, who tells that kind of refugee story halfway?"

"Fuck, you tell your story the way you can . . . Okay, now that Tuesday is a white man, does he understand how racist it is for him to thwart our plans for Black reconciliation in Ikot Ituno-Ekanem?"

Usen said there was no cause for alarm and promised to get Bishop Salomone to speak to Tuesday if need be. He explained he only wanted to share Father Kiobel's story because he had just learned that pro–Father Kiobel parishioners had already blunted Tuesday's attack: Ujai's grandparents had gone straight to warn the local bishop that if he transferred Father Kiobel just because of his fixation with new clothes, Awire Womenfolk had vowed to defecate on the bishop's court; they would feel the bishop was punishing him for enshrining rape discussion in our catechesis. The international parishioners had also told the local bishop they supported the reforms. "Usen, since

Tuesday is a rape victim himself," I said, "I expected him to back Father Kiobel, at least in this regard!" Usen said, well, the bishop had finally left our dear priest alone "to buy all the clothes in the world" because Two-Scabbard hinted that the youths wanted the bishop to account for Tuesday's diocesan donations.

A few days later, I woke up to a text from Caro saying Father Kiobel himself had just shared more details of his refugee journey. It contained a video clip of Father Kiobel addressing Our Lady of Guadalupe:

"MY DEAR FRIENDS, first, on behalf of Our Lady of Guadalupe, I want to thank you again for your generous novena for our Bronx children! Ofonime and Usen continue to send their gratitude, and Ujai herself confirms she's now okay. She says she and her friends are going to send us a thank-you letter. She tells me she wants to climb all the fruit trees in the valley and snorkel in the river. Knowing that we shall have a Thanksgiving Mass for them when they finally visit, she's practicing our dance steps and language, so she can roll out her Annang praises and proverbs."

Applause.

"Praise the Lord!" Father Kiobel said.

"Alleluia!" the church replied.

"Today, I've been forced to call you together, to finish my Biafran story. In light of the increasingly malicious versions making the rounds this week, I need to clear my name so our parish can move in one direction towards the memorial. I'm grateful to Ekong Udousoro, who has graciously agreed to head the planning committee."

More applause. Some were congratulating Caro in my name while she sipped from a bottle of water to stay calm. Two-Scabbard and others cheered and gave a thumbs-up to the poster of Brad, Alejandra, and I toasting in Chelsea. It was still smiling down from a wall like I was physically present. My heart leaped when I saw a few international parishioners sprinkled in the congregation, no longer in the front pews.

"Well, back to my story, if you like, my family's Stations of the Cross," the priest continued. "What I remembered most was that we stayed in Arinze's beautiful village for a year because Mommy was intermittently sick and wasted. Arinze's extended family footed her hospital bills and our sustenance. But it was like she'd never recover from Daddy's death, especially when Barisua and I failed to stop her from peeping at night at the bloody headtie.

"But just as she was regaining her strength, a crazy restlessness unsettled her mind: the Igbos themselves were angry our minorities had resisted Biafra, this Igbo-thing. It wasn't a good time to be trapped in Igboland. She warned Barisua and me daily to keep a low profile. Yet he and Arinze were carefree, sourcing for the sweetest and chilliest morning palm wine for the family, engaging their mates in keepie-uppie competitions, joining the crowds chanting the greatness of Ojukwu, daydreaming of enlisting in the Biafran army to avenge Daddy's murder.

"My dear parishioners, nothing prepared us for that hot humid noisy evening in mid-June 1967—two weeks after Biafra's declaration of Independence, and one and a half months before the first invasion of minority lands, when some Biafran militia ambushed them behind the makeshift synagogue, where loud all-night prayers used to be offered to Jehovah to send the Israeli army to defend Igboland against another holocaust by Nigeria, the Philistines, and to evacuate the willing to Tel Aviv. The boys were returning from watching an inter-village soccer match, when the militia beheaded my brother. Arinze, who punched someone out, lost his right ear. The girl who sliced it off as the mob pressed him down sold *agidi* in the market, and the guy who hoisted Barisua's head on a stick was the nephew of the synagogue leader. I was numb.

"As soon as Mommy finished soaking another headtie in my brother and Arinze's blood and rolling it up and bagging it, the mob had returned for the body. Some deity wanted the whole thing as sacrifice to weaken the minorities' anti-Biafra resolve. The shrine wanted the ear, too, to make every Igbo listen to Ojukwu, their supreme leader.

"Our neighbors, parishioners, and priest spent the night with us, crying and reciting the rosary. The police inspector condemned the murder, and the village chief said this wasn't the Biafra they wanted. Meanwhile, we had to lock up Arinze, who was bent on avenging Barisua's murder. The synagogue leader cut short their vigil and relocated to our yard, where he sat with his wife in literal ashes. They rent their prayer shawls, cuffed their hands behind their backs with tzitzits, allowed mosquitoes to feast on their faces, and chewed bitter leaves, *etidot* or *onugbu*, to denounce their nephew and new country. These reproofs were quite a big deal, if you saw the bullish mood in Igboland leading up to the war. They were already victorious, the African superpower, and could hurt anyone who hinted otherwise!"

Father paused to drink water before intoning "Eti Obufa Jerusalem," a Catholic dirge. The clip showed Caro and some folks crying and holding hands. In the background, it captured half of the poster of our New Jersey folks embracing us after the sacristy reception.

"Praise be to Jesus!" Father said.

"Honor to Mary!" the church responded.

"Three days later, Mommy decided we must risk the trip back to our village. After we'd gathered our belongings in two wooden boxes, Arinze, donning a headband of bandage and another that circled the top of his head and jaws, sobbed and begged to follow us, to be at his friend's headtie burial. His parents agreed this would help his guilt and also comfort me. Mommy refused, for we didn't know whether we could make it home because of militia violence. When they pushed, she argued the trip might bring infection to Arinze's wound.

"Her jaws set, Mommy opened the headgear bags and unfolded the blood-starched cloths. Arinze's mom helped her tie them around her stomach, like Ujai did in that New Jersey church, an Awire lady ready to fight her way home. Then Arinze's mom knelt and hugged me and said we'd be okay, that when we met again I'd tell her how the burials went. I nodded. Arinze opened his mouth to speak, but nothing came out. He felt his lips with one hand and where his right ear used to be with the other. I grabbed his hands and embraced him. 'Hey, no soccer till the wound is healed, okay?' I said. But, throttled by tears, he snapped out of my grip, bolted inside, and slammed the door.

"The synagogue leader and Arinze's dad carried our boxes on their heads. Arinze's dad's hand trembled with grief as he held mine all the way to the motor park where they bought us seats in a *gwongworo* truck. The other man gifted me with a brown tzitzit bracelet, tying it around my right wrist." Father Kiobel paused to show the one he was wearing now. "I don't want to bore you with the ethnic profiling on the road.[*] But I'd say things got terribly nasty towards Owerri. At each checkpoint, the Igbo militia asked if you were Hausa-Fulani or Yoruba or minority. They parsed your accent. If you sounded Hausa-Fulani, a whistle went off and you were dragged away. If you sounded Yoruba, you were disappeared 'in search of the lagoon,' to avenge the Igbos the Yorubas drowned in the Lagos Lagoon. If you were minorities, you were threatened or beaten or groped or robbed or raped—or all of the above. If you reacted, you became Hausa-Fulani or Yoruba. The new nation was like the old nation: we were unwanted minorities, aliens, in a foreign majority land.

"Near a market in Aba, I plucked up the courage to look a militia chief in the eye. He'd pulled Mommy's right boob from her green bra and wanted to suck it. I pushed his fingers off and put it back in and stood between her and the man. I wanted to protect her the way Ujai wanted to protect her brother in the New Jersey church; I was ready

---

[*] See Ntienyong Akpan's *The Struggle for Secession, 1966–1970: A Personal Account of the Nigerian Civil War* (Routledge, 1972).

to bite him. But, since it's an insult to maintain eye contact with an authority figure, as punishment for what he called 'stupid boy's ill upbringing,' they stripped us totally naked. Someone chopped off my tzitzit bracelet with a penknife before they paraded us as mad people. In some ways, it was worse than killing us, because, as you know, our tradition says once a mad person enters the market, he can't be cured. They mocked us, saying even our village would reject us. I felt I'd truly gone mad and cried for the first and only time in all that had happened to us, in spite of Mommy consoling me I had the Ogoni instincts for justice. But I was inconsolable when Igbo children laughed or touched our pubic hairs with broomsticks and sang of the mad *sabos* of Biafra. I thought even if I were allowed to wear clothes again, I'd always feel naked.

"If you read Wole Soyinka's *You Must Set Forth at Dawn*, you shall see how, shortly before the war, these ubiquitous Biafran militias had seized and roughened and stripped and jailed him butt-naked in Onitsha. Having failed to convince his Nigeria not to visit war on these grief-stricken genocide survivors, this Yoruba man was on his way to begging Ojukwu to back down, for the Igbos weren't prepared for war. But the militia thought he was a *sabo*. You shall also see how lucky the already world-renowned future Nobel laureate was that someone recognized his *ntagha-ntagha* iconic goatee the next morning at 'judgment' and freed him.

"Mommy thanked the militias for allowing us to roll up the headties in tight rings, to cushion the boxes on our heads. It was as if we were carrying our relatives' coffins, like Christ on the way to his crucifixion. I won't also tell you how we came upon the Simons of Cyrene and the Veronicas, who re-clothed and fed us with bread and Coke. They protected us like the Hausa-Fulani friends who evacuated us from Sokoto. They comforted us like the New Jersey friends who didn't even know of our people's sacristy disgrace. When we were totally exhausted, other Igbo militias had helped us with our boxes and new truck tickets. When we got home, Father Tom Flannery quickly improvised a requiem Mass for the headties, like

Ekong's father's secret requiem Mass. The headties were interred in shallow graves framed by ixora hedges under the purple bougainvillea trees beside our bungalow—"

Caro choked on her water and coughed as more people broke down and wept.

"Come on, Caro is faking her tears to *sabo* the tales of her grandpa's wonderful Biafra!" someone shouted.

"Like grandpa, like granddaughter!"

"Good thing her grandpa was nailed—"

"No, you can't praise murder in church!" Father defended her, shouting.

But they heckled and insisted their findings showed Father Kiobel himself later became a mad cold-blooded murderer as a child soldier, because of his humiliation as a mad person in the market. The hecklers sang that he was biased, for he and Caro's grandpa had committed the same unforgivable crime: joining the Biafran army. They called them sellouts like Ojukwu's minority deputy, General Philip Effiong. The Igbos stoutly protested they were giving Biafra a bad name. More commotion ensued when Caro insisted everyone must be allowed to tell their story. "If you're so sure Father is a war criminal, why don't you let him finish?" she hollered over the PA, trying to calm things. I had never seen her so angry. The international parishioners backed Caro, but they were also shouted down. Father and Two-Scabbard moved in to protect her.

Seeing he'd lost the faithful he'd worked so hard to unite, to calm things Father apologized and abandoned his story and peace plans. He bowed his head in shame and left.

THE HUMILIATION OF CARO and Father Kiobel by Tuesday shattered me.

She cried. When I called her, nothing I said could assuage the guilt. Apart from a one-line text saying it was not her fault, Father did not return her calls. I called him to sympathize and to beg him to call her. He did not answer. I texted. Nothing. In her nightmares, it was her "nailed" grandpa in Biafran fatigues, not Arinze, doing keepie-uppie with an earless head in blood-soaked bandage. She wept for Kiobel's mother and Barisua. I listened to her as if in a dream, afraid she might pull back; it was the first time she had opened up like this about her Biafran horror. I also let her know I was struggling with the images of the kids poking the refugees with broomsticks. We were learning how to mourn the war without mentioning our family tragedies. It had opened up a closed door in our relationship.

I called to thank Gabriel, or Two-Scabbard, for defending Caro. But when Father totally ignored me, it confirmed he himself was really hurting. I wanted to hear him out, to support him, to follow him to his father and brother's graves and cry together over a war that was still raging within us. It was the worst time to lose his friendship. Homesick, I drank and seethed with anger toward Tuesday.

To avenge Father Kiobel's supposed insult to his acquired white skin, Tuesday had sabotaged our memorial, which would have discussed our tribalism, which he himself thought was our main problem. He had turned against his roots. It was heart-wrenching how differently he and Father had handled their war childhoods and how the events in New Jersey had suddenly poisoned their relationship. My success in America—getting Father to tell his story, which had mobilized our spirits toward reconciliation—was stillborn. Tuesday had reduced the promises of our Thanksgiving Mass to ashes, unleashing all the ghosts of New Jersey. Like Ujai, I had become a child of the diaspora, consumed by the conflation of both American racism and Nigerian tribalism. My dreams were being shredded one after another.

I phoned Emily Noah for succor.

She listened to everything and said we would talk after she had watched the video. But, that afternoon, Jack called several times. I refused to answer. He texted that we really needed to talk. I ignored him. I was distilling my venom for December, when I would confront him. When Emily went to the gym and called, she apologized for his meddlesomeness. After watching the clip, she had lost her appetite. He blamed her for wasting time on videos. She accused him of being mean. He had shouted at her; she had retaliated by withholding the video. *Iya*, their spat devilishly excited me.

Emily strongly advised that we give Father Kiobel the space he needed to heal.

CHAPTER 32

Kelly King Rice, or Better Than Sex Rice?

THE FOLLOWING DAY, MY HEART GOT A LIFT FROM A GIFT certificate and Thanksgiving card from Greg Lucci. He praised me in a beautiful fragile handwriting for being a good squatter. I called him up and he had never been happier; he was purring, his voice clear as a concert flute. I sent a Thanksgiving card to the landlord. I stuffed into the envelope a printed-out crest of his beloved Italian soccer club, with "*U.S. Citti di Palermo*" boldly written on top. A few days later, Canepa left me a gracious voice mail asking me to call him.

When I did, as guarded as the first day, he said he had been thinking about our conversation. But, in the silence that followed, I feared he wanted to ask me to leave the apartment, effective immediately. I resolved not to beg and, already embarrassed, not to tell anyone. "Do you want your bottle of wine back?" I asked.

He said he had actually invited me downstairs so we could talk about the war, but then, unsure whether I was Igbo or minority, he had held off. But now, having ascertained my ethnicity from a google search of Nigerian surnames, he wanted to speak about the war. "I hope I'm not being patronizing when I say I'm also a victim of Biafra," he began sadly as I stood up and held my breath. "I was hoping Achebe's most important war memoir, *There Was a Country*, would outright apologize to you minorities. If after fifty years

he still insists Ojukwu went to war on behalf of the Igbos, why can't
he say it was wrong to drag the minorities through that valley of
death? Why does he write as though the minorities were in support
of Biafra?

"Anyway, as if it were yesterday, I still remember flying to Italy
for the burial of my favorite cousin, Marco, who was one of the oil
workers shot like a dog by Biafran commandos. As I used to tell
Greg Lucci, thirty years ago, when he had just become my tenant
and we were on talking terms, I should've been Marco's pallbearer
but there was no corpse to carry. His remains were buried immediately. Lucci even dropped me off at JFK on my way to Italy in
1994 for the twenty-fifth memorial Mass of Marco's passing. Of
course, he knew once he mentioned *Biafra* in the recent voice mails,
I wouldn't sue him!

"Ekong, my mourning, my obsession with Biafra, for good or
bad, has resulted in learning so much about your country, not just in
terms of soccer. I was heartbroken by your *sabo* disappearances and
the symbolic burial of shoes, belts—"

I hung up and sat down. I did not want to remember any burials.

WHEN I CHECKED MY PHONE, I saw that Canepa had called
back thrice. His voice mails said it would be nice to meet and talk.
"But, please, only if you want," he hastily added. He said he was
sad that Italians had been blind to both Biafran and Nigerian atrocities toward us, single-mindedly drilling their oil, until the Italian
deaths. He asked how many millions needed to die of hunger or how
many bombs needed to rain on Biafra before it touched the foreign
oil companies. He was ashamed racism provided the biggest push to
ending this war. He said after Marco's burial he spent days weeping
with the crowds in St. Peter's Square. He said, like our minorities,
this introduced him to abject powerlessness, as the Pope figured out
how best to appeal to Ojukwu to release the kidnapped Europeans
on death row.

I was too dejected to call back.

Father Kiobel's refugee journey, Tuesday's revenge, and Caro's fight back were still too fresh on my mind. What were the chances I would meet such Biafran heartbreak abroad? By beautiful Times Square? Today, my war trauma felt unbeatable. But the freedom Canepa gave me not to talk was the height of compassion. I set my boom box with Morehouse College Glee Club and Mahalia Jackson and Joan Baez on repeat, to mop up my country's floods of misery with their different renditions of "We Shall Overcome."

TUESDAY BEFORE THANKSGIVING, in the afternoon, I was reading a manuscript for the editorial meeting when Molly came out to announce the author of *Thumbtack in My Shoe* had accepted our offer. The offices erupted in excitement, as everyone stood up at once, praising the book and our good fortune. We were all so happy, it was like a pre-Thanksgiving party. Even though Bob had been fired, Molly did not have to sweat to convince the author's agent to stick with Andrew & Thompson because the bigger publishers had all rejected the book. My offer to help Molly draft the promo copy was universally accepted.

I was pleasantly surprised when Molly handed me a box of chocolates as my Thanksgiving gift. It came with a note apologizing that "by the time everything settled" we could no longer visit New Haven, as her parents were already in Florida for the winter. On my way back home from work, we texted back and forth, something we had not done in ages. When it felt silly, I called her and told her about Lucci's gift certificate. "That's so nice of him!" she said. "You know, he sent me a gift, too, and said to apologize again about his superbug comments."

"Oh nice," I said, laughing.

"Well, now that we can laugh about all this, I want to say I think he really likes you. Actually, that New Jersey Sunday, he'd called me because he was worried you might be suffering culture shock in

America. Almost in tears, believing you were depressed, he'd told me how you were cooking up a storm of Nigerian dishes, how he was using your mutual love for our U.S. women's soccer to calm you. I said, on the contrary, you were having a ball, either taking long night walks to the pier with your finger rosary or relaxing on the bleachers of Father Duffy Square, that Starbucks and the Food Emporium were your favs, that you'd visited your friend's family in the Bronx, that you preferred the Actors' Chapel to the cathedral. I even said you were making great progress on editing your war stories, some of whose victims you knew. Then he brought up *the little incident of bedbugs—*"

"No, wait, what, I . . . ah, understand what you mean," I fluffed my lines, realizing how this crook had scammed her for my details. "Well, Molly, Lucci is as inscrutable as the proverbial fowl in our proverbs. As the ancestors say, who can tell whether the fowl is dancing or scratching the earth for food? Hey, you have a wonderful Thanksgiving!"

"You, too."

When I hung up, I was seized by uncontrollable and inexplicable laughter, the very opposite of my feelings, the "Laughter of Ridiculous." Canepa was right: his fellow Italian American was a born gouger—an apt description for anyone who could deny me the joys of Starbucks by lying that I was being spied upon. I really missed Father Kiobel, who would have laughed with me. I texted him my good wishes. It was no use telling Caro; she thought Lucci was a saint. And I was afraid to tell Molly because she could call up Mr. Lucci, to scold him for bullying me. I could not stand another sleepless night in NYC. As they say, the crab that has just escaped a fishing net should not throw a party until it has finished counting its legs.

I HIT STARBUCKS at dawn on Wednesday as if to make up for lost time, because I had not been there since Mr. Lucci said I was being followed around NYC. My problems had melted away overnight, and the spirit of Thanksgiving hovered over the city, pure and festive. I could not remember the last time I'd had so much peace or anticipated a holiday with such gusto. I was halfway into my Chestnut Praline Latte when Caro called to give me an update on the parish. Armed with Emily's advice, she was adamant in telling the parishioners and even the cops—who could not relate with the new Father Kiobel—to give him space. It was the first time since the war so many weddings, baptisms, and confessions were postponed. Caro was emotional that they were listening to her, she who had been hitherto excluded.

My great feelings for NYC lured me back to Chelsea. Just to see the place again. Just to relive that dinner, where New Yorkers first helped me laugh at my woes.

In daylight, Chelsea was as enchanting as that night. But what excited me most was the unique view of the city I got walking the High Line. Today, I could understand Brad and Alejandra's obsession. Its elevated platform made me feel like I was a slow-moving train cutting through exclusive neighborhoods, peeking into homes and hotels and businesses. I got the distinct feeling of being in a park, and yet it was like no park I had seen before, a hallway with different walls. And the evergreen plants made it seem as though the denuded winter trees below us were fake, or vice versa. The whole atmosphere was so relaxing, so carefree, it did not feel like New York to me at all. I knew when I returned with Caro to NYC, we must certainly come here.

When the cold sun shrugged off the clouds, I sat on a bench and, from a distance, soaked in the water taxis and the birds skimming the brown choppy waters. The waves crashed on the piers, but the faint smell of the river reminded me of, not our village river, but of the sea at Oron. I became homesick, as though I were back in the Niger Delta. And reading my emails, I was happy to see the author of the novella "Biafran Warship on the Hudson" had accepted my suggestions and mailed me back a rewrite. Then I heaved out a loud laugh when a Thanksgiving e-card from the Bekwarras said their patriarch had safely arrived in NYC, was responding to treatment, and already was bugging his son for another gold tooth.

After a late lunch in Blue Fin, I relocated to Father Duffy Square to watch the intense Thanksgiving shopping until the cartoon characters came into view. Their presence rekindled in me that initial blinding obsession with the King Kong lady during my first days in New York. Today I did not mind seeing all these Scooby-Doos and Mickey Mouses in one place, like the ceremonial masqueraders of Ikot Afanga. However, when a Scooby and a Mickey started shoving each other, it was no longer fun to me. But the two cops nearest to them were laughing, pointing. Then, to have Hermit the Frog—whom I never warmed up to as a child because I liked to trap and roast bullfrogs in the valley—step in to beg Mickey to let go of Scooby's goatee almost spoiled my afternoon.

With earphones pumping out Rhianna, I bought bracelets and a handbag for Caro. I also bought colorful scarves and cards and endured long lines at the post office to mail them to Molly, Emily, and Jack; I felt he deserved something for not corroborating Angela's lies that I had threatened to beat him up over *egusi* and called Liam an "incurable racist." In their card, I specifically thanked Jack on behalf of the poor New Yorkers who benefited from his blood drive volunteer work. "Jack, God is pointing you to something," I wrote, "for I understand most of these poor folks are minorities."

And though Brad and Alejandra were going away for Thanksgiving, in memory of our Chelsea dinner I gave them a bottle of Riesling. They regretted this would have been a perfect chance to cook me Alejandra's *carbonada* or *asado*. Keith, Jeff, and I decided to feast in Jeff's apartment and do dessert in mine.

BUT, ON THANKSGIVING, I woke up still debating what to cook. Should I prepare Yoruba *egusi* or one of the six kinds of Annang *egusi* soups? I decided on jollof rice, but it became two things in my head—Ghanaian jollof and Nigerian jollof. Would these American friends of mine even eat any of this? The word *jollof* might even scare them, I worried, though it was one of the most popular West African dishes worldwide! Should I improvise a name, then, for them, like Tuesday calling himself Hughes? What if I called jollof rice *Kelly King Rice*, or *Better Than Sex Rice*?

I remembered Alejandra and Brad's little silence in Chelsea when the subject of my food came up, something I had not thought about since. Could I stand that kind of silence with my dishes served and steaming before us on such a glorious day? Would the silence grow into avoidance? Would they come very close but then scram like the Indonesian family of Times Square? The worst would be someone making fun of or trembling around my food, like I had boiled stones. Like Ujai after Tuesday's school visit, I thought of the jokes Keith and Jeff might make. I was more nervous than my village folks who asked if the Native American selfie cop had actually tasted our food.

I had never felt so vulnerable and restless.

Suddenly I knew there was not even a margin for humor in this business. I thanked my ancestors Brad was not home, with his fuck-this-fuck-that ways. That morning, just to rid myself of useless anxiety, I jogged to the New York Times Building, to the New York Public Library, to the UN building, to Waldorf Astoria and back. After doing that Hudson River–East River rickety rectangle twice without a drop of sweat because of the cold, my sense of being in uncharted waters was only heightened.

My food fears coupled with longing to hear about Father Kiobel made me call his cook. After coyly saying the boss was okay, the cook complained jollof rice was even "too American, too white." He insisted if these were really my friends, I should risk something, go totally Nigerian or Annang on them. He said if they pooh-poohed my food, I had only a short time left anyway in NYC. He told me their inability to eat the food would not bother him but mocking it in my presence would kill him.

Come party time, I showed up with coconut rice, chicken pepper-soup, a pot of chopped goat head, *iwuo-ebot*, which the Igbos call *isiewu*, spiced with *ujajak*. I had bought the goat head in Queens the day after the Chelsea dinner. My coconut rice was vegetarian, though, not because we eat it so in Ikot Ituno-Ekanem, but because I wanted to impress Hell's Kitchen. Keith brought sweet yam casserole, lobster stew, Thanksgiving meat loaf, and pumpkin pie, while our host served a half turkey, dumplings, rice cake, braised pomfrets, and shrimp fried rice, mashed potatoes, and spring rolls. We had a great feast.

My fears were baseless. Keith and Jeff tore into everything and swigged the palm wine. They thought it was funny the way I spread the mashed potatoes, their American food, on my plate, patterning it with my fork like Martha Stewart's tahini cookies, before over-loading my plate with assorted stuff. We did not spend time trying to teach each other how to eat the different dishes. We went at them the best way we could.

We were free.

The only thing that mattered to them was the names of the spices. They practiced these like kindergarten rhymes, and Keith said he wished he could capture and preserve the admixture of the scents from all three cultures. It was my best day in America, the day I was not ashamed to eat my food in public.

✂

KEITH WAS POURING the peppersoup's broth over his sweet yam casserole, when Caro called with holiday wishes. My celebra-tion was complete. Though she did not like the fact that she heard that her husband was cooking for the whole of Manhattan from the mechanic, who heard from the palm-wine tapper, who heard from Father Kiobel's cook, she was chatty and called me "Ekong Baby," nonstop. Jeff tossed a slice of goat ear into his mouth and blew out his cheeks and exhaled because of the pepper. I explained to Caro I had mistakenly put too much pepper in the food but that I was relieved it did not bother my companions.

"Well, Ekong Baby, you need to come home for the sake of Father Kiobel," she said, changing the subject.

"*Ade rie?*" I asked, cutting into the pomfret.

"He's lost his loud laugh. He comes late to Mass. Even his hom-ilies are all over the place, a market chatter of sorts." She lamented the Ogoni priest was driving longer and longer distances to buy clothes, to avoid scandal. I said he would be all right.

But when I said good night, Caro complained I had dismissed her too soon and insisted on greeting everyone, as if she wanted to bust Molly for cavorting with me. "Is it today you know I'm a jealous wife?" she said, laughing as I put her on speakerphone. Keith got her to laugh even more by saying the names of our spices, and Jeff said the large eyeballs in the goat-head dish were like over-boiled eggs, a favorite of his. She thanked Jeff for helping plan the Chelsea surprise dinner and photos.

WHEN JEFF LODGED a slice of goat tongue in his mouth and insisted on talking, Keith said he had a forked tongue like a snake. Keith and I were laughing like mad, but when he wanted to join us, we begged him to swallow the food first. As we were physically holding him, Keith worsened things by chirping that, being the dude with the baddest mouth in Manhattan, Jeff might actually have two tongues.

I did not remember how we got into the subject of my stairwell religion. But at this point I was comfortable with them, with the way they made me feel around my food. So I told them the truth about my religion. Initially, they thought I was kidding and continued to laugh. I repeated it nonstop and added I was Catholic. Finally, Jeff said he felt stupid. This allowed me then to share the import of the Chelsea photos on our villages. This brought a big dose of solemnity to our celebration.

Keith called up Brad and Alejandra to simply say this was his best Thanksgiving since childhood. But they blamed us for excluding them from the food and from talking to Caro. I promised to cook for them and gave Alejandra's phone number to Caro.

We went to my apartment to eat pecan pie with ice cream. We drank Mr. Canepa's wine. And that night, we layered up and walked around Times Square, taking in the early Black Friday madness. The King Kong lady was already in a Christmas outfit dancing to carols. I thought the rowdiness was worse than the Eleven-Eleven roundabout in Calabar before Governor Donald Duke came to power. My neighbors told me to move my wallet from my back pocket to the breast one to avoid pickpockets. I said I would return the next day to buy our J.Crew boots.

CHAPTER 33

Lead us through that beautiful valley

CARO INSISTED I TAKE MY NEIGHBORS ALEJANDRA AND Brad and others the following weekend to the Buka Restaurant on Fulton Street for the sake of variety. On the way, Alejandra spiced things up by saying she had been chatting with my wife since Thanksgiving and *they* had a surprise for me. When they all nodded, I knew the crooks were going to pull another Chelsea on me. Alert, I searched for clues.

We were among only a few in the train that Saturday evening, and this part of Brooklyn was the emptiest part of NYC I had seen. I could not imagine any commercial part of Ilorin or Warri being that *dead*. While I could tell apart Hell's Kitchen from Times Square, Chelsea, *my* part of New Jersey, and the Bronx, I did not know what to make of where I was. It was not beautiful. It was not ugly. It was not even boring. It was just Brooklyn, a place I was going to with friends, and already I loved the name so. Like the food joints of Urua Anwa, Buka was full of excited people, the sight of folks of all races a happy surprise. I ordered family-style and made it as diverse as possible, as though I were trying to represent all the ethnic groups of my country.

WHEN MOLLY SIMMONS WALKED IN wearing a yellow business suit, I did not recognize her, until Alejandra called her name and ran to embrace her.

"What are you doing here, Molly?" I exclaimed, standing up to introduce her.

"Oh, Alejandra invited me!" Molly said, giggling conspiratorially, as a waiter brought her a chair. She apologized for dressing a bit too formally, explaining she had just come from an author event. We told her it did not matter.

"This is a wonderful surprise, I must say," I said, and then raised a glass of Coke to toast her: "Hey, everyone, cheers to my great and only boss, Molly Simmons, my *oga* at the top, as we say in Nigeria!"

"Cheers!" everyone said.

"Don't listen to the boldest Fellow we've ever had!" Molly retorted as Keith quickly put a beer in her hand.

I made a toast: "Without her fighting for my visa and fighting off JFK immigration, I'd never have met you, great people of New York. Cheers again to you, Molly!"

"Cheers!" everyone said.

Alejandra told me how Molly did not want to come until Caro stepped in. "Molly, you've been talking with Caro?" I said, surprised, almost choking on my Coke.

"Yes, since Thanksgiving!" Molly said, laughing, explaining she could not say anything earlier, since it was a surprise. She added that they could not refuse Caro because they were all touched by our heartbreak about Father Kiobel's unsuccessful attempt to complete his story. She said Caro had also spoken to Emily, who could not come because Jack was sick.

I went to the restroom to make a call to Caro, to thank her for the gathering. She herself was in high spirits and said she was texting with Emily even now, while Jack was asleep. I became more emotional when Caro said arranging the dinner was also to apologize for all her bedbug accusations; Alejandra had finally convinced her America had bedbugs. Though I assured her I had no more infestations, I worried about these ladies chatting nonstop. I prayed that even if Molly knew I was drunk that bedbug Monday, she would shut her big mouth for Caro's sake.

The restaurant brought washbasins because everybody wanted to eat with their hands, like the Nigerians at other tables. Nobody wanted to touch the rice or bean dishes, complaining they looked too familiar. No, they went crazy and mixed things like we were competing for the weirdest combos. They did not bother to look up and see how the Nigerians at other tables were handling things. It did not worry me when Brad began his evening by sprinkling salt on *amala* to chew with Star beer, or when Keith ate *afang* soup with *akara* as entrée, even as he saw me moving from peppersoup to *amala* with okra soup.

Molly, who ate *ewedu* soup with stewed beans, was a different person here, unshackled from the officiousness of work. The more Nigerian beers she tasted, the chattier she became. She was already texting to thank Caro. Unlike Molly, though, Keith did not say a word or drink even water. He was lost in his world of *ogbono* and *egusi* and *oha* soups. He did not mix them. He just kept eating studiously from the different bowls as though he were judging a cooking competition. No one knew how he kept that level of focus in this atmosphere. When we distracted him, he impatiently said he was trying to decipher which one had *ujajak*. I said none, but he nodded and continued as if he had not heard me. It seemed the more we ate together, the more we learned about ourselves.

By the time Alejandra, like our Nigerian kids, wore little balls of pounded yam on the tips of her left fingers and *eba* balls on the right, the voices of my Nigerian compatriots from other tables had gone up in a cheer. Bending each finger into the bowl of *edikangikong* soup before transporting it to her mouth, she looked like someone experimenting on a strange harp. The restaurant owner came over to greet us.

We were on top of the world.

WE WERE WALKING MOLLY to her train. Brad, who was a bit drunk, said since I had outed myself about my stairwell "religion," he also wanted to confess that this outing was a greater occasion to appreciate my food than during the American Thanksgiving—something he said he and Alejandra no longer celebrated. Alejandra said they had been avoiding the holiday because it felt like a celebration of Native American colonization. "We always wish we could leave the country altogether on Thanksgiving!" said Brad, slurring and throwing an arm around Keith for support. "I'm sorry, but I guess I'm just tired of simply feeling this fucking guilt, you know. I get fucking mad because any white person asking people of color to return *home* should be the first to fucking pack up and ship back to fucking Europe! We need to do more than vote for Obama!"

"Well, Thanksgiving is particularly difficult for me and my family, too," Molly said timidly, and giggled and tripped on a stone and staggered. Jeff steadied her, as we all stopped to make sure she was fine. "I guess I just wanted to say I've got Native blood in my lineage," Molly announced, holding her ankle. "A child in whom the blood of the colonizers and the victims met."

"Oh, so sorry we brought this up," Brad said, and backed up, palming his head with both hands like he had suddenly gone sober. "It was just a private decision we made years ago."

"It's okay," Molly said.

"No, I'm sorry my boyfriend is drunk!" Alejandra moaned, covering her mouth. "We should never have brought it up."

"No, it's really fine," Molly said, and began to limp, pulling us forward. "My folks hit Florida shortly before every Thanksgiving. They stay around Lake Okeechobee, where our Seminole ancestors came from. And I, too, disappear during the holiday, locking myself indoors."

We all became quiet, a long, extended minute of silence dedicated to the history of her people. Yet, actually I was very loud inside, like my thoughts were catching fire. And since I had always thought of American Thanksgiving as a feast that united the whole nation in glory and nostalgia, I was demoralized that my best day in America—Thanksgiving—seemed to be my supervisor's worst, a day she and her parents had to hide from. When I remembered the unforgettable Thanksgiving feast with my neighbors, I felt so empty, like one who had worshipped at the wrong shrine.

Molly tried to recapture our earlier happiness, without success. The atmosphere was flat like overexposed beer. And when I looked at her face, I could see that her desire to cheer us up did not even touch her own eyes. They were beclouded by a shame I had not seen before: that of a child still struggling with the sordid history of America. I had never seen her so bereft of talkativeness and confidence, not even when we had talked about New Jersey.

Molly is a minority like the rest of us! I said silently to myself as I wondered why she had kept this from me. Nothing convinced me of the absurdity of race more than this Molly epiphany. I was mad that her white mask, as it were, was more perfect than Tuesday Ita's acquired skin. I remembered her apologizing to me after I told her about my father's rape: *Such stories really get to me . . . all this reminds me of the history of . . . Never mind.* Was this what she meant when she said while crying over her New Jersey bloopers, *I wish I could tell you why carrying these stereotypes is particularly shameful*? Or was this why she wished she could share what she called "my very complex childhood" with me? Today, her behavior was quite different from that of the Native American selfie cop who proudly declared his race.

MOLLY STOPPED BY my cubicle the following Friday afternoon, before the close of work. The offices were near-empty. We yakked about how daunting it could be shopping for friends and family, with Christmas looming. I said I would begin the slog next week.

When I told her I would really love to learn about her Native

American background, she said Caro had been asking for the same thing on WhatsApp. She spoke quietly, making sure no colleagues were near. She was happy Caro had, upon learning of her ancestry reveal from Alejandra, sent her a copy of the Native American cop selfie. "The gist is, unlike the selfie brother," she said, folding her arms, "I'm ashamed of myself, of what a part of me did to the other part of me. Maybe your delicious dishes opened me up. Maybe your strong beers. Maybe the sheer bottomless pain in Brad's confession."

"I love Brad."

"Perhaps, if I'd revealed my ancestry that could've made you feel a little less alienated around here all these months. I grew up hating, self-hating, my minority roots even as I used to follow them *home* to Lake Okeechobee to hide from Thanksgiving. Though my white looks give me all the privilege, I know the land I live on is both mine and not mine. Sometimes it feels beyond immigrants' pain, because there's no home country anywhere to return to or hope to rebuild. It's like something very strong in me is no longer visible, has been erased, disembodied, gone."

She apologized for not sharing this when I told her about Papa or when we talked about New Jersey or when I blasted the diversity workshop plans. She prayed someday she would have the courage of Emily or Father Kiobel.

We were the only ones left in the offices now, but it was like the place was screaming with vivid memories of my American experience. Molly was glowering, biting her lower lip. The fear that ringed her eyes after she stumbled and revealed her identity the other night was gone. Today I could see in her eyes my own pluck as I squashed Jeff and Brad's initial animosity, my defiance at that editorial meeting, my grit in Father Orrin's sacristy, my mulishness in boarding the train in New Jersey, my canniness in Jack's office, my prudence in planning a confrontation with Emily. And yet in this moment, too, my heart was also calm like the proverbial eye of the storm. It knew that, *k'akpaniko*, no matter how long, no matter where my friend Molly Simmons went, no matter her flaws, she would fight to bring minorities along, if only to complete her essence, to make the fullness of America visible.

MOLLY SUDDENLY REMEMBERED she had a letter for me in her office. Laughing a fake dramatic laugh to dispel the heavy mood, she dashed in and out with a white envelope. She apologized she kept it to ensure I got it since I did not usually get mail here.

"Seems someone is getting romance in the Big Apple, ha!" she said, her mischief at full bloom.

"Are you jealous?" I said, collecting the letter.

"*Iyo*, nope . . . *iyaaa uweiiii.*"

"*Iya*, it seems someone is learning Annang straight from Annangland, ha!"

"And how cool is that?"

She gave me a peck on the cheek; I hugged her. But as she was leaving the building, she pointed at the envelope and sniggered and said Caro was really missing me. I knew Ikot Ituno-Ekanem might hear about the letter even before I opened it. I did not recognize the bold writing on the envelope. Everything was capitalized. Yet the postage date was the day before, city NYC. No sender's name, no return address. At first I thought perhaps it was from Greg Lucci, but his writing was fragile, not bold.

When I turned it over, there was a big red X over the flap. The X was made up of little red heart stickers—which explained Molly's comment about romance. I opened it and "Your niece, Ujai" was written at the bottom of the letter.

To Best Uncle Ever, Uncle Ekong,
I and my friends know you're in this city. We know immi-
gration didn't deport or hurt you. We're happy because that
means you're not banned from America. But it's not your
fault that everyone lied to me, including my grandparents.
They even lied to Bishop Salomone, a whole representative

*of Jesus. But when the bishop visits us, all my friends agree
I must tell him the whole truth so I can really be worthy of
Holy Communion. During our Thanksgiving party, I overheard Uncle Hughes boasting to someone how they lied to
me you'd gone home, in case you still had bedbugs. But I
think he also forced Daddy to leave you out of the party
because he paid for it, just as he had paid for repainting our
house and bought us the beautiful ekpo-ntokeyen masks.
He thought you and Father Kiobel turned the village against
his new color and then told Bishop Salomone that he's a bad
person. He doesn't know Daddy ratted him to the bishop. But
we know they're lying against you, which is why my friends
say you must visit our school next time you're in NYC so that
others would stop calling us Team Liars. And if you publish
any books about dog valley cemeteries, we want copies in
our hands as proof. You must finally put Ikot Ituno-Ekanem
on the internet! We've edited this letter nonstop because we
want you to really really understand our stuff. Our white
friends really want you to know they, too, are part of our
group. We're not bigots. We all recite the Father Orrin Pledge.
We're good Americans. We love our country. When my parents wanted to bring Uncle Hughes to school in your place,
I cried nonstop to my grandparents though they lied to me.
Finally, Daddy listened but is still mad at me. It wasn't fair
to leave you out of our Thanksgiving party . . . secretly, I felt
really pissed like our Native American friend says they feel
on Thanksgiving though he doesn't admit it in class when the
teacher asks how the holidays went! If he whispers in your
ears about the wars America waged on them God knows
when, I tell you, they're worse than our Biafran War. He says
50 million of them were killed for their lands and natural
resources from Canada to Argentina. He's OK with sharing
this with you because you understand stuff. He says that's
how they were forced to become a minority or to disappear.*

We don't argue with him or cut in. We just allow him to talk. We listen. When the teacher mentions climate change in science class, he whispers in your ear so much of their blood was shed it changed the climate of America forever. When he says their dead weren't even buried, we become ashamed they were treated worse than our dead dogs of the Biafran War. I know my parents no longer talk to you. Don't worry I don't have bugs again. We've won our bedbugs war. I sleep well now. I no longer need to see a shrink. But I can't forget the days when we were so desperate and I agreed with Mommy to spray me with antibug spray, to avoid shipping bugs to school. It's no fun to be sprayed after a hot shower. You become cold like ice, then a bit oily, then completely dry like your pores suddenly drank up everything. But it's less painful than if your racist classmates found a bug on you. They'd say you brought it from Africa and bully you to death. It's better for my friends to find a bite, which I didn't even allow my friends to . . . But they'd never mock me. They hugged me every morning, knowing I was traumatized. We're really close. I told them the embassy called Mommy a whore and Daddy a pimp and bullied you to prove we Annangs exist. But I'm teaching my friends all the hip-hop moves of the Tiv guy who made everyone laugh in that prison of an embassy. I miss you big. Greet Keith, Molly, and Emily. When you go home, hug AuntieCaro for me. If you're still unsure of the bugs, do everything not to bring them to our dear village. Please, apologize to Father Kiobel we've not finished our long letter to the church yet. All my friends must agree on every word. I and Igwat will see you when we visit. Maybe Keith will come with us. You'll lead us through that beautiful valley, till the river changes color with the Harmattan.

***Please, don't reply so our teacher doesn't give it to Mommy and Daddy.

I sat back in my chair without knowing what to do, except to weep. It was like Ujai was confiding in me from another life. I read it again and again. It was written in blue ink on lined paper. With no breaks, no paragraphs, it overwhelmed me like the Cross River overflowing its banks.

Yet I was filled with hope that our children all over the world, irrespective of all the things that divide us, shall discover a language, a tenderness, a friendship with which to negotiate this increasingly complex world, this world we had so thoroughly messed up. I was filled with hope that these American children, especially those with recent roots outside these shores like Ujai and Igwat, would reach back as far as possible for the wisdom of balance, for the immigrant gifts that had always been the strength of this country. I hoped, too, in this reaching back, they would help their parents' countries to fix the dysfunction that drove them here in the first place. I hoped they would not turn around to hurt their people like Tuesday Ita.

Inspired by Ujai and friends, I vowed to write to Bishop Salomone. I vowed to even ask him to petition the compassionate, soccer-loving Pope Francis to send Dr. Martin Luther King's books to his native Argentina with its horrible racist history—instead of just presenting one to the U.S. Congress as he did last year when he visited America. If Ojukwu could listen to a Pope and free the kidnapped Europeans he had put on death row, we could reach the human heart anywhere. Like Mohammed Dib, I believed hope "enclosed in inaccessible places" was still hope.

ALAS, SUDDENLY I HAD the unshakable suspicion that bathing with anti-bedbug sprays was the *crazy bath* her parents fought over the night I had asked to move into their home. This. Was. The. Secret. This was what I thought I had demanded of the landlord in that angry voice mail. This was why Jeff had the two huge bags of empty sprays, and just as he had warned even in his drunkenness, now I could see clearly this was unhealthy.

That night, my dreams were heavy with a thousand replies to Ujai and her friends. But beyond prayers, I was powerless. It reminded me of Joseph Conrad's "Youth": "You fight, work, sweat, nearly kill yourself, sometimes do kill yourself, trying to accomplish something—and you can't. Not from any fault of yours. You simply can do nothing, neither great nor little—not a thing in the world . . ."

CHAPTER 34

Riskier than cooking for them

SUNDAY AFTERNOON, ON MY WAY BACK FROM THE HIGH Line, I saw a poster on the adjacent building announcing it would be exterminated in four days. I turned down the Tiwa Savage song I was enjoying and studied the poster carefully. I never knew there were posters like this, and I thought I knew everything about the bugs. It was a bad case because the building had sealed furniture trash in front of it.

Suddenly I felt completely vulnerable, naked, because I had trashed all my weapons. I did not sleep well and in the morning my head felt like I had light-headedness, though I did not. Afraid bugs in the adjacent building could somehow find their way to my apartment, I went proactive: I sneaked back to Washington Heights that evening. This time I bought a ton of just the anti-bedbug powder because this was more durable than the sprays. When the seller asked if the bugs were back, I joked I was merely stockpiling for all of Manhattan.

I poured the powder all over my apartment floor, window ledge, blinds, bed cabinet, even the bed edges. Everywhere was matted in eerie grainy white, like *ufok nduongo*, a native memorial shrine, and when I walked in, snicks of dust snapped at my heels. The heater kept it dry and unwilling to settle, like dust. I sneezed so frequently I went to bed in a mask. I left a clean rag in a plastic bag by the door, to wipe my shoes before I went out.

Now my only real problem with NYC was the plummeting temperature, because no matter the number of sweaters I wore under my coat, I was still cold outside. Unlike in my tropical Nigeria, I soon realized the brightness of the sun did not mean heat. Yet I was shocked how wastefully hot my apartment was, despite my initial concerns about the gaps in the windows. When I developed migraines and dizziness some mornings, I cracked the windows and slept better. Sometimes you got the impression that, the way these old heat radiators were groaning, even if you left your windows totally open they could keep out New York's worst cold.

However, one night, awoken by their crackle, I went to use the restroom. As I stood there urinating in the semi-darkness, my penis felt strange in my hand. I switched on the lights, trembling and wobbling my aim. I had been bitten in four places, a straight line across the tomato smoothness of the cap, a semi-ring of high welt hills, the distances between them modulated by tight valleys. Their volcanic eruptions, bloodshot and vicious, melted down the sides and would soon meet in the valleys. The trauma shrank my balls into one tight sack, a dried wrinkled passion fruit.

With the powder everywhere, I could not figure out when or how they got ahold of my dick. "*Iyo*, Ekong Otis Udousoro, there's no way you're confiding this one to your neighbors!" I whispered as I gingerly pulled my pajama trousers back up to cover my shame. "No, this is riskier than cooking for them or revealing a fake rail religion!" Afraid the bugs might be in my pajamas, or the babies or eggs between the plies of the toilet roll, I cast off the trousers.

But, as I bent down to inspect my bed, a bug parachuted in from on high. At first I thought it was falling from my head and subjected my hair to the roughest ruffle possible. Nothing dropped. When another bug dropped on the pillow, I looked up; they were rallying and gyrating on the ceiling, as though staging an elaborate *uta* victory dance. A few of them patrolled an invisible circumference, to protect the dancers. They had taken over the bedroom. I moved to the kitchen, like a man avoiding direct confrontation with the devil. I was trembling. I was too afraid to behold the ceiling. It felt as though they were roaring back to forcefully reclaim this little space of mine, like Dr. Zapata's fear of rebounded racism in America.

✕

I SHUDDERED as my dick's situation dredged up images of those of the victims in *Trails of Tuskegee*. I wanted to cry like Emily at that meeting when America first went wrong for me, that first moment I knew that in spite of my humanity I did not belong. Today I could not guarantee our landlord would make the entire block, like a country, safe for everyone. I could not stand eleven more nights in NYC. *I just have to return to Nigeria this evening,* I swore to myself, hoping to finish the last twenty stories of my anthology in Ikot Ituno-Ekanem.

Caro's phone was busy. Unable to sit down, I paced the length of my lodgings. The powder was disturbed when I moved too fast. When I coughed twice and a dog issued a low sleepy yelp, I put on my mask, to avoid coughing. Walking past the mirror, I noticed my eyes were bloodshot, like things bit by bugs. Yet, my mind was on the ceiling, to checkmate their next move. In the living room, when something moved in the chandelier, I backed away and hit the switch. The bulbs were dotted with black, as if birds were frozen in the filaments of lighting. Awakened by the glare and heat, they began to fall off like lazy raindrops through a flimsy cloud of white dust. They cut into my carpet of powder, dying instantly, bodies in shallow graves. I switched off the chandelier, for there seemed to be no point in killing them. Dead or alive, they had taken over the living room, too.

Naked, I placed my computer on the kitchen table to change my flights and made arrangements for a taxi to drop me at the airport, then forced myself to a marathon of the music videos of Gyakie, Wizkid, and Davido and drank instant coffee till morning. After showering, I dressed up in the baggiest of my jeans because my dick needed room. But the bugs had retreated from the ceiling to I do not know where.

I texted my neighbors and Molly and Emily to say I was leaving due to a family crisis. "Emily, I'll definitely call you from Nigeria for an important chat!" I promised at the end of my text. Keith apologized that he could not personally bid me goodbye, for he had lost all his free days to bedbugs. Jeff and Brad said they were around and would stop by. When I called the Bronx and was still blocked, I emailed them, to no avail. Later on, Alejandra and Molly phoned from work to express shock and to say goodbye.

Emily called midmorning. She said to hug Father Kiobel and Caro tight, but then—as though I might send greetings—announced she had dumped Jack. Relieved, I said she sounded happy. She said actually she was sad because Molly had just told her of all my shit with the Humane Society Two. "Ekong, I'm sickened by their endless bigotry," she said, her voice breaking. "I'm sorry I just didn't know of any of this. Please, still do call me from Nigeria, so we can talk, okay? This more than confirms I've made the right decision about Jack. Your friendship has been like a safety net for me since that editorial meeting. Do you know that when Jack and I quarreled over the Father Kiobel second clip, he almost beat me up? Ekong, now I realize he'd no business even meeting your people in that first clip."

Canepa regretted we would not meet again. When I mentioned the resurgence of bugs, he gasped and quickly said he would spray the whole building next week, whether Lucci let him into the apartment or not. I was so relieved my friends would get a reprieve. He also prayed Nigeria and USA and Italy would qualify for the 2018 Russia World Cup. We laughed as I gave him my home contact information.

CARO SAID FATHER KIOBEL had called once Usen announced my return to the village. This was how I knew my emails had gotten to the Bronx. But reconnecting with the priest pleased us so much I had no time to mourn the painful demise of my childhood friendship with Usen. Caro said Father Kiobel had apologized he was too depressed to acknowledge our texts and the shame of rejection had only compounded over time.

Of course, Caro herself said she did not understand my sudden return. She said Molly, Emily, Alejandra, and Father were asking her. "You'll *see* the reason very soon on their behalf!" I said.

When the priest called, I was shambling back from Rite Aid, where I had bought six cans of bedbug spray, to cleanse my entire luggage. "I'm not going to ask why you're fleeing from America," he said after pleasantries. "As the ancestors say, if the skies were that wonderful, why would the hawk be searching for food on earth?" I said I would love to listen to the rest of his story someday. He said he was in a better space now, that as frightening as life had been since he had started telling this story, it had strangely given him more peace. "Or rather, I should say, I can glimpse more peace than I've even known these fifty years," he said. "Some of these head voices that have harassed me since the war are gone!"

I leaned on the fridge as my body softened with joy; I knew a bit about head voices.

"Ekong, I might as well tell you the rest of my story now," he said. "Because by the time you arrive, I'll be away for a month attending the mass burials of the people of your beloved embassy dancer. I don't know whether I'll make it home, for the government-backed killers are even spray-bulleting burial crowds!"

"You shouldn't go, then!" I said.

"I must, because I know what it means to bury your beloved alone . . . The truth is I never joined the Biafran Army. I never killed anybody, as Tuesday's paid investigators and supporters claim. The truth is, one morning in 1968, less than a year after my father and brother's headtie burials, shortly before the fall of Port Harcourt, my mother and I were in the fields beside our house when a new batch of Biafran patrols arrived. I'd just turned eleven. I looked more mature and muscular than my age-mates. As a few shots rang out, we took cover on the ground, in between the yam mounds. Afraid of ambush, they were shooting from the low bushes across the road, securing the area from the Nigerian special forces that rumor said had come in from Calabar.

"The bullets were still chopping off yam tendrils and cocoyam stalks and snapping plantain and banana trees when Mommy blurted out Arinze's name. 'Arinze, my son, Arinze, my son! Barisua's mother!' she cried as he buckled and stopped shooting.

"He put down his AK-47 and signaled to the rest to stop, too. Without his right ear, the left one was very conspicuous, like an overgrown mushroom. When our eyes met, he pointed at me and opened his mouth to call my name. Nothing came out. He choked and felt himself with both hands, like he was searching for my name in his clothes. When he started touching where his ear used to be, Mommy got up and walked out into our driveway toward him, weeping and trembling. She crossed the street. He slowly pulled out of formation and came over, his hands raised in surrender. He was shouting something about my brother and father's graves. And I was pointing toward the bougainvilleas and ixoras—when his people shot him in the small of the back. He fell forward, almost into her outstretched arms."

Kiobel said the orders that she should not touch Arinze rang out, more shocking than that single shot. His mother ran toward the house. When she turned around and went for Arinze again, the neighbors screamed at her not to allow Biafra to orphan me, her son. She stood still, biting her forefinger, her body trembling like a *karikpo* dancer. Arinze writhed by the roadside. He was gasping and clutching his stomach, the ring of his blood eating the grass, his face jerking toward the sun, his brow shiny with sweat. In between him and the sun, she knelt to make her shadow big enough to embrace his face and torso. And when he finally kicked and lay still, he was on his side, his knees pulled in, his favorite position when he used to spend the night with Kiobel's family in Sokoto. But his face was still turned awkwardly toward the sun.

The neighbors led her away. Another group of soldiers arrived; they were in a panic as they relayed news of their losses elsewhere. They hurriedly rid Arinze of his gun and bullet belts and disappeared. Listening all day to his mom bemoan her failure to soak a third headtie in Arinze's blood, to take to his family after the war, listening to her weep for literally calling him to his death, Kiobel knew she would not survive the war. By sunset, she had descended into partial paralysis. Her right hand could no longer function, and she could barely walk.

"Still, like Mary, the disabled New Jersey lady who led the protest to Bishop Salomone, Mommy never stopped being her brother's keeper," he said.

"I'm sorry about your mom," I said when I finally understood the two women's connection. "May her soul continue to rest in peace!"

After Biafra had abandoned Arinze in the sun all day, seeing their neighbors did not know enough to sympathize with his execution, after night prayers his mother asked her eleven-year-old son to find a way to wash and pray over and bury Arinze. She wanted it done that night because they were all afraid rumors of Nigerian special forces meant an all-out war was afoot. "If they could recruit my baby son, your brother, Arinze, to hurt us," she had said, "you're old enough to cover his nakedness with the earth. Knowing the trauma of being paraded naked, we can't allow him to roam the lands and markets of the ancestors unclothed by the earth. We'll never escape the ghost of his twin brother, Barisua. He can't stare at us like this for another day. It's his Second Burial. His blood is ours forever. You're an Ogoni child. We stand together in life and in death. We never forget our people or land or waters or sky. We love fiercely."

So, after they had kept vigil till midnight—long after curfew had kicked in—and the patrols had not still made their tour, Kiobel's mother had hugged him in the dark, like she did not want him to see her tears. But they beat down on his neck all the same before she could cup them with her one functioning hand. "Go and do what you have to do," she said. "The spirits of your brothers and father shall not abandon you!"

He recounted how he had slipped out through a side door and locked it and stuck the key in his pocket. There was no moon, no stars, no fireflies, no bombs lacerating the skies of the big cities. It was pitch-dark. It was quiet. He felt he should wait for the patrols to pass and so hid in the farm, lying in between the yam mounds, covering himself with rotting plantain leaves. You never knew from what direction the patrols might arrive, or at what hours, and sometimes they did not use their flashlights. Some nights, they would have passed three times already. Lying there was eternity. It was like all his energy had left his body. Yet, he was trembling so much he thought the patrols would hear the rustle and shoot. "I'd never felt so lonely before," he said. "I'd never buried even a puppy. I didn't know where to begin."

WHEN A CRICKET CHIRPED and a bullfrog mooed, a flashlight stabbed the night. Father Kiobel said he had lain still. The glare revealed four men. They circled a neighbor's home. Then everything returned again to darkness. Their running footsteps told him they were already in his driveway. They cocked their rifles and circled the house, checking the doors. "They were stamping their boots like they wanted to wake my mother up, till they finally receded and went to stand over Arinze by the roadside," he recounted. "The beams of their flashlights slashed his body, picking out his face. He was still looking up, like he was waiting for sunrise, like he would see me if he opened his eyes."

Then Father Kiobel said, after they switched off the lights, one of them bragged about how this was the best punishment for Arinze's folks because he had heard of their obstinate anti-Biafran position. Someone else said the parents and their followers had been variously locked up and flogged and warned it was treason to openly denounce Biafra even as bombs rained on Igboland. "They're termites eating the wood from inside," another said, "so their ramshackle synagogue had to be burned down. If not for marijuana, Arinze himself would've run AWOL a long time ago!" As they spoke their Igbo-accented English, three Nigerian bombs had gone off far away, the lit clouds stagnant smoke plumes. The Biafran soldiers complained that the nonstop bombing of Igboland was against all laws of proportionality, nothing compared to the one rusty little thing Biafra had dropped near Yaba Market in Lagos, around my visa interview hotel. The soldiers were still committing the war to Our Blessed Virgin Mary when the commander received a radio signal about Nigerian special forces. He panicked and told the rest there was no time to bury Arinze.

I WAS SO MAD at the Biafrans, *ukpa-agwo-k'ikwa* mad, that I sat down on the stupid bed like I had been hit in the groin. I knew I would be haunted for a while by those voices floating over Arinze in the dark, cavalier as the sound of Jack's street phone call to Chad. I put the phone on speaker and set it on my lap because my fingers were trembling, my palms sweaty. I spat on my powdered floor. I felt they should have evacuated the body of their fellow soldier—even if they had no loyalty to him as an Igbo, a fellow Catholic or Jew or human, no matter their fear of ambush.

This was not the burial story Kiobel was supposed to tell Arinze's mom after the war. I was livid that these soldiers were more discriminatory than Father Orrin in that sacristy.

"Ekong, yes, you truly understand what I felt that night!" Father Kiobel said to calm me. "There's was no terror the Igbos didn't deploy to force the minorities to accept Biafra. There's nothing they didn't do to break our Ogoni or Annang resilience. Listening to them talk about Arinze was my first moment of pure anger in my life. When they killed my dad and brother, I felt loss and anger. When they abused my mom in Aba, I felt shock and anger. Even when they stripped us naked, I felt fear of madness and anger. Ekong, it's difficult to describe pure unalloyed fury, except to say it drove me to track the soldiers on the straight road to the edge of the village, where they turned onto another road." Knowing they still had three more villages to get to their post, Kiobel had turned around and run home, stumbling and crashing, his energy harnessed by that limitless fury, till he spotted the lantern by his mom's window. Inside, he had gathered a flashlight, a bucket of water, a towel, and a bar of soap. His mother was hard at prayer; he whispered loudly her son was almost at rest. He had neither time nor words to form any prayers himself, for, even kneeling on Arinze's dried hardened cold blood, he refused to believe he was dead.

"In that darkness, I rolled up Arinze's khakis and washed his face and feet and hands of his blood, since there was no time to wash the whole body," he said matter-of-factly. "I cleansed him twice, so he, too, could wash Barisua when they met. I added a third wash for Daddy. It seemed like the right thing to do. Then, with all the energy in my body, I grabbed the guy's head with two hands. I sharply twisted it back to align with the rest of the body. His weight and tucked legs swung me like in wrestling. I went with the momentum, rolling over. When I sat up and reached for him, he wasn't there. '*Lu' wa, Barisua, owa do wa?*' I said in Ogoni, bemused. 'But it's not really funny.'

"Groping around, I found him. He had tumbled and rolled. Now he was propped up on his knees and forehead, a Muslim touching the earth with his brow. I knocked him over and locked down his legs like in a tackle and levered and pushed and pulled and heaved to straighten them out. Then I dipped my thumb in palm oil to trace the sign of the cross on the boy's forehead, his palms, his feet, and his chest. I also repeated this anointment twice and whispered closely in his two ear holes to share with his twin and daddy in the grave, to tell them we're sorry we couldn't fight over or wash their bodies until now.

"My most difficult task that night was dragging him across the field to our family cemetery. When a headlock didn't work, I pulled him by his epaulets. Getting there, I asked him to stay calm, and I turned on the flightlight. The risk made me dig that shallow grave like a madman. When I switched off the flashlight, finally, I sat down and wept. First, it was relief the soldiers hadn't seen me and then that my two brothers and father were gone. I hadn't cried for them.

I didn't want to cry for them. But I guessed it was one thing to bury a headtie, a body another." Then he had rallied his spirits to disguise the new grave with wreaths of dry leaves and cassava stems. When he opened the door, he bumped into his mother, who had been waiting for him. He assured her it was done and helped her back to her room and disappeared into his, afraid his sadness might have completely paralyzed her. Kiobel said that night an angry rain had flushed the tracks Arinze's body had made on the field, releasing the fresh scent of the queen-of-the-night.

I WAS CAUGHT UNAWARES when my friend suppressed a laugh as he recounted the dawn visit of Father Flannery, the priest who had interred his father and brother's headties. I raised my hands in Hell's Kitchen as though I wanted to gag Kiobel, but then I reckoned he might have been healing his heart with the balm of self-mockery. He said the white man had taken a liking to him after the headtie burials a year before and given him shiny George Best and Bobby Charlton trading cards. This was how he became a die-hard Manchester United fan.

The war had turned this gentle Irishman into a drunken skeleton, his frothy blond hair mushrooming into a dirty Afro—a shadow of the ebullient priest whose Honda and yo-yo had been stolen in Ikot Ekpene Stadium. Kiobel said he hated his friend's overgrown nostril hairs, which tangled together and made it look like he had one nostril. And rumors said some days he was so drunk he gave absolution to the Biafrans—and later to the Nigerians—before they even committed atrocities. Some said he just entertained them with stories and stats of European soccer.

The Irishman had arrived at their home that rainy morning with a few things, as though he would stay the night. Before the mother could say what Kiobel had done, Father drunkenly said he had come to protect them because he had failed to secure amnesty for those who buried Arinze from the angry patrols who could not find the body of their fellow patrol. "They searched for his corpse in the rain to bury," he said. "I'm afraid they might be back to *ask* questions!" He stuck a rosary in Kiobel's hand and, dodging his eyes, told him to scram.

Yet, before the child wrote down his mother's directions to her friend's place among the beautiful creeks of Oron, the man had folded himself onto the couch and fallen asleep. "I cried, as I did not want to leave Mommy," Father Kiobel told me. "But she wept bitterly that she didn't want to lose her third and remaining child." She could not rouse Father to bless him, though. The boy himself shook him like a rag and even poured water in his left ear till it overflowed down his neck and into his dirty white soutane, but this human sacrament of protection was still snoring. Knowing the soldiers would not touch her with the priest around, he ran away, for as they say, the tears of a mother are deeper than prayers.

He returned from his refuge in Oron to hear she had died within three weeks. "Maybe someday Tuesday will realize that both of us were victims," he said. "Maybe we can hear each other for the first time. And, these days, I'm driving long distances, not to buy more clothes, but to see a shrink to stop dreaming about being paraded naked, to stop hearing the children chant, 'Sabos of Biafra.' This is key to ending my clothing obsession. Though I'm from another ethnic group and tongue, I'm entrusting you with these personal stories, my truth, my life. Not to discourage you, not to rile you up, either, but to open up paths to healing our peoples—in case I don't return from the Tiv burials."

CHAPTER 35

Thank you, my landlord

WHEN JEFF AND BRAD CAME TO THE DOOR, I WAS STILL trembling. Yet I could not but entrust them, too, with the whole truth of my new bites.

They pushed inside anyway.

They did not express any shock at my floor—though I knew their apartments were not yet re-infested—and I apologized to Brad because the dust made him sneeze. As they stood around silently like folks at the funeral of a fellow soldier, my mind churned with the details of the priest's war chronicle. His losses had whipped me so hard it broke the tension I had felt in my body since I went to pee the previous night. I needed to cry. But my eyes itched, for I had no tears left. Feeling a cold wetness in my shoes, I realized I had been sweating. Even though I also realized I had been too shocked to remember to thank Father Kiobel or wish him a safe journey, a strange peace had come over me.

Though there was no time to share Father's story with the guys, their quiet presence anchored me, like I had known them since childhood. I was grateful to them—folks who themselves had also been touched by the tragedy of war and were equally on their painful but invisible refugee journeys.

THEIR CLOTHES WERE MORE FORMAL than usual, like they were taking time to say a proper farewell. Jeff was in black Dockers trousers, black shoes, and black shirt. He had a black blazer with padded elbows. Brad wore black Birkenstock shoes, black trousers, and a black cotton shirt and a black knitted scarf. When they paced the apartment, they did so delicately to avoid kicking up the dust, but it felt dreamy, like watching zombies. When we finally found the words for small talk, they begged me not to scratch my dick, to avoid infection.

They asked if they could help me pack. I said yes. It was our last group activity. I instructed them we needed first to spray my suitcase and laptop case inside out and set them on the bed. But Jeff gestured to us to hold off as he grabbed the can to work on the bed first before we laid down the bags. Then he sprayed our hands and I did his. Next, one man held out a shirt or audiobook or belt or passport and the other sprayed—at close range—till it was damp. I folded and placed it in the suitcase. When I pulled up a big plastic bag of *ujajak* and other spices and sprayed, Jeff said he would like to keep the spices because he had already figured out how to use them. Brad insisted Jeff must share with him and Keith, who had bought Yemisi Aribisala's *Longthroat Memoirs: Soups, Sex and Nigerian Taste Buds* right after our Buka dinner. When Jeff nodded, I opened the top buttons of his shirt and shoved it down till it sat snug but uneven on his stomach. I buttoned up his shirt again like a child's.

Then I picked up the sealed envelope I had addressed to Canepa, containing proof of rent. I wanted to write on the other side of the envelope, "Thanks for sharing your Biafran story" or "I hope one day the Lord gives you peace over Marco's death." But I gave up, for this was not the time to talk about deaths. I settled for, "THANK YOU, MY LANDLORD!" and underlined it. When I gave the envelope to Brad, he received it with two hands, like a certificate. Then he raised and held it sideways so Jeff could spray without wetting it.

Then Jeff opened Brad's shirt buttons so he could slide it in, as I had done for Jeff with the *ujajak*. Brad patted his stomach as if he had just filled it with a pleasant meal.

I asked them to mail the envelope when I was gone. "And by the way, Canepa assured me this morning he'll exterminate the whole place," I said. They exclaimed that the old man had already left them a message to that effect.

I abandoned the beddings and suit and winter coat—all too thick to dampen. After closing the suitcase, we sealed it with another round of spray. Since I had used up my powder stuff, I was tempted to take some from the floor. But Brad shook his head and went and got some of his for my electronics. The first thing I did was to pour some into the envelope of Ujai's letter and seal and shake before placing it in the side pocket of the laptop case. The remaining powder was just enough for my laptop, wristwatch, phone, and headphones. I discarded the boom box and books. "Hey, you're not returning to Caro in these dusty loafers!" Jeff said at the door, picking up the rag from the plastic bag by the door to wipe my shoes. Then I locked up and handed them my keys and some money for Lucci so he could clean the place up.

By the stairwell where our friendship began, we made to hug, but pulled apart instead. It was our final humiliation, like Usen and me at that train station, this inability to say a simple goodbye on our own terms. We looked stupid, like children spooked by their shadows. Brad folded his arms; Jeff put his hands in his pockets; I looked down the stairwell. A text from Keith suggested they should help me pack. A few dogs in his apartment moaned and whined once his name was mentioned, as if they were standing in for him.

"Would you like to take the spray to the airport?" Jeff asked, seeing I was still clutching one can.

"Ekong, we could just toss or keep the damn thing, you know," Brad said, coughing. "You'll be fine!"

"Could you guys spray me?" I said.

They shook their heads, looking at each other, then at me. "Hey, dude, don't be such a wimp," Brad said to me, looking away with tears forming in his eyes.

"Ah, no . . . nope . . . not a good idea, Ekong," Jeff stammered, and stepped back.

"Yes, yes, just help your friend out one last time," I said, winking.

They exchanged glances again, and then Jeff shook his head and said, "I'm sorry, this is what I never wanted for any of my friends." Silence.

"Well, if not for you, my dear friends, my fears would've killed me," I said. "Now If the sprays succeed where those failed, at least, let my corpse travel home unafraid. As our people say, you're better off being buried by friends than by enemies . . . if you could clean my loafers for Caro's sake, you can certainly ensure I take no bug eggs to her."

Reluctantly, Jeff collected the can and led us downstairs. Brad thumped behind me with the suitcase. We descended slowly, Jeff setting the pace, conscious of my bites. I spread my stride and held the rails, worried my dick might have worsened. Then Jeff completely stopped on the next landing, because Keith's dogs were barking and crying and clawing at the door. I knocked lightly and rubbed on the door with a flat palm to say my goodbye to them. It gave them a bit of peace. We continued our descent silently, Jeff holding the can like a gun for a mercy killing.

By the mailboxes, Brad put the suitcase down and grabbed me in a breathless bear hug, blurting out that we should be okay, since they were going to spray me anyway. His stubbornness shattered the gloom. And, after Jeff's side embrace because of his spice *pregnancy*, we backslapped and exchanged bro fists and spoke and laughed in exaggerated whispers, like we did not want the bugs to know we had one-upped them.

We had retrieved a bit of our dignity.

When, finally, I stepped back and breathed in and pinched my nostrils and nodded, they knew it was time to cleanse me. Like relatives praying over you before a long journey, they asked me to close my eyes while they took turns to spray till I felt the balmy dampness all over my body. They sprayed till the fumes contracted my scalp like ice and drew tears from our eyes, and finally the pain I felt listening to Father Kiobel rained down my cheek. Next, in the manner of airport security, they asked me to remove my shoes. They blasted inside, over, and under them. They misted my socks before I put the shoes back on. When I picked up the suitcase, they sprayed the bottom. I promised to call from Ikot Ituno-Ekanem.

I wobbled out into the taxi with my load. I turned to wink at the guys. They gave thumbs-ups with both hands. When the vapors in my clothes drew a double sneeze from the driver, finally I relaxed in the hope that even if our nemeses were already in the car, I was safe.

Acknowledgments

There is no greater agony than bearing an untold
story inside you.

—Maya Angelou

I WAS BORN A YEAR AFTER THE BIAFRAN WAR (1967–70). For two and a half years, most of the ground offensive was in minority lands.

Its crazy stories shaped my 1970s childhood. In the last fifty years, they've followed me all over the world. These past ten years have been really difficult because, beset with self-doubt and despair, I was bent on fictionalizing this war from the perspective of the minorities of the Niger Delta. And I didn't always know whether I was weighed down by the prospects of writing a second book after *Say You're One of Them*, or by the very bruising war or wars I was trying to portray.

I ring my first bells of gratitude for Bishop Camillus Umoh of the Catholic Diocese of Ikot Ekpene in Nigeria. Between you and me, between me and our beloved diocese, you know how grateful I am for your support. When I finally told you I could no longer continue in the priesthood—because I needed to write—you made me know there's life beyond the stole. "Uwem, whatever happens, don't forget your God, for God is God," you said tearfully in August 2015. "At the end of the day, we do what we must do."

But I can never forget what you saw as a child of ten in Nto Ubiam at the beginning of the Biafran War, and in your subsequent refugee years in Abak, and what it meant to return with your family to homelessness at the end of the war, because Biafra had razed your home. According to you, this was when the war finally broke your stoic old man. He died shortly after.

Thanks for accommodating my vicious interrogations, as I came back again and again, like a bad dream. Still, I didn't get to ask you enough about the young boy who was conscripted on his way from school by Biafran patrols and your uncle who, after the loss of his home, refused to be a refugee even in other parts of Annangland; he chose to "sit out" the war in the forests, playing cat-and-mouse with Biafran sharpshooters. "My uncle wasn't the type to leave his land for anyone, even for a day!" you'd said that day in late October 2016. "We were shocked to see him alive when we got home." You said he told you how your home was burned. He was the one consoling your father, his brother. He and your mom were determined that the family would start afresh.

Though I heard my maternal auntie, Eka Ajimmy Udoh of Ikot Ama, has similar stories and was a refugee back in my village for the duration of the war, I couldn't subject her to any kind of serious questioning because she's now an old woman. Besides, they said she doesn't like talking about this stuff anymore.

I thank the late Lieutenant Colonel Etuk, our geography/English teacher at Queen of Apostles (minor) Seminary in Afaha Obong. You were the first ex-soldier I interacted with. As you tried to prepare us for 1988 WAEC exams, we teenagers were more interested in war stories than map reading or summary. We wanted to know why you joined the military. We wanted to see your rifle. Many times, we asked whether you killed somebody. Your reply was always that tribalism and corruption could kill a country. You could never satisfy us, even when I personally followed you to your Peugeot 504 station wagon after class. We repeatedly grumbled whenever you cut us off by uttering those lines: "Boys, make no mistake, war is not good for anyone. The best thing is not to start one, though some of you high schoolers look like folks who might start another civil war . . ."

I also thank you, Monsignor Kenneth Ennang, my high school rector and essay teacher, for the stories of Biafra ordering our people to surrender their weapons before the war, weapons they later used to kill us. And you still cringe when you recount how the Nigerian army later arrested, harassed, and almost executed Dominic Cardinal Ekanem near Ikot Ekpene's abattoir, accusing him of being pro-Biafra, because he insisted that killing and torturing Biafrans could never lead to reconciliation.

I'm grateful to late Fathers Linus Ntia and "Akwa Oku" Isidore Umanah and Monsignor Sylvanus Etok. Your war experiences were unique as young pastors. What you saw in this war, in the Biafran "camps," the eye cannot unsee.

Father Ntia, in 1971, a year after the war, you baptized an infant Uwem Akpan at Saint Alban's Parish in Inen, and then, ten years later, served me First Holy Communion in the Prince of Peace Chapel of the Generalate of the Handmaids of the Holy Child Jesus in Ikot Ekpene. A gentle soul, you were always reluctant to put your war experiences into words, because when you did it was incoherent. You literally fidgeted and wrung your hands, as you fumbled the explanations of God's love because of your memories of the camps, where our minority "refugees" were brought but were never released. As children, we hated your *idap-idap* (sleepy-sleepy) sermons and even prayed the cardinal should transfer you elsewhere, till we were old enough to realize you yourself never returned from the stupid war. But we always loved your confessional, because you never scolded us on behalf of God. Rest and enjoy the bosom of Abraham, where you don't need to preach.

Akwa Oku Umanah, the first Annang Catholic priest, you and I started a high school together at Saint Mary's Parish in Ikot Atasung/Ikot Obong Otoro, Umuahia Road, right after my high school. I couldn't fathom why you woke up before four a.m. to say the rosary, and I'm glad you quickly understood that kind of monkish Roman Catholicism was beyond me! Your account of some condemned *sabos* being handed over to Igbo masses by Biafran soldiers to kill just sounded unreal in my ears. But the closest you came to capturing the trauma for me was saying you'd become addicted to calling the Blessed Virgin Mary's name all night, to break years-long reels of memories of hearing the last confessions of folks you were convinced didn't deserve to die—for you knew them and their families back home—and yet couldn't save them.

Seeing my anger, one day in 1989, you told me: "My young seminarian and teenager, sooner or later, you'll learn that, sometimes, there's nothing you can do, except be present to the suffering around you." Akwa Oku, may the rest of paradise heal your memories.

Monsignor Etok, I'm unable to express my gratitude for you sharing your war experiences; I've heard of your abduction by Biafran forces and personal meeting with Ojukwu, the Biafran leader, from others. I treasure your advice to me in the Priest's Council in 2012 and your references to the war.

Thank you, Fabian and Francesca (Ekpoudom) Udoh of South Bend, Indiana, for your hospitality and for allowing me to dip into your memories of this war. Telling me of the deaths and terror this war visited upon your different families in different parts of Annanggland opened up new vistas for my project. Fabian, may the souls of the five members of your family, including your parents, who perished in the first two years of war rest in peace. Your details of Nigerian army jeeps repeatedly plowing through throngs of Annang refugees on Ikot Ekpene–Uyo Road during Biafra's 1968 Recapture of Akwa Ibom/Cross River—when the Nigerian army pulled out all thirty thousand troops in the "Atlantic Theater" to go free Port Harcourt, the oil city—have stayed with me, as well as the account of how your only surviving sibling still to this day has a stray bullet lodged in her waist from Biafran "spray-bulleting."

Francesca, thanks for sharing with me the story of your father who came back from "the camp" at the end of the war with a bullet in his head and died with it. He was a victim of that First Capture of minority lands, in 1967, when the Igbos stormed in and shot or disappeared folks who disagreed with the war or openly refused to be called *Biafran* or refused to join the army. His crime? Being an influential headmaster who refused to endorse Biafra.

Thanks to the Annang confessors who convinced the Biafran authorities to spare his life. He'd crawled out of a mass grave, soaked in blood, to startle even the executioners. In the pause this gave everyone, the priests, who used to visit your family before the war, testified that they knew him as an upstanding citizen of Biafra. Luckily, a compromise was reached to detain him till the end of war, because to release him would give our *sabo* ethnic groups the false hope that once you were taken across the Igbo border you could come back. No, once you were disappeared over that point-of-no-return line, you needed the extraordinary powers of resurrection, like Jesus, to reappear.

Since I met you in 2005, thirty-five years after the war, you've asked me repeatedly: where exactly did Biafra, this Igbo-thing, learn to torture like this? How do I get rid of the faces of the soldiers? What did Ojukwu and his think tank of intellectuals use to poison the hearts of our Igbo brethren against us? How many of our villages needed to burn before the International Red Cross took note? Like many of our people, you believe that Igbo propaganda was such that Catholic Charity even flew in weapons for Biafra, some of which would've been used against our minority Catholics! "Uwem, if the world only knows of three tribes in Nigeria, why are you shocked that it couldn't care less if two hundred forty-seven or five hundred ethnic groups were wiped out because of oil?" you've said many times.

SIR GABRIEL UDOH of Obot Akara, thank you.

I can't forget how much you said you wanted to join the Nigerian army once a Biafran soldier set your home on fire with a gas bomb and you had no time to rescue anything—and you couldn't even cry, as that could've been misconstrued as resistance. How you ran and prostrated yourself before the Nigerian army at Ikot Ekpene Stadium, begging to join, when they overran Biafra. You were already training with them when the tears of your widowed mother made you, her only son, leave. How up till today, in your late seventies, it still haunts you that you didn't go to war to rescue some of the minors whom Biafra had pressed into service, boys who finally returned, if they returned at all, destroyed by drugs or the trauma of being forced to terrorize their people. You noted that while Igbo boys were camped and trained in paramilitary ways, our children were simply abducted and thrown into war. Our children were "better" spies because they didn't have Igbo accents.

You were too ashamed, too angry to talk about the rape of our boys or men.

Your wife, Alice, kept telling me how much the war memories have tortured you over the decades and what it meant for me to listen to you. But, as soon as you told me sixty-eight villages were torched on that side of Annangland alone, I quickly said, "Sir, please, just give me, like, a detailed description of five or ten burning villages, nothing more!" I negotiated for a discount, just a small neat number for my fiction for the sake of my sanity. But you were ready to take me around to all the villages, assuring me they'd since all been rebuilt. After doing a tour of a few, where you introduced me to war survivors who were still seething, people with too many crazy stories for my own good, I rallied my spirits to listen to them.

For some, the saddest part of this war was the beheading and defacing of the tombstones by Biafran patrols. Some of these regal life-sized cement statues mounted on platforms in homesteads or on street corners had spooked the soldiers, especially at night. According to you and the villagers, the Biafran solution was to behead or chop off their arms with machine guns. When the people complained, you said they were told, "We've defeated even your ancestors forever! Any *kpim* from you, and you will join them."

Again, I refused to believe any of this, for my sanity. But I saw the pain on the faces of the children who'd gathered to listen to their grandparents tell me about the humiliation of their ancestors. It finally broke me. I gave up, gathered my stuff, and fled to my side of Annangland. I resurfaced the very next day like a bad coin with more questions, apologized for "abandoning you at the warfront," and explained I was also even tormenting the bishop and messing up his schedule over these matters. "My son, *iya uwei*, now you can't sleep anymore!" you said, laughing.

MRS. INIMFON (EKPENE) AKPAN, you and I go way back, and I thank you for everything. It was during our primary school days that I first heard your mother's accounts of Biafrans "securing" the maternity ward, while she was in labor, and what it meant for women to bolt in that state. Your mother was still mourning this particular newborn sibling of yours—who died a month later—till the last time I met her before her death in 2012.

Inimfon, you've harassed me for years as I struggled to find a setting for this novel: "Uwem, if you couldn't pull together a book like this, who then can do it for us? We don't care whether you set the book in Las Vegas or Beijing or New York! There must be a way for the dead to read . . . if I read it out loud by my mother's graveside, she must hear, for, as our people say, the dead are only dead in the eye, never in the ear!"

I'm also grateful to your husband, Dr. Martin Akpan, pastor and fellow writer, who recounted his experiences of the war as a ten-year-old in the present-day Ini Local Government Area in Ibibio-land. He bemoaned the difficulties around minority accounts of the war because "others from the same tribes that oppressed us in this war" have taken over and twisted our narratives, like the white colonial masters did to Africa. Martin, when you shared your memories of Biafrans smoking out your folks like bush animals, I could still see the burning flames in your eyes, the sight of homes popping like well-laid fireworks, your goose bumps like the flies that caked the bodies of the dead. Well, I liked our conversation about what fiction could do and how we must encourage minority writing.

Thank you, Fathers Tom Ebong and Emman Udoh for your accounts of the Battle of Afaha Obong Junction. Father Tom, I must also commend you for your detailed account of the malfeasance of the Nigerian army. Though you understood my novel was about Biafran atrocities in minority lands, you emphasized that minorities suffered from both sides of this war because of oil. To buttress your point, you talked about the Ikpe Annang man whom Nigerian soldiers executed by tying up and jeep-pulling him on the tarmac à la Patrice Lumumba, for supposedly supporting Biafra. My only consolation was that, at least, Akwa Ibom State government had apologized to the family when it unveiled its Biafran Memorial in 2014. "And what have we benefited *sef* from remaining in Nigeria?" you asked. "When will the federal government apologize? Look, the Igbo masses, who were being bombed nonstop for three years—people who didn't know of their army's bullshit in minority lands—did not and do not deserve the vengeful way Nigeria has continued to massacre them to this day."

Father Anselm Etokakpan, I thank you for confiding in me how frightened you were as a child of six seeing what Biafran patrols did to *sabos* week in, week out in Ikot Etokudo/Otoro axis. Father Gordian Otu, *sosongo* for taking me out to lunch in Abuja, Nigeria, once I touched down from Atlanta, Georgia, for research in 2016. I appreciate the nuggets of Nsasak and Odoro Ikot war stories and your prayers for me as I set out for Ijawland, Ogoniland, and Ikwerreland.

IT WAS MY FIRST TIME in Ijawland, and I shall remember it forever!

I'm grateful to my Isoko friend Anote Ajeluorou, political editor of the *Guardian Nigerian*, for goading me nonstop to write about this goddamn war. Thanks also for telling me of the war in Isoko/Urhobo region and for sending me an escort, Marcus, at such short notice so I could attend the annual Obe-Benimo-Oge Festival (Regathering or Liberation from Biafra Festival) in Tungbo-Sagbama on October 22, 2016.

Marcus, once I said my plan was to engage as many commoners as possible, you confidently worked out public transportation logistics and how I was to dress and comport myself, to avoid kidnappers. "Remember to speak pidgin only, not Americana o!" you warned. "My *oga*, your perfume smells too rich *na*." As reward, you only wanted me to visit your village and mention your Membe people in my book, that you exist, that you survived Biafra, that you're surviving Nigeria and the killer Fulani herdsmen. Like other Nigerians, it was so clear to you the federal government was unleashing these herdsmen on the country by staunchly supporting open grazing in the twenty-first century. You were shocked when I said you shouldn't only pray but save your tithe and "Tray Collection" money to buy your own two sophisticated guns for you and your wife, so you can take turns to protect yourselves. I'm sorry I couldn't visit your village.

Marcus and I arrived in the palace of His Royal Highness Amos Poubinafa of Tungbo-Sagbama at ten a.m., to ask for permission to attend the festival. The little peaceful coastal village is set on a sharp corner of the Tungbo River, a village where old men remember playing with crocodiles, their totem animal, like the friendly crocodiles of Paga Pond in Ghana. The shrine of the dreaded village deity—Akpolokiyai—is the last structure between the village and the river, a bulwark of sorts. It's unforgivable sacrilege to block this god's view of his beloved brooding brown river. Not even the fruits of the few plantain trees in between are edible.

Your Royal Highness, I'm grateful for the welcome that you, both as a gentleman and former naval officer, extended to us. Your hospitality included narrating the heartbreaking story of how the Biafrans desecrated the shrine by parking their lounge-boat in front of it, how the standoff between the soldiers and your subjects escalated into their torture and executions and finally the dispersal of the village—

and how important it was for the kingdom to institute this Regathering Festival right after the war.

I really enjoyed the delicious lunch of catfish peppersoup and rice and drinks, the fish fresh from the Tungbo. Carried away by Ijaw spices and the culinary skills of the queen, I ate a bit too quickly, till the pepper went down the wrong pipe. To the embarrassment and scramble of the royal household. You lightened my research work by asking Paul Ebikeseiye, then secretary of the Sagbama Branch of the Ijaw Youth Council, to show me around and explain how the different houses and bloodlines were preparing for the evening's war boat display on the Tungbo, the climax of the Regathering Festival.

Koko Kalango, I hit your office in Port Harcourt unannounced, straight from the killer-Fulani-herdsmen-infested road network and crowded buses from Yenagoa. You were shocked to see me dressed like a manual laborer and maybe smell even worse. But all I wanted, to decompress, was a bottle of Coke and *mmansang-ikpok* (boiled peanuts), because the ones I've found in American gas stations taste completely different. Thanks for letting me snack in peace.

I still remember the first time you invited me to your Rainbow Book Club in early 2009 to celebrate my first book, *Say You're One of Them*. I remember how happy you were when Oprah selected the book for her book club. But your secret game plan all along seemed to have been to encourage me to write about minority Biafra. You never got the chance to introduce me to Elechi Amadi before he died, the Ikwerre writer and soldier, who rallied his folks to fight against Biafra. I missed the chance to ask him why Governor Nyesom Wike and other Ikwerres—an Igbo-speaking group—insist they're not Igbo. Though you always prayed for my safety and insight in my crazy research forays, Koko, I avoided you for a few years because each time we met, I was drained by our analysis of the latest national misfortune. Blessings for all you've accomplished with the Garden

City Book Festival, your literacy campaign across Nigeria, and now your "Color of Life" Christian show.

When I left your office, I roamed the streets of Port Harcourt, eating roasted corn and *ube* or *eben*, until I found some chatty minority seller. Once I told him the Igbos were blaming us for the failure of Biafra—and I could prove to him I wasn't Igbo—he immediately suspended business to call up his grandpa to ask about the war. The narratives of Biafran atrocities that burst forth from this *chop-chop* chance encounter can't be printed here. It led to many more interviews in Ogoniland, and Ikwerreland than I'd planned.

LIKE IN TUNGBO-SAGBAMA, I learned this terror even contaminated the sacred spheres of Port Harcourt metro. An example was the Catholic Diocese of Port Harcourt, which was run by an Igbo bishop and clergy in 1967 when the war began. While some Igbo priests, nuns, and lay leaders mediated between their Biafran patrols and minority parishioners, others simply behaved like the Biafra secret police.

For me, a former priest, it was most heartrending to hear that some of the priests had broken the Seal of Confession and leaked minority "sins" to Biafra, which sent its killer squads to disappear the penitents and commandeer their properties. Nothing killed the trust between the Igbos and the minorities more than fucking *anwa*-shit like this. This *Biafranization* of the spiritual life completed the desperation and abandonment of the minorities. It was as though even God had rejected them.

You could only imagine the huge relief and feverish vengeance of these minorities against their Igbo brethren when Nigeria recaptured Port Harcourt in May 1968. The shameful killing of Igbos—sometimes aided by the Nigerian army, like during the 1966 genocide—and despoilation of their properties weren't restricted to here. Moreover, after the war, the minorities insisted they were better off without the Sacraments than to allow Igbo clergy to continue to run their diocese. I learned these folks would rather burn down Corpus Christi Cathedral. In 1973, Pope Paul VI appointed Bishop Edmund Fitzgibbon, a white man, as compromise.

THERE'S A SPECIAL PLACE in my heart for all my research contacts and interviewees and guides in Igboland.

I was quite afraid of visiting your villages to ask about the 1967 killings and harassment of our minorities and the Igbos who protected them. Initially when I revealed I was challenged by Professor Chinua Achebe's *There Was a Country* to present our side of the war, some of your IPOB* members wanted to expel me from Igboland, to say the least. Ashamed that tribalism, like the whiteness of American publishing or Catholicism, might deny this minority of minorities access to research, I allowed you to scold me for daring to critique Achebe, "our Igbo genius and Father of African Literature." My Owerri guides also soaked your *gra-gra* as you branded them traitors, *sabos*. You only relented when I stepped forward and lied that I was still a priest and Google yielded an old photo. You listened when I spoke about the kindness of your people in my last parish in Nigeria, Christ the King Church in Ilasamaja, Lagos, which was ninety percent Igbo. You cocked your ears when I shared how generous and inspirational Achebe himself was to me in 1997 when Father Dave Toolan (of *America* magazine) arranged for me to call him at Bard College, New York, for advice on how to become a writer. You were touched to hear how, in spite of his very poor health and doctor's advice, he'd answered that phone, as promised, and shared a few words of wisdom with this nonentity. "Well, they say a writer writes in spite of his fears and handicaps!" Achebe had said. "After all the exposure to good writing, you still have to want it, perhaps, more than anything else, to stand a chance."

* Indigenous People of Biafra, a pro-Biafra pressure group.

Now, as I explained to you, my Igbo interviewees, beyond the IPOB madness, you have the right to fight for an Igbo country. But, most importantly, you must continue to rid your forests and farms and homesteads of these Fulani militia masquerading as herdsmen. If you allow them to surround you, where would you run to during the next Igbo genocide? And, yes, your diaspora also have a right to send you weapons and/or bring your case before the international community. There's no other way to put this, having seen some of the gruesome photos of your slain relatives . . . though you didn't like my advice that reconciling with the Yorubas could actually help you negotiate for a better future, some of you hoped that my writing might even bring an understanding to Nigeria's history. Well, as your ancestors say, *egbe belụ, ugo belụ.*

Special thanks, too, to you my Fulani contacts, who're rightly worried about the evil things *your* Fulani government is dreaming for Nigeria. I encourage you to raise your voices in the mosques and everywhere against these current invasions and massacres done in your name. If white people could join Black Americans in Black Lives Matter protests, why can't Fulanis fight on the side of our indigenous compatriots, especially the Igbos whose pre-war genocide you masterminded?

AND, TO YOU ODIA OFEIMUN, poet and journalist—who told me how you became a war journalist at age seventeen, because the Nigerian army thought you were too young to enlist—I praise you for broadening my knowledge, not just of war, but of life. I learned a lot that hot day in November 2016 in your apartment in Lagos about the Biafran invasion of the Edo-Esan axis and the needless killing of Igbos by the Nigerian army once they chased out Biafra. It gave me the background to Biafra's using of minorities as human shield in three bloody days as they retreated toward Asaba in September 1967. Though history has detailed the Biafran massacre of minorities in the Urhonigbe Rubber Plantation, their drowning of more than three hundred adults and children in Ossiomo River,* etc., you were able to contextualize these events down to the more publicized four hundred Igbo men stripped and shot in Asaba by the Nigerian army.

Egbon, I appreciate your phone calls to monitor the progress of this book. You were thrilled by my plans to create Swiftian ironies between our Nigerian and American histories of violence, and of racism/tribalism in American publishing and religion. But you worried I might not find a publisher.

Professor Norman Thomas Uphoff, I appreciate our email correspondence in January 2013, sparked by my discovery of your 1970 letter to the *New York Times* about the glorification of Biafra by certain American writers. Your grasp of the ruthless ethnic politics within that entity and the *Lebensraum* and *Anschluss* philosophies of the Igbos surprised me. Your letter is completely different from Kurt Vonnegut's famous "Biafra: A People Betrayed," which reduces Biafra to only Igbos, thereby committing literary genocide against our thirty-some minority groups. I believe Vonnegut, my beloved American writer, had set out to show the agony of the Igbos in the last days of the war. But mentioning "Ibo" twice without any hint of the existence of other groups deletes us from that map and dispossesses us of our lands and oil resources. Of course, Professor Uphoff, the coverage of the war in the *San Francisco Chronicle*, where you suggested I search for what I needed, both gladdened and saddened me. But so did my trip to Ndiya, where your article said Biafra had buried sixty Ibibio people alive.

On three research visits to Nigeria, I had no heart to visit Ndiya. How do you even begin to ask questions about events like this? And I'd given up, until I ran into the beautiful art of Emmanuel Ekong Ekefrey online and learned he's from this same Ndiya. But, Mr. Ekefrey, after

---

* Read Dr. Nowamagbe Omoigui's "Biafra Midwestern Invasion of 1967: Lessons for Today's Geopolitics" and S. E. Orobator's "The Biafran Crisis and the Midwest," both online.

copious encouragement from your curator Bose Fagbemi in France, it was easier to visit your home in Okota, Lagos, on June 6, 2021, four hundred miles from your ancestral village. Thanks for all you shared about your art and life. I was still thinking about how to broach the war, when you asked what my next project was. As soon as I mentioned *Biafra*, your pain was so immediate, so complete, I couldn't resist your plea to visit Ndiya, though I'd already finished my novel.

To the people of Ndiya, I've never seen a Nigerian village with so many paved roads! Your story isn't easy to tell, like that of Tungbo-Sagbama. I couldn't process it. Chief Etop Ekefrey and Emmanuel I. T. Udoh, thanks for the trust even though I have no words to describe the logistics of such burials or what the general atmosphere was like as Biafra fought two wars in one—battling the Nigerian army and suppressing the Niger Delta minorities. I also have no words for our minorities' raw anger and bottomless angst that today's Biafran agitators, without consultations, have already included minority lands in the map of their dream Biafra. How could this Biafran attitude be the foundation of a new or better country? And I didn't know what to make of the fact that—unlike many Igbos—you didn't want to let your grandchildren know the details of these burials, to spare them the trauma. When should they know? How much should they know? I couldn't say anything because I felt overwhelmed, lost.

It was the last atrocity site I visited.

I MUST ALSO THANK all of you former soldiers I spoke to— ex-Biafran soldiers, of Igbo and minority extractions, and ex-Nigerian soldiers. Over the years, meeting you in Abuja, Umuahia, Ikot Ekpene, Eleme, Yenagoa, Lagos, Ossiomo Leper Colony, Owerri, Kaduna, Onitsha, Aba, Calabar, Badagry, in the U.S., Kenya, Benin, Zimbabwe, England, wherever, has been an unqualified honor. That simple question *Where were you during the war?* or *Where was your father during the war?* opened so many doors.

My heart goes out to those who're still bitter about being conscripted by Biafra. For soldiers who now regret what they did in our minority lands, I pray you let go of the guilt. I respect your plea for anonymity, for some of you, in retrospect, don't think what you did or didn't do in war could heal our country today. And it wasn't difficult for some on the Nigerian side to share the futility of it all, of feeling, most days, your sacrifices were in vain because of the pain and growing divisions today in our blessed country. Well, I was touched when a few of you mentioned how you still visited the families of fallen colleagues: to all of you, then, I say your struggles to handle the traumas are in themselves an interplay of sin and grace.

Thanks for your trust.

Even for those former child soldiers, who served in the Biafran Boys' Company, the BBC, though none of you agreed to reenter the darkness of that childhood with me, I sincerely understand your refusal. "A spy doesn't tell tales," one of you told me in Georgia, USA, as you served me *onugbu* soup and *poundo*. This was mere happenstance, as I'd no idea I was visiting the house of a former child soldier. But just showing me your war photos helped me a lot; your memories of Ikot Ekpene's *ekpo-ntokeyen* masks brought me nostalgia. For some of your former colleagues, elsewhere, who simply said if they'd had ten childhoods they'd give them all to the liberation of Biafra, I praise their honesty. And for those who subtly or bluntly told me to get lost, I respect their stand also.

WRITING A BOOK is a long, complex journey.

Big thanks also to Louise Erdrich for the generous endorsement of my first book, *Say You're One of Them*. By the time you sent that blurb, which you promised when we read together at the 2006 New Yorker Festival, my publisher had already said the cover was set in stone. I drank a shot of Malibu on learning that they couldn't resist your blurb. Also, that festival evening, it meant so much to me to chat with you and your friend about the beauty of literature and the formidable Catholicism of your Native American mother. You asked if I was going to set any works in America. Back then, I didn't know, but you were surprised when I said I'd already visited the Pine Ridge Reservation in South Dakota in the nineties and had played pickup soccer with Native Americans in Omaha, Nebraska, and Spokane, Washington. It's only thus natural that in this, my first attempt to set my story in America, I pay homage to your ancestors, the Native Americans, who first walked these lovely lands.

Thanks for your counsel on the lonely life of the writer and the narrative voice.

Reuben Abati, I often think of how happy we were to finally make each other's acquaintance in your office at the *Guardian Nigeria* in Lagos in early 2009. I was impressed by how much you knew of our old Cross River State ethnic dishes and hospitality. As I said, I'd come primarily to thank you for your 1996 article "An African in America is Baffled by Ebonics" in the *Baltimore Sun* while you were a Fellow at the University of Maryland, I a senior at Gonzaga University in Spokane, Washington. That syndicated op-ed intellectualized for me the bad blood between us Africans and the African Americans. I was already experiencing the strange complexity and painful "social distancing" between *us* and *them* at Gonzaga. And, as you can see, it's taken me just a quarter of a century to fictionalize this.

Alexis Gargaliano, my first editor at Scribner, in our initial conversations in 2012, as you tried to sign up this book, you were almost in tears when you told me racism had brought America to its knees and that you wished my kind of writing and imagery would hit at the immigrant foundations of America. God knows how many drafts you've read since then! Between us, words fail, except to say without my memory of your visceral understanding of racism, I would've given up.

Eileen Pollack, my teacher at the Helen Zell MFA Program of the University of Michigan, thanks for your brutal honesty about the book's flaws—but also, most importantly, its strengths. I also believe our experience of workshopping my *New Yorker* stories did make it easier for me to trust you with my naked frustrations with racism in general and in publishing in particular. I treasure our deep conversations since 2004 about anti-Semitism, the Palestinian question, your heartbreak about all these folks waving the Nazi flags at President Trump rallies, etc. As a Christian, I'm sorry about our history of cruelty and evil toward Jews. I pray we do better in the future.

You were so moved by the New Jersey church scenes that you quickly researched and sent me the link to a video of a white priest ejecting a bereaved Black family with their grandma's coffin from a Requiem Mass and calling the cops on them.* This sudden discovery revived my confidence in both my imagination and what I personally knew—as a seminarian and priest—of the racism/tribalism in my dear Roman Catholic Church.

I was touched when, on a research visit to NYC in December 2017, you invited me to your place for the liturgy of lighting the First Hanukkah Candle followed by dinner at a Ghanaian buffet in Little Senegal. I needed such enlightenment to rework the book. Eileen, now that you've retired from my alma mater, I want to thank you for your continuous kindness and presence, especially to us minorities and international students!

To cut short my long stories of rejections and rewrites and contract transfers, Alane Salierno Mason, my current editor at W. W. Norton & Company, you wanted to buy this book just a day after I sent it to you in the summer of 2020.

You loved the depth the Ekong-Ujai relationship brought to the work. I was very moved by your edits of our war scenes. But I really believed I could trust you when you said I'd be allowed to write about NYC bedbugs and the New Jersey church scenes!

* https://www.theroot.com/mourningwhileblack-priest-calls-cops-on-black-funeral-1827284231.

Today, I really want to thank you for taking me and Elif Batumen out to lunch in 2014 during my Cullman Fellowship with the New York Public Library, when I was still battling with this book. Without even knowing what I was writing about, your sad one-liner about the "hopelessly insular nature" of American publishing and the kind of fiction that could put this before the wider public had stayed with me. In the summer of 2018, sensing my own frustration with finishing this book, you were ready to take pictures of New York City, to help my research.

By the time Nneoma Amadi-Obi—a Nigerian American assistant editor at Norton—read the manuscript and laughed till she cried, three of us were already having a whole different conversation about diversity in publishing, edits, and maps. Nneoma, when you jubilantly told me your knowledge of American Embassy in Nigeria, editorial meetings in NYC, perceptions of our African food abroad, etc., resonated with those of my protagonist Ekong Udousoro, my overwhelming joy sent me on a ten-hour road trip and into making *akara* and then *ekwuong* okra soup all night. Thanks also to Mo Crist, assistant editor, and Erin Lovett, my publicist, for your energetic promotion of my book, and to Dassi Zeidel, my project editor, and Dave Cole, my copyeditor, for your patience with my endless edits.

Azafi Omoluabi and Femi Ayodele of Paréssia Publishers, my Nigerian publisher, your efficient communication skills, book publicity ideas, and insightful conversations about African Rights assured me my book had finally found a home on my two continents!

Maria Massie, my agent, blessings to you and your family. Suffice it to say when you warned me a long time ago that this book would need a lot of *politics* to fly, for publishing doesn't like being called out, I didn't understand what you meant. *Iya mmi*, now I do.

CRESSIDA LEYSHON, MY *NEW YORKER* editor, thanks for consoling me when I had bedbugs in your city in September/November 2013 during my Cullman Fellowship at the New York Public Library.

And I remember all our visits to NYC cafés when my landlord sued me in 2014 for squatting. Jean Strouse, then Cullman Center director, thanks for your immense support. As you can see, I more than loved your amusement that I could frame a whole book around my NYC housing woes; however, back then I was more concerned my infestation could endanger the precious tomes of your New York Public Library. I thank Marie d'Origny, your assistant, for accompanying me to court and giving me a treat in Chinatown. Paul Delaverdac, Julia Pagnamenta, and Sam Swope, I'm sorry for all the times I forgot my key and you had to stand up to let me into the center.

Peter Holquist of Princeton University, my fellow soccer-crazy Cullman Fellow, I've great memories of us sneaking out of our cubicles to watch European Champions League games at the Australian, instead of writing. Our mischief and obsession were such that we ensured others couldn't join us!

I also thank Pat Towers and Kristy Davies Albano for our conversations about race in publishing ever since you invited me to write for *O, the Oprah* magazine, in 2008. Thanks for reading the first versions of *New York, My Village*. You helped me with research and cooked for me and showed me around NYC. But I shall never forget our lunch of tongue sandwiches and beer!

And when you finally said I'd succeeded in writing about your city with the same intensity of our African cities, it gave me a real boost. Brad Kessler, you graced this book with a new depth by teaching me to rewrite the American dialogue to show how New Yorkers use coded language to talk around racism. I also want to thank the three bedbug victims, who've chosen to remain anonymous, because of the shame of having to abandon your apartments (with all your belongings) in NYC and Toronto, Canada.

I'd also enjoyed my fellowship at the Black Mountain Institute of the University of Nevada, Las Vegas (2010–11), thanks to Professor Wole Soyinka. Richard and Mini Wiley, your friendship in Vegas quickly helped me settle into Sin City. I thank the very compassionate Jesuit Superior General Adolfo Nicolás, who rescinded his earlier permission for me to leave the Jesuits but then failed to convince me to stay. I'm grateful for your insightful, kind, and prayerful emails. I'm sorry I could no longer stand the hierarchy dangling over my head as I struggled with the restlessness and fears of a second book. After three years of not being able to write a word in fiction, I knew something had to give. I'm grateful, too, to Danny Herwitz for bringing me to the Institute for the Humanities of the University of Michigan (2011–12). I'll never forget your support as I struggled to transfer my J-1 visa, alias "Leprosy Visa," from Vegas to Ann Arbor.

James O'Malley and Lelia Ruckenstein of O'Malley & Associates, my immigration lawyers, thanks for explaining again and again to this nervous immigrant that even if I lost my civil case with my NYC landlord, I wouldn't be jailed or deported. Getting to know how much protection tenants and squatters have in NYC courts has made me more appreciative of NYC.

I'm also grateful to Yaddo (Fall 2012) and Loyola University Chicago's Hank Center for the Catholic Intellectual Heritage (Fall 2017) for their fellowships.

AND HOW DO I thank you, Chinelo Okparanta? Hearing of how some editor had apologized that she wasn't courageous enough to publish this book, you took it as a personal challenge to strategize on whom to send it. But we couldn't stop laughing when another editor rejected it because it needed *more strangeness, perhaps.* "Did she mean we Africans should be walking on our heads or that no apartment in Nigeria could be better than those around Times Square?" you joked. You must also thank your friend Yang Wang, for all she shared about China, her fascinating country, when I visited Beijing in 2015. Unfortunately, I didn't realize my dream of comparing the racism in Chinese Catholicism to that of America in the book.

I thank Reverend Sisters Iniobong Akpabio, Philo Bassey, Imelda Effiong, and Magdalene Umoh. I also praise Shanari Williams, Clarisse Ncuti, Anne Okpohs, Ngozi Onuma, Marian Krzyzowski, Chika Unigwe, John Sanni, Dave and Trilla Bass, Aurelie Maketa, Jim Foster, Jim Shepard, Dan Grossman, John Bolen III, Elizabeth Yerkes, Pat and Rich Needles, Trish Roberts, Father Ehi Omoragbon, and Father Edmund Agorhom for your support. Anita Norich, thanks for your Holocaust class at the University of Michigan. Arua Oko Omaka, thanks for the research on Irish missionaries in Biafra. Delia Steverson, thanks for helping me with the Alabama African American vernacular. Chibundu Onuzo, I treasure the fact that when I couldn't download your BBC version of "Aka Jehovah, Hand of Jehovah," you sent me a private recording.

I thank you, Joe Nwizarh, Simeon Enemuo, Emmanuel Ugwejeh, Mekso Okolocha, all Igbos I could really thrash out the Biafran stuff with when I was a Jesuit. Your openness to the other side of the story, your dispassionate, inclusive analysis of our Nigerian politics, sadly enough, wasn't that common in our dear Nigerian convents, rectories, and seminaries. Simple courtesies like keeping an informal group conversation in English, instead of hoarding it in Igbo, so this minority could follow, went a long way!

AND FREDDIE OBIORA ANYAEGBUNAM JR., my former high school student in Nigeria, your Biafran War trauma, percolating to you two generations after the fact, stayed with me long after your reassuring visit to Atlanta, Georgia, in 2016. As our one-hour lunch meeting turned into six hours of endless driving around Georgia and catching up, you wanted to know about my minority experience of the war. What bothered you wasn't so much what the Igbos, your people, went through in the war, as what you saw as "complete, utter, or even snobbish silence" from other ethnic groups. You wanted to know why young Igbos marched for a new Biafra while everybody else carried on with their business. You asked what this meant in a multi-ethnic society. You were surprised by even the silence of your school friends from other ethnic groups. You wondered how your generation can commit to Nigeria, if you'd no understanding of the history—because the Nigerian government had banned the teaching of history, to hide its war atrocities from its children. You felt Nigeria hated your generation. You were really hurting that our compatriots were successful the world over while home remained a hot mess.

To your next question, abrupt and accusatory, "And, Father Uwem, why haven't you, teller of painful stories, written about this damn war?" I'd no ready reply, except to say, "Obiora, my man, perhaps it's exactly that—too painful." No matter how much you pushed, I promised you nothing, for I didn't want to disappoint you if I couldn't put a book together. I wasn't even sure my knowledge of Biafra would bring you peace anyway. But what I didn't and couldn't hide from you was my anger and shame that the Nigerian government—the same government that's protecting killer Fulani herdsmen—had just shot 150 peaceful pro-Biafra demonstrators, according to Amnesty International. Of course, I'm depressed to be from a country that is cuddling Boko Haram and herdsmen terrorists but continues to kill peaceful agitators.

Still, my advice to you, Obiora, and your cousin Jeni Giwa-Amu Wellington of Australia (your love for kangaroo meat helped me describe it in the novel) and others over the years, stands: My young passionate African diaspora friends, already Nigeria celebrates you because the funds you send from your diaspora are bigger than our national budget . . . When these global Western institutions employ you out here, could you leverage this privilege for the benefit of your *home* continent? And can you risk your privileges like Dr. Arikana Chihombori-Quao, the former African Union's ambassador to the United States, who lost her job to fighting the status quo?

But bombing our African issues only from abroad could lead to burnout or a disconnect, a certain win for whiteness. So to recharge your vision and represent us better, visit Nigeria or Biafra as much as possible. Meet up with your less successful childhood friends. Shop often in the open market. Visit public schools. Mentor poor children from another ethnic group—even when their elites are waging a genocide on your people. Sharpen your native language skills so you can understand the proverbs and oral poetry of your ethnic groups. Risk your palates on the most native of dishes. Welcome and dance with the masqueraders, for you can get rid of neither the past nor the future. If your big Cambridge degree hinders you from these things, you're losing the fight.

We, your teachers and parents, can only give you so much, and even our limited gifts are tainted. Imperfect. We've failed you in the Nigerian project. You must humbly remember all of this so you don't lose heart when your own children also begin to "cancel" you. Build deep friendships, especially with your Creator, because sometimes they'll be your only home left in the universe. Marry who you want to marry. And if all of this is stressful and confusing, take the long view, like the *ukim* tree, of this still-a-wonderful-world. Believe in the wisdom that if you live long enough to be grandparents, you may enjoy a different kind of love with your grandchildren, something less tense.

To my University of Florida students, you'll never understand how much your enthusiasm for writing has helped mine. Daily, I'm meeting my younger, more confident, hopeful self. I admire your interpretations of Rainer Maria Rilke's *Letters to a Young Poet* and Annie Dillard's *The Writing Life*. Yet, as I've said to you a million times already, too many institutions in our dear America are racist and sexist and homophobic. I stand before you because I believe your generation the world over seems poised to ask the hard questions, to fact-check on the spot, to re-create everything, to let everyone belong. I hope then my novel, if not these meandering acknowledgments, addresses some of your pointed concerns about how discrimination in publishing does shape the literary canon and ultimately your syllabi, about agents and editors, and about how to research and dialogue across culture and race and gender. You must remain brave and open and forgiving and hopeful, for, as Rilke says, "Let everything happen to you: beauty and terror."

I'm grateful to my colleagues—especially David Leavitt and Jill Ciment, Camille Bordas, William Logan, Ange Mlinko, and Michael Hoffman, and Sid Dobrin, my department chair, and Mary Watt, my associate dean. Melissa Davis, Carla Blount, Dennis Blount, and Lynn Harris, you know how much I depend on you in the administrative offices.

Jill, in the spring of 2019, a year before the #publishingpaidme *wahala* or publishing's reckoning with the Black Lives Matter phenomenon, I cried when you insisted on reading my manuscript though you were undergoing a ruthless regime of radiotherapy and could only read thirty minutes a day. You gave me the best advice on editing this crazy book: you said if you were me, you'd build the book around what average Nigerians didn't already know about America and vice versa. (It made me so happy because I know this NYC bedbug mess and rent racketeers or 419ers, for instance, would be a total shock to many in Nigeria!) You also warned I shouldn't allow editors and agents to control how I write about racism in publishing, because, "You know, Uwem, their noses are too in the bullshit to know it's bullshit." I'm lucky to have been your *student* before your retirement!

Iya uwei, I chime the last bells of gratitude to my dear friend Edie Hang Nguyen Weathers. Nobody cooks Vietnamese food like your mom! You were the one I turned to when the novel needed a huge infusion of research in 2016, for since 1995 you'd heard of my struggles with this war when we were undergrads at Creighton University. Even back then, you understood instinctively something about the inherited pain of war, because your own parents had fled to America as Vietnam War refugees. You were born and bred in the bitter memories of their war and deep Catholicism that withstood Vietnam's communism. Like Ujai, my child character, your love for both Vietnam and America is boundless—a perfect example of how any diaspora must balance her *Fiddler on the Roof* existence.

You sponsored that difficult decisive trip to interview Bishop Umoh and others in the Niger Delta and Igboland. But *k'akpaniko*, without you keeping in touch from Denver, Colorado, begging me never to give up no matter the obstacles, I would've *chopped* your money for nothing. When I was overwhelmed many times by the pain of my interviewees and the fears for my safety, your calls and emails brought me up for air.